THE MIRACLE MAN

THE MIRACLE MAN

JAMES SKIVINGTON

Matador
5 Weir Road
Kibworth Beauchamp
Leicester LE8 0LQ, UK
Tel: (+44) 116 279 2299
Fax: (+44) 116 279 2277
Email: books@troubador.co.uk
Web: www.troubador.co.uk/matador

ISBN 978 1848763 418

British Library Cataloguing in Publication Data.
A catalogue record for this book is available from the British Library.

Typeset in 11pt Palatino by Troubador Publishing Ltd, Leicester, UK

Matador is an imprint of Troubador Publishing Ltd

Printed in Great Britain by the MPG Books Group, Bodmin and King's Lynn

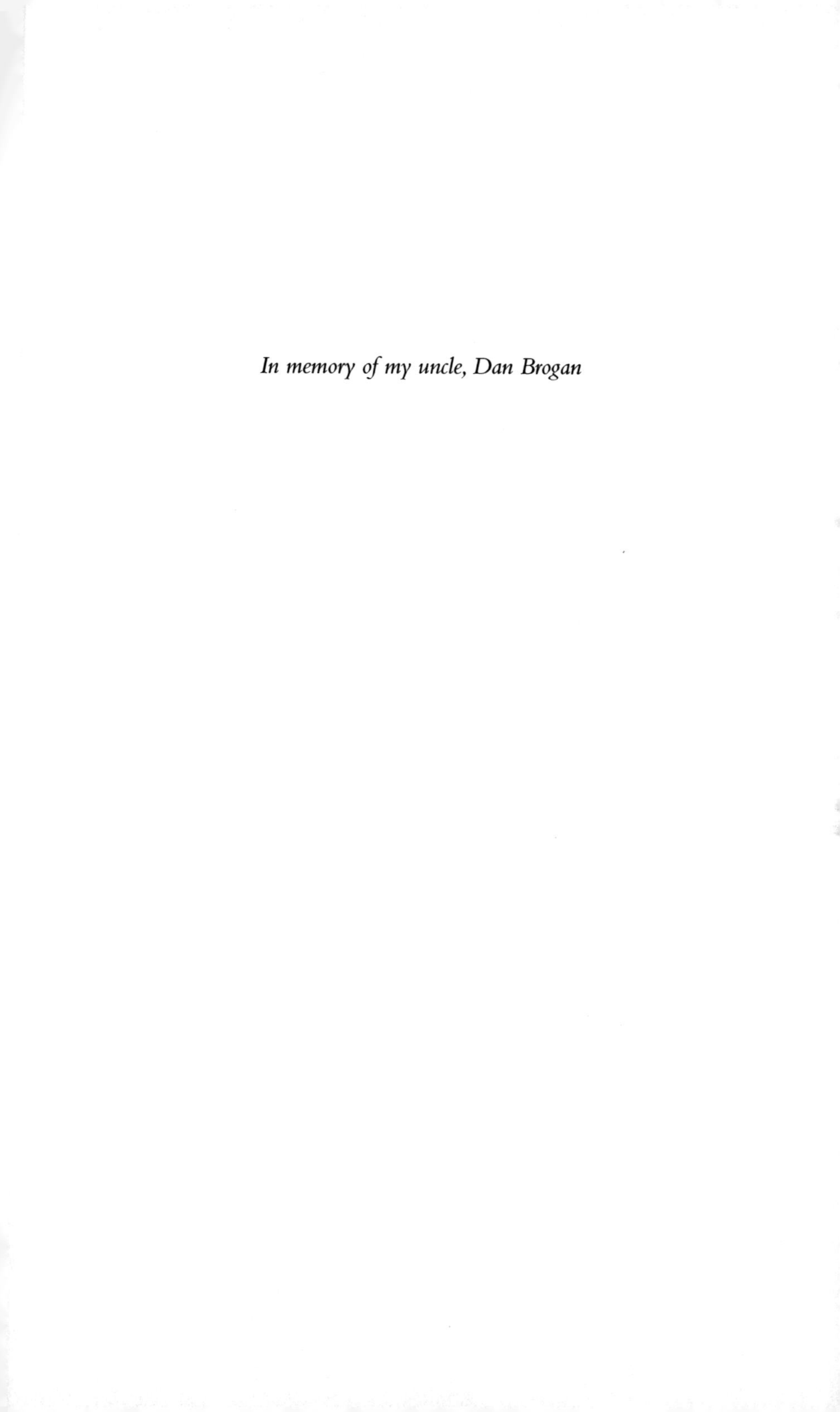

In memory of my uncle, Dan Brogan

chapter one

At a seat near the window of the Glens Hotel bar, Limpy McGhee hooked out his top dentures with his thumb and began poking at the brown-stained plastic with the blackened end of a spent match. On the other side of the table, young Danny Kyle was hunched behind a copy of the Northern Reporter in which he was reading reports of Sunday hurling matches and now and then saying in a doleful voice,

"Ah, Jasus," and "Damn it to hell, they don't deserve to win nothin'!"

Limpy's pouchy face, hoar-frosted with three days of grey stubble, contorted into gargoyle features as he concentrated on his task. From his mouth came alternate sounds of soughing and whistling and his top lip billowed and fell like curtains at an open window. Jabbing at the immovable matter on the dentures, he broke the match. "Whuck it!" he said and picked another one from the ashtray, scrunched the end of it on the table to remove the cindered head then began jabbing at the teeth once more.

At the next table three ruddy-faced men, just back from the sheep sales, sat and complained about the scandalously low livestock prices, unable to figure out for the life of them why the government had not intervened. But only, of course, when prices were low. When they were high, they certainly did not need the damned government poking its nose into a man's business. Beneath the table a black-and-white collie dog lay dozing, its long muzzle resting on its paws. For Limpy, further poking with the match was to no avail and so, throwing it down in disgust, he rummaged through the pockets of his ragged jacket until he found a stubby pencil. He was in the habit of taking this out now and then to hold poised before him and above a scrap of paper, so that an onlooker might conclude that the scruffy little man was about to record some gem of wit or acute observation. But now, he dug the dull lead into the offending material and heaved. The pencil skidded off the teeth, leaving the broken lead behind.

"Whuck it!" he said again, and gouged at the dentures. With an air of defeat, Danny Kyle slowly lowered his newspaper, saying,

"Hey, McGhee, did you read this bit about – ? What the hell are you doing?" His lips curled in disgust.

"Trying to sort whese whuckin' teewh," the old man said, digging viciously with the broken pencil. "Whem bloody sweets owh Kilbride's. A new sort of mints, he said. Fwiggin' concrete they are!"

"Jaysus, McGhee, you haven't the manners of a pig. Would you put them bloody teeth back in your mouth before I throw up!"

Young Danny averted his eyes and his hand went involuntarily to his mouth. Beneath the table, the dog opened one eye.

"How can I put whem back when where's a whing like a bloody gumboil on whem?" He bored at the remains of the mint with the pencil.

"Just get them back in, will ye!"

"Nowhing wrong wiwh whem? What the hell's what,

when?" He reached across the table, shoving the upper denture close to the face of his companion, who sprang back.

"Get away, you filthy old git!" His face was suddenly pale and his abdomen jerked as his stomach contracted.

"Look! Bloody concrete!" Limpy's jab at the teeth pushed them from his grasp and they plopped into Danny Kyle's glass of beer.

"Oh – jeez," the old man said. "Now look what you made me do."

"You – eejit! You . . . "

Limpy looked at the teeth which wobbled and grinned back at him from the bottom of the brown liquid. It was like smiling into a mirror at twilight. He lifted the glass and shook it. The teeth clinked against the sides.

"You'll need to drink some of what so I can get whem out," he said.

"With your teeth in it? Are you mad? You owe me a pint, McGhee!"

Danny Kyle's stomach heaved again.

"Ah, for Jasus sake, Kyle." A grubby hand with long, dirty nails was plunged into the glass, fingers wiggling to catch the teeth. "Where y'are," Limpy said, plucking them out and holding them up. He licked the beer that ran down his hand then shoved the beer glass in front of Danny Kyle again. "Here."

As the young man looked at the beer a kind of leaden pallor slowly suffused his face. "I'm not – drinking that," he said in a slow and heavy tone. "There's – bits floating in it." Then the chair legs suddenly scraped on the floor as he jumped up, wheeled and raced for the toilets, hand to his mouth and stomach churning. Limpy merely shook his head and turned his attention to the teeth once more.

This time he held them flat on the table, as if they were biting into the wood, and applied the edge of a coin to the sticky blob, leaning forward to exert the maximum pressure. The coin skidded, the hand holding the teeth lost its grip and they were catapulted off the table to land in front of the dog who opened his eyes and took an immediate interest in the object before him.

"Bugger!" Limpy held his hand out towards the dog, who was sniffing the teeth. "Good dog."

It gave a low growl and nudged the teeth towards itself. The men at the table with their backs to Limpy carried on talking in loud voices.

"Good dog," Limpy said, hunkering down on the floor and giving the animal the bottom half of a smile. "Give. Where's a good boy." Again the dog gave a warning sound, picked up the dentures in its mouth and turned back under the table with them.

"Whuck it," said Limpy.

As someone came to the punchline of a story, a roar of laughter erupted from the next table, the man nearest Limpy shaking his huge frame and drumming the table with his fist. From behind the bar, the hotel owner Dermot McAllister glanced up briefly from his newspaper. With some difficulty, Limpy got down on his hands and knees and began to crawl after the dog, but had barely got his head and shoulders under the table when a big hand grabbed the seat of his trousers and slowly dragged him out. He looked up to see three ruddy faces staring down at him. "Well what d'ye know, it's a leprechaun," he told his friends. And then to Limpy, "What the hell are you playing at?"

"That mongrel of yours. It's got my bloody teewh."

The men glanced at each other and smiled. They had always known that the villagers of Inisbreen were a little eccentric. That's what came of living beside the sea on the road to nowhere.

"I can assure you, Mister, that my dog's had the same set of teeth since he was a pup," the man said with mock seriousness.

"Damn it to hell," Limpy said, "he stole my whuckin' teewh!"

"I'd say," the man cocked his head to one side and looked at Limpy through narrowed eyes, "I'd say you probably look better without them. What d'you think, boys?"

All three of them began to laugh and the little old man's face twisted in annoyance. The sheep farmer pointed under the table. "You better mind how you go under there. He can be vicious when he takes the notion – and you wouldn't want to be bit by your own teewh."

One man struck up with a helpless, whining laugh, while the other two followed in a deep, rumbling chorus. Dermot McAllister, who had been observing all of this from the counter, simply smiled and shook his head as, red with anger, the old man began to crawl under the table, saying,

"Come on doggy, where's a good boy."

When he had at last recovered his teeth and finished his drink, Limpy McGhee hobbled out the front door of the bar, made his way round to the back of the building and went through a gap in the wall into the yard behind the hotel kitchen. Going quickly across the yard to the kitchen door, he looked around furtively before knocking on it. On hearing from inside the footsteps approaching, he at once hunched forward and composed a look of utter dejection on his face. There was a pause, and then the door scraped open to reveal his sister, Mrs Megarrity, known as the Winter Cook at the Glens Hotel. A small, stout woman, she wore a crumpled mauve jumper and a black skirt covered by a stained apron. Her feet were barely contained by soft shoes which listed like badly loaded barges. She nodded and gave a smile at her reprobate brother.

"Ah, it's yourself, John. Come away in and I'll make you a drop of tea. McAllister's down in the bar," she gave a sly smile as she turned away, adding, "though I daresay ye'd know that yerself."

Limpy hobbled through the doorway and stood there, his hands clasped before him, his head slightly bowed in deference to the sister from whom he was once more about to extract some money.

"I'll hardly bother with the tea, Lizzie. I was just passing and I thought I'd better call in and see how ye were doing."

The Winter Cook manoeuvred a large black kettle onto the hot-plate of the stove.

"Passing, is it? Haven't ye been in that bar this last hour or more."

"Ah well, I must admit I have, Lizzie. I have that." He gave a dry cough. "I was coming down the hill there and I was took breathless, and says I to myself, 'John McGhee, the hand of time's upon ye.' So I just popped into Dermot McAllister's for a wee whiskey to ease the congestion in the tubes. And sure enough, it did the trick." He demonstrated his newfound ability to breathe easily.

"Jasus tonight," his sister declared, "ye must have a chest like a cabin trunk, the amount of whiskey ye pour into yerself. Ye go whippin' in that bar door like ye was on rails."

"Ah now, Lizzie, don't be hard on me." He gave her a pathetic look whose frequency of use had rendered it all but ineffective. "I'm not getting any younger and it's no easy job getting about now, with the bad leg." He gave it a hefty slap. "An' with money short, an' all – well, it's hard enough getting good grub."

"Hmph, it's a wonder you've got any room for it. Ye'll do yourself no good at that drinking, I'm tellin' ye. I remember the day, John McGhee – when you were about nineteen or twenty – and not half a mile from here you took the pledge."

"So I did, Lizzie, so I did. Haven't ye the marvellous memory. And I swear t'God, only this leg wasn't making my life a living hell, I'd be off the drink to this day, so I would. Not a drop would pass my lips, I swear to God."

Mrs Megarrity gave a dismissive toss of her head. She'd heard it all before, and in a hundred variations.

"That'll be right. You'd probably take it intervenus."

"What's one of them, Lizzie?"

"Those things that go straight into your veins." When Limpy still looked puzzled, she offered, "Like them optics in the bar, with a tube coming out the bottom."

For a moment his eyes glazed over as he contemplated this wonder of modern science.

"Jeez, ye'd need some kind of brain on ye to think that one up. D'ye think would it work?"

Pulling him back onto the well-charted course, his sister said, "How much're ye after this time?"

Limpy looked hurt. She had seen that before, too.

"God forgive ye, Lizzie Megarrity. I come in here to see how my wee sister is, see if there's anything ye want fetchin' from the shop, and all you think is I'm after yer money. I don't know, ye try and do somebody a good turn, and all ye get's dog's abuse. What's new."

On cue, he turned towards the door. And on cue, she said,

"How much?"

The old man shrugged and shuffled his feet in a show of reluctance at the largesse that was about to be pressed upon him.

"If ye could see your way to lending me – a tenner – I think – "

"A tenner?" The Winter cook almost shouted. "Good God Almighty d'ye think I'm the Queen o' Sheba or what?" At which point in history the Queen of Sheba became famous for having a spare tenner in her purse, the Winter Cook neither knew nor cared.

"Did I say a tenner? Sure, ye know I meant a fiver. Ah, there's old age for ye, Lizzie. The brain's gone entirely. God knows, I'll hardly be long for this earth." His chest became concave and he gave a racking cough that would surely have been enough to summon any undertaker within earshot. Mrs Megarrity went to a drawer and roughly pulled it open, taking from it a battered purse from which she extracted a five-pound note.

"I'll pay ye back, mind," Limpy choked out the words. "I'll pay ye back, for sure."

"When? When ye find a crock of gold? I wouldn't need to be desperate. Here," Mrs Megarrity said, thrusting the note at Limpy, "I suppose it'll be in McAllister's till before ye can say 'Same again'. I don't know, I'm more stupider than you that gives it to ye."

The fiver swiftly disappeared into Limpy's jacket pocket, so that he might better explain his case with two free hands.

"Ah now Lizzie, don't be saying that. This here donation – gratefully received – it'll be used to buy grub. Build up my strength again." As he was seized by another paroxysm of coughing, his whole frame seemed to sag and he caught hold of the table for support. Speechless for a moment, his breath coming in short gasps, he shook his head in near despair at the parlous state of his health. The Winter Cook's face clouded as she looked at her brother intently.

"You all right, John? Dammit, haven't I told you before to eat proper?" She gave a snort. "Ye've never grew up, have ye?" She went to the refrigerator and brought out a plate with a large piece of cheese on it. Then she cut the cheese in half, wrapping one piece in greaseproof paper.

"Here, take that with ye," she said. "I can't give ye nothing else just now. That bloody McAllister's poking into everything, so he is. He'll be counting the sugar lumps next."

"Ah, God love ye. Ye always did look after yer big brother." He put the cheese inside his jacket. "Listen, Lizzie, I was wanting yer advice on something. To do with money."

"I haven't got one penny piece more to give ye. Ye've had all – "

"No, no, ye've been more than kind. More than. It's this. I thought that, seeing as how old Quinn has died and left that bit of land my wee house is on to young Nancy, maybe this could be a good time to ask her for a reduction in my rent. She'll maybe be a softer touch than the old fella was."

"Well, it's not as if your rent's very high now."

"Always worth a try, I say."

"Ye know what them Quinn's is like as well as me, John. They'd wrestle a ghost for a ha'penny. But she could hardly be tighter than that old bugger was. Ye've got nothing to lose, I suppose."

"Right," Limpy said, "I'll call round and see her. Give her a bit of my charm, ye know?" He winked at his sister and gave a crooked smile that showed his brown-stained teeth.

"Get away off with ye," she said, and gave him a playful slap on the shoulder, "before I change my mind about that fiver."

"Thanks, Lizzie. I won't forget it," Limpy said and quietly slipped out the back door, closing it gently behind him. From a pocket beneath her apron, the Winter Cook drew out a quarter bottle of whiskey and uncorked it.

"I'm sure ye won't, for you always know where to come back for more." She put the top of the bottle to her lips and took a long drink.

Outside, Limpy looked around before making his way across the yard and through the gap in the wall. He seemed happier now, with a broad smile on his face and a certain swagger in his limping walk. His health, it seemed, had dramatically improved.

"Knock and it shall be opened unto ye," he said aloud. "Ask for a tenner and ye shall receive a fiver. Thus saith the Lord."

A little further along the lane that ran behind the hotel, he drew out the little parcel from inside his jacket. Weighing it in his hand, he said, "Bloody cheese," and threw it high over the hedge.

It had been a wet spring that year in the Glens of Antrim, and the village of Inisbreen and the surrounding countryside had seen the steady rains of March and April saturate the high bog-land and send torrents of water cascading down the steep hillsides, through deep gullies over-arched with bracken, fern and hazel. The small river which ran the length of the valley floor, at one point taking the middle ground through broad, flat meadows, then crossing to reach the sea beside the village, was frequently gorged with brown peaty water that drew a dark trail across the green expanse of the sea water in the bay. With the flood had come its usual casualties, the low branches of riverside trees festooned with uprooted vegetation, blackfaced sheep swept from the slopes and floating downstream with their distended bellies uppermost, along with a procession of wooden boxes, planks and other assorted debris.

Under the bridge at the village there had come floating one afternoon a woman's nightdress, spread out on top of the water and rippling seductively in the waves, as if worn by a river siren who was beckoning to the men who watched its progress from above. As they observed its approach there was speculation amongst them as to whom its former owner might be and the circumstances of her disrobement, with someone suggesting it was a signal and that she could even then be observing them from some riverside haunt, naked and awaiting their attentions. There was even talk from some of a search party, with declarations of intent more appropriate to the search for the source of the Nile. And then Seamus McAvoy, a man who had once given serious consideration to

working for a living and who had m
as a haberdasher's assistant, gave it a
that the size of the nightdress was at t
and that its former owner would the
a build and temperament as to requir
with the power and stamina of a p
men's interest in the nether garme
passage towards the mouth of the riv... and thence to the sea, where a being of more mythical proportions, they fancied, might take up the challenge that it offered.

Now the days of driving sleet, of torrential rain or grey mist creeping down the hillsides had gone, and the sun probed its warm fingers into wooded crevices and rocky fissures that had lain dark all winter. On the slopes above the valley, heather and bog cotton put on new growth and high above them the skylark sang of them and of the growing lambs and the black turf banks. The sheep lay on the warming grass and on the road, their starkly stupid faces turned towards the North Channel with the Scottish hills beyond, ranging in colour with their proximity, from dull green and brown to a faded purple, from the near to the far distance. Here and there, at the side of the winding, rutted tracks that led off the road and into the bog, stood turf stacks depleted from winter usage, like the ruins of some ancient clachan. Curlews called across this treeless landscape and snipe flew zigzag to hidden nests among the tiny pools.

From the topmost hills could be seen the whole valley, from the steep-sided upper slopes where the viaduct bridge crossed, past the plantation of oak and sycamore, the chapel and graveyard held in the crook of the river's arm, to the broad strand and sandy crescent bay. At one end of the bay stood the village, its main street continuing over the bridge and making a sharp right turn to climb the hill above the river. To the left, a y the side of the river and in front of the Glens ring out a few hundred yards farther on where a of rocks was washed by the sea. The yellow-painted of the hotel – with the name picked out in brown Gaelic-yle letters – looked across the bay, the building's ancient bulk seeming to have settled back into the hill behind it at a slight tilt, an old boy with his hat at a rakish angle, someone had said. And like an old hand too, it had been around and seen a few things in it's time and it's past was a little mysterious. Some said it had once been a ropeworks and others a warehouse to store the produce wrested from the land and the mouths of Irishmen for shipment to the groaning tables of mainland landlords. A retired schoolteacher – and self-appointed chronicler of local history – had even claimed evidence of a meeting between Charles Stewart Parnell and a Prussian count to plan a German invasion of Ireland, but this story was dismissed by locals on the grounds that the schoolteacher's brother, as the owner of a nearby taxi business, had a vested interest in the tourist trade. In any event, the small, sleepy-eyed windows and heavy oak door of the Glens Hotel were giving no clue as to its past life.

The hotel's tourist business was highly seasonal, running from the beginning of June to the end of September at best and was largely comprised of expatriate families on a two-week break from mainland cities, as well as the odd – sometimes very odd – American, French or German couple on an overnight stop during a tour of the North coast. There were a few permanent residents in the hotel – three to be precise – and they had something of a second-class status, guests who were tolerated rather than attended, serviced rather than served. Dermot McAllister had tried in a number of ways to increase the off-season business of the hotel, but to little avail. He had advertised weekend breaks for two with a champagne breakfast and fishing holidays with warming alcoholic beverages supplied. He had even considered bringing in busloads of men for an evening meal and strip show at an all-inclusive price, but he had a wife to reckon with, the formidable Agnes, and an eight-year-old son who somehow, sure as hell, would have managed to sneak into the proceedings. And of course there would be the clergy to contend with. The trouble was that Dermot, first and foremost, was a man of the land, more at home climbing steep acres after sheep than bowing and scraping to people who, having paid his modest prices for a fortnight's full board, appeared to think that they had bought the hotel and could therefore enjoy certain rights in perpetuity.

Like the people of the glens, being of the land, Dermot had its scale of time upon him, a reckoning that dictated that things happened in days or weeks but never in minutes or hours. Nothing was so urgent that it could not wait until a few words were exchanged with a neighbour or a final drink was taken to keep the previous ones company. Time was marked by the passage of the seasons, by sowings and lambings and harvestings, and not by the three o'clock bus to Ballymane or the school bell that drew reluctant children to the rigours of grammar and arithmetic. And being a man of the land, Dermot had always been interested in acquiring as much of it as possible. Boggy tracts high on the mountain or the broad and lusher pastures of the valley, land was the only truly worthwhile possession. It gave a man status and power and a sense of belonging. So when Dermot had heard that the young piano teacher Nancy Quinn had inherited a few acres next to some of his own land, naturally he was interested. While she was still considering whether or not to let him buy the land, he had started an affair with her which, he fancied, would go some considerable way in compensation if she decided not to sell. If he could manage to enjoy the benefits not only of the land but also of its current owner, he would be a happy man. Until, that is, another piece of land became of interest to him, or the flick of a different skirt caught his eye.

From his armchair by the window of the Glens Hotel sitting-room, Mr Pointerly looked out at the river, placid beneath the calm evening sky, then above and beyond it to the green-marled waters of the bay. The scene could have been from last year, he thought, or half a century ago. Nothing much seemed to change. Oh, they had built a few houses at the back of the village – ugly, black and white things that looked more like police barracks than domestic accommodation – but that was all. And neither had he changed. Older, of course – who wasn't? Yet he still walked out every day to his haunts of six decades, and his mind was as active and sharp as ever. Well, perhaps a little misty at the edges. Only to be expected when you were getting on a bit. "Blessed with a poor memory," he would say, and "Selective forgetfulness". Slowly the memories came drifting back to him of warm summer days on the strand with Celia and Mother in her straw hat that was almost the colour of her hair, of afternoons beneath the shade of the wild rhododendrons, those that Seumas the gardener was always going to "blast the buggers out with dynermite". That was where his and Celia's hide-out had been, where they had laid their plans to ambush some passing tribe of Red Indians. But the Red Indians had never come. Now, if he cared to speak her name, lifted his head and said clearly, "Celia!", she would answer him from the rhododendron bushes. It was possible. Anything was possible. He had his dreams, always had done. Dreams in the past that his parents would understand him, dreams of the present that some day he would turn and there before him would be . . . well, he had his dreams. So many of them had gone over the years, ground away to nothing by the cruel abrasion of time, or dashed from his hands with a laugh of derision. Like the grains of sand on the beach, he decided, in a flood of self-pity. If only they could have understood him, made some kind of effort. But they had never even tried.

The door to the sitting-room opened and the Misses Garrison came in, first Margaret, the older one, the larger one, with her severe look and sharp voice that reminded him a little of Mother, and then Cissy, small and thin, always one step behind like those Indian women, she being more of a sympathetic nature like himself. He had watched them so often – observed them with his artist's eye – and overheard their little bickering conversations while he pretended to read one of the mildewed Vicki Baum or Jeffrey Farnol volumes from the bookcase in the corner. There was "A Brief History of Ireland" there, so old that it was itself part of history, and a "Highways and Byways of Donegal and Antrim" with ink drawings of scenery through which wound unsurfaced roads walked by quaintly-clothed men in munchkin hats – halfway between humans and leprechauns. He had read all the volumes in the bookcase, or at least flicked through them. He really should buy some books, he thought, keep himself up to date with what was passing for literature these days. But books were so expensive, and if the one a visitor had left behind last year had been any indication, he would stick with the classics. He glanced down at the copy of "Chrome Yellow" by Aldous Huxley which lay on his lap, one of his slender fingers a bookmark at page eight. Now there was a writer, he decided, at least judging from the first two chapters, which was all he had ever managed to read.

"Good evening, Richard," Margaret Garrison said, as if by using his Christian name she was paying him a compliment. It was "Richard" when she felt kindly disposed towards him and "Mr Pointerly" when she did not, and there was no reason he could ever fathom for either attitude. He nodded gracefully at both women and smiled. Margaret took her customary seat in the armchair by the empty fireplace while Cissy sank into the couch, the broken springs offering so little support that when she finally came to rest, her eyes were almost level with her knees. Only when she was in company could she risk sitting on the couch, as she generally had to be assisted to her feet from it. She fussed at the folds of her dress, pulling it down taut over her knees. What a look she might otherwise receive from Margaret, who was saying to Mr Pointerly,

"And what d'you think we might expect for dinner this evening, Richard?"

Mr Pointerly gave a rueful smile, lifted and dropped a languid hand.

"Ah, who knows, my dear? Who knows? We are entirely at the mercy of the Winter Cook."

"Hmph! A cook, she calls herself? The woman hasn't the slightest idea what the word means. If she's boiled potatoes for pigs, that's about the height of it. And have you seen her hands? There's bears' paws that are cleaner. It's a wonder we're not all poisoned." She gave a sniff. "I ask you, how much longer do we have to suffer the depredations of that woman? We'll all be in an early grave." Frowning, she glanced over at Cissy who was as usual off somewhere on thoughts of her own. "Where are we now, Cissy?"

Her sister blinked at her. "Why – the sitting-room, Margaret."

For a full five seconds Margaret closed her eyes in silent martyrdom before opening them to gaze up at the ceiling.

"The date, Cissy!" She said. "The date, for goodness sake!"

"The – second week in May – I think," Mr Pointerly volunteered. "Don't know the exact date, I'm afraid. Don't possess such a thing as a calendar now – or a diary." He shrugged. "Used to keep one years ago, of course. We all did. Hardly seems much point now." His voice trailed away as his gaze drifted from the sisters to the sunlit scene on the other side of the window. Margaret Garrison tutted and gave a little flick of her head. Like a favourite cat, her large macramé bag sat hunched on her lap and from it she took a lighter and a packet of cigarettes, screwed a cigarette between her pouted, magenta lips, lit it and puffed smoke out without having inhaled it. It was a habit of some sophistication that she had picked up in London in her twenties, during the year she had spent there with her cousins, the Hennessys.

"Cissy," Margaret said without looking at her sister, "as I believe I've mentioned before, I really don't think that cardigan goes with that dress. Perhaps you should go upstairs and change it before dinner."

Pinched between two fingertips, the cigarette was held aloft, a symbol of her authority and superior knowledge in matters of couture.

From the couch Cissy peeped over her knees and gave a vacant smile.

"Well – I rather like it, Margaret," she said, smoothing the rumpled fabric over her flat chest. "And it's not as though we're going to dine with the Queen, dear."

"Puts me in mind of fuchsia. This is the place for fuchsia," Mr Pointerly said, as if revealing a great truth. And then he said simply, "Ballerinas."

Margaret ignored this irrelevance and said to him,

"I don't know about you, Richard," with the clear implication that she meant the opposite, "but I intend to make the strongest possible representations to Mr McAllister about the food we've been forced to endure at the hands of that – woman. Indeed, I fully intend to demand a reduction in my bill – and I would strongly advise you to do the same."

Mr Pointerly opened "Chrome Yellow" and glanced down at the beginning of Chapter Two.

"Perhaps," he said, half to himself, "if the food was better, the bill would be higher."

At that very moment the banshee wail of Mrs Megarrity, the Winter Cook, came hallooing down the hall, an inescapable call to account. Margaret groaned and Cissy valiantly tried to struggle from the grip of the couch. Without the page being marked, "Chrome Yellow" was closed and laid on the water-marked wood of the windowsill, long since devoid of varnish. The cooking smell that was beginning to drift from the kitchen into the sitting-room was really quite pleasant. Perhaps this evening's meal would be different.

Although all three of them, the Garrisons and Mr Pointerly, had been residents in the hotel for a number of years and in the off-season were frequently the only people who were dining, two tables were set and always the same ones, Mr Pointerly's beside the huge black sideboard with its cabinet full of grubby glassware, and the Garrisons' in the middle of the room. All three of them sat, heads slightly bowed, silently awaiting their sentence. For, what would it be this evening? Tasteless fish in a watery white sauce, accompanied by lumpy mashed potatoes and peas which, fired from a gun, would have brought down a rabbit at fifty yards? More of that tough beef, so rare that, as another guest had remarked, a good vet could have got it back on its feet? Or the now famous curry made from unspecified meat – the chimera curry, Mr Pointerly had called it – so vicious and glutinous that it could have been used as rat poison and was certainly instrumental in depleting the hotel's stock of stiff and shiny Bronco toilet rolls. With every swing of the pendulum on the old grandfather clock, the gloomy mood of the room deepened.

From the direction of the kitchen came the ominous squeak of Mrs Megarrity's tea-trolley and in a moment she appeared in the doorway, bent low and with arms straight out in front of her as if pushing a load of boulders up a steep incline, instead of the three bowls of soup which wobbled on the trolley's top shelf. One leg of the trolley was badly askew and every few inches gave a judder which threw the vehicle sideways and brought a mumbled oath from the Winter Cook as she fought to bring it back on course. At last she came to a shuddering halt between the two tables, the soup dribbling from the bowls. She drew herself up to the full five feet two of her height. As usual, she had made an effort to dress for her secondary role as waitress, with a little white waitress's hat, frilled but starchless, jammed on the front of her head and drooping over one eyebrow, and a crumpled white apron to match, worn over a black skirt that was a veritable menu, a sampler of all the meals cooked since she had last changed it a fortnight before. The cuffs of the black polo-neck jumper she wore had been turned back three or four times to fit her short arms and now hung like tyre inner tubes on her wrists, wobbling back and forth at every movement.

"Jasus tonight!" she breathed, her great chest heaving. "If I've got to put up with this thing one more day, I'll throw it in the tide – an' him along with it." As though it were McAllister himself, she kicked the bad leg of the tea-trolley and sent more soup slopping onto the top shelf. Mr Pointerly peered hopefully into the soup bowls. With a bit of luck, she might spill it all. On Margaret Garrison's face a kind of restrained anguish was in evidence as she stared straight ahead.

"God alone knows why I stay in this place," Mrs Megarrity was saying as she shoved a bowl onto the table in front of Mr Pointerly, driving more of the soup over the edge and onto the table-cloth.

"You're – not thinking of leaving us, Mrs Megarrity?" There was a quiver of hope in the old man's voice.

"And where would the likes of me find another job around here?" she demanded of him. "Tell me that, Mr Pointerly."

"Well," he said, hastily taking up his spoon, "I only meant that perhaps . . . "

Mrs Megarrity swept the remaining bowls from the trolley and planted them in front of the Misses Garrison.

"Ye slave your backside off for pittance wages," the Winter Cook was saying. "Cook, waitress, toilet attendant, jack of all bloody trades – and what thanks d'ye get for it?" She stuck her face near that of the elder Miss Garrison. "I'll tell ye. Damn all, that's what. The amount of work I have to do, he must think I'm twins. Get that down ye before it gets cold." Turning away, she laid hands on the trolley as if about to give it the thrashing it had so long deserved and wildly swung it around to face the kitchen, the momentum almost throwing her off balance and into the sideboard full of glasses. Margaret slowly lowered her eyes and looked at the grey liquid with the globules of fat floating in it. Around the inner rim of the plate there was already a dark tideline beginning to form and lumps of some unknown substance moved turgidly beneath the surface.

Mrs Megarrity was halfway to the kitchen when Margaret Garrison's voice boomed out.

"What – is this?"

The squeaking of the trolley stopped abruptly. The Winter Cook turned on her heel, her eyes glaring.

"That," she said, with the authority of an official declaration, "is the best of mutton soup."

Mr Pointerly gave a muffled cough, his spoon clinking against his plate.

"Mutton – soup?" Margaret Garrison said, her face contorting. "Who ever heard of mutton soup? It's disgusting."

Cissy, who had been craning over her bowl, spoon gently parting the rapidly-forming crust of yellow fat, gave a little shriek, dropped her spoon with a splash and squeaked, "There's a piece of wool in my soup! A fleece!"

"Jesus save us!" From the trolley Mrs Megarrity came stamping across to the table and peered into Cissy's bowl. "What is it, for God's sake? I never met as fussy people in my life. Holy

God, if this was in our house, they'd have this lot cleared and the hand ate off ye as well. Where is it?" she demanded of Cissy who had one hand clamped over her mouth. She jabbed a finger at the bowl. With practised ease Mrs Megarrity's grubby finger hooked out the half dozen strands of curly wool. "Ah, sure it's only a bit of oul' wool. Clean meat never fattened a pig," she said, and with a deft flick of her hand fired it away behind her. Mr Pointerly, who had been straining for a sight of Cissy's bowl, as though expecting to see nothing less than a crocodile hauled from its grey depths, was caught in the eye by the projectile, dropped his spoon and sent half the contents of his bowl down the front of his trousers. At his frightened yelp, Mrs Megarrity turned and came towards him as he leapt to his feet. "God Almighty, what're ye doin' to yerself now, Mr Pointerly? You're a terrible man for accidents." He stood with his hands in the air, steam gently rising from the front of his trousers. "Here, let me get that." So saying, the Winter Cook took a tea towel from her apron strings and began to rub vigorously at Mr Pointerly's crotch.

"Please – Mrs Megarrity – please – stop!"

"Now now, Mr Pointerly, don't be getting yourself into a sweat. I'm a married woman and a former nursing assistant. If I'd a pound for every one of them I've handled, I'd be wearing fur knickers." She gave a final sweep with the cloth, making Mr Pointerly flinch. "There now," she said with a wink, "that'll put a bit of colour back in your cheeks."

Wide-eyed, the Misses Garrison had sat watching Mrs Megarrity. As the Winter Cook returned to her trolley, Margaret regained her composure and demanded of her,

"What, might I ask, is for the main course?"

"Well, boiled mutton, what else! Waste not, want not."

"But – I don't like boiled mutton!" Margaret Garrison said with a stamp of her foot, her voice leaping two octaves in perfect parody of a spoilt child. The Winter Cook's face took on a savage look.

"It'd be a fine thing if we only got what we wanted in this life, so it would. Most've us've just got to take what we can get and lump it. The food money I get from him upstairs wouldn't keep a cat in fish heads. Mutton it is and mutton ye'll get!" She grasped the handles of her trolley, bent low behind it and began to push. "And I'll thank ye to be quick about it too," she threw over her shoulder. "I've still got them toilets to muck out before I finish and by the state of that one at the back, there must've been an acrobat in it." And, mumbling to herself, she squeaked her way into the kitchen and slammed the door behind her. Margaret Garrison gave a long, shuddering whimper, her sister, hands clasped before her as if in prayer, stared into the murky depths of her bowl, while Mr Pointerly sat slumped in his chair and vaguely wondered why he should have been so naive as to think that this evening's meal might just have been better than any of the others.

chapter two

Mrs Megarrity came out of the back door of the Glens Hotel kitchen, glanced around the cluttered yard and up at the rear windows of the hotel before giving a low whistle. After a few moments the bushes at the rear of the yard parted and a boy of about ten poked his head out. The Winter Cook silently beckoned to him. Out he came, to be quickly followed by four others, ranging in age from about six to fourteen, all of them tousle-haired and scruffy, with torn and patched clothes. Without exception, their hands and faces gave the impression that they had at that very moment emerged from a coal mine, rather than from the lane at the back of the yard. One after the other they ran across the yard and into the kitchen, crowding together just inside the doorway, their dark faces turned expectantly towards the mound of sandwiches and the blue jug of milk that sat on the table. She crossed the kitchen and turned the keys in the doors that led to the dining-room and to the corridor. At the table she poured out five cups of milk.

"There yez are now, boys. Get yourselves tucked into that," Mrs Megarrity told them, taking a step backwards as her four sons and Mrs O'Hagan's boy Sean surged around the table, hands darting in at the great slabs of sandwiches, mouths sucking hungrily at the milk.

Through the sounds of jaws chomping and the slurping of milk broke the high-pitched voice of the youngest boy, Jack Megarrity.

"That's bloody mine, that is! Give it here!"

"Is not!" Anthony retorted, running round the table and stuffing as much of the sandwich into his mouth as he could manage.

"Shut yer mouth, will you?" Mrs Megarrity hissed. "Yez'll have McAllister down here."

But Jack had launched a flying tackle at Anthony and the two of them fell in a heap to the floor, spitting and clawing like a pair of cats, bringing a plate and two cups down after them to smash on the floor. With a speed that belied her bulk, the Winter Cook was beside them, a long wooden spoon in her hand. The other three boys headed for the doorway. With indiscriminate aim and matching each word with a blow, she hissed at them,

"Give – over – ye – pair of – buggers – and get up – to hell – out of that." For a few seconds they carried on fighting, but the blows were falling on them with such ferocity that they at last scrambled to their feet and out of her reach, to stand panting and glaring hatred at each other, even more dishevelled than before. Mrs Megarrity advanced upon them again, spoon upraised, and had but half a stride to go when she was brought to a halt by the sound of the dining-room door handle being rattled. Then there was a knock on the door.

"Mrs Megarrity, are you in there?"

"Jasus, Mary and Joseph!" she hissed, "didn't I tell yez? It's McAllister!" Her voice took on a soft tone, with a politeness of address that she generally reserved for talking to members of the clergy. "I'll be with ye in just one moment, Mr McAllister, so I will." She turned and hit the nearest boy a sharp crack round the head with her wooden spoon. "Get out that door, ye bunch of whelps" she said in a harsh whisper, "and don't make a sound!"

Gladly they pulled open the back door and one by one slipped into the yard beyond.

"Why did you have the door locked?" Dermot McAllister asked when Mrs Megarrity finally opened it to him.

"T'was that bloody cat, Mr McAllister. Running about like a mad thing, it was." She nodded towards the broken plate and cups on the floor. "It hasn't been right since the vet took the nippers to it. I didn't want it upstairs bothering the guests, so I didn't."

Dermot gave a little smile.

"Of course not, Mrs Megarrity. That's your job." She gave him a puzzled look but he continued, "I came in to see what was holding up the dinner."

"The dinner is it?" She hurried to the stove and swept the lid off the casserole dish. "It'll be with you in two shakes of a lamb's tail, Mr McAllister, done – I might say – to perfection. I know how yourself and the Missus likes the very best."

Dermot McAllister moved towards the door then hovered near it as the Winter Cook began rapidly to prepare the meal.

"Yes, I've been meaning to ask you about that, Mrs Megarrity. The size of my food bills, I'm beginning to think we're feeding a night shift I don't know about. I mean, we only have three guests, after all."

"Well, you've hit the nail right on the head, Mr McAllister, if you don't mind me saying so. If you want my opinion, some of it's taking legs." She gave him a knowing look over a dish of steaming potatoes. "That Mary one. I'll say no more."

"You think – Mary might be taking food home?"

"Well, that's not for me to say, Mr McAllister, but – she is a

Hanlon, after all, and them's the biggest tribe of tinkers God ever put breath in. They'd take the eye out your head and come back for the lashes."

"The bill I got from the breadman the other day, I thought we must be feeding the five thousand." Wearily he shook his head. "I'm going to have to think about how we can make some economies around here – and get some more customers in while we're at it, otherwise we'll all end up in the poor house." Going towards the door he turned back and said, "Mrs McAllister was getting a little agitated about the dinner not being ready. So if you could hurry it up a bit."

"Mr McAllister," the Winter Cook said expansively, "I've got you the loveliest bit of cod that ever swum in God's green ocean, brought round special by Wee Henry himself, God love him. And a white sauce to go with it," she indicated the very saucepan, "that'll melt in your mouths."

Dermot smiled and then winked at her. "Mrs Megarrity, I only wish I was a few years older."

She smiled coyly, not realising what he had said, but when the door was safely closed behind him she pulled a face and said in a whining voice,

"'Mrs McAllister's getting a wee bit agitated.' Well, tough bloody luck, Mrs High-and-Mighty!" She slapped a spoon into the sauce, sending drops of it spitting and sizzling onto the stove top.

It had been in Dublin twelve years before that Agnes Friel had met Dermot McAllister, the big auburn-haired man from the North, with his freckled face and smiling green eyes. She had been attracted by his good looks and ready laugh, held by his easy manner and strange Northern accent, with its short vowels and lilting cadences. As she got to know him better in the following days and weeks, she began to discover and grow fond of his personality – so unlike hers – that made him by turns carefree to the point of recklessness, and a little melancholic, though never without a streak of kindliness which she thought at once admirable and endearingly naive. Those were the reasons, she had decided, or had perhaps imagined, as she lay alone at night in their bed, lulled to a half sleep by the sound of the waves lapping along the shore, while below in the shuttered hotel bar Dermot served drink for the laughing, garrulous faces. What she had never admitted to herself was that she had been attracted to Dermot because her friend Colette had seen him first at the party and accidentally bumped into him to strike up a conversation. A Wexford Friel could hardly let such a challenge go unheeded. And after all, Colette Grogan was only a grocer's daughter and could hardly be expected to compete with a scion of what Agnes in her greater flights of fancy liked to think of as "landed gentry", or in more sober moments, "gentlemen farmers". She had gone up to Dublin for a few days in the hope that the boredom of rural life might be temporarily replaced by the modest excitement of shopping trips and Francis Cooley's party. Dermot had come with two friends to the city for the All-Ireland Hurling Finals at Croke Park and had made acquaintance with Francis in The Long Hall pub in South Great George Street after the match. Of course, if Agnes had known that at the time, she might well not have spoken to Dermot at all. It was tantamount to him having picked her up in the pub. But that night she had enjoyed herself more, had laughed longer and louder at this humorous storyteller, than she had done for as long as she could remember, and most telling of all had abandoned, at his repeated request, her usual glass of sweet white wine for the whiskey and water that he drank with his stout. On reflection, the jollity of the night and the next morning's hangover, could have served as a metaphor for their subsequent marriage. The fact that he was a hotel-owner, she would admit, may have had some little part to play in his attractiveness to her. She had fondly imagined some large establishment called the Strand Palace or the like – Colette said that Agnes read too many romantic novels – which would generate enough cash and provide the setting for her to hold court in the manner in which her mother did more modestly in Wexford. Now here she was, stuck in this Northern glen by the sea, not entirely unhappy, because she had her son and she did care for Dermot, but had grown tired of what she called "the parochialism and determined ruralism" of its inhabitants, where she still felt like what the locals called "a blow-in". Her ready smile was still there, but now it was tight, almost painful. In her imagination other worlds beckoned, but if the Wexford Friels had nothing else, if they were lacking in humour and frugal with affection, they had a sense of duty. And she knew where her duty lay. Unfortunately for Agnes, Dermot was not quite so principled.

Agnes slipped the small piece of cod from her fork, chewed it, tasted it and then said,

"Yes, well, I suppose it is all right." She neatly separated another few flakes of fish and with them poised on the end of her fork added, "But it took her long enough to prepare it. And these peas – they're like buckshot. I wouldn't be surprised if she was too busy eating – and feeding that tribe of hers – to concern herself about serving us."

"Now Agnes, you've got no proof of that at all."

"Dermot, I know she does, and I wouldn't be surprised either if she's stealing food to take home as well."

Their eight-year-old son Patrick, who disliked fish and had been poking through it in the hope of finding a bone as big as a whale rib in order to demonstrate the mortal danger in which he had been placed by being ordered to eat it, looked at his mother and said,

"I looked out the upstairs window one time and there were

kids all round the back door. Hundreds of them. Ah! Why'd you kick me, Dad?"

"Get on with your dinner and mind your own business. You've got your music practice to do."

Patrick stabbed viciously at an innocent potato. "I hate music."

"I'm not surprised, the way you play the piano."

"Dermot, leave him alone," Agnes said. "He's doing very well for a beginner. You'd be better employed deciding how you're going to get rid of that Megarrity woman."

"Yes," Patrick said, seizing his opportunity, "I don't like her. She smells – and she's got a big fat arse."

"Patrick McAllister!" his mother almost shrieked. "Where did you learn a word like that?"

Dermot busied himself with his dinner, his eyes narrowing against the expected tirade. Patrick, who had developed a considerable degree of low cunning for one so young, turned to his mother and said primly,

"Mrs Megarrity said it. I thought it was all right – seeing as she's a grown-up."

"Well, that's it, Dermot! The woman will just have to go. I won't have her – polluting my son with her bad language and uncouth manner. There's little point in sending him to a good school if he comes home to hear that kind of language."

"Oh, for goodness sake, Agnes, it was probably at school he heard it."

"Did not, smarty."

"That's no way to speak to your father. Get on with your dinner. Dermot, you'll have to get rid of her. I've been telling you that for years. I know I said I wouldn't interfere in the running of the hotel, but enough's enough."

"Now Agnes, you know how difficult it is to get anybody around here. And besides, she's not exactly expensive. I'll have a word with her. Leave it to me." His roguish smile was met by an obstinate stare. "And you know, beneath that rough exterior, she's got a heart of gold. Anyway, I've got more important things to worry about than Mrs Megarrity."

"Such as what?"

"Such as this hotel. I'm not doing much more than breaking even, except in the summer season, and you know how short that is."

"And when was it any different?"

"Well, it wasn't – much. But that was alright as long as the farming income kept up. Now that's on a downer too. Sheep prices dropping, store cattle hardly worth the raising. I tell you, for two pins I'd sell this place – if I could find an eejit with enough money."

Agnes looked a little taken aback at this suggestion from her husband. Being the wife of a hotel owner, even of the Glens Hotel, carried a degree of prestige that would not be easily obtainable by other means.

"Dermot, your father would turn in his grave. You couldn't possibly sell the hotel."

"Well, I don't know. Maybe not. But I tell you, something's got to be done, otherwise we'll be eating spuds and milk."

With this, a sort of sullen silence descended upon the little group as they finished their main course and turned to the ice-cream, a dish that not even the Winter Cook could spoil.

From the windows of her house in the main street of Inisbreen, Mrs McFall was in the habit of keeping an eye on the activities of her neighbours and of any passers-by. It was nothing personal, it was just that she was nosey. Now that obnoxious little McGhee man with the limp was standing across the street, staring at her and daring her to continue looking at him. She tossed her head and quickly turned away from the window, while Limpy smiled and continued on his way up the street and past the Inisbreen Stores, the brownpaper parcel under his arm containing a fresh trout, fetched out of the river the evening before by Dan Ahearn. A brown trout, Limpy had said to someone on the bridge, not one of those foreign bloody rainbow things. It would do nicely for his tea, so it would.

He passed the stores and turned the corner to where the road ran parallel to the beach with a low wall separating them. Now at low tide lay exposed and glittering in the sun great swathes of bladder wrack and small rocks worn round by the constant pawing of the waves. The smell of salt and seaweed was strong in the air. Up ahead of him, looking out to where a flock of birds floated on the water and quarrelled noisily over some tidbits, a small figure in a raincoat stood with her hands resting on the wall. Limpy stopped and screwed up his eyes. It was Cissy Garrison. He glanced around but her sister Margaret was nowhere to be seen, a situation which was unique. "Must be joined at the hip," people would say. Limpy quickened his pace and in a few moments was approaching her, saying,

"Is that you, Cissy?"

She gave a little jump as she turned towards him, alarmed.

"I'm sorry, I didn't mean to scare ye." Like an awkward schoolboy he shuffled his feet and gripped his parcel tighter. "It's been a long time. How've ye been?"

She glanced back nervously towards the corner. He had always thought she looked like a little bird, one of those kingfishers he'd seen away up the river where the banks were high and sandy.

"I'm fine, John, thank you for asking. I keep very well." She gave the briefest of smiles. "We do a lot of walking, you know."

"Indeed ye do and many's the time I've seen ye, striding out there. It wouldn't be me that could keep up with ye."

She shot him a glance from beneath lowered brows.

"You were able to at one time."

Limpy gave a little snorting laugh.

"Ah, I think ye were good enough to walk slower."

Standing side by side, they both looked out to sea, suddenly overwhelmed by the memories that crowded in on them.

"Ye'd wonder where the years went, wouldn't ye? Me away in Derry, you down here."

"I suppose it's just life, John," she said. He wanted to say, "No it wasn't just life, it was your father and then it was your sister," but instead he shuffled his feet and said,

"I was just wonderin', Cissy, if you and me could, well, maybe have one of them walks again some time. Of course," he added hurriedly, "maybe you're too busy for the likes of that."

Before she even had time to formulate a reply, the strident voice assailed her from the corner, like a mother calling her child away from a dangerous encounter.

"Cissy!" Margaret boomed. "I haven't got all day." She stood glaring at them, one of her arms akimbo, the other holding her little bag of purchases. Cissy gave another little jump.

"It's Margaret. I've got to go, John. Nice speaking to you again." She turned and hurried away towards the corner, head down, shoulders hunched, as Limpy stared after her and said, more to himself than Cissy,

"Why d'ye have to go, Cissy? That's the question," the last words dying on his lips.

"What d'you mean wandering off like that?" Margaret said as she set the pace and strode out for the hotel. "You could've been anywhere. And talking to that – unpleasant little man. He hasn't changed, you can be sure of that."

Although he would normally have walked home by the road, Limpy went through the gap in the wall and onto the broad expanse of greensward that stretched between the wall and where the bluey-green spikes of marram grass grew on the first sand of the beach. Sitting down on the green-topped sandy bank above the beach, his legs dangling over the edge, his patched jacket flapping in the wind, he drew out a tobacco pouch and papers and rolled himself a cigarette. As the exhaled smoke was snatched away by the wind, he looked down at the place near the black rocks where they used to gather, all those years ago, watching as others ran to dive into the cold water, splashing and chasing the squealing girls. And as he couldn't chase Cissy, she had stayed beside him and they had talked about every subject under the sun, as young people in their late teens do, whilst they still know everything. He had never understood why it had to end. It was obviously to do with Cissy's family. Her mother had been a nice enough sort of a woman, a bit stuck up, maybe, but polite and quite friendly. Her father had been a different kettle of fish, a right old bastard, with his Rolls-Royce and his camel-hair coat and his way of tapping the side of your leg with his cane when he wanted you to move out of the way, like he couldn't bring himself to talk to a peasant, far less let his daughter be friendly with one. Probably wanted her to marry a rich man like himself. And she ends up marrying nobody, just like her sister. Limpy struggled to his feet, stood facing into the wind and stuck out his chest. He was as good as any man and better than most and he should have stood up to them, taken Cissy away with him and to hell with the family and their money. He clamped his trout under his arm and started towards the road. That had been a very long time ago. All those wasted years in between, where that horse-faced Margaret had taken over from her father the guardianship of Cissy. Margaret and old Garrison. Two peas in a pod. Sometimes he wondered if it had really happened. Still, there was nothing to be done about it now, and as he hobbled out onto the road again he consoled himself with the thought of the brown trout for tea, washed down by a glass or two of best poteen.

chapter three

In the comfortable and well-appointed living-room of the chapel house that overlooked a hay meadow sloping down towards the river, Canon Daniel O'Connor moved his ample midriff a little to one side and found himself a more comfortable position on the couch. His fat fingers with their square-cut nails were intertwined on his lap and his shiny shoes were reflections of each other, brought face to face by the crossing of his plump ankles. He leaned back comfortably, looking around the familiar room as though taking his leave at that very moment, his eyes narrowing momentarily here and there as they lit upon an object of particular memory – the signed picture of the Pope from the Marian Year pilgrimage to Rome, the statuette of Our Lady of Lourdes. Canon O'Connor sighed contentedly and from his inside jacket pocket drew out a fat cigar which he slowly unwrapped, taking care to leave the band in place, before rolling the end between his lips and applying a flame from a lighter which he took from a pocket in his bulging waistcoat. The perfect circularity of the smoke ring which he blew might have been an apprentice piece for his own halo.

The door opened and Father Burke came bustling in to drop

down on the other end of the couch, bouncing the Canon from his comfortable perch, so that the cigar end brushed past his lips and almost went up one of his nostrils. He turned and looked at the new parish priest, whose nose was puckered against the acrid smoke.

"A parishioner," the priest said, "wanting to know if it was all right to have – relations – with her husband when she was fasting before Communion. God help us."

"Mrs O'Hagan," the Canon said without hesitation. "The woman's paranoid about – " he smiled at the young priest, " – relations." The cigar was a baton of authority in his hand. "And what did you tell her, Father?"

"I told her that of course as she was fasting, nothing should be allowed to pass her lips – " the Canon raised his eyebrows, " – and that anything that could lead to such an event presented a grave risk and should be avoided."

"And what did she say?"

"That the question didn't normally arise because by the time she'd finished her prayers, her husband was usually asleep and then she spent more time thanking the Lord for answering her prayers. I'm going to visit her to-morrow."

"I wouldn't bother, if I were you. You'll come out stuffed full of soda bread, tea and nonsense. Did she tell you she had nine children?"

Father Ignatius Loyola Burke looked surprised. "Really?"

"Really, Father" the Canon replied, and took another pull on his cigar.

On a low table before them, Mrs McKay the housekeeper prepared tea, pouring the tawny liquid from the fluted china teapot into the matching cups. Before handing the Canon his tea, she stirred in the milk with delicate strokes.

"It's a fine parish altogether," the Canon was saying. "Very good Mass attendance – and regular communicants. Good, down-to-earth people, you know? Call a spade a spade. You'll like them, Father. Mind you, you will find a bit of drunkenness, but not much else in a serious way of going."

Father Burke tried to remember where the Canon had said he was from originally. His accent and manner of speaking closely resembled those of the locals.

"Well, maybe a bit of extra-marital sex as well."

The priest glared at him and then rolled his eyes to remind the Canon of Mrs McKay's presence. She had taken a seat and was drinking tea.

"Ah, you needn't worry yourself about Mrs McKay, Father. Mh?" He gave her a conspiratorial smile. "You know, one man told me he'd had extra-marital sex." The Canon leaned forward, smiling. "I told him that was all right as long as he hadn't used a hyphen." Like a volcano erupting, the Canon started with a low rumbling in his chest that grew in depth and loudness and then broke out into a rich chuckling laugh, his fat jowls shaking in accompaniment. "Laughed so much we near blew the doors off the confessional." Father Burke did not so much as crack a smile. "It's a matter of developing a relationship with your parishioners, Father. A little give and take, you know?" But seeing the grave face of the young priest, he added, "Within the laws of God and the Church, of course."

"If you don't mind me saying so, Canon," Mrs McKay said, bracketed by two slurps of tea.

"And even if I do," the Canon smiled round his cigar.

"I think you're giving this parish too much benefit of the doubt. I mean, look at some of the things that – "

"Now, now, Mrs McKay. Let she who is without sin cast the first stone."

"Well, those that live in glass houses should take the consequences, I always say."

This apparent non sequitur briefly sent a furrow across Father Burke's brow before he turned to his housekeeper and said,

"Mrs McKay, would you very much mind taking your tea in the kitchen, please?" As though about to give him a reply in kind, she glared over her teacup at the priest. She caught the Canon's eyes indicating that she should leave, so she rose abruptly and said,

"Whatever you wish, Father."

The door closed behind her as the Canon said, "If you would take a piece of advice, Father, from one who knows. You'd do well not to make an enemy of Mrs McKay. When it comes to running this parish, she can be a very useful ally. Knows everybody – and all their business. Many's the time she's got me out of a hole." His eyes drifted up to a high spot on the wall, as if it showed a living frieze of events during his time in the parish.

"Thank you, Canon, but I don't think I'll be needing my housekeeper's advice in running the parish. I do have plans of my own."

The Canon chuckled. "Well now, they're not very big on plans around here, Father. I wouldn't make too many of them if I were you."

It was on the tip of Father Burke's tongue to say, "Well, you're not me," but there was no point in falling out over it. Very soon the Canon would be gone, although no doubt the attitudes he had helped to engender would take a little longer to remove. The man had plainly been there too long and had obviously gone native. He, Father Ignatius Loyola Burke, knew how to run a parish – hadn't he virtually run his previous one in the face of a weak parish priest – and knew that there could be no compromise with sin or the perpetrators of it. Since the day he had started his studies at Maynooth, hadn't he prayed fervently every night for the Lord to show him the way? Hadn't he promised his mother, who had given him support and encouragement since boyhood, that he would be steadfast in his faith and would accept any burden the Lord chose to lay upon him? What was this appointment – he was one of the youngest parish priests in Ireland – but a sign from the Almighty that He had chosen His humble servant for special service? He knew where his duty lay and it was not in going native with a bunch of crafty glensmen. Despite their Catholicism, the dash of Scottish blood in their veins gave them a pragmatism and hard-headedness that was not conducive to unquestioning acceptance of the Church's teaching. But he was a Dublin man, and more than a match for any of them.

The Canon was saying something about salmon.

"So whenever you fancy a piece of salmon, Father, you just give the nod to Mrs McKay. She knows where to get it for the right price. I tell you, we had one last summer, it was so fresh it swam round the pot three or four times before the heat got the better of it. And rabbits – or a pheasant, if you've got the taste for it – just let her know and she'll do the rest. Mind you, some'll come your way without the asking, just handed in at the back door of an evening." His grey eyes gleamed with mischief. "But for some reason, the salmon mostly seem to appear on the doorstep overnight."

There it was in a nutshell. The man had been eating poached salmon. And the Lord knows what else had been happening in this house. The Canon was not long in telling him, lowering his voice to a stage whisper.

"And if you're partial to a drop of poteen," he gave a little nod of his head, "you're in the right place, Father."

Father Burke momentarily closed his eyes. Cigars, poached salmon, illicit drink, indeed any kind of drink. What sort of image would the parishioners have of the Church? They must have thought the chapel house was Liberty Hall. The task that he had been set by the Lord was clearly going to be more difficult than he had anticipated.

"Thank you, Canon, but my tastes in food tend to be simple. Porridge for breakfast, a light lunch – no more than a collation – and a dinner of perhaps soup, potatoes and vegetables and a little meat or fish. I'm also in the habit of fasting one day a week. Eating, I think, should be regarded as a necessity, not an indulgence. And I never touch alcohol. I've seen what it can do."

The Canon regarded the priest's spare physique with some distaste.

"So have I, Father. That's why most people drink it. Listen, by the time you've been here in the sea air for a few weeks, you'll be eating and drinking like a navvy."

Father Burke gave a self-satisfied smile.

"I hardly think so, Canon." He just wished the man would go. They had nothing at all in common except for their religious function and he was even beginning to have doubts about that. The sooner he got started on the work of rehabilitating the parish, the better it would be. Scarcely had the thought formed in his mind than Mrs McKay came into the room and said in what the new parish priest regarded as an overly-familiar tone,

"You'll be staying for a bite to eat, Canon? I'm just putting a wee something on now."

The Canon was undecided. His big eyes widened in questioning anticipation. Father Burke tried to make a signal of disapproval to the housekeeper but decided that he had been blatantly ignored.

"What're you doing, Mrs McKay?"

"Trout and mushrooms in a white wine sauce, Canon, with asparagus tips and new potatoes, and then apple turnovers and cream to follow."

There was plainly annoyance in the lowering of Father Burke's head and the set of his shoulders. The Canon's lips twitched and a hand moved involuntarily in his lap, as though the feast was already before him.

"I know how much you like your apple turnovers," Mrs McKay added.

The smile was benign, conferred upon a child eager to please.

"Thank you, Mrs McKay, it sounds delicious, but I really do have to be going. It's a long drive to Armagh I have."

Father Burke glanced out of the window at the large BMW which sat in the driveway, the latest in a long line of splendid cars supplied by the business of the Canon's family. It wouldn't take long to get to Armagh in that. He himself had been thinking about eschewing the use of a parish car altogether and buying a bicycle. Example was everything. Later, in his prayers, he would seek guidance.

Father Burke was on his feet before the Canon had made a move. The Canon struggled to his feet, the cigar a smouldering stub in the ashtray beside him. He crossed the room to Mrs McKay, who stood with a tea-towel in one hand. Grasping the other hand he shook it vigorously and like the action of a water-pump, tears welled up in the eyes of the housekeeper.

"Goodbye dear lady and thank you for all your kind assistance over the years. I'll remember you in my prayers."

The housekeeper gave a great sniff.

"Canon, I – God bless you. Who's going to look after you now, might I ask?"

Canon O'Connor, with Mrs McKay's hand now held in both of his, leant forward and kissed her firmly on the cheek. Father Burke turned away, unable to conceal the surprise and disapproval on his face. "God bless you, now, and look after yourself – " the Canon gave a wicked little smile," – and Father Burke too, of course." He gave her a wink unseen by the young priest.

"Goodbye, Father."

He turned and shook the other man's hand. "I hope you'll be happy here, Father. For a young man such as yourself, now, it's a great opportunity. You'll find there's more to this place than meets the eye." He threw a glance over his shoulder at

Mrs McKay who was dabbing her eyes with the tea towel. "I'm sure the bishop and Mrs McKay will see you all right."

"I'm sure," said Father Burke coldly, "they'll both be very helpful." The audacity of the man, to even suggest that a housekeeper, of all people, would "see him all right". At their very next meeting, he would need to make it quite plain to the Bishop the state to which the parish had been allowed to deteriorate.

He led the Canon out of the room, Mrs McKay feebly waving her tea-towel as she might have a handkerchief at a departing ship bearing away a loved-one, her face brimming with restrained emotion. On the driveway, the vast BMW was stroked into purring life, and with a little wave of his hand, Father Burke watched as the car was backed out and raced off down the narrow road that led to the village. Hand on the gleaming brass door-knob, he stood there for a moment, the upper valley stretching before him to end in a great rounded hill, the browns and greens of its slopes merging in the soft evening light. Now he was quite clear as to the nature of the task the Lord had laid upon him and he would carry it out to the best of his ability. The closing of the front door, he felt, was symbolic, the end of a chapter and the opening of a new and exciting one to meet the challenges of the future. And the first challenge was that specimen in the kitchen who was cooking him trout and mushrooms in a white wine sauce, with apple turnovers and cream to follow.

Heading the big car towards the village, Canon O'Connor passed the Misses Garrison out for their evening walk. As he had always done to every local, he waved a greeting to them, although they were not parishioners of his. Along with a mere handful of others – Frank Kilbride, owner of the Inisbreen Stores was one – they were Protestants, and now and again, on what the visiting minister considered a special occasion, the sisters would attend a service in the little Church of Ireland church that sat among pine trees near the shore road. In the small graveyard beside the stone building, their father and mother were buried, and sometimes, if Margaret only wanted a short walk and was feeling particularly sentimental, she would announce to Cissy that it was the graveyard this evening and would she hurry up and get ready. But this time it was the longer route they would take, from the village to the bridge a half mile up-river, then along the chapel road, but going in the opposite direction, and finally across the strand and through the village back to the hotel – about two miles in all. Margaret insisted on it. It was good for the constitution, she said, and yet she dismissed Cissy with tutting and a wave of her hand when she asked why, in that case, did she always feel on the point of collapse when they finally reached the foyer of the Glens Hotel.

Now they walked silently side by side between the burgeoning hedgerow fuchsia and honeysuckle, each woman with a walking stick from their father's collection. Ever since they could remember, they had taken walking sticks on outings such as these. They were a sign of purposefulness. Not just a stroll, such as the locals might take, but a walk. Quite different. For want of anything better, most of the locals had always gone on foot in the old days, and certainly without walking sticks, whereas the Garrisons – father, mother and two daughters – had done so out of choice. And didn't the walking sticks say who they were.

They had passed the chapel house garden and were approaching the row of cottages on the other side of the road that ran down to the bridge when Margaret cleared her throat as she always did before she made what she called "an announcement", and said to her sister,

"You know, Cissy, that since Mother died, I've always taken care of the – financial side of things." It was probably the first time she had ever broached the subject with Cissy, or anyone else apart from her adviser in Belfast, Mr Rowan, who was even older than she was.

"Yes, Margaret," Cissy said with her usual air of indifference. She was watching a large bird which had settled on a tree by the river.

"And with what Father left us – and Mr Rowan's invaluable assistance, of course – we've been quite comfortable over the years. Mr Rowan has advised me on investments and so forth – I won't bother you with the details – but generally I left it to his superior knowledge. And he's done well by us. Very well. But now, as he says, unfortunately money is tight, and we have perhaps even been living a little beyond our means." A small sigh escaped her lips. "Although, heaven knows, it has been a modest enough existence." Dreams of another life of grand houses, extended tours and a respected place in high society had faded and gone like the morning mist from the hills. Still, the two women had never worked a day in their lives, nor had the thought of doing so ever entered their heads. "The fact is, Cissy, that according to Mr Rowan, there is very little left in the bank and even if we sell the few remaining shares – which Mr Rowan's son has kindly offered to buy from us at a very reasonable price – we will only have enough to last about another three or four months. Then – I simply don't know what we're going to do. I've been at my wits' end about it for weeks." Her feeling of despair momentarily gave way to one of resolution. "But I believe there is a possibility of getting something from the government – much as the thought of it pains me – after all of the taxes Father paid. I just don't know if I could bring myself to ask for it. Mr Rowan said he could perhaps look into it for us, but of course, as we soon won't have the resources to continue paying him . . . "

Cissy was intently watching the bird as it flew to the river bank and began pecking at something in the undergrowth.

"Have you been listening to me, Cissy?"

"Of course, Margaret."

"And don't you have anything at all to say on the matter?"

"I suppose we'll have to apply for Social Security."

Margaret looked at her younger sister in surprise.

"For – what?"

"Social Security. They give you money if you haven't got any."

"They – give you money? Who gives you money? And – how do you know about this?"

"I've heard the locals talking about it. Lots of them do it. If they don't have a job – and sometimes even if they do – the Social Security pays them. They get a cheque every fortnight in the post."

"A cheque – every fortnight?" A slight tremble crept into Margaret's voice. "And how do you get this – cheque?"

"I'm not sure. I think you just apply." She had lost sight of the bird now and was looking around for something else to occupy her attention. "It's some kind of government thing."

Margaret gave a little smile at the mention of the government.

"Indeed. A government thing. Well, that sounds very much like what we require. Social Security." The words had a kind of warm, protective feeling about them. "Of course, we should need considerably more than the locals, what with hotel expenses and the higher standard of living that we need to maintain, but I'm sure Mr Rowan could sort all that out for us. He's coming down to see us in a week or two. I'll discuss it with him then." She bestowed an unusually warm smile on her younger sister, and with a fresh spring in her step and a renewed vigour in the swing of her walking stick, she stepped out for the bridge over the brown river. Three or four times along the road she said slowly and under her breath, "Social Security," savouring each word and its golden prospect.

Later that night, on the mountain road to Castleglen, Dermot McAllister pulled his car off the tarmac and into a clearing shielded by bushes from the few passing vehicles. Switching off the ignition, he sat for a few moments and looked down at the glen below, seeing the pinpoints of light scattered on the slopes grow more numerous as they reached Inisbreen, where they coalesced into a tiny cluster of house lights and street lamps. Above, the last light in the western sky tinged pink the few fingers of cloud that rode above the valley, stragglers lingering there before making their passage eastwards across the sea. From this position, Dermot could almost see the piece of land adjoining his, which was across the road from the house of Nancy Quinn who was at this moment sitting beside him in the car, the land which he had yet to persuade her to sell to him. But he was working on it, and tonight he would bring the big gun to bear. He smiled in the darkness. If he got the timing right, she would give in without a fight. Having taken a long look at the scene, he gave a sigh before turning to Nancy who slipped her hand onto his arm and said dreamily,

"You thinking the same as me, how beautiful it is?"

"Well, sort of. I was thinking how beautiful it would be if I could join those fields of mine with that one of yours. Then I could run sheep across the whole lot and get access directly to the road."

"Oh you're not still on about that, are you? Is that all you brought me up here for? To talk about land?" Her lips thrust forwards into a pout. "I wonder sometimes why I ever took up with you at all." She turned away from him and hunched her shoulders into a sulk. "I don't think I like you any more, Dermot McAllister."

"Ah now, don't be like that, Nancy," he said, caressing her leg with a big hand, "Sure you know I couldn't do without you. But that land's no use to you on its own. What are you going to do with it, eh?"

"Don't know. Haven't made up my mind yet."

Dermot's hand slipped further up her leg and underneath the short skirt.

"I could help you out there."

She slapped his hand away, though not too hard, then pulled herself nearer the door. "You only ever wanted me for one thing," she said.

"Well, one thing at a time, I always say. I was never greedy. And I couldn't think of a person I'd rather steam up car windows with than you, Nancy. Now come on over here and I'll show you how much I love you."

By gentle teasing and slow cajolery he gradually drew her to him, and the embrace into which they fell soon quickened into a flurry of wild kisses and frenzied gropings, fingers racing here and there amidst an embarrassment of fleshly riches.

"Oh Dermot!" Nancy gasped as she tore at her skirt to remove it. "God save us, we shouldn't be doing this!"

"I know," he said, his hands diving for his belt buckle, "but nobody's perfect. Put the seat back, Nancy! Put the seat back, I'm coming on over!" Fumbling down the side of the seat she pulled on a lever, throwing the back of the seat and herself flat all at once. Nancy gave a little shriek followed by a louder one as something hairy pressed against her face. She went quite rigid.

"What? What the hell's wrong, for Christ's sake?" Dermot demanded.

"A rat! There's a rat on my face! Get it off, Dermot! Get it off me!"

Reaching out in the darkness, he felt the offending article.

"It's not a rat. It's a – bit of a sheepskin rug I was taking to a fella." Dermot grasped the dead lamb which he had meant to take to the vet that very day and pushed it further back on the rear seat.

In the confined space they struggled to remove the

appropriate garments. When his hand finally guided hers to the protrusion beneath his shirt, she gave a little gasp and said,

"Oh – my – God!" with a shudder of fear and pleasurable anticipation. And then, "Oh – yes, Dermot. Yes!" Dermot reached out to steady himself on the door. He found that no further movement was possible.

"Come on Dermot – please!" Nancy reached up for his shoulders.

"I – can't. Jasus, Nancy, I can't move."

"What d'you mean, you can't move?"

When at last he spoke, his voice was grave. "I think – one of my legs is – paralysed."

"What? Jesus Mary and Joseph! Paralysed? God, I knew we shouldn't have done this, I knew it. It's a judgement on us. What's my mother going to say when she finds out her unmarried daughter's been shagged by a cripple?"

In the enclosed space, Dermot's shout was like an explosion.

"What the hell's your mother got to do with it? My life could be hanging in the balance and all you can think about is what your mother's going to say."

Through sobs, Nancy asked,

"Which – leg is it?"

Slowly she felt down the leg he indicated and then she began to snigger.

"Oh, I'm glad you think it's funny."

"You eejit," she giggled, "you've pulled your trousers down over the gear stick."

"Well it's not bloody funny. I could've been paralysed for life."

Her hand slipped round from the side of his leg to the front of him.

"As long as this isn't paralysed," she said, and guided him towards her. As they commenced a slow and steady rhythm, the car springs creaked, setting up a counterpoint to a dull clash from two buckets in the boot.

"God, this sounds like a tinker's cart," Nancy said, between gasps.

"How's that, Nancy? Okay?"

"Oh, that's – fine, Dermot, just – fine."

"Good. There's something you could do for me."

"Oh God – yes – anything."

He suddenly stopped moving.

"Sell me that field. I'll give you a good price for it."

"Dermot, don't stop." She pulled him tightly against her. "I'll think about it. I promise you. Only – don't stop now."

With the movement of the vehicle the dead lamb on the seat began to rock back and forth, one outstretched leg slowly moving towards Nancy. After a few seconds she said in a timid voice,

"Dermot. There's something – tapping against my head."

"Ah, come on now, Nancy," he said with a chuckle, "I'm not that well endowed."

"What? I said there's something touching my head." Awkwardly, she stretched an arm behind her and slowly her fingers closed around the cloven hoof. Her voice was a high-pitched whine. "Jeeesus! It's the devil! He's come for us!"

"What now? What, for feck's sake? This is like sleeping with a banshee."

"There's – something – in this car! Jesus, Mary and Joseph make it go away, Dermot! Make it go away, pleeease!"

"God Almighty would you stop leaping about, woman. You'll have it wrenched off me." He reached up and thrust the leg away. "Dammit, it's only a lamb – and it's dead."

"Dead? You told me it was a sheepskin rug!"

"Well it is nearly. Now come on for God's sake. Where were we?"

"I'm not doing anything with a sheep watching me."

"Jasus wept! It's dead!"

"I'll still know it's there. Those big eyes. You'll need to get rid of it."

"Give me patience. All right, all right, I'll get rid of it. Mind your knee there, for God's sake!"

Nancy moved to allow Dermot clear passage to the driver's seat, and then she said, "What's that?" She reached down with her hand to feel what was resting against her knee and then gave a little giggle.

"What?" Dermot almost shouted. "What the hell now?"

"It's – " Nancy broke into laughter, " – it reminds me – the other day in the butcher's – there was a sausage on the floor – " she gave a shriek of laughter, " – and somebody had trod on it!"

"Is it any bloody wonder, with all your shrieking? Let go of me."

"And this woman says to her husband – " Nancy gasped, "thinking I couldn't hear – 'I see,' she says,'somebody's stood on that sausage. What's your excuse?'" As Nancy shook with laughter Dermot angrily flung himself towards the driver's seat, catching a blow from the gear stick that temporarily put all notion of sex out of his head and banging his back on the steering wheel. Throwing open the door he hauled the dead lamb after him. Then standing with his trousers round his ankles, with Nancy hanging out the door pointing and laughing, he held the lamb by the leg, whirled it once round his head and flung it away into the darkness. When he got back into the car, she said to him through her giggles,

"Oh God, you should've seen yourself!"

"Very bloody funny, I'm sure," he said."

"I couldn't help laughing, Dermot. You were such a sight. But darling – you know I love you, don't you?"

"Oh yeah? I sometimes wonder."

"Oh but of course I do. Don't you know I'd do anything for

my big hunk?" Nancy gave him a kiss on the cheek. "Including sell you that piece of land."

Dermot sat upright in his seat.

"You would? Really? Ah, you don't know how much that means to me, Nancy." He leant over and gave her a hug. "Thank you. I won't forget this."

"Mind you," she said, "there is a drawback."

"Oh yeah? What's that?"

"You'll have John McGhee as a tenant and him hardly paying a penny in rent. You know the old rogue actually came round yesterday looking for a rent reduction? I couldn't believe it."

"Never misses a trick. So what did you say?"

Nancy laughed. "I told him some people would pay big bucks to live so near a holy place like the Mass Rock and in fact I should be putting his rent up, not down."

"I'm sure that made a big impression on that old heathen."

"You're right. He said it hadn't done him any good and him a cripple all his life." Nancy slowly began to run her hand up Dermot's leg. "So I told him he'd just have to keep praying for a miracle. You know what he said? 'The only miracle'll be the day a Quinn parts wi' money.' The cheek of him."

But Dermot hadn't heard the last part of what Nancy had said. He was staring out of the windscreen and through the trees to where the village lights glowed in the valley below, as an idea, a wonderful idea, slowly formed in his mind.

chapter four

One evening about two weeks after Dermot McAllister at last acquired the piece of land near the chapel from Nancy Quinn, Limpy was sitting in the small crowded bar of O'Neill's public house in the village of Inisbreen. Behind the counter Mrs O'Neill presided over the proceedings from her high wooden stool beside the cash drawer, her wrinkled hands plucking coins and notes from hand and counter and dropping them into the till with the speed and skill of a conjurer. While her son Danny pulled pints, wrenched the caps off stout bottles and measured out whiskey and rum for the thirsty customers – and all at a trot – "the Mother", as he called her, sat serenely in the corner surveying the bar, her eyes and ears missing nothing. Her hawk-like features and formidable bulk had made many a customer give second thoughts to challenging her ruling on standards of language and behaviour in her establishment. Arbitrarily, using no known logic or published code of conduct, and with the plaintiff having resource to no court of appeal, least of all his peers, she would eject customers without explanation as to reason or length of sentence. "You! Out!" was her declaration, accompanied by the pointing of a long and unsavoury finger at the miscreant who, unless he was very swift, found himself in the village street with his unfinished drink still on the bar. She kept it to sell to other customers, they said, but not within her hearing. Humour was not a strong point with Mrs O'Neill, any more than was conversation. Many years before, when Danny was still at "the wee school", Mr O'Neill had run off with one of the barmaids, young enough to be his daughter, as Mrs O'Neill would have it, a black-haired temptress with scarlet lips, low-cut tops and skirts so short you could clearly see her intentions. Years passed before word began to drift back to the village that Mr O'Neill and his seductress were running a pub in Birmingham and had three children. There was renewed speculation as to how Mr O'Neill had managed to have even one child with Mrs O'Neill, or indeed had succumbed to marriage at all, as it was generally agreed that he should have legged it in the opposite direction the moment she hove into view. It was also an established fact that, ever since, she had been taking it out on Danny and her customers.

On a stool at the counter, Limpy sat hunched over his Guinness and Bushmills whiskey, an unlit roll-up cigarette dangling from his brown-rimmed lips. His brown hands and face with its deep-cut lines were evidence of the time he had spent outdoors, "watching people working", some said. But there was always money for a few drinks, they noticed. Maybe he had found a crock of gold. He was certainly small enough for a leprechaun. And if nine o'clock in the evening passed and Limpy was not leaning against the bar counter, there would be talk in O'Neill's of sending out a search party. He would have done no less for any of them. Kings and queens could come and go, empires crumble, but Arthur Guinness and Old Bushmills remained the cornerstones of their social life. They were, as someone had once said, members of the legal profession who had been called to the bar at an early age.

"Listen," he was saying to one of the young Moore boys, the one that had left for Scotland with a teacher's wife and returned home with someone else's, "what the hell has Europe ever done for the farming people round here? Eh? Tell me that. They don't know a damn thing about this land. Sitting over there in – wherever the hell it is – telling us – " he prodded his chest with a forefinger, " – bloody telling us how to run our own places." He pushed back his greasy cap to reveal a startlingly white expanse of skin and swayed gently on his stool. To young Moore's disparaging look he said, "Listen, boy. There's been McGhees in this glen for – thousands of years – "

"Aye, and you're one of the originals," somebody said from the back. Limpy smacked the counter to dispel the laughter.

"Thousands of bloody years, boy. And they're telling us how to farm this land?"

Johnny Spade, so-called because his father had once made his living by hiring himself out as an agricultural labourer, turned to the other patrons who were craning forward at the promise of a lively argument and said,

"Jasus, would you listen to him. He never did a decent day's farming in his life. He wouldn't know the difference between a yow and a cow."

"What? I wouldn't what?" Limpy was on his feet, his face thrust forward pugnaciously. He stuck up two dirty hands. "You see these here hands? They've done more work on this land – more work than any other living man, so they have." The crowd gave a groan. "And by God, I could still match myself against any man, even I am over sixty – and with a bad leg." He dipped down on one side to show just how bad it was. John Breen, a big, raw-boned hill farmer from the top end of the glen looked straight ahead and said in his slow drawl,

"Bad legs ran in your family, didn't they, McGhee?" "There was never nobody ran in his family unless it was away from work," someone else chipped in, to added laughter. Limpy was off the stool and hopping up and down on his good leg.

"Who said that?" he shouted, vainly trying to see past those who towered over him. "Who said that? Let him step out here and I'll face him. Yous wouldn't know what a day's work was, the half of you. One day cutting turf on that mountain and you'd be carried home on a shutter, every damned one of yez!"

"Sure what would you know about cutting turf, McGhee? You only ever got it from somebody else's stack."

In frustration and anger, the little man stamped a foot on the floor.

"That's it!" he said. "Bloody well that's it. You bunch of back-stabbing gits. I'll take no more drink here this night." The fact that it was almost closing time and that he might be called upon to stand a round of drinks did not go unremarked by his fellow patrons. They knew well his mode of operation, and it seemed that a night was not complete until he had had at least one argument and come near to blows, although never actually engaging in violence, as it was, he said, against his pacifist principles. In quick succession he threw back his whiskey and the remainder of his stout, banging each glass on the counter, so that even Mrs O'Neill, who had been taking little interest in this nightly event, looked towards him and narrowed her eyes.

"Clear the road!" he said as he pushed his way through a throng of people to the door and threw an insult over his shoulder before stamping out of the bar. When the laughter had subsided, John Breen said with a smile,

"Maybe you were a bit hard on him, boys."

"Ah, he's always in here shooting his mouth off," young Moore said. "What the wee bastard needs is a good kick up the arse."

One by one the other voices in the bar fell silent as all eyes slowly turned towards Mrs O'Neill whose basilisk glare turned on young Moore who grew suddenly pale and had difficulty in getting his words out.

"I'm – eh – sorry there, Mrs O'Neill." This was accompanied by the gesture of a forefinger almost touching his brow. "Sorry about that." A good piece of scandal was one thing, but calling a man's parentage into question was another matter entirely in Mrs O'Neill's book. Breaths were held as they watched the face of she who was the final arbiter of taste and decorum, and then shoulders dropped in relief as she gave a little toss of her head and looked away.

"Last orders please, gentlemen! That's the time now!" Danny O'Neill announced, revelling in the only moment of authority kindly allowed him by "the Mother". Later, under the pretence of taking a walk to clear his head of smoke and drink fumes, he would meet Annie Curran in the Church of Ireland lane near the beach for a few fleeting kisses. But that relationship too had its problems, given that Annie embraced the principles of creative conjugality, that is, with no possibility of a ready-made man able to meet her exacting standards, she would need to create a bespoke one from the common clay that was the generality of men. And the first requirement was that Mrs O'Neill would play no part in their married life. Danny was still thinking about it.

In the wan light from a moon half hidden by cloud, Limpy McGhee started out on the walk home across the strand and then up the chapel road that ran alongside the river. "The oul' feet know the way on their own," he would say, and that was just as well, given the frequency with which they had to perform the function without aid from his reeling brain. His gait was like the movement of an eccentric wheel, made worse by the peculiar action of his limp, so that he proceeded by a series of gradually rising hops that, after four or five, subsided and began their ascent once more. In the late evening the wind changed direction and freshened and now blew in from the sea, bringing with it the tang of the sea-weed strewn on the beach by the receding tide. Limpy stood on the grassy bank above the sand, his body swaying slightly from the combined effects of drink and the onshore wind, and he looked out over the bay towards the horizon, there being just enough light to see where the sea met the sky, almost in a uniformity of colour. There was something magical about the sea at night, the moon's reflection riding on the waves that crashed and hissed their way up the beach, the wind whistling in his ears, the dark bulk of the land looming behind and on either side of him. There were plenty of people who wouldn't go along the beach after dark, but it didn't bother him. Been used to it all his life, he had. Go anywhere. Eyes like a cat. Oh, they liked to poke fun at him, they did, because of his bad leg, because he spoke his mind and would face any man in an argument. Like those boys in O'Neill's, taking a hand out of him. They thought they knew him, thought he was just an ignorant old cripple. But that's where they were wrong. He was smart, a lot smarter than most of them realised. Did some deep thinking at times, came up with tremendous thoughts on all sorts of things. There was that time that he'd come up with that great idea on . . . . Well, he couldn't remember exactly what the subject had been but he definitely remembered it had been a great idea. Time would prove him right. If he could remember the idea.

He began his tortured progress once again, rising and falling with the action of his bad leg, exacerbated by the uneven ground. A few ragged notes from some half-remembered air escaped his lips as he made his way through the thorny whin bushes on the strand, drawing his jacket collar tighter around his neck. Then abruptly he stopped walking and stared out at the water again, screwing up his eyes to improve his vision. Had he seen something out there, some object bobbing between the dark waves? He leant forward and peered at the spot, confused by the jumble of waves and troughs and wind-patterned water. A branch of a tree, was it, or a beach ball? Could be a seal, but he didn't remember having seen one of those at night. He concentrated even harder on the spot. Was . . . was a mermaid possible? He already half believed in the Little People, had heard too much evidence to deny their existence. Maybe this mermaid had come for him, to lead him slowly into the breaking waves to a watery paradise. Well, he wouldn't be found wanting when it came to it, old and all as he was. He'd picked up a thing or two about women in his time, and enough never to have married one of them. That one in Portrush whose father had been a butcher. He had been doing all right there until he found out she had been flogging her own mutton at the back door to any man that would slap a tenner in her hand. Limpy looked out again at the water and blinked. He could no longer see the object, and as he set off again on his way homeward, he reassured himself that it was probably a seal. And what use would a mermaid have been to him anyway? Didn't everybody know they were fish from the waist down.

Underneath the tall sycamores of the chapel road Limpy hobbled, zigzagging back and forth across the road, knowing, as someone had said "all the soft places in the hedge to bounce off". He stopped once, where the road ran close to the river, and stood for a moment listening to the water chuckling over the stones. "I'll have a salmon or two out of there soon," he said, perhaps confusing past achievements with future possibilities. Years before, he would have been down there with his little net after dark, wading waist-deep in the brown water and throwing two or three of the great silver fish onto the grassy bank. There was always a hotel would buy them at the back door. Those were the days.

He started forward in a sudden, headlong rush at a pace hardly sustainable by his mismatched legs, as though wanting to leave those memories behind him by the river. Further along the road he passed the graveyard and the chapel, dark against the last vestiges of light in the sky. With difficulty he climbed the gate on the other side of the road, paused swaying on the top as his bad leg scrabbled for a foothold, then plunged down the other side, barely able to remain upright on the steep ground. In the top corner of the field stood his house, a two-roomed, tumbledown affair with tiny windows that Canon O'Connor said had raised neglect to an art form. The pigs that had been its former inhabitants were long since gone, although it would have been difficult for the untrained eye to know of their departure. At the upper side of the field, the trees of an ancient plantation ended in a rocky outcrop and in this, partly shielded by overhanging branches, was set a crude stone carving of a crucifix some three feet high and surrounded by other Christian symbols. This was the Mass Rock, brought there, some said, at the time of the Penal Laws and for many years used in secret worship. On certain holy days a little procession would come to it from the chapel and now and then a tourist or two who had read the footnotes in the guidebooks. Apart from that, it lay quiet and undisturbed in its wooded seclusion, its former religious significance lost on the agnostic Limpy, whose sole observation on the subject had been, "You wouldn't know what the hell it was supposed to be. The boy that carved that must've been straight out of O'Neill's bar."

Slowly, Limpy began to climb his way up the slope, three steps forward and one back, so that at times he teetered on his heels and threatened to fall and roll down to the road again. The trees blocked out most of the remaining light from the western sky, making the rock itself invisible and causing pools of darkness on the uneven land. How often had he crossed this field in the dark – more than once on his hands and knees – with only his homing instinct to guide him to his front door?

The door that had no lock on it and led straight into a kitchen which also served as a bedroom. Had there been any sheets on the bed, they would have been torn to ribbons by the boots he wore, but he had long given up using sheets for the sound reason that it saved undressing at night and dressing again in the morning, as well as a deal of washing of both himself and the sheets.

"Efficiency," he would say, "is how man has learned to survive and prosper on this earth." He plunged on through the clumps of grass and benweed, and then all at once he felt as if he had lost contact with the ground and was being borne aloft by some invisible force. Trees and bushes and the ground leapt and spun, against the black sky white light streaked into his vision. Then, as suddenly as he had been flying through the air he was falling in the pitch darkness, farther and farther, until he found himself lying on the ground, which seemed to be swaying and heaving beneath him. He lay there for a few moments, the grass cool against his unshaven cheek, his befuddled mind trying to place himself in the subsiding kaleidoscope of swirling grass and trees and glowering sky. With an effort, he hauled himself to his knees and peered about him.

Dark shapes swam into vision and then out of it. High up somewhere – surely in the sky – there was something white, something moving, a person maybe, and a voice talking to him, saying words that he couldn't quite understand. Or was it the old eyes? They weren't so good these days, but he'd be damned if he'd ever wear glasses. He craned forward. It was somebody, surely. A woman, dressed in white and high above him, her two arms extended and a heavenly glow all around her. Again she might have spoken, but still the words weren't clear. At the third attempt, he struggled to his feet, to take a few tentative steps towards her. His head ached where he had hit it on the ground and a sharp pain gnawed at his bad leg, but nothing a drink wouldn't put right. Now the woman, if woman she had been, was nowhere to be seen, so after shaking his head to clear it, Limpy started again for his little house, the terrain easier now, more even and with fewer of the boulders strewn from a broken wall. With an unusual turn of speed he strode across the grass. Indeed, he fairly flew over it. Need to ask O'Neill what the hell he was putting in the drink. Best poteen, for sure. It's the only thing that would do it. And then Limpy came to a dead stop, to stand rigid at the entrance to his front yard, his mouth wide open and a gentle swaying motion moving his entire body. First one foot went forward gingerly and then the other, as though he were treading with bare feet on hot coals. He considered this for a few seconds then tried another few steps, less cautious than the first ones. Then quicker they came, across the yard and back again with lengthening stride, wheeling at the top like a guardsman, faster and yet faster until his legs raced to pass one another in a frenzy of movement. And when he finally scrunched to a halt in the middle of the yard, his breath coming in short gasps, Limpy McGhee lifted his arms and eyes heavenward and in a voice soft with reverence said,

"Jasus Christ Almighty – it's gone. It's bloody well gone!"

Limpy stood outside the house of his neighbour, John Healy and once more battered on the door.

"John! Would you get up to hell and open the door." Taking a step backwards he looked down at his legs, shook his head and said softly, "Jasus, Mary and Joseph." Above him came the squeak of a window being raised and before he could look up at it a boot hit him on the shoulder and Mrs Healy's gruff voice shouted,

"Get away out of that to your bed, you drunken, foul-mouthed being, before I set the dog on you." The window screeched then banged shut. Leaping back, Limpy shook his fist at the darkened window.

"You oul' witch, I'll throttle your bloody dog!" He ran at the door and gave it a kick. "John Healy, are you going to let a woman run you? Would you open this door for God's sake! I'm a dying man!" There was a short silence and then, "John! Would you let me die out here alone?"

Again his boot thudded off the door. After a few moments the light in the upstairs room came on and there was a loud exchange of voices, quickly followed by a thundering of feet on the stairs, before the door was flung open to reveal the tousle-haired Healy in his pyjamas.

"Listen, ye wee bugger . . . "

Limpy fairly flung himself at Healy, shouting, "John, for Christ's sake listen to me! It's a miracle! I swear to God! I can walk, man! I can walk!"

"At this time of night, it's a miracle you can stand."

"No, no. Look." The little man walked up and down in front of the house and there was no trace of his limp. "D'you see, John? My bad leg, it's gone! Over there." He jabbed his finger excitedly, "I was coming across and I saw this woman above me." He held out his arms. "Like this. And she called me and – I fell down. And when I got up – Jasus God – the limp was gone. Look!" He gave another demonstration of his new-found ability, executing brisk steps and fancy turns with the skill of an Irish dancing champion.

"John!" Mrs Healy's voice came bellowing down the stairs, "would you get rid of that wee eejit and come up the stairs!" But her husband's interest was thoroughly aroused.

"Bloody hell's teeth, McGhee" he said. "Show me that again."

It was well after midnight when Healy drove Limpy to the chapel house and with a steady banging on the front door roused Father Burke and Mrs McKay from their beds. Persuaded that it was a matter of great importance and that anyone looking like Limpy could only have been snatched from the jaws of death in a wet ditch, the priest showed the two men into the living room, ignoring the whispered protests of Mrs McKay, swaddled in a huge old dressing-gown, that the wee one was a drunkard and a crackpot that would need fumigating for a week before a living Christian would let him over the doorstep. Her insistence that he would be "lepping with fleas" fell on deaf ears. In the living-room there was a garbled explanation from both John Healy and the miracle man which only served further to confuse the priest. Then, with a broad grin, Limpy McGhee marched up and down like a toy soldier, leaving a trail of mud on the carpet. A silent snarl set itself on Mrs McKay's lips.

"God knows, Father, it's a miracle right enough," Healy told the priest as they observed the performance. "The wee man here's had that disablement since ever I knew him. It would've pained you to watch him go."

"You say this happened at the Mass Rock, Mr McGhee?"

"The very place, Father. I was going home, across the field thonder and suddenly – this figure appeared above me. Jasus Christ! It shook me, I can tell you."

The young priest look puzzled. "You're saying that – Jesus Christ Himself appeared to you?"

"Ah no, Father. T'was a woman. All in white, she was, with her arms out – like this – and floating above the rock. Well, I needn't tell you, I fell over at the sight of it." His eyes grew wide and he leant towards the priest. Mrs McKay was slowly shaking her head at such gullibility in a man of the cloth. "And then – she spoke to me."

The priest drew back at the acrid breath assailing his nostrils.

"Spoke to you? And what did she say, Mr McGhee?"

"She says – 'John McGhee, you've had that there limp too long, and you never deserved it in the first place. So I'm going to do a miracle on you.'"

"She said that?"

"Them was her very words, Father. Or similar to."

"Disgraceful old liar," the housekeeper said under her breath.

"And did she say – who she was?" Father Burke inquired.

"Who she was?" It was Limpy's turn to look puzzled, but only for a moment. "Well – not exactly. But she didn't need to. She had this gold thing shining round her head and she says to me, 'I want people to say their prayers and lead good lives.' Well, I knew straight off who she was." And as he assumed that the priest, being a man of God, also knew, Limpy did not elaborate. Father Burke shook his head.

"This is quite remarkable, to say the least, Mr McGhee. Very remarkable indeed. You are in effect claiming to have seen a vision of the Virgin Mary."

"Another night it'll be pink elephants," Mrs McKay murmured.

"Tell me, Mr McGhee. Was there by any chance a witness to this event, this – apparition that you saw?"

Limpy leant forward, his face alight with religious intensity.

"A witness, Father? Well, of course there was a witness." The eyes of the other two men widened in anticipation, and even Mrs McKay leant forward to catch his words. "The Good Lord himself," Limpy said, with a reverential glance heavenward. "Didn't he see the whole thing."

chapter five

It was stuffy in Doctor Walsh's small waiting room for the morning surgery. Fourteen people with various ailments or none sat staring at the wall to avoid each other's eyes, conversing with their neighbours in hushed tones or flicking through ancient copies of Horse and Hound, The Field and Shooting Times. Mrs Maguire's four-year-old darling James, having tired of scattering the magazines on the floor, crawled beneath a chair and popping his head out between both chair and human legs looked up the skirt of the woman above.

"Don't do that darling," his mother told him, "you'll get your clothes filthy."

Between a young pregnant woman and a fat woman with varicose veins in her legs, sat Dippy Burns, his thin frame hunched forward, his pale face under the lank hair showing signs of anxiety. Over the past few months he had been steadily working his way through the illnesses in his copy of "The Home Doctor", and having been mentally if not physically debilitated by the vicissitudes of anaemia, botulism, two minor cancers, (with a temporary diversion by way of ovarian cysts), some physical benefit had at last accrued by the yoga-like contortions he undertook while examining his toes for Foot,

Athlete's. Now he was in the grip of an unknown fever, and was also momentarily expecting an attack of haemorrhoids so severe that he wondered whether he should really be standing up. Having sneaked a preview of Verrucae, he had pondered the fascinating possibilities of simultaneously suffering these and haemorrhoids, in which case neither sitting nor standing would be possible. This was the first time that he had succumbed to two illnesses at once, and he looked forward with pleasurable dread to the many combinations he might exhibit before finally expiring, his place in Irish medical history secure.

In his consulting room, Doctor Walsh paused before pressing the bell-push to summon his next patient. He turned and gazed out of the window to where a couple of fat wood pigeons sat in a fir tree. Slowly he put his head to one side, raised his arms and squinted along an imaginary shotgun barrel. Bang! He had got both of them with the one shot. Then he watched with glazed vision as they tumbled from the branch, wings flapping in a parody of flight, as though even in death they were attempting to soar to safety. That's what he should be doing on a fine day like this. Or perhaps he could be along the river bank with a rod, stalking those elusive brown trout in the deep pools beneath the overhanging hawthorn and hazel or on the deck of his little boat, straining to haul a large cod up from the depths. He sighed and turned back to his desk, his hand poised over the bell-push. Perhaps, just perhaps, there would be one interesting case amongst today's lot, one person for whom he could really make a difference, save a life, or just change a life for the better, rather than the usual crop of ingrown toenails, imaginary cancers and problems that should be dealt with by a social worker. He sat a little straighter in his chair and pressed the white button at the corner of his desk.

The outside door to the surgery opened and Father Burke came into the waiting room, closely followed by Limpy, wearing the same clothes as he had been the night before – a pair of dark trousers with bulbous knees, a dirty tweed jacket frayed at the edges and one pocket flap torn off, cracked boots and a plaid shirt stiff with dried sweat. As the patients stared at the unlikely duo making their way directly to the consulting room door, they drew back with nostrils twitching at Limpy's passing. He smiled and nodded to his audience. Maybe some of them had heard already, but if they hadn't, they soon would. And a celebrity like he was shouldn't have to wait in a queue. On the contrary. They'd soon be the ones forming the queue to hear his story, to touch the miraculous leg – "the celestial transplant", sounded better, he had decided – or even to ask for his advice on religious matters.

The man who had risen from his seat at the sound of the buzzer and was reaching out for the door handle of the consulting room, suddenly found a smiling Father Burke at his side.

"I'm sorry," the priest said, grasping the door handle, "parish business."

After a peremptory knock by Father Burke, the two men marched into the consulting room and closed the door behind them, leaving the bewildered onlookers to stare in wonderment at each other. What could that old eejit and the new parish priest possibly have in common and why would they be seeing the doctor together?

Doctor Walsh looked from Father Burke, who had taken the only other chair in the room, to the individual who stood before his desk grinning like he was about to be pronounced sane.

"It's very good of you to see us at such short notice, Doctor," the priest said. "This is the man I was telling you about – Mr McGhee."

The odour that wafted across the desk caught the doctor

unawares and he drew his head back sharply, leaving Limpy under the misapprehension that the doctor was mightily impressed by him.

"How're ye, Doc?" Limpy said. "I've never had the pleasure of being unfortunate enough to need yer services. Thank God," he added, for Father Burke's sake. Limpy judged that his new status demanded a more formal manner of speech. After all, he wasn't just anybody now.

Doctor Walsh regarded him with a distaste that would have been obvious to anyone but Limpy.

"You said something about – a leg – Father?" The doctor looked down at Limpy's lower limbs as if they harboured a virulent plague, something that was not outside the bounds of possibility.

"Yes, Doctor. Mr McGhee appears to have undergone – shall we say an instantaneous recovery from a lifelong affliction. A severe limp."

Limpy held himself a little straighter and beamed.

"And how long have you had this limp, Mr McGhee?"

"I inherited it from me father. He had one the dead spit of it."

"You – inherited it." The doctor sighed, saying under his breath, "Dear God." Aloud he said, "I see. And now its completely gone?"

"Devil the sign of it. In fact, I would venture my opinion, Doc," Limpy wound himself up to it, ready to deliver the phrase so lovingly fashioned and burnished in his mind, "that it was nothing less than what you might call – a celestial transplant, thanks be to God." He slapped his restored leg and said, "She's as good as new." And then with his little choking laugh said, "In fact, better than new!"

Doctor Walsh gave a pained look to Father Burke, who did not reciprocate. A strange light gleamed in the eyes of the young priest.

"A celestial transplant," the doctor said through clenched teeth. If he had had that shotgun, it wouldn't be the pigeons he would be aiming it at now.

"I'd like you to examine him, Doctor, if you would. To verify that the leg is in perfect working order."

Doctor Burke's gaze slowly descended from Limpy's matted grey hair to the toes of his battered boots.

"A visual examination, I think."

There was a riverful of fish waiting to be caught and he had to be stuck with these two fools. He waved a hand.

"Just – walk up and down there a bit Mr McGhee, will you?"

Limpy promptly complied, with an enthusiasm born of novelty, and almost goose-stepped back and forth across the small room, whirling round at each end by means of a fancy three-step routine that seemed to have come naturally to him, as it had been entirely unpractised.

"Amazing," Father Burke murmured. "Amazing."

"Mr McGhee," Doctor Walsh barked, "I didn't ask for the Highland Fling. Just walk up and down in what passes for a normal manner."

When Limpy had done so, the doctor asked him to get onto the low examination table and slip down his trousers. This revealed two skinny and hairless legs and a pair of tattered underpants, all of which were covered in a grey patina of dirt. Limpy looked down at his legs as though he had just made their acquaintance.

"It's this one, Doc. I swear to God it could run a mile on it's own."

Doctor Walsh regarded the miraculous leg.

"Now that would be a miracle." He took a pencil from his desk and poked the flesh around the hip joint. "Judging by the colour of this limb, Mr McGhee, it would appear that your so-called "celestial transplant" was from a donor of somewhat more Asian origins than yourself. Tell me – and I hesitate to use a profanity in front of a man of the cloth – but, do you have such a thing as a bath in your house?"

"Ah, you obviously don't know his house, Doctor," the priest said. "Pre-Renaissance Celtic."

The doctor nodded.

"Our family was never very big on washing," the little man on the couch replied. "My old Da used to say washing takes the bloom off yer skin."

"If I could see yours," Doctor Walsh said, "I might venture an opinion."

Then the doctor had Limpy turn this way and that, stretch and bend his leg while he watched the action of hip, knee and ankle, after which he sat down behind his desk and motioned Limpy to dress.

"As far as I can see, Father, the leg is perfectly normal – apart from the colour, of course, which is not. But naturally, as I haven't seen his previous disability, I'm unable to comment on the nature of the recovery."

Father Burke looked so pleased that he might have effected the miracle himself.

"Thank you, Doctor. Thank you very much indeed. I think we may have something very exciting here. Possibly even – " he stopped to savour the word, "miraculous."

Limpy stood dressed and ready for further instructions. Doctor Walsh rose to indicate that they should leave.

"In this trade, Father, there's not a lot of room for miracles," he said, glaring at Limpy. "Soap and water – and a lot less drinking – those are the only miracles that are required here."

"Ah now, Doctor," said the parish priest with an indulgent smile, "everything in its place. The Good Lord sometimes works in mysterious ways."

Perhaps he could see his way to working on these two, Doctor Walsh thought as he prodded the little man through the doorway. When both of his visitors had gone, he rushed over to the window and flung it open.

Dermot McAllister sat in his tiny office under the front stairs of the Glens Hotel and wondered how best to break the news to the Garrison sisters. He had been over it four or five times in his mind, rehearsing different approaches, now hard and unyielding – the ruthless capitalist who pursued old women for money – now caring and understanding, ready to accept that it was merely a hiccup in their financial affairs and that they would soon be placed on a sound footing once again. No doubt the South African diamond mines had been having a difficult time, the Shell and Esso dividends had been a little disappointing, or else the rise in the birth rate had done the London Rubber Company shares no good at all. No, that wouldn't do. Best keep it simple. And yet it all seemed so unlikely. Everybody knew the Garrisons were well-heeled, had been for decades, and it would surely be just a matter of days before they came up with the cash. There was probably no need for such an unpleasant confrontation. But unfortunately Agnes had been looking through the accounts and had noticed the missing payment from the previous month. It was pay up or get out, she had said. The place didn't make enough as it was, without entertaining freeloaders. And of course she was right. Hadn't he only been saying something of the sort himself a few weeks ago. Dermot sighed and began to go over the last few months accounts again. Perhaps he had made a mistake.

There was no-one in the foyer except Mr Pointerly, who was standing at the window looking forlornly out at the rain which came drifting across the bay in waves, obscuring the far shore and scarring the glassy surface of the river water. Now his walk would have to be postponed. He squinted in the other direction, the one from which the prevailing weather came, up towards the round-topped mountain that was the infallible barometer. "If you can't see the top for cloud," a local would tell a tourist, "the weather's going to be bad. And if you can see it – it'll be worse." The mountain-top was covered in cloud, so perhaps in a short time he could take a stroll – up the river would be nice – see if there was anyone about, any boys fishing there. He could talk to them, tell them about how that place had been a favourite fishing spot of his as a lad, give them the benefit of his years of experience and perhaps even share their sandwiches with them. A little frisson of excitement ran through his stooped frame and he wished that the rain would hurry away. He turned to see the two Misses Garrison coming down the stairs. He nodded gracefully.

"Ladies."

"Mr Pointerly," they replied, almost in unison. Like himself, he thought, from the old school. He almost regarded them as family, they had been residents together for so long. As he turned back to check on the progress of the rain – another reason why boys might be fishing, he happily realised – the two sisters opened the door of Dermot's office and squeezed themselves inside.

"Ah, Miss Margaret, Miss Cissy," Dermot said, taken a little unawares and rising so quickly that he bumped his head on the sloping ceiling. He sat down abruptly. "Please – take a seat."

"Thank you, Mr McAllister," Margaret said, and with some difficulty they wedged themselves into the available space, with Cissy noisily passing wind. She gave a little smile, and her sister and Dermot pretended not to notice.

"We received your message, Mr McAllister," Margaret said superfluously.

"Ah, yes. Thank you for coming down, ladies. I – " Dermot shuffled his papers. "There is a matter of some – well, delicacy – and importance – that I need to talk to you about." Not for the first time he remarked to himself on the fact that when he conversed with either of the two sisters, he tended to adopt the same somewhat stilted manner as they did. "It concerns the payment, or should I more properly say the non-payment, of your monthly bill." He lifted a cheque and held it up to show where it had been stamped in red on the front. "I'm afraid to say that this cheque, Miss Margaret, has – well – bounced."

Cissy Garrison looked at the slip of paper as if she had never seen a cheque before in her life, which may well have been the case, while Margaret gathered her huge handbag to her bosom, glared at Dermot and said,

"Bounced, Mr McAllister? Bounced? Garrison cheques do not bounce!" She waved a hand dashed with large freckles and when she spoke again her pouted lips lent yet more disdain to her voice. "There's obviously been some administrative error at our accountants. I have no doubt whatsoever that it will be corrected very quickly."

"Well, I hope so, Miss Margaret, I really do. But I have to say – it isn't the first time this has happened. The cheque for the previous month, it also bounced. I had to re-present it."

"Mr McAllister, you have my assurance," her voice rose half an octave, " – my absolute assurance – that I will speak personally to my accountants immediately. I'm quite sure there is nothing with which you should concern yourself. Nothing at all."

Dermot shook his head. This was harder than he had imagined.

"I'm not a hard man, Miss Margaret, God knows, but I do need to tell you that, if another cheque bounces – well – I'm afraid that's it. I really don't have any choice. You and Miss Cissy, I'm afraid, will have to – go."

Margaret looked at Cissy and then turned to stare at Dermot.

"Go?" she said. The word went through Dermot like a lance. "Go where, might I ask?"

Cissy passed wind with a squeak but this time she did not smile.

"I – I don't know where, Miss Margaret. That would be up to you."

The elder sister looked at him in frank amazement.

"But we do not have anywhere else to "go", as you so crudely put it. We sold our house all those years ago, when we came to live here, when we made this our – home. My sister and I are not "going" anywhere."

With a long sigh and a scratch of his head, Dermot tried again.

"Miss Margaret, you must see my position. I'm not a charity. I simply can't afford to keep people here free of charge. I am running a business, after all."

Cissy nodded in agreement and Margaret glared at her.

"You would do that? After all the years we've been here? After all the money we've paid? Oh, how times change. It certainly would not have been like this in your father's day."

"I know," Dermot said. "That's why he nearly went bankrupt. And while we're on the subject of money, Miss Margaret, I have to say that your monthly rate has not gone up by one penny in over five years. I mean, if I was to charge you the proper rate, it would be about another ten or fifteen percent at least."

Margaret looked at him as if she had never stooped to doing anything so common as calculating a percentage. Her sister looked blank and said, "Ten percent."

"Mr McAllister, I do not wish to hear another word. I will speak to my advisers forthwith."

"Is that sooner or later than this afternoon?" he asked.

Ignoring this remark, the elder Miss Garrison tapped her sister on the arm and indicated the door, while Dermot gently fanned himself with a sheaf of bills. But Cissy did not depart without leaving a final memento, and Dermot made a mental note to have Mrs Megarrity crush a few charcoal tablets into the younger Miss Garrison's food – if the two sisters were still around, that is.

Margaret Garrison strode through the foyer towards the front door, Burberry buttoned to the neck and yellow sou'wester pulled tight around her head. Mr Pointerly approached, swiftly removing his hat.

"Do forgive me, Margaret," he said very quietly, "but I couldn't help – well – overhearing some of your earlier conversation with Mr McAllister, regarding your little financial difficulties."

Miss Margaret glared at him as at one who had been caught loitering in public toilets, but Pointerly pressed on.

"I'm not a rich man, as I'm sure you know, but – well, I do have more than enough for my needs, and I would deem it an honour, indeed, a privilege, if you would allow me to – "

Margaret's upraised hand stopped the words in his throat.

"Enough, Mr Pointerly! Do not say another word! There has been a minor administrative error by the guardians of my late father's estate. Nothing more. And I would be thankful if this matter would now become what it should have remained all along, private and confidential." She started for the door. "We are now going for a walk."

Mr Pointerly hastily drew aside, hat pressed to his chest, his features crestfallen at the manner of the rebuff. As she passed the coat stand, without pausing in her stride Margaret swept two walking sticks from it and tapped one against the leg of Cissy who, similarly attired to her sister, let out another riffle of wind as she struggled to open the heavy front door. Outside, the rain fell straight and heavy.

"But it's raining, Margaret," the old man said, stupidly pointing.

"A little rain, Mr Pointerly, never stopped a Garrison," she said, and the two women marched out abreast, leaving the door wide open behind them.

Ten minutes later, Dermot looked up from his pile of papers on hearing the wailing sound that came from the direction of the kitchen. He listened. Then it came again, more distinct as words now, although he could not make out their meaning. What he could make out was that the noise emanated from the Winter Cook, and she was heading his way. He had barely laid down his pen and stood up when there was a thudding of feet on the floorboards and she was standing in his doorway, one hand at her throat, the other grasping the sleeve of her brother's jacket, her great chest heaving and wobbling beneath her black jumper. Limpy stood beside her smiling broadly, the prize exhibit.

"Oh, Mr McAllister, God save us," she panted, "you wouldn't believe what's happened!"

"What, Mrs Megarrity? What's happened?"

"Oh, you wouldn't believe it! I swear to God, you wouldn't!"

"Well you're not giving me much of a chance. Tell me what happened."

"A miracle has been done on me," Limpy said in a measured tone. He was quite getting used to these announcements regarding his new status as a miracle recipient and probable future object of veneration. "Last night the Virgin Mary cured my bad leg."

Dermot could not have looked more surprised if Margaret Garrison had just paid her last two month's bills in hard cash.

"What?"

"Show him," the Winter Cook instructed, poking Limpy in the shoulder. As Dermot came to the door of his office, Limpy took off down the corridor like a greyhound from a trap, executed a brisk turn at the kitchen door and almost sprinted back to where he had started.

"Good God," Dermot muttered. "How did that happen?"

"Last night, at the Mass Rock," Limpy told him. "The Virgin

Mary appeared to me and then – wham! – the leg was as good as new. You'd hardly believe it, Dermot, only you'd seen it with your own eyes."

"Jesus," was all that Dermot could venture.

"It's a miracle, Mr McAllister!" Mrs Megarrity said reverently. "It's a proper miracle!" She blessed herself. "Oh, thank God. Thank God Almighty." She clapped a congratulatory hand onto Limpy's shoulder. "That's what comes of leading a good life."

But this contentious statement was lost on Dermot as he stood with a puzzled look on his face but the beginnings of a smile creeping across his lips. He slowly shook his head.

"Well, Mrs Megarrity, you might be right," he said. "It may indeed be a miracle."

When Father Burke called, it took a long time for Bishop Tooley to come to the telephone. Age had slowed him, and the only reason he didn't use a walking stick was the little touch of vanity against which he had fought for so many years. And to no great effect, he thought. He should have gone long ago, of course, back home to Cavan to live out whatever time the Good Lord allowed him, but because of the shortage of priests, he had been asked to stay on, long past normal retirement age. And these days half the parish priests were mere youngsters. Either that or they were decrepit, like himself. Oh, he had prayed hard and often for more vocations to the priesthood, for more young men to take up the call, but so far the Lord had not chosen to answer his plea to any great extent. Now there was this new one in Inisbreen who had the kind of light in his eyes that usually spelt trouble. Perhaps it had been a mistake to give him a position of authority at such a young age, but what choice had there been?

"Good evening to you, Father." The Bishop's voice was soft and reedy.

"Ah, Bishop, there you are. I'm sorry to disturb you, but there's a matter of considerable urgency that I'd like to discuss."

With a sinking heart the Bishop noted the enthusiasm in Father Burke's voice.

"Oh, I see. Will it take very long? Only I am rather – occupied."

Dozing in an armchair had long been an essential part of his afternoon routine. "Only a moment or two. I just wanted a piece of advice, really." Father Burke cleared his throat. "I think, Bishop, I have a case in my parish of," he paused for effect, "what appears to be a – miraculous cure."

"You – what?" Bishop Tooley's degree of deafness was often dependent upon the subject under discussion.

"An apparent case of a miraculous cure, Bishop," Father Burke repeated more loudly. "I believe I have one in my parish."

What had he said? A miraculous cure? Not another priest with a drink problem. And there was no use him blaming it on the communion wine.

"And what makes you think it's miraculous, Father? People are cured all the time using the unmiraculous technique of medicine."

"Ah no, Bishop, no. This was instantaneous. No doctors involved at all – except that a doctor has declared the limb in question perfectly normal. No, this was a man cured of a major and long-standing affliction while passing an ancient shrine last night – the Mass Rock here in Inisbreen. And he claims to have seen – and been spoken to – by the Blessed Virgin herself."

Bishop Tooley waited for a respectable period before asking,

"He didn't by any chance have – drink taken, Father?"

Father Burke's voice was taut as his words crackled down the line.

"He may possibly have had a little drink taken, Bishop, but that has no bearing whatsoever on the fact that a very severe and lifelong limp disappeared in an instant and the man now walks completely normally."

Bishop Tooley breathed a heavy sigh. Television had a lot to answer for.

"Father, Father, my advice to you is – forget the whole thing. It's probably somebody's idea of a joke. You can be sure there's drink involved somewhere." A weary sigh from the bishop whispered down the line. "Now, I'll say good evening to you. God bless, Father."

Father Burke stood looking at the receiver in his hand, hardly able to believe that the Bishop had ended the conversation so abruptly. Here he was with an event in his parish – indeed an event of which he was virtually a part – which had all the hallmarks of a miracle, and the Bishop dismissed it as the ramblings of a drunkard. Was it any wonder the state of the diocese? God help him, the poor man was the common butt of their humour when two or more of the clergy got together. Well, bishop or no bishop, he knew where his duty lay. Not only his duty but perhaps even his destiny. When this was shown to be a miracle, which he, Father Ignatius Loyola Burke had recognized and brought to the attention of a sceptical world, it might well start a revival of devotion to the Blessed Virgin, bring pilgrims flocking to Inisbreen and perhaps – yes, it was possible – make his name known inside the very walls of the Vatican itself. He allowed himself the ghost of a smile. And he had been bemoaning his lot about fetching up in this backwater, this remote village where nothing ever happened and he would have no chance to shine. Well, it was now clear to him that, not only had the opportunity arrived, but that he had recognised it and so he was now going to seize it with both hands.

chapter six

At the far end of the main street from the bridge, the Inisbreen Stores was an emporium of such a diversity of goods that any request for something out of the ordinary was a voyage of discovery for its owner Frank Kilbride and his assistant, Peggy May, who was generally regarded as simple, although not so simple that you could give her a fiver and expect the change from a tenner. As there was no other shop in the village, the windows did not need to perform the usual function of attracting customers with pleasing displays. Set up long ago, the window dressings comprised a pyramid of assorted cans with faded labels – prunes supporting cling peaches which in turn held up processed peas and tuna steaks – another pyramid of custard packets buckled with age, and two cardboard signs, one for sewing thread and the other for sheep dip. In the second window, throughout all four seasons, languished a pile of children's plastic buckets and spades, their bright colours washed out by the sun, an inflatable duck whose head had gradually drooped as the air had leaked out or from disappointment at being unwanted, and a clutch of small wooden frames with green fishing line wrapped tightly around them. On the back partitions of each window, as occasion demanded, were pinned notices of cattle markets, auctions and dances, an appropriate grouping, some said, in that the latter activity in the halls around Inisbreen often appeared to be a combination of the two former ones.

Inside the store Kilbride stood behind the counter at the hardware section, poring over a ledger, bundled yard brushes and axe shafts set in galvanized pails to one side of him and flanked on the other by rubber boots and sharpening stones on the counter and boxes of baler twine piled on the floor. Behind him, shelves bulged with little boxes of wire nails, bolts, screws, washers and hinges for every conceivable application, while the fronts of the shelves were festooned with coils of wire and rope, bunches of leather work gloves, waterproof hats and up near the ceiling a clutch of metal devices whose function had long since been forgotten but which had been retained by Kilbride in the certain knowledge that one day someone would walk in and point and say,

"Give me a half dozen of those," and Kilbride would say, "They're two pounds each," as if he had just sold some the previous day.

The grocery and drapery were operated under similar confusion. It might take an hour to find what was wanted, but found it would be, along with a handful of other items, the locations of which had long since been forgotten. On a bench that ran at an angle between two of the counters, and close by a stove that was kept lit from Monday to Saturday lunchtime during the winter months, sat Dan Ahearn. Tall, thin and sinewy, with a shock of dark hair and a melancholy face, he looked like one of the wind-bent trees that were on the slopes of his sheep farm, from which he wrested a meagre income. He habitually wore dungarees, and the only concession he made to fashion was that at Sunday Mass he wore the same pullover outside his dungarees as he had been wearing all week underneath the bib and straps.

Beside him sat Francis Cully, who had over the years variously described himself to the tax man as rabbit-catcher, farmer, fisherman, cattle dealer, unemployed and "considering a number of business opportunities", none of which, according to Mr Cully, had ever produced enough profit to render him liable for income tax. He sat with his short, fat legs splayed out from his short, fat body, his ruddy face beneath the sweat-stained cap at odds with the small cunning eyes. When he spoke, his voice was the squeak of a porker. And they called him Pig Cully to his face.

"Well, hey," he was saying to Ahearn, "they tell me she's moved in with yer man McLenihan or whatever the hell his name is – the minute his wife stepped on the bus. I tell ye, ye needn't walk too close to that house this night, for they'll be shaking a few tiles off the roof. And sure, yer man must be fifty if he's a day."

Master of the grand gesture, big Dan Ahearn clapped his hands onto his bony knees and leapt to his feet, turning to face the prostrate Pig.

"Jasus McGonagle, if that doesn't beat all! Wasn't he saying to me only last week that he was for selling up and going back to Limavady." Wildly he flung out an arm. "On that very street there!"

With a glance over his shoulder towards where Peggy May was making tea in the back shop, Kilbride said,

"He'll be going back to Limavady on his knees after a few days with that lady, so he will."

Pig added his medical opinion on the illicit affair. "Aye, and maybe taking home more than he bargained for."

Ahearn sat down, punched one hand in the other and said, "Well, damn me. Six months ago the man was at death's door with the bad back. 'Dan,' he sez to me, 'they took me in the hospital and had the gall bladder out of me and then they find out it wasn't the gall bladder after all.' 'Well,' sez I, 'did they put it back in?' 'Bugger me, d'you know what, Dan? I never thought to ask that,' says yer man."

From the back shop Peggy May came with a big mug of tea, but despite her rigid carriage a quarter of the contents were spilled on the journey.

"And how're you today, Peggy May?" Pig Cully looked at the young girl with lascivious eyes.

"I'm doing very well, Mr Cully," she said pleasantly, having put down the cup beside Kilbride. As she turned towards the back shop she added, "And Mr Simpson said that I have the nicest wee arse he's seen in a month of Sundays." With a prim little smile she went through the doorway to a squeak of laughter from Pig Cully and a frown of disapproval from Kilbride.

"Holy God," Ahearn bellowed, giving his knee a loud slap, "would you listen to that."

Pig Cully's laughter had no sooner died to a whine than the door opened and Limpy came in, his old greasy cap perched jauntily on the side of his head, his face registering a frown as he looked at Cully and Ahearn.

"Well, well, the things ye see when ye haven't got a gun." Then he broke into a smile and said, "How're we doing this fine day, boys?"

Kilbride barely glanced up from his ledger as Limpy walked in measured steps towards the counter. In an exaggerated manner Pig Cully looked at his watch and said,

"Well, if it isn't Lazarus himself. Must've been a bloody miracle to get you out of the bed before midday, McGhee. It's hardly gone eleven."

Limpy's smile faltered. Had somebody told them already and denied him the pleasure of breaking the news? Ahearn grabbed Cully's wrist and pulled it round to read the watch, almost hauling the unfortunate Pig off the bench.

"So she is, Cully! Eleven o'clock and no more." He threw

back the wrist with a force equal to that with which he had grabbed it. "Well, that beats all hell," he said, but did not elaborate.

"What got you out the pit, McGhee?" Pig Cully asked. "Fleas having a banquet?"

"I'll ignore them remarks, Cully," Limpy said grandly, "in the spirit in which they was intended." Kilbride glanced up and shook his head. Limpy came and stood with his back to the counter. Beside Kilbride, Peggy May had come to stand and watch the comical figure. At least he'd never tried to put a hand up her dress.

"Did yous boys notice anything when I walked in here?"

"I thought the air smelt a bit different," said Cully with a snigger. Ahearn's eyes narrowed and he scrutinized Limpy from head to toe. Limpy strutted towards the door, his old boots clacking on the tiled floor, before executing a neat turn which was almost a pirouette and marching back again.

"Well? Did you get her? Eh? What's different about me?"

"There's another hole in your jacket, Mr McGhee?" Peggy May ventured.

Limpy gave another walking demonstration, half way through which Ahearn leapt up, clapped his hands and shouted,

"Jasus and his wee brother, I've got it!" He hit Pig Cully a thump on the shoulder that raised him from his reclining position.

"It's the legs of him! It's the bloody legs, man."

"What the hell about his friggin' legs?" Cully said angrily.

"The wee bugger can walk. His limp's gone!"

Limpy gave a huge grin and slapped his hands together.

"Spot on, the big man!" he declared.

Then several times Ahearn punched one hand into the palm of the other as he walked around and around Limpy and stared down at the miraculous leg. Frank Kilbride, who had been smiling quietly to himself as if he knew something the others did not, began to take an interest and asked to see a further demonstration, which they all watched with fascination.

"I decided to take a short cut – by way of abbreviation – across the field beside the house. Just when I was passing the Mass Rock, this woman in a white get-up and a kind of a light around her head is sort of floating above the Rock, with the arms out, looking at me. Well, I needn't tell ye boys, I nearly fell over."

"Ye were pissed," Cully told him.

"I was damn all of the sort, Pig Cully. God forgive ye. 'Mr McGhee,' sez she," he stuck his arms out in front of him, "'I have long been troubled by your haffliction, and this very evening you will receive permanent relief from it.' And then there was this dazzling light came flying down to my bad leg – " he gave it a resounding slap, " – and the next thing I knew – I was walking perfect." Limpy slowly looked from one face to the next for approval.

"Damn me," Ahearn said softly. "The Virgin Mary herself." He crossed himself and stretched out his hand towards Limpy's formerly bad leg.

"Would ye mind if I touched the article in question?"

"Not at all," said Limpy, "not at all," almost indicating with a nod of his head that they should form a queue. "That's what it's there for. In fact, I sometimes feel as if it's almost no longer mine. Like, it's been given over to – " he searched for the appropriate word, and having found it, held it aloft with evident satisfaction, " – the faithful." He must remember that. Father Burke would like it.

Ahearn's trembling fingers pressed against the torn and grubby material of Limpy's trousers.

"Jasus McGonagle," he almost whispered, "you can feel a – a sort of – electric thing running through it." He quickly withdrew his hand. "Boys," he said with slow deliberation, "if this here isn't a miracle – then Ian Paisley's a Fenian."

And Limpy puffed out his chest and smiled and smiled.

Mr Pointerly stood on the bridge and looked out towards the mouth of the river, where the incoming waves met the steady flow of brown water. From time to time the spit of sand across the river from the hotel would change shape or partly disappear, depending on the tidal action of the sea and on the river's flow, but apart from that, everything looked the same to him as it had done all those years ago, when he had first rowed his little dinghy in and out between the moored boats and cast his line in the hope of bringing a salmon – or at least a brown trout – home to Mother. Now, as he wandered around the village and the strand, the faces of the young people echoed those he had known, so that he was never quite sure of the generation to which they belonged and sometimes even fancied that it could be one of his boyhood companions who had never grown old, and that he himself was still in his youth. It was most disconcerting. But then so had been many things in his life. He had wanted to be a painter, or a poet – something of that sort – but Father wouldn't hear of it, and Father had held the purse strings. So he had been forced to go into the family business, to spend long boring hours in that hateful factory with its clattering machinery and meaningless metal parts turned out by the thousand, and then in the office with its ledgers of interminable rows of figures. But in the years since he had acquired the time and the income to indulge his artistic leanings, he had never once been able to resurrect them. They had been tragically stifled at birth. It really was too bad.

Glancing to one side and up the village street, he saw a small figure approaching. Quickly he turned his head away to look across the river. It was that dreadful McPhee chap, the one with the bad leg. Rarely sober, he was. It made you wonder where they got the money. Mr Pointerly watched as a large car pulled up in front of the hotel and a man, a woman and a boy of about ten got out and went into the foyer. He watched the front door intently, until the man came out again and began taking suitcases from the boot to carry inside. They were staying. They were actually going to be staying at the hotel. Would he make their acquaintance? He gave a little shiver of excitement. And then the McPhee person accosted him.

"And how're we this fine morning, Mr Pointerly?" Limpy leant on the parapet beside him and looked as if he was settling down for the day. At least he was down-wind.

"Very well, thank you." The man was a perfect pain. Why didn't he go and bother someone else? Mr Pointerly anxiously watched the front door of the hotel.

"Have ye heard the news?"

There was no reply from Mr Pointerly who stood like one of the herons to be seen up river, eyes locked on its objective.

"Well, ye wouldn't have, would ye? My leg, the bad one, ye know? It's had a miracle cure, Mr Pointerly." Limpy looked up at the silent man who was gazing into the distance. "I know, I know, it's hard to believe, but that's what it was. A miracle cure, as sure as this leg's walking straight – or will be as soon as I start it off again. Got the power of two now, Mr Pointerly," he slapped the leg, "the power of two. I swear to God, it could walk two ways at once."

Mr Pointerly half turned towards Limpy and gave a wan smile, his gaze remaining firmly on the hotel door. "Is that so?"

So Limpy began to tell his tale once more, adding a few little flourishes here and there for effect, while Mr Pointerly nodded and said "Really?" and watched the luggage being taken piece by piece into the hotel and the sturdy boy with the golden hair darting in and out of the front door. Here he was trying to keep an eye on things and this idiot beside him was banging on something about a leg. They loved to talk, these people. Any old thing as long as it was talk. Why, when he was a boy there used to be three men and when the weather was fine they would stand on the bridge – this very bridge – and talk the whole day, disputing and arguing, alternately laughing and cursing each other. Sometimes he came out of the hotel in the morning and half expected to see them still there, still arguing about things of little consequence, still laughing about less.

"What d'you think of that, Mr Pointerly? A bloody miracle. As sure as a gun's iron. You can touch it if you want to."

"I – beg your pardon?"

"I said you can touch my leg if you want to."

"Wh – Why should I want to touch your leg, Mr McPhee?"

"Then you'll feel the tingling. Other people do."

The old man turned and gave Limpy his full attention.

"Good grief, man, not in the street. D'you want to get us both arrested?"

"What?"

"How was I supposed to know? You've never given any indication before."

"Any indication of what, Mr Pointerly?"

Mr Pointerly nodded and winked. "You know. I mean, if you had come to me – discreetly. Got to be discreet, old fellow. Good Lord, you must know that. Look," he glanced around him before delving into his pocket and pulling out two five-pound notes, which he crumpled in his hand and then held out to Limpy, "get yourself a drink. We can have a little private talk sometime soon, mh?"

Limpy glanced down at the two notes that had been thrust into his palm and his fingers quickly closed around them. This was better than working for a living, although as he had had no recent experience of that, he had to rely on his imagination, which fortunately was prodigious. Clearly, he should've had this miracle years ago.

"Thanks very much, Mr Pointerly."

"Not at all, McPhee, not at all. Now you run along, like a good man." He winked. "I'll be in touch with you soon, don't worry."

Limpy touched the peak of his cap.

"Good luck to ye, Mr Pointerly," he said, then quickly added, "and God bless ye." He was a man of religious significance now, a living example of the power of the Lord, so he had to keep on the right side.

He set off across the bridge towards the hotel at a jaunty pace. Mr Pointerly looked after him and wondered if at last his luck had turned. Here was someone right under his very nose, and he hadn't even noticed. Not the most appealing of specimens, of course, but then how particular could he afford to be? A bit of a wash and brush up would work wonders. Mr Pointerly gave a little shiver of excitement and anticipation. He would have to arrange a meeting with him, somewhere discreet. Perhaps up in that little old house of his on the back road, where they would be undisturbed. That sounded ideal. And if the man was a little shy, which was understandable in the circumstances, then no doubt a pleasant surprise would easily overcome his reluctance.

At the end of the bridge Limpy turned onto the narrow road that ran alongside the river and towards the Glens Hotel. Ten quid for nothing. Maybe he should chat to Mr Pointerly every day. Ever since the miracle, things had been looking up, so maybe now was the time to take the bull by the horns, while his luck was in, and do what he should've done years ago. Only it would need to be done on the sly, at first anyway. Given half a chance, Lizzie would have her nose poked into his business. And that sister of Cissy's, Margaret, treating her like a child, "Cissy come here, Cissy do that". He sure as hell didn't want to get the rough edge of her tongue. So as he approached the sitting room window of the hotel he paused to check what was supposedly stuck to the sole of one of his boots and then took a swift sidelong glance into the room. It was empty. He smiled and carried on walking, past the hotel, past the bar – a unique event which substantially tested his determination – and round the corner to the lane at the back.

Standing just inside the back door Limpy looked around him and listened intently. He thought he could hear some noises from the kitchen. That'd be Lizzie getting the grub ready. All he had to do was make it to the back stairs and he would be okay. All at once and up on his tiptoes he ran down the hallway and was climbing the stairs two at a time as if both Lizzie and Margaret Garrison were chasing him. Unused to rapid movement or indeed any substantial physical exertion, Limpy rapidly became breathless, so that by the time he reached the landing of the first floor his sides were pumping like bellows and he had to cling onto the banister. Maybe this was a job for a younger man. But he'd come this far and he wasn't going to give up now. He'd given up before, all those years ago, and look what had happened. He pulled himself upright, smoothed his hand over his hair and surveyed the four doors on the landing. One sunny afternoon he'd caught a glimpse of Cissy looking out of her bedroom window, the one directly above the hotel entrance, and he'd taken a mental note of which one it was. It wouldn't be difficult to work out which was her bedroom door. It was obvious that only the two middle doors led to rooms which faced the front of the building and after a few moments reckoning Limpy decided that the left hand one was Cissy's. That had to be it. He'd worked it out.

Quickly he ran over in his mind the little speech he had prepared and then he stepped up to the door and clenched his fist ready to knock. This close, the squiggly marks on the paint of the door that were supposed to look like wood grain made a funny pattern in his eyes. He stepped back, blinking. It had been so long, so very long. Oh, he had talked briefly to Cissy the other day at the sea wall but that had been a casual meeting, albeit the first one where she had been alone. This time it was entirely his responsibility and was therefore up to him to justify. His clenched hand fell to his side. What if yesteryear was just that, yesteryear? What if she thought he was a joke and laughingly wondered how she had ever had anything to do with a person like him? Limpy looked down at his dirty cracked boots his baggy trousers and his worn jacket. As he nervously thumbed a lapel, he saw as with her eyes the stubby hands with the dirty fingernails. He'd been kidding himself. What lady in her right mind would want to take up with the likes of him?

He didn't hear a thing, not a footfall on the stairs, not a creaking floorboard, until the voice bellowed into his ear,

"What business have you got here?"

Limpy gave a jump, pitched forwards and thumped his forehead on the door. Now he really was seeing funny patterns. Then he felt the index finger poking into his shoulder. Just like her father.

"I asked you what your business was here."

Limpy turned to face Margaret Garrison, to see the brows drawn together, the mouth in an angry pout.

"I just came – to have a word with Miss Cissy. But I wouldn't want to disturb her if she was having a visitor or anything."

Margaret's voice rose to the higher pitch which she reserved for addressing the locals. It was the verbal equivalent of a poke in the leg with a walking stick.

"My sister's social arrangements are none of your concern. But I can tell you that she has no wish whatsoever to converse with you."

"But I was only going to ask her if . . . "

"I have made the position clear," Margaret interrupted, "now if you please," she waved her hand, "move on."

Watched by Margaret, Limpy gave a last forlorn glance at Cissy's bedroom door and walked towards the stairs. Why did he think there might still be something there after all those years. It was true what they said, there's no fool like an old fool. He started down the stairs with heavy tread. Maybe two miracles had been too much to expect.

chapter seven

On the Sunday, almost a week after Limpy McGhee had received his celestial transplant at the Mass Rock, there was a hurling match at Inisbreen. The game against the visiting team of Culteerim was to be held in the hurling field by the beach, at the far end of the bay from the village, and in the warm spring sunshine of the afternoon the perimeter of the field began to fill with cars and spectators on foot. Malachy McAteer, who said his brother in London was making a fortune in the commodities market – or had the brother said Camden Market, Malachy was never quite sure – had at the entrance to the field a ramshackle ice-cream van that now and then broke into laryngitic chimes and had drawn a good crowd around it, a gathering which might not have been so keen to sample his wares if they had seen how he had made the ice-cream.

Around the pitch was a wire fence against which people took up positions, couples, groups of friends, whole families together in a clutter of bicycles and prams and dogs fretting on unaccustomed leads. Yet others sought a better vantage point on the higher ground at the side of the field away from the sea. While the majority of spectators were aware of the main rules and conduct of the game and simply wanted their team to win, the aficionados, who were mostly middle-aged and older men who had played the game in their youth, gathered here and there in small groups and argued the finer points of form, stamina and gamesmanship. A small number of spectators, who neither knew nor cared about the outcome of the match, had simply turned up in the hope of seeing a fight between the players and possibly a contribution from some of the more partisan spectators. Mass pitch invasions followed by widespread fighting were not unknown.

From the sidelines, spectators would exhort individual players to greater efforts, only to curse them later for their mistakes, pointing out how obvious the correct course of action had been and wondering at the tops of their voices whether the player in question was blind as well as useless. They would bang their fists on fence posts, throw their arms wide in delight when Inisbreen was given a free, or pull their caps down over their faces in frustration at a missed opportunity, so that at the end of the game they would leave the field as exhausted as the players. When the Culteerim team came out first onto the pitch for a warm-up, practised eyes from the sidelines narrowed in scrutiny before pronouncements were made as to the capabilities of the opposition. And it did not pass unnoticed that the referee was the self same one who had robbed Inisbreen of a match-winning point the previous season, and if he was rash enough to resort once again to bloody crookery, he would be lucky to leave the field, as one spectator put it, "with his arse facing backwards".

Pig Cully wore his cap pulled down so low over his eyes that he had to hold his head back to see under the skip and alongside him Dan Ahearn, who kneaded one hand in the other while shrugging and shuffling in a fever of anticipation, stood at the section of fencing nearest the Inisbreen goal. Now and then quarter-bottles of whiskey would be drawn from inside pockets and a few mouthfuls taken to join what had already been consumed in the lounge bar of the Glens Hotel. A few yards away the two Moore boys, along with Johnny Spade and John Breen stood together and argued about Inisbreen's chances of winning the Intermediate Cup later in the year. Peggy May, standing a little apart from them and with a huge muffler in the team's colours of yellow and brown obscuring half her face, had already set up a shout for a player who was not even in the team that day. With a friend in whom he was trying to arouse an interest in medical conditions – specifically his own – Dippy Burns stood at the corner of the field nearest the gate and divided his attention between the match and the skin on the back of his hands, where he expected to see the first signs of yellowing presaged by his reaching the "Jaundice" section of his "Home Doctor" manual.

Dan Ahearn was nudged by Pig Cully who nodded towards a tall young man with wire-framed glasses and a brush of red hair who was leaning against the fence, a notebook and pen in his hands. He was showing a singular lack of interest in the preparations for the forthcoming match which were taking place on the pitch but was looking around the crowd as though expecting to see a friend. Ahearn looked past Cully to the young man and said,

"Looks like he's taking orders for something. D'ye think maybe he's from one of them burger vans? What d'ye reckon?"

"For feck's sake, Ahearn, are ye blind or stupid or both. He's one of them buckos from the newspapers."

"Jeez-o," Ahearn declared, "I think ye've got her spot on, Cully! Good man yerself!" And so saying he gave his companion a slap on the back that might have felled a lesser mortal.

"Well now, let's go and find out what's in the news," Pig Cully said and walked towards the young man, cautiously followed by Dan Ahearn who eyed their target warily, as though expecting him to turn on them and bite.

Pig Cully tilted his head back and looked out from under the skip of his cap, giving the object of his gaze a fine view of his nostrils and thus confirming the appropriateness of his nickname.

"You'll be one of them reporter boys, I suppose."

Fergus Keane had been with the Northern Reporter for less than a month – his first proper job since scraping a pass in his finals at university the previous year – during which time he had covered funerals, local council meetings, minor sports events and little else. At the advanced age of twenty-three, he was beginning to wonder if he would ever realise his ambition to become an ace reporter whose incisive questioning and investigative skills would lay bare the cankers at the heart of society and rock the very Establishment to its foundations. Perhaps he had already missed his chance. Now he had been sent on some wild goose chase – even his editor, Harry Martyn thought that – following an anonymous telephone call to the newspaper about somebody that claimed to have been the subject of a miracle. It just showed how desperate the paper was for material.

"Yes, sir." Always better to be extra polite until you knew who they were. He stuck out his hand. "Fergus Keane, from the Northern Reporter."

Pig Cully was a little taken aback by this familiarity but had automatically responded in kind and so felt obliged to shake the reporter's hand. Dan Ahearn kept his hands firmly in his pockets. Handshakes were for weddings, wakes and funerals and when you had concluded the sale or purchase of sheep or cattle, not something to be dished out like they meant nothing. The usual toss of the head and, "How y'doin'?" would suffice. So saying, he took half a step backwards. The fella might have extra-long arms.

Further words from the young reporter were drowned out by the shout that went up from the crowd as the Inisbreen team ran onto the field and began to spread out, hurley sticks swinging and chopping the air, chests expanded and contracted, muscles stretched and kneaded. Then the crowd began to get into the spirit of the occasion.

"Did you forget your drawers, short-arse?" John Breen shouted at Tim Sullivan, a diminutive left half-back whose shirt was three sizes too big and came to just above his knees. A series of whoops and shouts came from around the perimeter fencing – "C'mon Inisbreen, show them how it's done!", "Run them off the bloody field, boys!", or "Watch that wee baldy-headed get or he'll hit ye with his pension book!"

Pig Cully took out his quarter bottle of whiskey and amidst the general excitement forgot the habit of a lifetime and offered the reporter a drink.

"Here, get some of that down ye and ye can shout for the right side. I tell ye, this could be history in the making here."

"Ah, ye're right there, Cully," Dan Ahearn said, slapping his thigh. "History in the bloody making right enough."

"And I hope ye're going to report this match fair and square, young fella. We don't want any – "

"I'm not here to report the game," Fergus Walsh said, but his reply was drowned out by the shout that went up as the game started. He shrugged, looked at the whiskey bottle and then took a long swig from it. His subsequent smile of thanks as he handed back the bottle quickly changed to a grimace.

After a few minutes of play an angry shout went up from the spectators as Culteerim were awarded a free. The face of Pig Cully grew redder as he threw a string of abuse at the referee and line judges, each of his remarks echoed by Dan Ahearn at his side. Pig Cully rapped the virgin page of the reporter's notebook.

"Get that down, boy. Get her down. `Biased referee gave

unfair free to a bunch of foulin' gets from Culteerim.' Chapter and verse." Then he looked more closely at the page. "Bejasus ye haven't even put pen to paper yet. What hell kind of reporter are ye?"

"I tried to tell you, I'm not here for this match. I've come to talk to a man called – " he turned over a page in his notebook, " – John McGhee? They told me in the village he'd almost certainly be here. Could you point him out to me?"

"Ye want to talk to Limpy McGhee? What the hell for? Even people that know him don't want to talk to him."

"Especially people that know him," Dan Ahearn threw in.

"Well, somebody phoned the paper and said John McGhee was supposed to have had some kind of miraculous cure."

Dan Ahearn looked at Pig Cully.

"Jeez-o."

"Oh, it's the Miracle Man ye want, is it?" Pig Cully scoffed. "Knowing that wee hoor, it was probably him that 'phoned ye."

"Well, I – Is he here?" Fergus Keane asked. This was going to be more difficult than he had anticipated, and all for what? Some cock-and-bull story about a miracle, no witnesses, no corroboration. From beneath the skip of his cap, Pig Cully carried out what appeared to be a comprehensive survey of the crowd.

"Oh, he'll be here somewhere," was his conclusion, "only I can't just see him right now." He turned his attention to the game once more, and after watching it for a minute or so, said,

"If this match doesn't end in a barney, I'm a feckin' Dutchman."

He uncorked his whiskey bottle again and sucked noisily at it. Dan Ahearn also took a bottle out, drank from it and after wiping the top with the sleeve of his jumper, stuck the bottle under the nose of Fergus Keane.

"Here." The young fella would probably need another

drink if he was going to have any dealings with the wee man.

To the young reporter the taste of the whiskey might have been horrid but the warm glow from it was strangely attractive and comforting.

"Thanks," he said and took a pull from the bottle, remembering to wipe the neck of it with his sleeve before returning the whiskey to Ahearn, who took another drink.

"Yes sir!" Dan Ahearn clapped his hands together and rubbed them in anticipation. "A barney's what it'll end up in. Ye have her off to a tee, Cully."

A bad shot from the Culteerim free-taker brought a cheer from the crowd and then the game settled to a series of poor tackles, missed catches and runs that got nowhere. At half-time the score was two goals and two points to Culteerim and seven points to Inisbreen, who were still grumbling about the unfair free that had resulted in their opponents going one point ahead. As the two teams lay back on the grass or sat drinking from bottles of water, Pig Cully, Dan Ahearn and the man from the Northern Reporter finished the last of the whiskey from both bottles.

"Never fear, my friend," Pig Cully told Fergus Keane, who was beginning to look a little unsteady on his feet, "Never fear. There's another one not too far away."

"Damn right," Dan Ahearn said, gently swaying back and forth.

From behind them a voice said,

"Well now, boys, how are we doin'this fine day? Enjoying the game' eh?" It was Limpy that stood there, his chest stuck out like a bantam cock. He was wearing an ancient double-breasted suit that, many years before, he had been asked by a member of the charity, the Saint Vincent de Paul Society, to convey to an old man up the glen. On the road, a neighbour had told him that the old man had died in the night and so Limpy had, as he had put it, "diverted" the suit to his own abode, and now wore it on major occasions, regardless of the fact that it had been made to fit a man a stone or more heavier than himself. Now, of course, every day was a major occasion. He had religious standards to maintain.

As Limpy stepped forward, Dan Ahearn swayed back at the overpowering smell of mothballs and stale sweat.

"Well, bejasus, if it isn't the Miracle Man himself," Pig Cully said, sweeping his arm in front of him and giving a gracious bow.

"None other," Limpy said, with a broad smile induced as much by drink as by his burgeoning fame. "None other."

Throwing his arm round the reporter whom he dragged from his refuge on a fence-post, Pig Cully said, "This here's the man you were looking for, Limpy McGhee – or maybe we should call him ex-Limpy McGhee – now that he's a walking miracle man. And this here's – what's your name again, son?"

"Fergus Keane, from the Northern Reporter" the young man said mechanically. He seemed to have some difficulty in breathing.

"Well well, the newspapers, eh?" Limpy said, with barely concealed glee. "Word travels fast. So I suppose you'll be wanting an interview, young Fergus Keane?"

"Eh – if you wouldn't mind, Mr McGhee," he replied, although he looked in no fit state to conduct one. He glanced around him, as though seeking somewhere to lie down.

"Ask away, young fella. I'll tell you all you want to know about the celestial transplant," Limpy said grandly. He slapped the limb and rose a puff of dust from the leg of his trousers.

"As good as new," Dan Ahearn averred. "Walks like a regular leg, so it does. You could go far with a leg like that."

Pig Cully winked at Ahearn and said to the reporter, "No doubt about it, Fergus, you're witnessing a living miracle in this man here. Brought about by – " he lowered his head a little, " – the Blessed Virgin herself."

"The Blessed Virgin," Dan Ahearn repeated, as if proposing a toast.

Limpy looked a little put out by these two muscling in on his new-found fame.

"Ye need to hear it straight from the horse's mouth," he told Fergus Keane, "and it's got to be told in the right order."

"After the exchange of a twenty-pound note," Pig Cully threw in.

Whether it was because of the bracing sea air or the all-embracing whiskey, Fergus Keane's lethargic attitude was rapidly dissipating in the face of his mounting interest in Limpy's case.

"Are you saying, Mr McGhee, that – a miracle really did happen to you?" He turned to a fresh page in his notebook and held his pencil at the ready.

"I certainly am. Five nights ago at the Mass Rock." He snapped his fingers. "Just like that. One minute the leg was good for nothing – and the next it was a new instrument entirely."

"As good a leg as ever a man had under him," Dan Ahearn said.

"Well, no offence, Mr McGhee, but you must realise that it's a bit, well, difficult to believe. You know, miracles and all that."

"No offence taken, Young Fergus, but I've been certified by the doctor – and the priest, so I have. There's no doubt about it. I had a limp since the day I was born. They tell me when I was a nipper I even crawled with a limp and they say it was a pitiful sight. And after the other night it was gone entirely. Didn't she speak to me and tell me she was going to do it."

"Who?"

"The Virgin Mary, who else?" It now appeared that Limpy had been on familiar if not intimate terms with the mother of Jesus.

"The Virgin Mary – spoke to you?" The young reporter's

eyes widened in wonderment before commercialism intervened. "Have you – talked to any other newspapers about this?" He scribbled something in his notebook. This was more like it. He might even have – the prospect of it made a little shiver of excitement run through him – a scoop.

"Oh not yet, not yet, but it's only a matter of time, isn't it? Newspapers, radio, tv. Interviews, photographs. I soon won't be able to step outside the house for them journalists and photographers. Bloody paternazis. Ah, I tell ye, that bastard Hitler has a lot to answer for."

"Paparazzi," Fergus murmured, and then, "You said it happened at some – Mass Rock. Where is that exactly?"

Limpy considered this for a moment and then said,

"I tell you what I'll do, Young Fergus. If you and me go to the hotel, where we can have a bit of privacy, I'll tell you the whole story and then I'll show ye the place it happened. I can't say fairer than that."

"Thank you, Mr McGhee. Thank you very much," Fergus said. "That would be fine." This was a front-page story if ever he'd seen one, although he had seen very few in his new role as junior reporter, and he was going to be the one to write it. He could see his name above it now, in letters almost as big as those of the headline.

"And we'll come along to see fair play," Pig Cully said quickly, turning and winking at Dan Ahearn, who stuck up a wavering thumb and said,

"Fair play, Cully."

"Just in case any details slip yer memory – Mr McGhee," Pig Cully added. He slipped his arm round the reporter's shoulders. "Have ye a car, son?"

"Yes, I have. It's parked just over there."

"Then, lead on, boy, lead on."

After paying for yet another round of drinks, which his three companions seemed able to quaff almost as quickly as he could draw the money from his wallet, with a spinning head but mounting excitement Fergus Keane went to the little wooden telephone booth in the foyer of the Glens Hotel. Judging by the stories which usually made up the front page of the Northern Reporter – "Facelift for Sewage Farm" and "Mother of Twelve Children Is Only Support Of Her Husband" – the editor, Harry Martyn, would be as excited as Fergus about this one. Fergus Keane, ace reporter, was on his way. The only problem was that, as it was Sunday, he would have to telephone the editor at home. Before lifting the receiver, Fergus stood for some moments, rehearsing in his mind what he was going to say, thinking that he should have jotted something down, some bullet points, as Mr Martyn liked to call them.

"Hello? Mr Martyn? This is Fergus." He could picture the round face and the bald head with its fringe of dark hair above the ears. A thumb and forefinger he could imagine stroking each side of the man's chin, as though searching for a beard. There would be a large mug of tea handy.

The loud voice came barking down the line.

"Fergus? Fergus who?"

There was a short silence, during which time the young reporter was overwhelmed by a feeling of panic and Harry Martyn's memory caught up.

"Oh yes, Keane. Where the hell are you, Keane? And why're you 'phoning me at home on a Sunday? Good God, as if I didn't have enough to put up with from Monday to Saturday without being badgered in my own living room."

"Eh – I'm sorry to have to phone you, Mr Martyn, but I think this is very important. I'm at Inisbreen. Don't you remember, there's this man – "

"Inisbreen? What are you doing at Inisbreen, for God's sake? I thought you were supposed to be covering that dancing competition at wherever-the-hell-it-was? Does nobody tell me anything around here?"

"But – " Fergus could feel his whole journalistic career slipping away, "it was you that sent me here, Mr Martyn."

"Oh, it was, was it? Well, alright then, but next time – keep me informed. How can I run a newspaper if I don't know where half my bloody staff are?" There was the sound of slurping. "Anyway, what d'you want?"

"Well, Mr Martyn, I think I've got – a scoop."

The slurping suddenly changed to a choking noise.

"A – what?"

"A – scoop, Mr Martyn."

"A scoop? You've been reading too many comics, Keane. A scoop's what you use to lift dog-shit off the pavement."

With a pained expression on his young face, Fergus swallowed hard and wished he'd taken his mother's advice and become a teacher.

"Well, Mr Martyn, there's this man and he claims he's seen a vision of the Virgin Mary and that he's undergone a miracle cure to a life-long illness. He definitely appears genuine to me."

Fergus waited expectantly for the praise that was undoubtedly on its way. Instead, a long sigh slithered down the line from Ballymane.

"Genuine to you? In your long experience in these matters, is that?" But then Mr Martyn softened a little. He'd been young once, although definitely never as green as this guy. "Look, son, your job is to expose these nutters, not take their side. I mean, I hate to disappoint you and all that, but there's hardly a day passes in Ireland without some lunatic claiming he's seen a vision or he's been cured of Christ-knows what. Let's get back to the real world, eh?" the editor said, his voice rising. "The harsh realities of life, the cut and thrust of politics, the broken homes, the – the – dog mess on the pavements. That's what this newspaper's for."

"For – dog mess, Mr Martyn? Didn't you just say that's what a scoop was for?"

"No, not for clearing up bloody dog mess, for . . . Jasus!" There was a short silence and then a barely audible, "God give me patience," and then louder, but softly, "For community issues, Mr Keane!"

"But this is a community issue, Mr Martyn. And I'm absolutely certain it's genuine. In fact, positive. And both the Church and the medical profession have upheld his claim."

Harry Martyn took a little longer than normal to reply.

"They have, have they? The Church and the medical profession?"

"That's what I've been told." Fergus grasped his

opportunity to impress. "But of course, I'll be checking it all out. This could really be something big, Mr Martyn. I think maybe I should stay here for a day or two and follow this up. Dig out the facts, you know?"

The "Yes" that came in reply was non-committal. "I suppose there just might be something there. Although I'll take a lot of convincing, I'll tell you." But his interest had been aroused. "Keep me posted on this one, Keane. We might just be able to wring a story out of it."

"Will do, Mr Martyn. No problem."

"Okay, speak to you tomorrow."

And then Fergus remembered what was probably the most important thing he had to say.

"Oh, I meant to say. I'll be needing some – " Fergus grimaced and closed his eyes momentarily, " – expenses, Mr Martyn."

There was another silence before a verbal hand grenade was lobbed down the line.

"Expenses! What the hell d'you want expenses for? Even if we could afford them. If you'd ever seen the bills I get here you'd know better than to ask for expenses!"

"Well, I'm sorry but – I'll need to stay somewhere to-night and, I don't know, I might have to pay this man something for the exclusive story. How much do you think that should be, Mr Martyn?"

Again, silence, before a strangled cry indicating that the editor of the Northern Reporter had spilt hot tea into his lap.

"What? Chequebook journalism? That's totally against my principles, Keane, especially where our money's involved. For God's sake, this isn't bloody Fleet Street. Scoops, expenses, money for stories! You're living in cloud-cuckoo land, kid." There was a slurp of tea and then the editor told Fergus, "Look, you can have today and tomorrow to follow this up, but I want you back at this office on Tuesday morning, bright and early. And you needn't come to me waving a bunch of extravagant expenses, because you won't get them. And Keane, this better be good."

"Oh, I'm sure it will, Mr Martyn," Fergus Keane said, his mounting excitement tempered by the knowledge that he had already run up a substantial amount for his three companions in the bar. There was no reply from the other end. Mr Martyn had rung off. Fergus Keane stood in the telephone booth and squared his shoulders. This was it, he thought. This opportunity, this chance of a big scoop – he had a mental image of a little plastic shovel sliding under a dog turd and realised that the word had now been ruined for him by his editor's callous description – had landed squarely in his lap. Was he going to seize it or let it pass and regret his action for the rest of his life? Of course he would take it. Wasn't he going to be an ace reporter? Leaving the telephone booth and walking down the hall he swayed a little, but he put it down to the unevenness of the floor.

The car came racing along the narrow road and slewed to a halt beside the gate that led to the Mass Rock field, sending a shower of stones into the ditch. The driver's door was flung open and with some difficulty Fergus Keane hauled himself out to stand swaying in the middle of the road while the other three men extricated themselves from the small vehicle. Limpy was the first to emerge, followed by Pig Cully and Dan Ahearn, who stumbled to his knees and had to be helped up by the other two. Side by side they drifted across the road like an errant chorus line, before running forwards in unison towards the gate.

"Jasus McGonagle," Dan Ahearn said, "I'm full."

Pig Cully, whose small, glazed eyes looked out from a face of bright red that seemed to wobble independently of his neck, said nothing.

Limpy stated, "She doesn't open, boys. It's up and over."

All four of them started together onto the wide gate which squeaked on its rusty hinges. Dan Ahearn was the first to the top where he clung quivering to the gnarled wood before giving a shout of "Ah, Jasus!" and falling headlong over the other side. Fergus Keane slithered over the top to join him on the ground, but Limpy picked his way nicely up one side and down the other, long practised as he was in the art of drunken gate climbing. Somehow Pig Cully had managed to get himself stuck on the top and cursing loudly had to be helped down.

"We can do without that kind of language, Cully," Limpy said in an officious tone. "This here's a holy place." And for good measure, he made the sign of the cross.

The four of them progressed slowly across the uneven ground, with stumbling runs down inclines and teetering backwards on the upward slopes. At one point Fergus suddenly ran ahead on his own and fell into a clump of bracken. From beneath the green fronds he looked up at the three faces spinning above him and said,

"Now I know why some people stop going to Mass."

Then he turned his head and was sick into the bracken. The

other three simply staggered away and left him to crawl out by himself. When Limpy reached the clearing in front of the Mass Rock he held up his two arms before him.

"There she is, boys." A sideways stagger threw him off balance but he righted himself with some dignity. "The Mass Rock herself." He appeared to give a little bow. Fergus staggered past him and stood looking open-mouthed at the ancient symbol of Christianity carved into the grey rock overshadowed by the surrounding trees.

"How – old is it?" he said softly.

"Ah, now your asking," Limpy said. "Hundreds of years. Hundreds."

Behind them, Pig Cully stood stiff as a statue, while Dan Ahearn, head sunk to his chest, was stepping back and forth to maintain his balance.

"And this is where it happened, Mr McGhee?"

"The very spot, Fergus. I was proceeding in this direction – "

"You wouldn't know how to proceed, McGhee, if your bloody life depended on it," Pig Cully slurred. Limpy ignored the remark.

"I was proceeding in this direction here," he indicated with a great sweep of his arm and fell against the reporter, "like this," he said and suddenly set off across the field in an exaggerated imitation of his former limping gait. Fergus Keane was clearly impressed. Tilted to one side, Limpy executed an arc and came hopping back towards the other three. "And then," he said, "it happened. Flash of light. Your woman appears hanging above that rock, speaks to me and then – bang! I'm on the friggin' deck and she's gone." He stopped to get his breath back.

"Like you said, this is a religious situation," Dan Ahearn declared in a grave if indistinct tone. "There's no call for foul language." He looked up at the rock and crossed himself before his legs gave way and he sat down heavily on the ground.

"When I got up there was a helluva pain in the oul' leg, but as I headed for the house there, she got easier and by the time I was halfway across, the leg was fair flying." Again Limpy set off at a brisk pace, careening across the uneven ground, until he disappeared with a shout over the top of a hummock.

"I think," said Pig Cully, "the Miracle Man just fell on his arse."

His boyish features upturned and his eyes fixed firmly on the Mass Rock, Fergus Keane walked slowly towards it. As though expecting to see the Virgin Mary appear before him at any moment, his eyes were wide and his mouth hung open. Limpy's head and shoulders appeared as he crawled over the top of the little hill, mouthing obscenities, his cap slewed sideways on his head. Then slowly down the fair-skinned face of the young reporter large tears ran and he moved forward, closing his hands before him in an attitude of prayer. Step by step he drew nearer to the rock. There was a splash from beneath his feet.

"Shit!" he said and drew back from the little stream of water that flowed between the stones. He began to stamp his feet. Limpy came puffing up the slope and stopped, looking from the young man's wet shoes to the running water. He gave a low whistle.

"By Christ, boys, come and see this! C'mere!"

With some difficulty, Dan Ahearn and Pig Cully joined the other two and they all looked to where Limpy was pointing near the base of the rock.

"A stream!" he said, hardly able to contain himself. "A stream, as sure as God! It's a sign, if ever I seen one! Maybe now yous'll believe me. That, Pig Cully, is holy water."

Dan Ahearn slapped his thigh and said, "Damn me," but Pig Cully said,

"Holy water ballocks! It's a bloody spring, McGhee. There's hundreds of them up and down this glen."

"Listen, Doubtin' Feckin' Thomas, in all my born days there was never a spring next or near there. I'm telling you, that's miraculous water – so you want to show a bit of respect, Cully."

While the two of them began to argue about the source of the stream, Fergus Keane slowly lowered himself to a kneeling position, said softly,

"Jesus, Mary and Joseph," and dipping his fingers into the water made the sign of the cross on himself. Now there was no doubt about it at all. The story must be genuine – and he would be on his way. This was going to be the biggest thing ever to hit the front page of the Northern Reporter.

chapter eight

In the sitting room, young Patrick McAllister sat hunched up on the couch and awaited the arrival of Miss Quinn. His hair had been wetted, parted with precision and slicked back, his grey school socks – unusually for him – were pulled tight to his knees and his crisp white shirt gave him an air of elegance and composure entirely foreign to his nature. This was the way it was every Thursday afternoon at four o'clock when he had his piano lesson in the apartment at the top of the Glens Hotel, his Mum out playing golf with her friends, his father hovering around somewhere, putting his head around the door now and then to say something like, "Very good, Patrick. When d'you think he'll be ready for the Albert Hall, Miss Quinn?" There was nothing he disliked more than piano lessons, with their interminable scales and those little black dots dancing before his eyes, each one looking very like all the others. And Miss Quinn always made him play things over and over and over until he got them exactly right, even although sometimes he could hardly see the piano keys let alone the little black dots on account of the tears of frustration welling up in his eyes. But Miss Quinn did smell nice, especially when she leant close to him to show him what to do, with her chest – which was much bigger than Mum's – sometimes rubbing against his cheek. And she smiled a lot and had long red hair and sometimes when his lesson was finished she would play the piano and sing a song and Dad would come in and listen to it and smile. But Patrick still didn't like piano lessons and would much rather have been out on his bike or clambering over the rocks to look in pools for little fish and crabs and those bright red squidgy things that clung to the side of the rock and squirted water when you squeezed them.

He looked at the clock on the mantelpiece. It was almost ten past four and his spirits suddenly rose. Maybe she wasn't coming today. He jumped to his feet and went towards the door, giving the piano a dark look as he passed it. Then he stopped, went back and closed the lid, a smile of satisfaction on his plump little face. Outside his bedroom door he stood, trying to decide whether to change into older clothes and go out to play or go as he was while the opportunity lasted and risk his mother's wrath. It was better to go now, he decided. His father could appear at any minute and even if Miss Quinn wasn't coming he would be made to practice until five o'clock, the time at which the lesson normally finished.

With exaggerated steps he began to tiptoe towards the stairs. He would have to remember the squeaky floorboard on the landing outside his parents' bedroom. If he could get past that to the stairs, he had made it, and he would be off down the back way and through the kitchen to the yard. And Mrs Megarrity wouldn't tell on him. It would be their secret, just the same as it was a secret between them the stuff he had seen her drink out of the little bottle that smelt like the bar and was for her health.

And then he heard the noise, a sort of springy sound, like the time he and his cousin Joseph jumped on the bed like one of those bouncy castles and Mum came in and shouted at them.

There was another sound, too. He leant towards the door of his parents room and listened. Somebody's voice, but not talking. A sort of groaning, and maybe there were two voices because sometimes it was high and sometimes it was low. The springy sound went quicker. A voice said, "Oh, Dermot," and it was definitely Miss Quinn's voice and his eyes widened in bewilderment at the thought of her being in his parents' bedroom because he had definitely never seen her in there before. He heard the deeper voice groan – it sounded like his father's – and the scrape of something on the floor and Patrick thought that maybe they were moving furniture although it was usually Mum and Dad that shifted the furniture around. But why was Miss Quinn helping Dad do that instead of giving him a piano lesson – he still didn't want the piano lesson – and if she liked that better maybe she could always move furniture when she came, and forget about the piano lessons.

Slowly he stretched out his hand and grasped the door knob. He should go down the stairs now, when they were busy moving furniture, but he was curious. Maybe they were doing it as a surprise for Mum when she came home. But Dad might be angry if he wasn't practising his piano. He would just have a little look and then go. Remembering to step over the squeaky floorboard, he slowly turned the handle, pushed open the door a few inches and listened. Somebody was puffing and blowing and then Miss Quinn said, "Oh," again. It was bloody hard work moving furniture. Dad always said so. Edging his head through the gap, Patrick looked into the room. He couldn't see either of them. They must be behind the wardrobe. Miss Quinn said, "What's wrong?" and his Dad's voice said, "It's gone again, dammit." If they had lost something, he could help them look for it. He was good at finding things. When Dad had asked Mum what had happened to the bowl his sister Geraldine had given them as a present, Mum had said it was lost. But Patrick had found it, underneath a pile of old clothes at the back of a wardrobe and borne the navy and yellow striped bowl to his parents in triumph. Mum didn't seem very pleased and said he'd been told before about "raking around in places" that didn't concern him and then Mum and Dad had an argument and Patrick left the bowl and went off to his own room. Sometimes you couldn't work out what parents really wanted you to do.

Peering through the bars at the end of the bed, he saw his Dad lying face down on top of Miss Quinn, with her looking up at him. What could he be looking for there? His face was stuck up against her chest. Maybe her necklace had fallen down the front of her dress. Except she didn't look as if she was wearing a dress. And she said, "It's flat. I knew we shouldn't have done this, Dermot." Patrick tried to see what could possibly be flat, and thought the only thing might be Miss Quinn, with Dad lying on her.

"Bugger it!" his Dad said, which Patrick knew was a bad word that was never said when Mum was there. It seemed obvious to him that there would be no piano lesson that day and the best thing he could do would be to sneak off down the stairs and leave his Dad and Miss Quinn to whatever kind of grown-up thing they were doing. He began to move back, slowly pulling the door closed, only to step on the loose floor board which gave a loud squeak.

Patrick jumped with fright, stumbled forward and fell head-first against the door which swung open and banged against the wall.

"Jasus Christ!"

"Oh my God!" Miss Quinn and his Dad spoke and jumped up at the same time. His Dad was pulling at his trousers and Miss Quinn's chests were all bare and wobbly until she saw Patrick staring up at them and covered them with her hands. "Oh my God!" she said again. "I thought you said you'd locked it?"

"Patrick!" his Dad shouted, "what the hell are you doing?"

Slowly Patrick got to his feet. Would it be better to help them look for the thing they had lost? One look at his Father's face told him otherwise. He stared at both of them for a few long seconds then turned and ran from the room, with his Dad calling after him down the stairs,

"Patrick! Come back here this minute! Patrick, do you hear me?"

And then he ran even faster. He ran down the stairs and through the rear hallway towards the kitchen door. In the door, across the kitchen – even if Mrs Megarrity was there – and out the back door, and he would be free. Later, his Dad wouldn't be so angry. He never was. Patrick slowly opened the kitchen door. It would be better to walk, or Mrs Megarrity might shout at him. She was standing at the sink peeling potatoes and she looked over when he went in. He was breathing hard from his run down the stairs and his cheeks felt hot.

"Well, Master McAllister. And what can I do for you?"

Patrick moved steadily towards the back door.

"Nothing, Mrs Megarrity, I'm just going out to play."

She dried her hands on a cloth and came towards him.

"In your good clothes?" She narrowed her eyes and looked at him more closely. "And what've you been up to? You've a face like a beetroot and you're breathing fit to bust. Eh?"

He was close to her now, almost overshadowed by her great chest.

"I was just – I haven't been doing anything." Why didn't she just let him go out the back door? And his Dad could arrive at any minute.

"You've been up to something. You've got that guilty look about you. What happened?"

Unlike Mrs Megarrity, she sounded almost kindly.

"I'm just going out to play for a while because I can't do my piano lessons because Miss Quinn's helping Dad move furniture."

There. Now could he go out to play? Mrs Megarrity's face screwed up and she leant closer to him and he could smell on her breath that stuff that was good for her health.

"Moving furniture? Where?"

"In my Mum and Dad's bedroom."

Mrs Megarrity looked like she was pleased at this.

"Were they, now? And did you see them?"

"Just for a little minute when I – fell in the door."

"I see. And what furniture were they moving?"

"Well – they weren't moving any furniture when I saw them. They were on the bed and Miss Quinn had lost something and Dad was looking down here at her." He prodded his fingers against his chest.

Suddenly Mrs Megarrity wasn't interested any more, because she turned away and went towards a cupboard, saying,

"Well, well, there we are now. So you're going out to play. Good man." She opened the cupboard and Patrick heard a rustling sound. "And how about one or two chocolate biscuits to keep the strength up, eh?"

He was surprised. Mrs Megarrity had never given him chocolate biscuits before, only dark looks. But he remembered his manners.

"Thank you very much, Mrs Megarrity."

And then she came to him smiling and with a whole lot of chocolate biscuits – loads – and said,

"There you are son. Now off you go and have a play to yourself, but mind those good clothes."

"I will. Thank you, Mrs Megarrity."

When he had the back door almost closed behind him the biscuits began to slip and he stopped for a moment to get a better grip on them. He heard the clap of hands and Mrs Megarrity saying something like,

"Ha! I've got you now, McAllister," but he didn't know what it meant and anyway he wanted to run to his hideout in the bushes on the hill above the village and eat his chocolate biscuits very slowly, as they were probably the only food he would get for the next few days whilst he waited for the pirates to discover him and mount an attack.

That night in the village, just after ten o'clock, the main street was empty except for Mrs McFall's cat making its nightly round of the dustbins, which Mrs McFall said must be "in the nature of the beast, for it gets well enough fed at home." Curtains were drawn in the windows of the houses and in O'Neill's public house, where a tipsy Fergus Keane was filling the pages of a notebook with observational scribblings which later would prove impossible to read, Limpy and his miraculous limb were the subject of heated debate. Despite having demonstrated two or three times in front of the bar his new ambulatory dexterity, there were still doubters who were not prepared to believe the evidence of their own eyes. Someone even said, although not within the hearing of the sainted one, that Limpy had never actually had a limp, but had been faking it all his life in order to avoid work. To the amazement of his companions and with a degree of charity that would have been unthinkable a few weeks before, Limpy gave a magnanimous wave of his hand and said, "Ah well, if they're slagging me off they're leaving somebody else alone." This more than the cure to the leg, convinced some people that perhaps Limpy McGhee had indeed seen the Virgin Mary. He appeared to be a changed man.

In his house in the village square, old Sean Larrity dozed peacefully in his chair before the fire, dreaming of his time in the merchant marine so long ago, his first sight of New York from the heaving deck of his Anchor Line ship, the smell of Lagos four or five miles before they could even see the African coast, that beautiful girl with the dark, dark hair and scented skin that he had almost jumped ship to be with in Buenos Aires and ever after wished he had and cursed himself as a fool, for he had never found one that even came close to her and he had been a lifelong bachelor. Even now, when he remembered her in his waking hours, it still brought a tear to his eye and a dull ache to his chest.

Next door Mrs McFall had embarked upon a crocheted cardigan for her dog Denis – renamed after her late husband on account of the poor creature's age and lack of control over its reproductive organ. As there had been no children from the marriage, whilst Mr McFall may not have had any control over the organ, Mrs McFall evidently did. And Sean Larrity had remarked to someone, "Ah, but which came first, the chicken or the egg?"

Above the houses turf smoke swirled down from the chimneys and into the street, then up again, to be caught by the wind above the rooftops and borne away over the river and out across the dark bay. At the end of the street nearest to the beach and beside the Inisbreen Stores, the telephone box stood lighted and empty, casting a barred pattern on the pavement and as if in answer to it, at regular intervals the bright beam from the lighthouse on the Mull swept across the undersides of the clouds. All that could be heard was the gentle breaking of waves on the beach, a shimmer of sound now and then from wind-blown leaves and the piping of bats as they patrolled above the hedges and flittered between the branches of the sycamore trees.

At first it was like the faraway call of a seabird, a great white gull swooping to the waves for food, but as it grew nearer it was heard as a series of wails, interspersed with an echo of a higher pitch. Mrs McFall looked up from her crochet and listened again, while people in other houses stopped talking and were attentive. Even old Larrity jerked awake from his slumber, just as the dark-haired girl from Buenos Aires smiled and took his face in her soft hands. Only in O'Neill's did the raised voices drown out the strange sound and that not for long. In the wind the sound died away then grew stronger, sending a shiver of fear and apprehension amongst those who believed in the harbinger of death, the Banshee. In a momentary silence, old Larrity turned his face to the fire and settled again. In his younger days he'd had a few nights like that himself in O'Neill's, or if it was the Banshee come for him at last, he'd been ready for many a day. Then he plunged back into the catacombs of his dreams, desperately seeking his beautiful lost love. Suddenly the noise grew louder and seemed to be coming from the very street itself, curtains here and there were edged open by men with women at their backs and worried glances were exchanged.

"There she is boys, the Banshee. I wonder who she's for tonight," Johnny Spade said and nobody knew whether he was joking or not. Young Danny O'Neill kept working, in the knowledge that, even if it was the harbinger of death who had come for him, he would need to keep his nose to the grindstone until his mother gave him permission to leave, Banshee or no Banshee. Limpy, self-appointed arbiter of all things spiritual, declared,

"Banshee? Them's just peasant superstitions. How can grown men believe in that pagan rubbish? As sure as hell it'll be a cat with it's tail caught in a gate." He marched out of the pub, obviously intent on consolidating his new position as village seer and with that the bar emptied behind him.

The noise from the street was now discernable as that of a tortured human voice, or rather two. Doors were opened and people stepped out cautiously, to see a woman and a girl, hands held, standing in the middle of the street and howling a duet with which Mrs McFall's cat might have felt a strong affinity, had it not at that moment been engaged with the remainder of a pork chop from a dustbin. The woman, it was seen at once, was Mary McCartney and her ten-year-old daughter, from the wee white house with the funny windows. In common with her house, Mary McCartney was seen by most people as a little eccentric, although in yet another moment of frustration with her, Doctor Walsh had gone somewhat further and described her to a medical colleague as "a well-known eejit and hysteric."

Around the pair a crowd from O'Neill's and the surrounding houses quickly gathered, with people pressing forward to see the cause of the commotion.

"What the hell's up with the woman?" Pig Cully asked.

"I seen it," she seemed to be saying, while the child simply screeched in response. People stared and talked in whispers to their neighbours. Dan Ahearn said,

"D'ye think, Cully, she's finally flipped her lid?"

From the back of the crowd Limpy pushed his way through, saying,

"Make way there, make way," and surprisingly, they did. Notebook and pen at the ready, Fergus Keane followed him through, whilst at the edge of the crowd new arrivals strained for a sight of the phenomenon and questioned those nearest to them. Mary McCartney fell silent for a moment while a great gulp of air soughed in her throat. Then she started up again, trying to tell something to a woman at the front of the crowd. Johnny Spade stepped forward and grabbed her by the shoulders.

"What are ye going on about? The last time I heard a racket like that was when Tim Hanlon ran off with the wife's savings."

Mary McCartney tried to explain.

"I – seen it!" She whined. "Walking past! I seen it!"

With each word he uttered, Johnny Spade shook her, so that Mary McCartney's lips slapped together.

"What – the – hell – did ye – see, for – Jasus sake?"

At the back of the crowd Pig Cully said,

"The woman's obviously drunk," and staggered back towards O'Neill's, fearful that it might close before he had had his quota for the evening. The tearful child looked up as her mother said, more calmly now,

"Up at the Mass Rock – we were walking past – her and me – and we seen it." The crowd leaned forward expectantly. "A woman in white – above the rock." Mary McCartney swept her wild eyes around the faces that were pale in the wan light from the street lamps. "I swear to God. Wee Mary and me both seen it."

"Hah, now they'll believe me," Limpy declared, then turning to Fergus Keane he tapped the young reporter's notebook and added, "Get that down, boy. 'Another vision at the Mass Rock'."

On every side there were muted sounds of excitement and incredulity. And then Mary McCartney began wailing again. Mrs Murphy who lived in Captain Kelly's old house at the top of the village stepped forward and tried to calm her, imposing her bulk between Mary McCartney and Johnny Spade, thus dismissed as a loudmouth and a bully and entirely typical of the male species. Mrs Murphy said to Wee Mary,

"Don't be crying now, love. That woman on the rock – she would never do you any harm."

"It wasn't," the girl sobbed and sniffed, "the woman on the rock. I dropped my bag of sweets on the road – and Mum wouldn't let me go back for them."

At this, a titter of amusement went round the crowd, but they had caught the excitement of the moment and as the woman comforted Mary McCartney and Wee Mary, people began to talk animatedly in groups, some of them dismissing the incident as the product of the darkness and the pair's imaginations, while others said that whilst she could be a little eccentric at times, there wasn't a steadier woman in the glens than Mary McCartney and if she said she had seen something at the Mass Rock, then seen something she had.

With the assistance of Fergus Keane, Limpy climbed onto a low wall and called for silence. People stopped talking and turned to face him.

"Since the Virgin Mary appeared to me at the Mass Rock and did a miracle on me, there's been more doubting Thomases than there were in the Bible." Limpy's acquaintance with the New Testament was not intimate but he pressed on nevertheless. "It says in the Bible to love your neighbour. Mind ye, the Good Lord obviously didn't know I'd have John Healy and his wife living next door to me." There were a few chuckles from Limpy's audience. Then the little man stuck out his chest and grasped both lapels of his jacket. He was actually beginning to enjoy this, the first proper speech he had ever given. "But that's what the Virgin Mary said for me to tell people, be good to everybody." Fergus Keane looked up at Limpy with a fervour verging on the religious, though whether inspired by the proximity of miraculous events or on account of the whiskey he had drunk in O'Neill's was not immediately clear. "Some of yous didn't believe I'd seen her," Limpy continued, "and accused me of being a liar and a fraud." He stuck out his chin and slowly looked across the crowd, lingering here and there on catching sight of his principal detractors. Then he flung out his arm towards Mary McCartney. "Well, there's the proof I was telling the truth. Mary McCartney – ye wouldn't meet an honester woman in a week's walking – she and her wee girl there saw the exact same as me. And there'll be more," he shouted, leaning so far forward to make his point that his acolyte had to grasp his legs to stop him falling off the wall. "There'll be more. You mark my words."

"Fergus, me son," Limpy said as the crowd around Mary McCartney and her daughter melted away, "ye don't have to worry yerself about getting a bed for the night. Ye can stay up at my house. The prices that Dermot McAllister charges is bloody scandalous. And anyway, a young fella like you is far better off with the home comforts – ablutions just out the back, bed near the fire, and dammit, ye can reach right out and pull a bottle of stout when ye've a mind to. Ye're giving me a helluva write-up in yer newspaper. The least I can do, young Fergus, is see ye all right for accommodation." He looked at Fergus and beamed. "After all, the Good Samaritan didn't pass by on the other side, did he?" As they set off in Fergus's car towards Limpy's house, he could not help but feel a glow of satisfaction from his new status as miracle recipient and prophet. Wasn't it truly wonderful the ways of the Good Lord.

The drive home was a miracle of good fortune, with Fergus clinging onto the steering wheel, one eye closed, as his car hurtled through the tunnel of light formed by the headlamps. Humming tunelessly and tapping time on his knee, his passenger seemed to view the prospect of imminent death with equanimity. They raced at bends and somehow went round them, from hillocks they flew and landed unscathed and when they finally slithered to a halt amidst the screech of brakes and the rattle of stones, Limpy hopped out and said,

"Ye're steady enough at the driving, young Fergus. Kept her between the hedges, so ye did," then wandered off into the darkness, apparently under the impression that Fergus's head bowed over the steering wheel was in thanksgiving for a safe journey.

When he staggered after his host and caught up with him at the door to his cottage, Fergus knew that he was running on reserve. He hugged the rough-hewn wall and from somewhere far away heard Limpy say,

"Jasus wept! That bloody dog's pissed on the matches again! I'll kick his arse when I can see which end of him is which." There was the sound of furious rasping and the tinkle on the floor as another useless match was thrown down. Then a dim glow sprang up as a match sputtered into life followed by a brighter light from the lamp that had been lit. "Don't stand on ceremony!" Limpy said, waving his arm. "Come on in! Make yerself at home!"

Fergus swayed around the door jamb, blinked in the light as he looked into the room, and almost instantly became sober. Before him was a scene of devastation. In the far corner of the room stood a narrow bed, the pillow the colour of a coal sack, the huddled blankets, once the creamy white of new wool, now uniformly grey and stiff with grime. On the floor – what could be seen of it – were empty beer bottles, newspapers torn and crumpled, a dog bowl, old shoes, some pieces from a tractor and a collapsed heap of assorted turf and firewood. Supporting itself against a wall, a crook-legged table held an array of dirty crockery, cracked and handleless cups, chipped plates and a teapot with a broken spout, beside which stood a chamber pot whose internal colour had clearly not been of the manufacturer's devising. On the wall, which was liberally draped with cobwebs, an arthritic clock ticked painfully, as if every swing of its pendulum would be its painful last. And on the mantelpiece above the black stove a cornucopia of oddments. Between the tins, cartons, bottles and boxes, wads of envelopes and papers stuck out, all topped by a further row of random gleanings in the form of pieces of string, broken cork floats from a fishing net, an open carton of rusty screws and an assortment of tobacco tins. Above all of this hung a framed photograph of a country scene, so dark and ancient that it might have seen the reign of Queen Victoria. Fergus averted his eyes from the far end of the room, fearful of what fresh horrors might become apparent if he peered too long into the semi-darkness.

"Bloody hell's teeth," he said under his breath, and longed

for the sweet excess of a warm clean bed in the over-priced Glens Hotel.

Limpy swept some debris from a wooden chair and with the magnanimity of a maharajah welcoming a stranger to his palace, said,

"Make yerself comfortable, now. There's no rules nor regulations about this establishment. I'll just put the kettle on for a drop of tea."

Fergus sat gingerly on the chair and gathered himself to avoid touching anything else, lest he should come into contact with the virulent microbes that undoubtedly seethed unseen on every surface and in each crack and crevice. Could he possibly make an excuse and leave? Sleep in the car, perhaps, or rouse them at the hotel and demand medical asylum? But if he did that he would upset the old bugger and he wouldn't get his story. In the midst of his thoughts, the smell came to him. It was a mixture of dampness, stale sweat, turf smoke and – dog excrement. Fergus's stomach heaved and he wished that he was still drunk.

When he and his host had taken their tea – with Fergus searching in vain for somewhere to tip the contents of the cracked cup – Limpy went to a cupboard and pulled out two blankets.

"I'll make up the bed for ye," he said, and slammed the blankets against the wall, producing a cloud of dust that temporarily obscured him from sight. He fell into a paroxysm of coughing and came staggering into view like someone who had just survived an explosion. "Christ knows – " he gave a great sneeze, " – when these were last used. But, they'll do the job, so they will. Gets a bit cool in here sometimes."

Fergus turned away, his shoulders sagging and his head drooping almost to his chest. This wasn't the breathless adventure of the ace reporter that he had imagined. Still, he had to stick with it.

"Mr McGhee." The old man was spreading the blankets on a wooden couch affair across the room from his own bed. "I'd like to do a series of articles on you and your miracle. You know, something about your past life, about growing up in this community, and then building up to how the miracle actually happened. Talk to the priest and the doctor, that sort of thing. And I'll get a photographer down to take some pictures." He cleared his throat. "An exclusive, Mr McGhee, all right? That means you don't talk to any other papers."

"Oh, I know fine what an exclusive is, son." A maid at the Ritz could not have patted the blankets into place with more tenderness. "It means ye're going to pay me some money."

"Well – I – it's not usually our policy to – "

"Ah now, policies are no good to me, young Fergus. I can't spend a policy. What a man in my position needs is hard cash. For the necessities of life. Otherwise one of these winter nights – without so much as a fire in the grate – I'll be found in the morning, stiff as a board. And all for the want of a few pounds for my – entirely exclusive – miracle story. A bargain, young Fergus, at – five hundred quid."

"Five – hundred?" Was that a lot of money for this kind of story? It didn't matter. If he told his editor that he'd paid that kind of cash, Harry Martyn would make it sound like a king's ransom. But surely part of an ace reporter's job was to make decisions – whether or not to follow up a story, how to get his copy back in difficult circumstances, where to get receipts so that he didn't lose out on expenses. He was out in the field and operating on his own. It was all up to him. Decision time.

"Done!" he heard himself saying. "Five hundred pounds." And then reluctantly he put out his hand to shake the grubby one of Limpy's that had shot out to meet his.

"Good man, Fergus!" Limpy said. "I knew we could do business."

Without removing an article of clothing, Limpy got into his

bed and pulled the old blankets over him. With less enthusiasm than if it had been a coffin, Fergus stood looking down at the resting place that had been prepared for him. But then, something like this was all in a day's work for the man who was going to get the story of the year for the Northern Reporter. What would he do if he ever had to live rough with a tribe on the plains of Africa in the furtherance of his journalistic career? Brushing aside the thought that a pride of lions would smell sweeter and a mud hut be less noxious than the McGhee redoubt, he boldly threw back the covers, lay down on the wooden seat and wrapped himself in the blankets, being careful not to let them touch his face. Death would smell fresher.

"I can see you and I are going to hit it off just fine, young Fergus. Ye're a man after my own heart. What for would you be wanting to spend fancy money on sheets, when all they do is make washing," Limpy said, and then blew out the lamp to throw the room into total darkness.

Fergus lay uncomfortably on the hard wooden bench, his face contorted by a swarm of imaginary agonies, from cholera to swine fever, and by the very real ones of Limpy McGhee's snores and muffled farts from the other side of the fireplace. At least, Fergus consoled himself, he had the man's agreement for an exclusive story, and cheap at five hundred pounds, he hoped. No doubt when the other papers read it in the Northern Reporter – he managed a little smile – they would be round the old man like vultures in no time. But he, Fergus Keane, had beaten them all to it. After a few more of these happy thoughts, the excitement of the day and the effects of the drink began again to crowd in on him, and despite his unpalatable surroundings, the ace reporter slowly drifted into sleep.

Fergus was reaching out to accept the Pulitzer prize for journalism when he felt the hand on his back. Before the admiring audience, his smile became a little strained, and he wondered what Limpy McGhee was doing up there on the stage and touching him. The smiling presenter seemed to fade before him as the upturned faces of the spectators became blurred and he couldn't hear their clapping any more. The hand at his back slowly moved downwards. Casually, he attempted to move away but it was still there, down near his waist now. With difficulty he kept smiling, fearful that the presenter would not give him the prize if he created a scene. And after he had worked so hard to get it. Then he felt the warm breath on the back of his neck, the body moving closer to him, and heard the gasp of the crowd as they realised what was happening. Suddenly there was total darkness as everything disappeared – the stage, the presenter, the audience and the bright lights – everything, that is except the warm breath in his ear and the hand on his backside. No longer was he in the wide auditorium but huddled on the hard wooden bed with the musty blankets over him. For a moment he lay rigid and awake, checking his senses to be sure of what they were telling him. Then he was scrambling to his knees and lashing out in the darkness.

"Get off, you filthy old bugger! No wonder you offered me a bed!"

Fergus retreated against the wall. There was the sound of a match being struck, then a curse from Limpy, followed by another scrape before the guttering match was applied to the lamp wick. Fergus had two surprises. A bleary-eyed McGhee looked out from his bed on the far side of the room and said,

"What's the matter, son?"

Both of them saw the elderly man by Fergus's bed at the same time. He was tall and slim, with a long, pale face that showed more surprise than either of theirs. His hands he held up before him as though he had just snatched them from the jaws of a trap.

"Jasus. Mr Pointerly," Limpy said softly.

"Ah – Mr McPhee. There you are." Mr Pointerly was finding it hard to keep his eyes off Fergus. "I was – passing, and – I thought why don't I call in and see my friend Mr McPhee. But – " he nodded towards Fergus and winked at Limpy, " – I can see you're – entertaining. So I'll bid you a good night. No doubt we can meet soon and – have a little confidential chat."

The tall figure gave a little bow. Considering the debris on which he had to tread, Mr Pointerly made rather an elegant retreat through the door and pulled it shut behind him. As Limpy and Fergus turned to look at each other in surprise, there was the sound of growling from outside and Mr Pointerly's raised voice, which rapidly grew fainter.

"Jasus, he's a bugger that dog. If he doesn't get ye coming in he'll get ye going out. I knew by the look in his eye that his teeth would be in somebody's arse this night."

After the light had been blown out again and both of them had settled down, Fergus said,

"Mr McGhee, did you mean what you said about that exclusive interview?"

"Well of course I did, son. Of course I did. There's one thing about a McGhee you can count on. His word is his bond, every time."

"Thank you, Mr McGhee," Fergus said, smiling in the dark and snuggling down on his wooden bed which, now padded with good prospects for its occupant, seemed surprisingly comfortable.

chapter nine

In the following days, news of Mary McCartney's vision spread fast around the village and into the surrounding countryside, the story gradually growing in the telling, so that by the evening there was a version that had Wee Mary offering the Blessed Virgin one of her sweets and the Virgin eating the whole bagful. In the Inisbreen Stores and the post office, around the bars of O'Neill's and the Glens Hotel, and from behind cupped hands in the chapel pews, the word was spread that the woman in white had once more been seen floating above the Mass Rock, as a consequence of which something miraculous would surely happen soon to Mary McCartney, like her husband giving up betting on three-legged horses. Old Mrs Gallaher, a daily communicant and normally a woman of the most moderate language, shocked her neighbour by saying that that McGhee one had always been a cocky little bastard and it would've suited him better to have stopped drinking rather than limping. "Now that would've been a miracle, and no mistake," the neighbour had replied.

Mrs McKay commented on the news which had been conveyed to her early in the morning by the milkman, with the usual snort of disapproval that she reserved for any sign of religious fervour amongst the local population, like when the chapel was crowded every night in Mission Week. She had said that most of the congregation only came because they felt so much better in the pub afterwards. "You tell those Redemptorists, Canon," she had once said, "to give it to them hot and strong – and not to finish till after the pubs are closed. It's only the contrast they're after." And now she noted with a weary countenance and a sinking heart how Father Burke's eyes lit up when he heard about Mary McCartney and Wee Mary and said triumphantly,

"Well now, Mrs McKay, perhaps there's more to this miracle business than meets the eye after all, hm?"

"Piece of nonsense if you ask me, Father," she said as she served him his breakfast of porridge and black tea. If she had had a tendency to irritableness before, the plainness of the diet of what Father Burke called "good basic food" made her much more so, and as she scraped at carrots or hacked the bad bits out of big, woody turnips she often longed for coq au vin or some mussels in garlic and a white wine sauce to lift the gloom of a dark evening. But that was all gone now, and rather than being a pleasure to eat, every meal was like a kind of purgatory to her.

"Oh ye of little faith," he chided her, in one of his rare attempts at humour. "I have a feeling about this, Mrs McKay. A feeling deep down in my bones." The bones to which he referred were primarily his knees, given the hours he had spent on them praying for guidance, for some clear signal on the matter from the Almighty. And now here it was. Not conclusive, of course, but was anything ever in life, or – he shied away from the thought but it assailed his consciousness nevertheless – in faith? But this errant thought only served to make him fight back the stronger. Was it not typical of the low tactics of the Devil that he should seek to undermine this simple priest at the very moment of his triumph of faith? And faith he had in abundance, dinned into him firstly by his mother, with love, and later by the Christian Brothers, with determination and ruthlessness. Thus they had passed on a precious gift to him and he would cherish and protect it – his soul the Ark of the Covenant – and hand it on to others, and that faith would be with him all the days of his life, sustaining him in the grind of daily life, bearing him up in times of particular trial, like the present.

"Indeed, I'm going this very afternoon to discuss it with the Bishop," he said to his housekeeper. "As I told you, he wasn't all that receptive when I first broached the subject, but this time when I 'phoned him he seemed, well, quite amenable. Ah, the Lord works in mysterious ways, Mrs McKay," he said, "and of course, a little prayer now and then doesn't go amiss."

Mrs McKay stabbed at a lump of porridge with her spoon, more out of spite than necessity.

"Are you sure the Bishop knows what you're going for, Father? You know, he's quite often away in a wee world of his own, God love him. The Canon used to say he was already halfway to heaven. But then, the Canon is a particular friend of Bishop Tooley. They were always very close."

"Mrs McKay," Father Burke said with a patience worthy of a holy martyr, "I am perfectly capable of making my intentions clear, even to an elderly man who is, shall we say, slightly hard of hearing," but her question had rekindled the tiny doubt that had been lurking in his mind ever since he had made the telephone call.

When Mrs McKay sat down to her afternoon cup of tea and cast an eye over the front page of the Northern reporter, she saw in the bottom left-hand corner the headline which said, "Glensman Claims Miracle Cure". Slowly raising her eyes to heaven she said,

"God Almighty save us," and then began to read the small article underneath the headline.

'In the Glens of Antrim village of Inisbreen, John Henry McGhee, a single man in his sixties' – "That's a lie for a start," she interjected – 'has claimed that he has undergone a miraculous cure to a severe and lifelong disability – a "devastated leg". The cure happened, Mr McGhee said, at the site of an ancient Mass Rock about a mile outside the village, where Roman Catholics used to worship in secret during the days of the Penal Laws of the eighteenth century. Mr McGhee claims that a woman in white, possibly the Virgin Mary herself, appeared to him at the time and said that people should lead good lives and look after each other. Since the incident last week, a small stream has appeared at the base of the rock, which some local people are declaring is a miraculous stream of holy water. Local parish priest Father Ignatius Loyola Burke, 36, one of the youngest parish priests in Ireland, a member of the prestigious Burkes of Mountjoy family, and a graduate of Dublin University who trained for the priesthood at Maynooth' – "Well, I wonder who gave them that information" – 'said yesterday, "It is of course too early to make a final judgement on this, but there can be little doubt that it is not simply the fevered imaginings of religious people. I believe that in our little village something very significant has happened that may grow to have world-wide importance. There is every likelihood that the Good Lord has now rewarded this corner of Ireland for all the love and devotion it has shown to Him over so many centuries." The Bishop of Down and Connor, Bishop Desmond Tooley, was not available for comment, and neither was the local physician, Doctor Walsh, who has given Mr McGhee a clean bill of health after the incident.'

Mrs McKay let the newspaper fall to her knees and said aloud,

"Did ever you hear the likes of it? That drunken wee skitter McGhee has done it now. Played right into the hands of this fella here," she said, nodding towards the empty study across the hall where Father Burke's rough sketches for a shrine, a car park and a two-lane highway to the Mass Rock lay spread out on his desk.

Walking a little stiffly because of the arthritis gnawing at his knees and hips, Bishop Tooley came into his sitting-room, where he saw Father Burke reading a breviary and sitting in his chair, no less. The young parish priest continued to read for a few seconds before looking up. Piety, the Bishop thought, or just a hint of arrogance? On the other side of the fireplace he slowly lowered himself onto the hard, straight-backed chair which should have been taken by his much younger visitor. Father Burke got to his feet and they shook hands.

"Good afternoon, Bishop Tooley. I trust you are keeping well?"

There was an eagerness about this young man, a kind of missionary zeal that the Bishop didn't much care for. It almost always spelt some kind of trouble. Couldn't they find any priests that were, well, ordinary? If it wasn't rabid Republicans who wanted to convert all Protestants to Catholicism by force – like those Spaniards in South America did to the natives a few centuries back – and have the whole of Ireland speaking Gaelic within a decade, it was young sophisticates who openly advocated, Liberation Theology and married clergy and talked about "packing it in" – God forgive them – if they decided it wasn't for them. And what was it this fellow had said he wanted anyway?

"Good afternoon to you, Father. Don't let me keep you from your breviary."

"Oh, not at all, Bishop, not at all." He closed the book and patted it lovingly. "It's very good for passing a spare moment. Always have it within easy reach," he said and then added quickly, "as I'm sure you do yourself."

Bishop Tooley remembered the fellow now. Difficult to

make out what he was saying sometimes, what with the hearing going a bit and his Dublin accent. If only there were more vocations to the priesthood from local young men. Look at that time in Ballymane when they had a priest from Clare. Nobody could understand a living word out of him. Nor could the priest make out a word of theirs in the confessional. Weren't there some people coming out of confession not knowing whether they had been given absolution or not and others claiming to have gotten away with adultery at the price of just a Hail Mary and a Glory Be. One old woman had been in tears, convinced that she'd been told to say a hundred decades of the rosary by "that clown from County Clare", as he had come to be called, simply for having put salt instead of sugar in her neighbour's tea because of some minor slight. There were even parishioners who demanded that a tariff of each possible sin and its penance be pinned up on the church noticeboard so that each person could check if he or she had been sentenced in an equitable manner. What's this his name had been? Father Finnerty? Finaghy? No, wasn't that where the Orangemen held a parade every year?

"Thank you for sparing me the time, Bishop", the young priest broke into the bishop's thoughts. "I know how very busy they keep you."

Busy, did he say? He glanced at the clock on the mantelpiece. Yes, at this time he would normally have been busy – taking a nap.

"What can I do for you, Father?" The name just escaped him for the moment, but it would come, it would come.

"You might recall, Bishop, that a few days ago I telephoned you to discuss a rather unusual occurrence in my parish – Inisbreen – where a man had apparently experienced an instantaneous cure to what had been a lifelong affliction."

Burke, that was the fellow. He'd once known a family by

that name, from Galway, wasn't it? Father was a headmaster. Lovely man. Obviously no relation to this man.

"At the time, Bishop, I think you were – quite rightly, I'm sure – somewhat sceptical, although I must say I never had any serious doubts about it myself. Now, however," in a burst of enthusiasm Father Burke sat forward and clasped his knees, "my suspicions have been totally vindicated. Yesterday evening, two independent witnesses saw the self-same thing at the precise spot where the previous incident occurred, what would appear to be a vision of the Blessed Virgin herself." The young priest sat back with a smile of self-satisfaction, but the Bishop regarded Father Burke with some incomprehension. Of course people had to bear witness to the Blessed Virgin, had to have a vision of her, as Mother of the human race, as intermediary with the Lord. That went without saying. Surely the man hadn't come all this way to tell him that. In the circumstances, though, it might be better to humour him. At least he hadn't come to say he was "packing it in" or wanting to discuss Liberation Theology, thank the Good Lord.

"I agree with you, Father. Yes, indeed I do."

"You do?" Father Burke looked surprised. "Well, I'm very glad to hear that, Bishop." He smiled and nodded. "Very glad indeed. So, what do you think I should do about it? I was thinking of perhaps," Father Burke held his hands apart, as though the thought had just occurred to him, "having a shrine built. Oh, nothing elaborate of course, and naturally it would be paid for by public subscription. I mean, it's early days yet and confirmation is needed, but we really should plan ahead."

"Plan ahead, did you say? Isn't the Christian life all about planning ahead, Father? Planning, by our actions in this life, for our existence in the next one? There is nothing – " he held up an emphatic if wavering index finger, " – nothing, that will repay an individual as much as devotion to our Blessed Mother – after the Lord Jesus, of course." What did they teach them nowadays, that he had to come and ask questions like these? He should've learned these things at his mother's knee. Unless, of course, he had been the product of a mixed marriage. Or, given his age and zealousness, had he been ensnared by the principles of Liberation Theology – whatever they were?

"So I have your support in this, Bishop?"

"My what?"

"Your support, Bishop. Your – blessing."

Bishop Tooley looked at Father Burke for what seemed like rather a long time and then, suppressing a shake of his head, slowly raised his right hand and made the sign of the cross, whispering,

"In nomini Patris, et Filiis, et Spiritu Sanctum, Amen." The Latin still came easiest to him. The young priest at first looked a little bewildered, then smiled hugely and told his superior, "Thank you, Bishop. Thank you very much indeed. You can safely leave this matter entirely in my hands. I'll keep you fully informed of developments – " he smiled again, " – both literal and figurative. And I'll get to work on plans for that shrine right away."

Bishop Tooley was happy at seeing the young priest smile. A little shrine to the Blessed Virgin would be nice. It obviously didn't take much to please the fellow. A blessing and a few words of encouragement. Perhaps he wouldn't be so difficult after all. Now perhaps he would go away, settle into his new parish and run it quietly and efficiently. He had met one like this many years before. Made a big fuss at the beginning and then quickly settled down. Hardly ever heard from him after that. Or was he getting him mixed up with the one who ran off with the headmaster's wife? God willing, this one would go about his business and ensure that both of them had a nice, quiet life.

Just after lunch-time, and with two stiff whiskies inside him to fortify himself for the coming ordeal, Fergus Keane called Harry Martyn, his editor on the Northern Reporter.

"Mr Martyn? It's Fergus Keane here."

"Keane? Oh, yes, Keane. What's the point in saying, 'It's Fergus Keane here'? Where the hell is 'here'?"

"Inisbreen, Mr Martyn. You know, following up the Mass Rock Miracle story? You printed my piece this morning."

"Did I?" There was a pause. "Yes, I suppose I did. It's a wonder I can remember my own name, the amount of work I've got to do around here."

"And – it's an exclusive, Mr Martyn. A complete exclusive. Can you put that on my next piece? I negotiated that with the Miracle Man himself."

That was the way to do it. Give him the good news first, and then while he was expressing his approval, slip in the bit about the five hundred.

"Oh God, you didn't promise him any money, did you? If I've told you once, I've told you a hundred bloody times, Keane. No chequebook journalism. Apart from the fact that it costs money – which this journal does not possess – I don't hold with it. It's against my principles. So you'll just have to tell him he's getting nothing, d'you understand, not a penny, not a brass razoo. Tell me that you understand, Keane."

Fergus Keane, being a university graduate, had thought of this possibility, and had devised a stratagem.

"But – Mr Martyn, I've signed an agreement on behalf of the paper. Doesn't that constitute a legally binding document? I mean, I wouldn't want him to sue us or anything. It could cost a fortune. Perhaps even put us out of business altogether."

"Oh, God Almighty, how much for, Keane? How much have you signed a bloody document for, you pillock?"

"Only – five hundred pounds, Mr Martyn."

"Five – hundred – pounds!" Each word sounded as if it had been wrung from the very heart of the editor of the Northern

Reporter and as such intimated that he would break down and become incoherent at any moment.

"Five hundred – ? Have you gone totally out of your mind, Keane? Have you any conception," Mr Martyn's voice rose to such a pitch that he could have been in contention for female lead at the Royal Opera House, "any clue whatsoever of how many small ads that represents?"

"But, it's a world exclusive, Mr Martyn – and the Northern Reporter's got it."

A pitiful groan escaped the editor and slithered down the line to Inisbreen.

"And you believe it's a genuine story?"

"Oh yes, Mr Martyn, I certainly do."

"And you think it's going to run and run, do you?"

"Definitely, Mr Martyn. Or should I really say, absolutely indefinitely." Fergus's modest attempt at humour, which he thought rather good in the circumstances, evoked no response in kind.

"Well in that case – we'll pay the money."

"Really? Oh, thank you, Mr Martyn. That's terrific. I can't say how pleased I am that – "

"And it'll be deducted from your salary."

For a moment there was complete silence on the line.

"But – Mr Martyn – I can't afford that!"

"I'll take it out of your salary rise."

"Oh, I didn't know I was getting one."

"You won't be. Not for the next three years," the last two words were shouted, "at least!"

"But it's an exclusive, Mr Martyn. Think of the increased circulation."

"The only increased circulation around here will be mine – at the thought of paying five – hundred – bloody – quid!" And then the editor's voice sank low, taking on almost a pleading tone. "Keane, Keane, Keane. Where the hell've you been all your life? It's only an exclusive until some rag comes along and offers him a few quid more. And anyway, it's dull, Keane, dull, dull, dull. Isn't there any sex angle you can put into this? What readers want is something to brighten up their drab lives, take them out of their pedestrian rut. You know, 'Geriatric sex addict runs off with schoolgirl bank robber.' That sort of thing. Bring back a story like that, Keane, and promotion will be rapid and substantial. So this old guy's leg's been cured. So what? End of story. He's not going to have a miracle happen to him every week, is he? Has anybody else had a miracle happen to them?"

"Well, no, but I'm sure it's only a matter of time. But other people have now seen the vision and there's a stream that's appeared beside the Mass Rock. The locals are saying that it's holy water."

"Well, that might run, Keane, but this story bloody won't. Next week it'll be as dead as a dodo. So you can tell your man that we're not writing his story and he can forget about the five hundred – agreement or no agreement, signature or not. You get yourself back here, pronto. There are two art exhibitions and a council meeting coming up and I've got nobody to cover them." There was a slurping sound from Harry Martyn as he gulped another draught of tea the colour of rust. "And don't come in here waving a big bunch of expenses, son, because you won't bloody get them."

"But Mr Martyn, I can't come back! This is a big story, an exclusive. All the newspapers in Ireland will be onto this now. And then the English ones, not to mention tv and radio. I've got to stay here and follow it up."

Fergus Keane heard a long and painful sigh.

"Keane, believe me, I've had plenty years of experience of this kind of thing. Miracle stories are ten-a-penny in Ireland. Too many tossers wandering around with their heads full of drink and bloody leprechauns. This is a bummer, Keane. In a few days you'll probably find out it was a hoax."

"Oh no, Mr Martyn, it's genuine. I know it is. In fact, I would stake my reputation on it."

"Keane, you little prat, you don't have a bloody reputation! Now would you get yourself back up here, in double quick time."

Fergus stood for a moment, heart beating fast, watching his reflection in the glass of the telephone box as he composed a determined countenance, more for the impressive reflection of his face in the glass than for any effect it might have on his voice. Then he said, slowly and very evenly,

"I'm afraid I can't do that, Mr Martyn. It's my duty to stay here and uncover the truth. And you'll see, I'll prove to you that I'm right."

And then to his own amazement Fergus gently replaced the receiver and stood for a few moments trembling with excitement at his own audacity and the prospect of success that lay before him. Just before he stepped out of the telephone box, he squared his shoulders and allowed a casual grin to slant one side of his mouth. That too looked good in the reflection, he felt good, his instincts were good, and he had now mastered every aspect of this job. He didn't need any editor, and certainly not Harry Martyn, to tell him when he was onto a big story. He would send in the best damned pieces that had ever been printed in the Northern Reporter, or any other paper, for that matter. And when The Times and The Daily Telegraph were chasing him – The Washington Post flitted through his mind but he thought it was a little premature for that – when the big London dailies were offering him a fortune to go and work for them, he would tell Harry Martyn where to stick his job. But if he didn't pay the miracle man his five hundred, there would be no exclusive, no fame, no fortune. So, he would just have to take it out of his own meagre savings. It would be an investment in his talent. And after the story went nation-wide and every paper was clamouring to get the inside track, Harry

Martyn would be rushing to pay him back his five hundred, and a nice fat bonus on top of it as well.

With a piece of meat in one hand and a rolling pin in the other, the Winter Cook went searching behind the furniture and boxes in the kitchen of the Glens Hotel for the cat, which had stolen a piece of lemon sole from a plate and her only turned her back for a second, the filthy brute. As she went, she hummed a little tune, an action which was entirely foreign to Mrs Megarrity's cantankerous nature.

"Here, puss puss puss," she said, holding out the meat and hefting the rolling pin. "Come and get it!" She bent low and peered under a table. No sign of it there. Tiptoeing across the room, she gently opened a cupboard door with her toe, the meat waving before her, the rolling pin held aloft. Then she searched among the packets, tins and jars stored there, but saw no sign of the fat, sleek animal that seemed to be able to disappear like a wisp of smoke after each of its many crimes. And still the Winter Cook kept up her tuneless humming as she pulled out boxes and looked inside, peered behind piles of nested pots and even looked in the oven in case the cat, in desperation, had decided that a slow baking was better than a cracked skull.

Having failed to find any trace of the animal, the Winter Cook laid the piece of meat on the table and was turning to put the rolling pin back into the drawer when she heard behind her the little thump of four paws landing on something. She glanced round, the wooden implement still clutched in her plump hand. Standing on the table, the big tom cat was lowering his head towards the piece of rump steak. A gleam of triumph illuminated Mrs Megarrity's eyes as she silently turned, at the same time raising the rolling pin to shoulder height. She took one step across the kitchen floor. The cat's mouth was round the meat. The cat bit into the red flesh. Mrs

Megarrity's final step was more of a leap, with the rolling pin slicing through the air towards the animal's head. At the last possible moment, the cat leapt clean off the table onto the sink and from there out of the open window. The rolling pin thudded into the slice of meat, Mrs Megarrity shouted, "Jasus tonight!" and then Dermot McAllister walked into the kitchen.

"Mrs Megarrity! What the hell are you doing?" he said, a puzzled smile on his face. Again the Winter Cook thumped the rolling pin on the rump steak.

"I declare to God, Mr McAllister," she said, "this meat's tougher than old boots. When I get that butcher, I'll give him rump steak, so I will. This has been in his freezer that long it's near fossilised."

"Well, never mind that for a minute. I've got something important to tell you." He gave a broad grin. "I just had bookings for three single rooms for tonight. Can you do three extra dinners for this evening? I think they're newspaper reporters from the South. The first of many, I hope, coming to report on the miracle story." He rubbed his hands together. "This is just the start of it, Mrs Megarrity. Just the start. Tell me, how's the Miracle Man keeping?"

"Oh, the Miracle Man's just fine," she retorted, "but I'm not a miracle bloody woman. How am I expected to get meals ready for people when I don't know they're coming? Would you tell me that?"

"But – I just told you, Mrs Megarrity."

"That's all very well, Mr McAllister, but I can't be going out now to buy a whole rake of stuff to put on a menu, and if I was to keep it in case somebody did turn up and then had to throw it out, you'd be onto me about the cost of the food."

"Ah, Mrs Megarrity, I'm sure you'll rustle up something. You always do. I'm sure these reporters are not that fussy."

"And another thing," she said. "If I'm to be doing all this

extra work, I don't think a rise in wages would go amiss."

"Mrs Megarrity," Dermot said, approaching as if he was about to put his arm around her. The temptation was not difficult for Dermot to resist. "Believe me, I would like nothing better than to give you a wage rise. I really would. But until business gets better – and maybe this is the start of it – there isn't much I can do without bankrupting the place."

The Winter Cook smiled sweetly at him.

"Ah now, I'm sure there is, Mr McAllister, I'm sure there is. In fact," she turned the rolling pin in her fat hands, "unless you want Mrs McAllister to find out about the shenanigans upstairs in the bedroom with the piano teacher, I would think there's quite a lot you could do."

The look on Dermot's face was a mixture of pain and puzzlement.

"The – piano teacher?" he said, adding under his breath, "I'll kill the little bugger."

She held up her hands in protestation of innocence.

"Not that I would sit in judgement on any man, Mr McAllister. 'Judge not, lest ye be judged', that's always been my motto. But I'm not so sure your good wife would see it that way. I'd say another – fifteen pound a week would save any problems in that department."

With tight lips and narrowed eyes, Dermot regarded the Winter Cook for what seemed like a long time.

"Five," he said.

The Winter Cook gave this some thought.

"Ten."

"Seven fifty, dammit, and that's my final offer."

"Done," said the Winter Cook, with only a modest smile.

"Of course, you know what this is, Mrs Megarrity. This is blackmail."

"Oh, I know, Mr McAllister, I know fine. And thank God for it."

chapter ten

Mr Andrew Rowan, senior partner in the firm of Rowan, Rowan and Pettigrew was a small, dapper man in his mid sixties who liked to dress well, dine on the best and in general enjoy the good things in life, whether provided by his own efforts or unwittingly by those of his clients. His thriving solicitor's practice in Belfast had long ensured that he could maintain an expensive lifestyle, and since his son had joined him as a partner, he felt that the family fortunes were now doubly secure. On recently inserting the second Rowan into the name of the practice, he had reflected on why he had never removed that of Pettigrew all those years ago, but Rowan and Pettigrew had a ring to it, and anyway it was always better to give the impression that a practice was not simply a one-man band. It had only been a few years after he had set up the practice with Pettigrew that the unfortunate incident of the widow's legacy had occurred. Poor Pettigrew. For a solicitor, he had been so naive, and Rowan had been happy to benefit from the money while his partner took the blame. Naturally, Rowan had made great efforts to cover things up for his friend and partner, and had certainly succeeded in preventing charges from being brought, but some kind of justice had to be seen to be done, and so young Pettigrew had had to leave and sell his half of the business to Rowan. At a price which was very advantageous to Rowan, of course. On reflection, Rowan realised that it had been a blessing in more ways than one, as it showed that Pettigrew would never have made either a good solicitor or a long-term partner. He was too naïf – that was Mr Rowan's euphemism for "honest" – and would certainly have brought misfortune upon the firm sooner or later. And Pettigrew's departure had certainly been the start of Rowan's success, the other major part of which had been the handling of legal affairs for the Garrison family. When old man Garrison had died, who better to advise on both legal and investment affairs for his two daughters than Mr Rowan. And advise them he did, on investments in land, in property, in stocks and shares and, as he had determined at the outset, he kept on advising them about their money until it was all gone.

In mid morning the wind had changed from the west to due south and now sent a warming breeze across the strand at Inisbreen, where Mr Rowan and the two Misses Garrison were taking a leisurely walk back to the Glens Hotel for lunch. The solicitor walked with a sister on either side of him, stopping here and there to ask about various points of interest – the strangely-shaped hill at the top of the glen, the derelict house on the strand – and Margaret regaled him with little anecdotes of times past and how nothing was what it had been in their young days.

Cissy took little part in the conversation, pre-occupied as she was – and as she had been for the last few days – with thoughts of John McGhee. She knew that everyone called him Limpy, but she could never think of him like that. And now, apparently, she would have no need to do so, as they were saying that he'd had a miraculous cure to his leg. It had only been after their recent brief conversation that she had realised the possibility of there still being a spark of interest on her part, a spark – indeed it was then a flame – that she had assumed extinguished many years ago by her father and Margaret. By turns she thought a relationship so long over was incapable of revival, then in the next breath decided that true love never dies, except perhaps beneath the dragon breath of Margaret. She was reluctantly being drawn towards the conclusion that it would have been better if John had not spoken to her that day at the strand.

"I'm so glad you came down today, Mr Rowan," Margaret was saying to the solicitor. "This whole money business has been such a worry to me this last few weeks, I feel quite exhausted by it. But now that you're here, dear Mr Rowan, I feel sure that we can have the whole matter resolved and then we can get back onto an even footing, don't you think?"

Mr Rowan gave the obsequious smile that he kept exclusively for elderly female clients and in particular for those like Margaret Garrison, who, whilst trying to give the impression of being knowledgeable and sophisticated in financial matters, were in fact not only naïf but gullible.

"Now, now, Miss Margaret, didn't we promise that we wouldn't talk about nasty business matters until lunch? After all, you can't expect me to be subjected to your sharp intellect on an empty stomach, mh?" he said, and as she gave him a coquettish smile, he sounded his little chirruping laugh and breathed deeply of the fresh sea air.

At first they were the only customers in the dining-room of the Glens Hotel. Later, an old couple came in, both of them talking loudly to overcome the other's hardness of hearing, the man drumming his fingers on the table with impatience at the woman's repeated questions, she giving a snort of derision at each reply he gave her. The Winter Cook came out from the kitchen with three tatty menu folders which she put on the Garrisons' table, then stood tapping a pencil against her pad and sucking at her teeth. The rolled-up sleeves of her black sweater bobbed at her wrists.

"Right, what d'yez want?" she demanded when they had barely opened the folders, inside each one of which was a small piece of paper that had written on it in scrawly writing:

Soup

Fish (depends)

or Steak and Kidney Pie

Ice Cream

Coffee

Mr Rowan looked at the menu, pulled a face and demanded,

"Is this it?"

"No, the steak and kidney pie's off," the Winter Cook said. "The cat got at it. Well, there's maybe about enough left for one, if anybody's interested. So, what is it to start? Three soups?"

"What is this," Mr Rowan persisted, "'depends'?"

"Depends what kind of fish is available at the time."

"I see. And what kind of fish is available today?"

"White."

"White? What kind of white fish?"

"Look, mister, I'm not a biologist. I just take the guts out and cook them. D'ye want it or not?"

Mr Rowan took a very deep breath and his lips drew to a point and his eyes narrowed.

"This is ridiculous. You have the effrontery to call this place a restaurant. Of all the establishments I have ever been in – "

Margaret Garrison laid a restraining hand on his arm and said frostily to Mrs Megarrity, "Three soups and three fish please. Boiled potatoes and carrots."

Mrs Megarrity walked away without writing anything on her pad. Mr Rowan looked at the menus and then said to Margaret Garrison,

"How did you know there were boiled potatoes and carrots?"

"Because it's always boiled potatoes and carrots."

Mr Rowan slowly shook his head.

When Mrs Megarrity brought the soup, which looked as if it might once have had a casual acquaintance with vegetables, Mr Rowan said,

"Could I see a wine list, please?"

"Ye could," Mrs Megarrity informed him, "if ye had a pair of binoculars. The nearest wine list's in the Strand Hotel, five miles away." She turned and walked off towards the kitchen.

Mr Rowan looked at each of the Garrison sisters in turn.

"And this is where you have lived for the last seventeen years? My dear ladies, you have my undying admiration."

Over the first course, Mr Rowan at last broached the subject of the Misses Garrisons' finances, when he pulled a face at the thick and oily consistency of the soup and replaced the spoon in his bowl. Then he gave a smile of such ferocity that a passing shark, having seen it through the window from the bay outside, might well have claimed kinship with the smart little solicitor from Belfast.

"Well, ladies – to business. As you are aware, for many years now my practice has acted on your behalf in the administration of your late father's estate and the ensuing investments and disbursements. In accordance with what was decided immediately after his death, I was given power of attorney over your financial affairs and have therefore in the intervening years been able to manage them as dictated by the prevailing financial climate – ," Margaret Garrison nodded sagely and Rowan continued, " – in order to save both of you any worries or concerns regarding the best way to deploy your assets. And from time to time, as prudence dictated, some assets were acquired and some assets relinquished," he held his hands wide, palms upwards, in a display of acceptance of the vagaries of long-term investment, "by dint of which substantial gains – and some losses – were made." He paused for a moment, allowing the significance of this statement to be realised. “In the case of equities, it is of course in their nature that values can fall as well as rise, and it was indeed sometimes necessary to sell at a loss – in order to avoid further losses, you understand.”

Margaret Garrison smiled her understanding. Cissy gave no reaction but, unusually for her, she had fixed Mr Rowan with a steady look. Had Margaret Garrison seen this, she would have assumed that her sister's thoughts were far removed from the subject of her gaze.

Mr Rowan continued,

“One must also understand that what was a substantial monthly income twenty-five years ago would nowadays be regarded as – well – rather a paltry sum, to be honest. Your expenses have – very understandably – risen, whilst income has tended to – decline.”

Cissy pushed away her soup, which she had hardly touched, and leant forward, as though to hear Mr Rowan the better. “The result of all of this, dear ladies, is that your assets have been reduced to the point where – to be brutally frank, as I am honour bound to be – there aren't any. Except for about five thousand shares in Commonwealth and Orient and about the same in Consolidated Uranium, for which my son has, very generously I have to say, instructed me to offer you, on his behalf, fifty pence each. He would like you to know that he is prepared to take the loss in order to assist you dear ladies in this lean period – and of course in the hope that some day the price might rise a little. A forlorn hope, I told him, but he absolutely insisted.” Mr Rowan smiled indulgently at the thought of his dear son, who had learned so very well from his father. “The impetuousness of youth, mh? He has his mother's charitableness. `Johnson,' I said to him, ‘this is business.' ‘No Father,' he told me, ‘these are the Misses Garrison.' Even for a hard-nosed old realist like myself, it really was quite a touching moment. I would have to say that it is an excellent offer, and I would urge you to take it. Now," he clapped his hands together as though all had been amicably resolved, "where has that white fish of ours got to, I wonder?" He gave what sounded like a little chuckle but was in effect the death rattle of the Garrison assets. "I doubt this is not an eating place I would care to recommend."

A glazed expression on her face, Margaret Garrison sat looking at Mr Rowan, whom she had hitherto admired as the financial wizard who had smoothed their path through life with a modest income and many reassurances.

"Are you saying, Mr Rowan – ", her normally strong voice was now light and quavering, " – that we have – nothing left at all, apart from these shares? Nothing – at all?"

Mr Rowan bestowed a beneficent smile on his client, who was soon to be an ex-client.

"One thing that has always kept me on my toes over the course of our long relationship, Miss Margaret, is my knowledge of your perspicacity, your ability to grasp in an instant the essential details of a complex situation and draw a logical conclusion, and over all those years I have from time to time regretted a little that you did not wish to be taken more fully into my confidence in these matters. I feel sure you could have made an invaluable contribution. You are, as always, perfectly correct in your financial assessment. The ten thousand shares to which I referred represent you and Miss Cissy's total worth. Yes, indeed."

"You mean – no more property?"

He shook his head. "No more property."

"And – the land – ?"

"All gone, I'm afraid, sacrificed to maintain what one can only call a comfortable lifestyle." This was perfectly true, except that he did not reveal that the comfortable lifestyle was his own. "But please," he continued, the soul of reasonableness, "why not look on the bright side? There are still the shares," he leant forward and said in a conspiratorial manner, "and I just might be able to persuade Johnson to part with a little more for them, perhaps sixty pence each." He waved a hand. "He can afford it."

Cissy aimlessly moved a knife on the table-cloth then said,

"I assume you have some kind of – record – of all these transactions, Mr Rowan?"

Mr Rowan's eyes were suddenly narrowed as he looked at Miss Cissy with a new wariness, but he smiled and said, "My dear Miss Cissy, one couldn't possibly keep records of everything over such a lengthy period of time. The paperwork would be staggering – and very expensive to maintain. But – why would you want such a thing, for goodness sake?" He laughed lightly.

Miss Cissy had begun to move her knife again.

"So that we could see if you had been cheating us or not."

Taken aback, Margaret glared at her sister and then almost shouted,

"Cissy! How dare you!"

Mr Rowan's smile transmogrified into a grimace.

"Well now, I think perhaps Miss Cissy is a little overwrought. Perhaps understandable in the circumstances."

"Thank you, Mr Rowan, but absolutely nothing can excuse such behaviour. Cissy, you will please apologise at once to Mr Rowan."

"I will, Margaret, if he can show us that what I said isn't true." Her knife came to rest pointing straight at Mr Rowan and she looked directly at him with her weak green eyes, which hitherto had been seen as reflecting her general dullness but suddenly appeared merely to be cloaking a sharp intellect. "It can't all have gone, Mr Rowan. Not the whole of our father's estate."

It was the solicitor's turn to have a little quavering sound in his voice.

"Miss Margaret, I am a patient man and well used to dealing with – difficult clients. But your sister has gone too far and has questioned not only my honesty but also my professional integrity. I simply cannot accept that."

"You could sue me for slander," Cissy said mildly, "except that if you won – I wouldn't have any money to pay you."

Mr Rowan stood up quickly from the table and a spoon clattered to the floor. With a sweeping gesture he wiped his mouth with his napkin and threw it onto the table.

"That's it, Miss Margaret. I'm sorry, but I'm not prepared to hear any more of this, especially after all the work I have done on your behalf over so many years. I have explained to you how the present unfortunate situation came about and yet – either deliberately or through lack of wit – your sister does not seem to understand." He buttoned his silk and mohair jacket and stood erect. "I would be pleased if you would, as soon as possible, let me know about the sale of the shares I have mentioned. Despite what has happened, I will endeavour to persuade my son to keep his excellent offer open. Then, our business relationship will be at an end. Rather a tawdry end, I fear, but an end nonetheless. Farewell, dear lady." He shook the outstretched hand of a tearful Miss Margaret. "I'm sorry, Miss Cissy, but in the circumstances, I do not feel that I can extend the same courtesy to you. Goodbye."

And with this he gave a little bow and walked briskly out of the dining-room. Unperturbed, Miss Cissy carefully repositioned her knife, while Miss Margaret, shocked beyond previous experience, sat staring into space, tears brimming in her eyes.

Later in the day, when Father Burke was driving to the Mass Rock field to see the new stream for himself, he saw Peggy May walking along the road in the same direction. He pulled up his car, which he had not yet quite decided to sell in favour of a bicycle, reached across and opened the door.

"Can I offer you a lift?"

Peggy May looked at him, executed a partial genuflection by the roadside, and climbed into the passenger seat.

"Thank ye, Father. I'm very grateful. The elastic in these new knickers is like cheese wire. It near has the backside cut off me. I tell ye, I'd be better with them off."

A look of mild panic swept across the young priest's face.

"I – eh – I'm sure they'll be all right when you – in a few days." Father Burke squirmed in his seat and wished he had left the wretched girl to walk wherever she was going.

"Oh, Father, I wouldn't wear them for that long! They'd be walking on their own, so they would. My Mammy says that cleanliness is next to Godliness – especially round the nether regions."

Father Burke rolled his eyes to heaven, and then said quickly,

"I've been interviewed by a journalist, you know. From the Northern Reporter. About what's been happening up at our Mass Rock here." The priest glanced over to see how impressed Peggy May was by this. "It was in this morning's paper. Did you see it?"

"We don't get a paper in our house, Father. My Da says all they're good for's lighting the fire or wiping your arse."

Father Burke sank a little lower in his seat.

"That's where I'm going now, Father. The Mass Rock. D'you think we'll see the Virgin?"

"Well – it is a possibility, but I doubt it."

"Why not, Father? I prayed for her to come so I could ask her to get Saint Anthony to help our Margaret."

Father Burke sighed.

"Why does your Margaret need Saint Anthony's help?" He braced himself for the answer, which he felt would not be capable of prediction by a score of logicians, or, in this woman's case, illogicians.

"Because I heard our Margaret saying she was pregnant and she didn't know who the father was and I'm going to ask Saint Anthony to find him."

Father Burke's car swerved a little on the road and around the steering wheel his knuckles showed white.

"Well, I still don't think you can count on seeing the Virgin Mary at the Mass Rock."

And Peggy May glanced over at the young parish priest as if she had just decided to reconsider her belief in the infallibility of the Church.

From the gate into the Mass Rock field they saw small groups of women kneeling in a semicircle round the rock and praying, some aloud with the rosary beads inching through their fingers, while others with hands clasped before them mumbled into their chests. Now and then a woman would break away from a group and go to the stream to fill a plastic container or an empty whiskey bottle. One old woman walked away clutching two vacuum flasks, happy in the thought that her rheumatism would now be a thing of the past. The overcast sky and the drizzle of rain that fell softly upon them gave Father Burke the impression that the scene could have been one from long ago, dark, distant days when the Mass Rock had been regularly used for worship and in sympathy with the oppressed peasants the sun had rarely shone on the benighted land. He stood at the gate, enthralled.

"Now isn't this what we see before us the very essence of Catholic Ireland?" he said, addressing no-one in particular and certainly not Peggy May, who stood beside him, similarly overwhelmed by the spectacle, although perhaps for different reasons. "The Faith kept throughout the ages – the dark ages – handed down from one generation to another under the guidance of the servants of God. It was like a living flame that had sometimes to be hidden in a deep cave and at other times could be revealed for all the world to see, carried aloft – " his hands rose to the level of his face, " – to the huzzas of the faithful, with incense and bells and benedictions. And it can be that way again. Here in this glen there can be a statement of God's love for man, a place of pilgrimage to which people will come – like these women – the tired, the sick, the hungry, even those of little faith who seek a new path in their lives, a way back to God's love."

Peggy May, while barely understanding the words the priest had spoken, was looking up at him in awe, occasioned by his staring eyes, his dramatic posture and his missionary tone.

"We could build a shrine – over there!"

He could see it before him, built around the rock to protect the holy place, perhaps to a height corresponding to halfway up the trees above it. No, higher than that – and wider. How could he put a limit on the glorification of God? But should they not start out with grander plans, for a church, perhaps, or even – he gave a little shiver of excitement at the thought – a basilica?

"A basilica," he almost whispered.

But Peggy May's enthusiasm had quickly waned. She had a thumb hitched in a leg of her knickers and was attempting to ease the cutting action of the elastic.

Of course, the field in front of the Mass Rock would need to be cleared and paved to accommodate the multitudes and a great stone pulpit built from which he, Father Ignatius Loyola Burke, would preach to them. And roads. There would need to be roads built, wide and straight, that would carry the faithful to this holy place which in time would surely come to rival Croagh Patrick and even Armagh itself as the true repository of the Faith of the nation.

"Ah," he said, "what a wonderful prospect and vouchsafed to me to make a reality." He basked in the glory of his own creation.

"Father, d'you think would Mr McBride take these knickers back after I've worn them? He wouldn't take a cream bun back from Mrs McAuley because he said there was a fingerprint on it."

Behind them, a car went through a puddle at speed. Father Burke jumped back, but it was too late. The car threw out a great wave of muddy water that missed Peggy May completely and caught the priest around the back of his legs.

"Bastard!" he said, quite forgetting Peggy May's presence.

"That's what Mrs McAuley said too, Father."

All of the women stopped praying and collecting water when they saw Father Burke approaching and they began to gather round him, one or two casting puzzled glances at his wet feet and trousers. Peggy May was ignored. Many of them began to speak at once, pointing towards the stream or holding up their water containers.

"Father," said one woman, "d'you think she'll come again? Will we see her, Father? God Almighty I'd drop dead if she came when I was here, so I would."

"Somebody was supposed to have seen something up in the trees last night," said another.

"Have you come to bless it, Father?"

"Now now, ladies, please, don't get carried away. There's been nothing proven yet, although – "

"But Father, what about the vision – and the stream? There must be something."

"Would the water sort cats, Father?" The old woman had managed to wriggle her way to the front, carrying a large ginger tomcat. Father Burke smiled at her, although he had a worried look on his face and someone else told the cat woman that she was taking some of the water home to give to a goat that was ailing. With the women crowding round him, Father Burke made his way to the Mass Rock and saw the little stream that flowed from the ground beneath it.

"Has there ever been a stream here before?" he asked.

"Not within living memory, Father."

"That's very interesting indeed. Of course, it may only be a coincidence, but if it is, it's rather a large one, to my way of thinking." Stepping back, he looked up at the top of the rock. It was just the kind of place one could imagine the Virgin Mary appearing. The fine rain drifted like mist in front of the trees and across the face of the rock to land as tiny silver beads on his black jacket. He seemed to sparkle with white light.

"Ladies," he said suddenly, "I think we should say a prayer together," and he knelt down facing the rock, oblivious to the mud that squelched around his knees. The women followed suit and even Peggy May knelt down, albeit a little awkwardly. When Father Burke blessed himself the women did so too, with Peggy May lifting a paw and doing the same for the cat, presumably on the grounds that, with an injured limb, it was unable to do this for itself. Father Burke said three Our Fathers, three Hail Marys and the Memorare. He had intended to say a prayer specially for the occasion, one that he would compose as he went along and give out in ringing tones, but whether because of the dismal weather or the earlier taxing of his imagination, nothing appropriate came to mind.

When he had finished and stood up – the women rose in unison – he turned to see a man standing a few yards away from them, the light glittering on his waterproof coat. It was John Healy, Limpy McGhee's next-door neighbour. He came forward a little hesitantly and gave a nod of his head.

"Hello, Mr Healy," Peggy May said brightly and waved one of the cat's paws. He nodded towards her and then began awkwardly,

"I don't know if you know, Father, "but these people here are all – well, trespassing."

"What?"

John Healy moved uneasily from one foot to the other.

"You're all trespassing, you know," he said to the women. "This land here belongs to Mr McAllister now. Private property. There's no access allowed without permission."

Father Burke took a step towards him.

"No access? What're you talking about, man? People have been coming to worship here for hundreds of years without let or hindrance. Now away home like a good man and don't be making a fool of yourself."

Father Burke turned away. From an upstairs window the stolid gaze of Mrs Healy met her husband's nervous glance backwards. He cleared his throat and tried again.

"I'm Mr McAllister's agent, Father. And from tomorrow onwards there'll be a charge made for anybody coming onto this land." From the women there were gasps of disbelief. Father Burke stared at the unfortunate Healy who seemed to shrink beneath the visual onslaught of his wife from the rear and the priest and women to the fore. Angrily the parish priest moved to within inches of the new land agent. The women drew closer.

"You would make money from people coming to pray to the Lord Jesus? What sort of men are you at all?"

"A bloody pagan!" one woman shouted, and another started, "A money-grubbin' little f – ", before being elbowed into silence by her neighbour.

"That's the sin of simony," Father Burke thundered at Healy, but this failed to make any discernible impression on him. In any competition between Satan and his wife, Healy knew who his money would be on.

"A man's got to make a living, Father. When people start crowding in here, devil the bit of sheep can go on it. Mr McAllister says it's simply a – " he readied himself for the deliverance of the phrase, " – a commercial undertaking."

"Oh he does, does he?" Father Burke almost shouted.

"Well, we'll see about that, Mr Healy. We'll soon see about that."

Having delivered his piece, John Healy turned abruptly and walked off towards his house, congratulating himself on having had the nerve to see it through. Maybe there would be a price to be paid for this in the next life, if there was one, but unlike Satan, his wife was very much in this life, he could reach out and touch her, and much more importantly, she could reach out and grasp him. Behind him, from the arms of Peggy May, the cat waved a cheery goodbye.

When Limpy received the five hundred pounds for his exclusive story from Fergus Keane, he did not even open the envelope but straight away put it at the back of the cupboard next to the fireplace. Normally, if he had any money besides that which was in his pocket – a rare event – he would stuff it into one of the tins on the mantelpiece. His "savings", he would call it, but the money only remained in the tin until that in his pocket ran out, which was never more than a few days. Then it was off with the tin lids, one after the other, rummaging amongst the pieces of string, the foreign stamps which, if he had ever collected more than half a dozen would one day have netted him a fortune, the assorted buttons, badges, nails and screws. Now he couldn't be too careful. There was an increasing number of people coming to the Mass Rock site and as his little house was adjacent to it, he was now subjected to complete strangers peering in his window and attempting to use his outside toilet, although it was unlikely that any of them, having used it once, would venture back without a gas mask and a flame-thrower.

He had thought up hill and down dale, as he liked to put it, about the best use for the money and had come to no firm conclusion. He could buy a new bed, of course and some new clothes, he could put a lick of paint on the house. With each possibility, he had decided that he was happy enough the way things were, so why waste the money. He had even considered giving some of it to the Church, on account of it having been the result of a religious event, but he didn't much take to the idea of the money going into Father Burke's coffers to be used for who knows what.

The five hundred pounds in its tatty brown envelope lay in the cupboard for the best part of a week before Limpy removed it and laid it out on the table. It was more money than he had seen at one time in the whole of his life. He gazed at the creased and crumpled ten- and twenty-pound notes for a long time, hoping that the sight of such wealth would conjure up all sorts of delights on which he could spend it. He considered a foreign holiday, but what use would that be on his own? He pondered the amusement of a small boat in which he could potter around the river and the bay but when he remembered that he could be seasick just looking at a moored boat bobbing up and down, he quickly dismissed that idea. A car, now there was something that would be a major benefit. He could go where he wanted when it suited him. He could drive around the countryside, visit friends in Ballymane and Castleglen and wouldn't be a slave to the erratic bus timetable. And all he would have to do was put a drop of juice in the machine now and again – and pay for repairs and tax and insurance and . . . maybe a car wasn't such a good idea after all. He gathered the money up, put it back into the envelope and replaced it in the cupboard.

News travels fast in a village and Inisbreen was no exception. Whether by way of Mr Pointerly, the only other person besides Dermot who knew of the Garrison sister's financial problems, or from Dermot himself, it was not long before most people heard that they had fallen on hard times. Some refused to believe it. People like that knew how to hold onto money and the Garrisons had always been loaded. And anyway, they must still have it because what the hell did they spend it on? When Limpy heard the news he also refused to believe it and in O'Neill's bar almost started a fight with Pig Cully who, being in favour of the distribution of wealth as long as it was primarily distributed in his direction, had taken delight in the story. Later, when he went to the hotel kitchen to visit his sister Lizzie, who was pleasantly surprised that he didn't tap her for a couple of pounds, he learned from her that the Garrisons had indeed fallen on hard times and she related the snippets she had overheard from "that little weasel of a lawyer boy that came from Belfast." And if Lizzie said it, it must be true. She had long since cornered the market for gossip in Inisbreen. On his walk back home Limpy was deep in thought, so much so that he quite forgot he had intended to make his daily visit to the Glens Hotel bar for a few restorative drinks. Mrs Megarrity, her suspicions raised when he left without having asked her for money, covertly watched him from the door of the hotel as he walked up the road and past the bridge. He clearly wasn't going to O'Neill's bar either. She might have lectured him long and often on his drinking, but when any creature strayed from its natural path, there was obviously something wrong.

Glancing into the sitting-room, where Margaret sat staring sightlessly at a book propped before her, Cissy stuffed inside her cardigan the bulky envelope which she had taken from the letter rack in the foyer of the Glens Hotel and began quickly to climb the stairs towards her room. Her receiving a letter – or a communication of any kind – was such an usual occurrence that she could hardly contain her excitement. And the envelope could only have been placed in the rack a short time before, otherwise it would have been spotted by Margaret who would have intercepted it with the excuse that any such missive would require her interpretation before the contents were communicated to Cissy in the simplest of terms. After the incident with Mr Rowan, it was clear that Margaret was just waiting for a chance to get back at her.

As Cissy climbed the stairs, she felt the envelope beneath which her heart pounded from her exertion and unconcealed excitement. It must be more than a letter, it was so bulky, and yet what it could possibly be she had not the slightest idea. It was most probably a mistake, with the letter having been intended for Margaret. She stopped on the landing outside her room. Should she take it to Margaret now and thus avoid the embarrassment and reprimand that would inevitably follow her opening of it? She pulled the buff envelope far enough out from her cardigan to see again the details of the former addressee scored out and her own name written above in ill-formed letters. "Miss Cissy Garison" it said. She barely noticed the mis-spelling. Giving herself a little hug of excitement and with a smile broadening on her lips, she went into her bedroom, where she closed and locked the door behind her.

With trembling fingers she tore open the top of the envelope, which had been sealed by a great blob of some sticky substance and then in a paroxysm of anticipation, she paused. It was a joke. Someone was playing a cruel joke on her and when she drew the contents from the envelope something would flutter into her face or make a terrible noise or stick to her fingers. And it was probably Patrick McAllister. After all, he had once put a squeaky cushion on her chair in the dining-room and she had jumped up and spilled soup over Margaret who had never forgiven her. Pulling a face, and with the envelope held almost at arms length, Cissy slipped her fingers inside it. There were pieces of paper. Lots of them. She frowned and drew them out. Then her eyes sprang wide open and her jaw dropped as a wad of ten- and twenty-pound notes emerged, to slip from her nervous fingers and fall on the bed.

Cissy sat with her hand clutched at her throat, eyes staring and her chest heaving rapidly. Such a pile of money. Then she noticed the piece of white paper underneath the notes and drawing it out she unfolded it and read what had been written in the same poor handwriting as that of the envelope.

"Dear Cissy. I was sorry to here about yer finanshal trouble. I dont want you to think I was poaking my nose into yer bisness, but Inisbreen isnt the best place for keeping secrets. It was great bein able to talk to you the other week only yer sister came and spoyld it. I know I agreed not to see you after what yer father sed all them years ago but I coudnt see you in a bad way an not help. I had a bit of good luck and got this £500. At least Ive got a roof over my head and you might not have soon, so Ill pass it on to you. I hope itll be sum help. You can say its a preznt for a fine wuman and from my memory of old times. Maybe we can meet again some time soon, just you and me. Good Luck.
John."

Cissy read the note several times and then sat looking from it to the money and back again. Slowly she shook her head and her face began to pucker as tears welled in her eyes.

"Oh, John," she said. "John McGhee."

Cissy sat with four of her father's old cigar boxes in front of her on the bed. Slowly and painstakingly she was examining the pictures which they contained – small passport types of her mother and father long ago, medium-sized ones taken by members of the family, and large ones with protective covers done in studios by professional photographers. Some were very old and faded, the people in them long since dead, and others were so dark that she could make out little detail in them. Here were she and Margaret as children playing in a garden with big rhododendron bushes, and again with their parents, standing in front of one of her father's shops. Over some of the photographs she lingered, while others received the merest glance. In the third box she came across a photograph that showed about ten or twelve young men and women on the beach at Inisbreen – all smiles and horseplay – with herself and Margaret at the front.

Cissy studied each face in the photograph, holding it very near to her eyes and moving it the better to catch the light, then glanced at the back which was unmarked, before returning it to the box. The rest of the contents in the third cigar box were examined and then she started on the last one. Halfway down it, she picked up a small black-and-white photograph, examined it for a moment and then drew in her breath sharply. It showed her and a young man – both in their twenties – sitting on a grassy slope, he with his arm round her waist and she posing for the camera by resting her head against his shoulder and smiling broadly. Cissy Garrison turned the photograph over. On the back was written in faded pencil, "John McGhee, Inisbreen, August 19—". The last two digits of the year were indecipherable. After looking at it for a long time, she slowly ran her fingertips over the surface, caressing the image on the shiny paper.

chapter eleven

"Wake up, McGhee, for Christ's sake!"

It was almost midday and John Healy was standing ankle deep in the litter beside the bed, shaking the recumbent Limpy, who gave a huge yawn which his stained dentures failed to follow. He opened one eye.

"Jasus, would ye leave a man to get his sleep, Healy. What the hell time is it?" He pulled the grubby blanket tighter around his chin.

"It's after twelve o'clock. Would ye get up out of that. I've got something to tell ye."

"What the hell are ye doing waking me up at this time? Don't ye know the sunlight's damaging to your skin at this hour of the day?"

"Come on, McGhee, get up! The sunlight'll never get near your skin. I've got something to tell ye – about money."

The old man took a little more notice of this.

"I don't owe nobody nothing. Go away. Us personalities have got to get our beauty sleep when we're appearing before the public."

"Look, ye old eejit, I'm talking about you getting some money."

Limpy lay quiet while this momentous statement registered in his drowsy brain, and then propping himself up on one elbow he said warily,

"What do I have to do for it?" If there was a suggestion of anything that could be classed as "work", his interest would be at an end. Anybody could get money for work, that was easy. It was getting money without working for it that was difficult.

"Clean this place up, for a start."

"Clean it up? What the hell's wrong with it?"

"For feck's sake, man, I can't even see my feet! The place is a dump."

"Now look, Healy, I don't come in criticising your house, do I?" The fact that what Limpy called "that hallion of a wife of yours" would not have allowed him over the threshold with a fire hose had she been ablaze, went unmentioned. "What you don't realise is that everything here is positioned exactly, so I can put my hand on it at a moment's notice."

"Listen to me, McGhee. There's money to be made here – for nothing."

Limpy pulled himself upright in the bed. "For nothing? Why didn't ye say that in the first place?"

"Ah, ye're interested now, you graspin' old bugger. Look, there's people already coming around here to this Mass Rock and before ye know it they'll be arriving in droves, so they will. Dermot McAllister's going to be charging them very nicely for the privilege. So while they're here seeing the rock, can't they pay a bit extra to meet the very man it happened to and see his wee house? I'll go ye halfers on the money I take for visits to your house." He gave an exaggerated wink. "And McAllister needn't know nothing about it."

"Halfers? Bloody halfers? Why should I go halfers with you?"

John Healy smiled. He really had to hand it to his wife.

"Because they can't get to your house without crossing

McAllister's land first," he jerked a thumb at his chest, "and I'm in charge of McAllister's land."

Limpy screwed up his face and glared at his neighbour.

"Ye bloody robber. You'd wrestle a ghost for a ha'penny, so you would."

"For God's sake, man, all ye need to do is give them a guided tour of this great establishment of yours – the drawing room, the servants quarters, the library. Money for old rope."

Limpy's cracked and dirty fingernails rasped on his stubbled chin.

"And ye say I'd need to clean the joint up a bit?"

"Of course, man. Ye couldn't take people on a tour of this feckin' place like it is. You'd lose one or two on the way round."

"And what would ye be charging them?"

"Well, I'd say maybe – a pound. That'd be fifty pence for each of us."

"Fifty pence, eh? And how many people would you get?"

"Jasus, I don't know. Maybe – two hundred in a good weekend. That'd be – a hundred quid to you."

"A – hundred quid? In two days? Man dear," Limpy got out of the bed with an agility that belied his age, "ye've got yerself a deal there, Healy!" He looked around the room. "And I'd say the first thing is to do a bit of clearing up around here. Damn it to hell, you can't be showing paying customers round a tip like this."

Outside Limpy's front door the pile of debris from years of indiscriminate collecting – usually without the owner's permission – was growing steadily and included one and a half orange boxes, a stuffed bull's head with one horn missing that had been thrown out from a butcher's shop, an assortment of tractor and car spares, two broken hurley sticks, a number of cardboard boxes and an old toilet seat. Against the wall leant two bent brass curtain rails, although since their acquisition a decade before, his windows remained uncurtained. In order to remove other bulky objects and after a struggle accompanied by much cursing and swearing, Limpy had dragged his battered kitchen table outside and in a fit of pique thrown it on its face, its legs pointing skyward like some wild animal that had at last been vanquished. For a moment he supported himself against the wall to catch his breath. Despite what Healy had said, this looked and felt suspiciously like work. The big black dog came round the corner of the house and stopped, eyeing his master and the junk suspiciously, as though fearing that he would be next to be thrown onto the heap.

"Ye're never here when you're needed, dog. All you're good for's eating and pissing."

The dog lay down on the grass and watched Limpy in anticipation of some entertainment, something which had not been in short supply since he had come to live in this outsize kennel. Then John Healy came running across the field that separated his house from that of Limpy, and he was waving a newspaper.

"McGhee! Hey, McGhee! Have you seen this?" He arrived outside the house breathless, his big moon face redder than usual. Limpy emerged into the sunlight, smothered in a dusty bearskin rug. With its front legs over his shoulders, it looked as if it was carrying him. Unable to see where he was going, he fell onto the pile of junk.

"Ah – shit!" He struggled to his feet, said "What the hell are you gawping at?" to the bull's head and kicked it viciously.

"McGhee! Look at this," John Healy said.

"Oh, it's you! Come when I'm nearly finished, eh? How is it, Healy, I'm doing all the bloody work and you're getting half the money?"

"Never mind that, McGhee. There's a bit in the Northern Reporter about you and the miracle. Free publicity, man. They'll be streaming in."

Limpy smiled and tossed his head.

"I knew young Fergus would do a fine job."

"Listen I'll read it to ye."

And so as Limpy continued to bring further articles from the house and dump them on the grass outside, John Healy followed him back and forth, both of them stumbling over old boots, beer bottles and a mildewed curtain that had been unearthed from the bottom of a cupboard. The piece in the newspaper under Fergus Keane's name began with a fanciful description of the miracle and its subject, John Henry McGhee, followed by two sentences about the Mass Rock and its supposed history.

"'Father Ignatius Loyola Burke'," John Healy read as he followed Limpy who was carrying two chamber pots, "'a native of Dublin and one of the youngest parish priests in Ireland' – well, we know where he got that information – 'has taken a direct interest in the case of the Mass Rock miracle since the beginning and is strongly of the opinion that it is genuine. He says that signs of a miraculous power at work have been clear from an early stage, with medical opinion backing the miracle claim, subsequent sightings of The Apparition and the sudden appearance of a stream from beneath the Mass Rock itself. Says Father Burke, "I don't think it's any exaggeration to say that what we have here might in due course come to rival the phenomenon of Lourdes." There has, however, been at least one false alarm, when a pair of crutches was found propped against the Mass Rock. A local disabled man was later questioned by police and may face charges of indecency for relieving himself in a public place.' Would ye believe it? It was that stupid old git Wag O'Donnell."

"Never mind him. Does it say anything about the doctor?" Limpy enquired. "He's the man. Nobody listens to them priests."

"I'm coming to that bit," John Healy said, following the lines of print with his finger. "Here we are." He cleared his throat. "'A doctor, who for professional reasons did not wish to be named, recognised the medical signs of a possible miracle cure. "It was really quite remarkable,"' he said, "the amount of functionality that had been restored to the crippled limb and virtually in an instant. I have seen many rapid cures in my lengthy medical experience, but I have to say that Mr McGhee's is in a class of its own. It was all the more remarkable for the fact that the subject himself was unwilling to believe that he could have been the beneficiary of such a thing. I found his humility quite touching. However, after a thorough examination of the patient, I was in no doubt that an extraordinary phenomenon had taken place, the results of which would appear to be permanent." The small village of Inisbreen nestling beside the sea and at the end of a sandy beach, has been buzzing with talk of the miracle and the subsequent events. Already, people are coming from miles around to visit the site and take away bottles of what they now refer to as holy water. While there was a guarded "No comment" from the office of the Bishop of Down and Connor, there is little doubt that the faithful, the people of Inisbreen and the local countryside, have come to their own conclusion on the Miracle of the Mass Rock.'"

Both men had stopped beside the pile of rubbish and Limpy was standing with his eyes wide open and looking into space.

"Man, that's a class piece of writing from young Fergus Keane, if ever I heard one. Yer man Shakespeare couldn't hardly do better nor that."

"Shakespeare wrote plays, McGhee. He wasn't a reporter."

"Well he needn't bother applying. That's one great piece of writing. They'll be piling in here now, so they will, to meet The Miracle Man."

He pouted, lifted his chin up and gave a handshake of great gentility to an imaginary admirer. "Pleased to make your acquaintance, yer honour."

"At a pound a time," John Healy said, with a smile and a nod of satisfaction at the riches in prospect. "At a pound a time, McGhee."

John Healy had no better means than Limpy of transporting the heap of rubbish to the traditional dumping place in the river, and even if he had done, his wife would have come up with a number of reasons to disallow it, not least of which would be that they might "catch something from that boggin' little scoundrel or that bug hutch he lives in". For some time, therefore, Limpy wandered back and forth from the house to the heap of junk he had gathered outside, viewing it from every angle whilst drinking from a bottle of stout. The big black dog lay by the wall, watching him come and go and awaiting developments. And after some time an idea did seem to develop in Limpy's mind, so that he smiled and looked at the dog before giving a little skip and clapping his hands together. He almost ran into the house and after some banging and the sound of falling objects, he came hurrying out with a long knife and a great tangle of rope stiff with age and dirt.

"I have her cracked now, boy," he said to the dog, whilst untangling the rope and straightening the kinks in it. "Ah, isn't it marvellous the power of the human brain. Is it any wonder boys like me have reached the peak of civilisation, while the likes of you dogs are still lying about in the dirt?"

Limpy cut two lengths of rope, each about eight feet long, and tied one to each of two legs of the table which still lay top-down where he had thrown it. Then he rummaged in his junk heap and pulled out the old toilet seat. "Here we are! By God, this is going to be some machine!"

He tied the two free ends of the rope to the toilet seat, one on each side, then laid it on the ground and began to fill the underside of the table with junk from the pile. When the junk was almost the height of the upturned table legs, with some of the objects teetering on the top, he went over to the dog and grasped its collar.

"C'mon, dog. At least once in your life you'll work for your living."

The reluctant dog was stood facing away from the table and the toilet seat placed over its head and onto its shoulders, forming a kind of harness. Limpy's conveyance was ready for action.

Standing behind it and trying unsuccessfully to crack a makeshift whip, with shouts and threats Limpy managed to set the precarious sled in motion down the sloping field. Railing against the chafing yoke, the dog went this way and that, stopped and then started again under strokes from the whip and verbal abuse from its master.

"Ye useless, God-forsaken, flea-bitten old whelp! Get your arse into gear! Hup! Hup!"

And so they proceeded, Limpy running to keep up, then almost pitching forward into the rubbish as the dog came to a sudden halt and barked long and loud. At the gate onto the road, Limpy came forward to open it and had to do a quick side shuffle as, teeth bared, the dog went for his miraculous leg.

"Ye ungrateful cur! Ye'd bite the feckin' leg that feeds ye! Too used to the soft life, that's your problem. Back! Get back!"

With some difficulty, he urged the dog through the gate and out it went onto the main road with the impromptu conveyance dragged after it. This made for an easier passage, as there were no hillocks or clumps of rushes with which to contend, and the dog at least had to keep between the two hedges. Every so often it would stop to sniff a verge or cock its leg, only to give a yelp and a growl as Limpy's whip caught it on the hindquarters. The charioteer, attempting to steer the table by his grip on one of its legs, strode along behind it with such an air of self-importance that he might have been acknowledging the cheers of the crowds in the Coliseum. The pile of junk wobbled precariously but somehow managed to remain intact.

"By God, she's a great machine altogether!" Limpy shouted. "Marvellous! I've been wasting my time all them years. I could've been a – any damned thing I wanted. Bloody hidden talents," he shouted at the dog. "That's what I've got. Hidden talents! Hup! Hup!"

The car horn that blew behind him almost had him jumping over the table.

"Would you get that bloody contraption to hell off the road, you old lunatic!" the man shouted out the car window. "Jasus, they're not all locked up yet."

Limpy hauled on the two rear table legs until the dog nearly throttled itself trying to pull the table. Turning, Limpy glared at the man and began,

"Listen, shortarse, I've just as much – " but the driver pulled the car out and went racing past, giving one long blast on his horn as he did so. This set the dog off and it went down the road at a gallop, towards where the river almost met the road at the dumping place.

"Bloody – fascist!" Limpy roared after the car. "Feckin' dog! Stop, damn ye!" He ran down the road after the table from which the bull's head fell and rolled into the ditch followed by two old pans clattering onto the tarmac. The whole pile on the table wobbled and threatened to topple to the ground. When Limpy caught up with his chariot, the dog was drawing level with the opening to the river. He hit it on its outside flank with the whip.

"Round, ye bugger! Round!" The dog headed for the opening. "Now, slow! Slow, damn ye!" The dog responded in the specified direction but not at the required speed and it fairly plunged through the gap in the hedge and raced down the short slope to the riverbank, with the table and Limpy following as they might.

"Bastard! The river!" Limpy managed to shout as his legs flew past each other in a blur of motion. "Stop!"

And the dog did stop, very suddenly and near the edge of the bank. Behind it, Limpy stumbled and fell flat on his face, his upper dentures thrown clean out of his mouth. The table sailed over the bank and across the water, its momentum yanking the toilet seat from the dog's neck and almost removing one of its ears. There was a kind of slap as the table landed on the water, its load largely intact, and floated off down the river. Pushing himself up from the ground, Limpy watched it go.

"Whuck it!" he said. "Me bloody table's gone – and the fwiggin' pension book in the dwawer."

Then, seeing the narrowed eyes that were turned upon him and the whip clutched tight in the white-knuckled hand, the dog took off into the bushes without waiting for a verdict. Limpy pulled himself round to a sitting position and stared at the table, which was slowly sinking in the brown water.

"And how many whifty whuckin' pences will it be to buy a new table? Right awhter I strangle that whucker Healy!"

From the doorway of the Glens Hotel a cat shot out three feet from the ground, drop-kicked by the Winter Cook, who bellowed after it,

"Get out to hell! God curse ye for a dirty skitter! D'ye want to give us all dire rear like yerself? Jasus to-night, if I catch ye pawing round that steak pie again I'll chop yer bits off ye, so I will!"

Mrs Megarrity watched the cat as it scurried down a little slipway towards the river's edge, and then she turned back into the foyer to put her head round the door of the residents' lounge and say,

"Good evening to ye, Mr Pointerly. And the Misses Garrison. Good evening, ladies."

"Beautiful evening, Mrs Megarrity," Mr Pointerly said with an enthusiasm he usually reserved for occasions other than talking to the Winter Cook. "Just the thing for a brisk walk, mh?"

"Ah well," Mrs Megarrity said, "I'm sure that'd be very nice for them as had the leesure for such diversions, Mr Pointerly. It's an ill wind that blows nobody anywhere. Some of us has to keep slaving away, so we have, mucking out toilets and making the meals."

Margaret Garrison winced at this unfortunate conjunction.

"Not, I hope, in that order," she said quietly from behind the book she had been pretending to read. Mr Pointerly said nothing. He had never been quite sure how to respond when under attack by a woman.

"And what, might I ask, is for dinner this evening?" Margaret said in a voice heavy with dread.

"I've done yez a nice steak pie – in between mopping up after that bloody cat. It's been coughing up them balls again. I swear to God, it was going at both ends. Ten minutes ago you would've needed galoshes in that kitchen. D'ye know, I had to fire the mop out the back window, it was that bad."

The colour in Margaret Garrisons face quickly faded to a sickly grey, her book was closed and her hands fell listlessly to her lap. Cissy's face took on a pained expression, her lips curled at the corners as though she already had some of the horrid pie in her mouth. Mr Pointerly swallowed hard.

"Well," the Winter Cook said in a doleful voice, "it'll soon be your last meal, so it will."

"Wh – what?" Cissy managed to get out. Although all three of them had often felt when eating the Winter Cook's culinary efforts that it might be the last one they would ever consume, it was something of a shock for this to be announced in advance.

"Aye. Soon be yer last meal from me. McAllister's putting

me out to grass for the summer, as usual – and that hallion Standish is coming in early. Ah, now – " she held up a hand to restrain the expected wave of protest, " – there's no point in saying nothing. His mind's made up. 'Ye need a rest, Mrs Megarrity,' he said. 'It's been a long winter.'"

"You can say that again," Margaret mumbled.

"What's that, Miss Garrison?"

"I say, 'Will you be coming back again?'"

"Don't be worrying yourself on that score. Come the first of October, I'll be back." She gave a smile. "Now wouldn't it hardly be the same if the four of us wasn't together through the winter months – just like a wee community. If McAllister would only pay half-decent wages, wouldn't it be a pleasure working for yez."

And with that she turned and headed back towards the kitchen to check the steak pie for fresh paw-prints.

In his chair by the window, "Chrome Yellow" lying unheeded beside him, Mr Pointerly sat looking with unseeing eyes at the far wall, his long yellow teeth working at his thin lips. Towards her sister Cissy, Miss Margaret was coldly silent, her book thrust before her face, although she had not turned a page in the last five minutes. Miss Cissy, only partially visible in the sunken seat of the couch, was clearly deep in thought, cocking her head first to one side and then the other as she considered something of obvious importance. At last she gave a smile and began to struggle out of her seat, her two little legs waggling like those of a trapped insect, until her feet reached the floor and gave better purchase. Her elder sister ignored her efforts and Mr Pointerly, who would normally have gone to her aid, was oblivious to everything save his own thoughts. When she got to her feet, Miss Cissy gave a little smirk at her sister – unseen from behind the book – and left the room.

A few minutes later she returned with a newspaper, sat

down again and began to leaf through it. From behind her book Miss Margaret sneaked a look at her sister, and was surprised at what she saw. Cissy had never been known to read a newspaper in her life. Up and down the columns, page after page she scanned, until she came to a section near the back of the newspaper. She smiled and started to move her index finger slowly down a column tightly packed with small print. Miss Margaret gave up watching her and retreated behind her book. By the window Mr Pointerly was slowly shaking his head at some remembered incident. Suddenly Miss Cissy gave a little squeak of delight and examined more closely what she had found. Smiling, she turned to Mr Pointerly.

"Would you have a pen I could borrow, Mr Pointerly?"

Margaret looked out sharply from behind her book. If Cissy was going to do a crossword puzzle, it would be the first time, as far as Margaret knew.

"Of course, of course." His long bony hand dived inside his jacket like a heron after a fish. "I always carry a pen," he said, withdrawing a Parker, burgundy-coloured and with gold trim, which he held out to her, "although nowadays, there doesn't seem to be anyone left to write to."

"Thank you, Mr Pointerly," Cissy said and after checking the print once again she carefully made a mark against one of the columns. Margaret was intrigued beyond measure but would not lower herself to ask her sister what she was about. With the pen now as a pointer, Cissy set off down the columns again, after some moments stopping with a "Ha!" of satisfaction and making another mark against this second column. Then, holding her finger at the first mark on the page, she struggled from her seat and went to where her sister sat, the book even closer to her face.

"Margaret," Cissy said. After a moment Margaret slowly lowered her book.

"There you are, Margaret, I knew it. The man is a crook."

She thrust the newspaper towards Miss Margaret who reluctantly put down her book and looked at what was being pointed out to her. It was the page which gave the prices from the previous day's London Stock Exchange trading and next to "Commonwealth and Orient" was the figure of 998. "Almost ten pounds a share, Margaret! And look here." The tip of her small finger stabbed at the second mark. "Consolidated Uranium, 843, eight pounds forty-three pence each. Those are just a little bit more than the fifty pence each he offered us, aren't they?" Miss Cissy smiled broadly, and the newspaper rustled as her hands trembled. "And with about five thousand shares in each, that makes over – " she looked at some figures she had written in the margin of the newspaper, "ninety thousand pounds! Ninety thousand, Margaret! I think perhaps that should be enough to live on in the meantime, don't you? At least until we get a good lawyer and sue that little crook."

Now she wouldn't even need to think about using any of John's five hundred pounds and could give him the good news when she returned it to him. Her eyes wide in disbelief, Margaret stared at the figures until her sister lowered the newspaper and folded it. And when Cissy left the sitting-room to take the newspaper back to Dermot, Margaret blinked, raised her book very close to her face and let the big tears roll down her cheeks.

Dermot took the newspaper with him when he went upstairs for his evening meal. She was like a little timid mouse, Miss Cissy, and always in the shadow of her sister. He didn't know what was going on between them, but since that man had come to have dinner with them, something had changed. He hoped it was to do with their finances, because the time was fast approaching when he would have to ask them to leave, and although he would happily have put Miss Margaret out – and smiled while doing so – he would find it much more difficult with Miss Cissy. Of course, if this miracle business really took off, he could well manage without them – and old Pointerly. That would be three more rooms to let at premium rates. He might need all he could get. Today he had taken another two bookings, one for two nights from a man with a Dublin accent, and another from an Englishman who had rung up and asked if he had any vacancies for Wednesday and Thursday nights – with ensuite bathroom and shower, no less. Dermot had told him that it was the Glens Hotel in Inisbreen, not the Shelbourne in Dublin, then the man had laughed when he was told the price, asking if that was for one night or two and saying that he would take it. They could be very peculiar sometimes, these English.

In their private sitting-room, Agnes sat on the couch reading a golfing magazine, her hair tied back with a red bow, her nails filed and painted to perfection, the make-up on her pretty face a complement to her brown-checked skirt and oyster-coloured silk blouse.

"Isn't she just like something out an advert," Mary Hanlon had said.

"Aye, for frozen fish," had come the Winter Cook's reply.

Dermot tried to get to the small kitchen unnoticed but only made it halfway across the room.

"And what's keeping Mrs Megarrity with the dinner this time?"

"Oh, I'm sure it'll be here in a minute, Agnes. I think she had trouble getting a pot big enough to put the cat in."

As of late, Agnes ignored his attempts at humour.

"And where's Patrick? I don't know. I try to instil some discipline into that boy, but I get precious little help from you."

"I told him to come up. He'll be putting the bike away."

"Ah yes, the new bicycle. What prompted this sudden fit of generosity?"

"Agnes, he's been wanting a bike for ages."

"Yes, but why now, Dermot?"

Dermot shrugged and moved towards the kitchen.

"Why not?"

It had been worth it to have the little bugger keep his mouth shut. It was bad enough having that conniving old bitch Megarrity screwing him for another seven fifty a week over it. God alone knew what would happen if Agnes ever found out about Nancy. In the kitchen, which had been a storeroom before it was converted and still had an old black telephone screwed to the wall, Dermot rang downstairs. When he asked how long it would be before dinner was sent up, Mrs Megarrity said,

"Beggin' your pardon, Mr McAllister, but do I look like an octopus?" and when Dermot was stuck for an answer she put the telephone down. He went back into the sitting-room and said,

"Mrs Megarrity says dinner'll be up in a couple of minutes."

"Very likely," Agnes said.

Dermot poured himself a whiskey and settled in an armchair with the newspaper, idly wondering what was in it that Miss Cissy had been so anxious to see. Agnes said to him,

"I've been asked by Father Burke to join a committee."

Dermot grunted from behind the newspaper.

"He's setting it up to help him decide what should be done with the Mass Rock site."

Dermot lowered his paper.

"Well, you can tell Father Burke he's relieved of that responsibility. I own the land now, and I'll decide what's happening to it."

"Including charging people for visiting a religious site? Dermot, you can't possibly do it. It's the first thing they're going to ask me about. It's immoral – making money out of religion like that."

"You mean, like the Church does? I can see why he wants

you on his crusade committee. It's just a way of getting at me by the back door."

"Oh, is that all you think of me as, a back door?"

"You know what I mean. This is a business I'm trying to run, Agnes. I can't put sheep on that land now that people are trampling all over it. Don't you see? It's a golden opportunity to make some money – and you ought to be interested in that. You're good enough at spending it."

"Oh, I see. I might've known it would come down to that eventually. So it's all my fault, is it?"

"Did I say that?"

"Oh, I know the way you think, Dermot McAllister."

Dermot sank behind his newspaper.

"Dear God. Save me from mind readers."

"All I know is, I'll be there at the first committee meeting tomorrow night. At least someone around here is interested in the Church."

Dermot gave her his full attention.

"Tomorrow night? Where is this meeting?"

"In the chapel house, of course."

"You're going to the chapel house tomorrow night?"

"Unless you can find some way of transporting it here."

"But I told you I was going out tomorrow night. I've already arranged for someone to do the bar."

"Well, you'll just have to stay in. You won't get Bernadette Tierney to babysit at this short notice. I can't miss this meeting. It's an honour to be asked."

Dermot loudly shook the creases out of his newspaper before sinking behind it again, a thunderous look on his face. There was little point in arguing. When Agnes got something into her head, there was no deviating her from it. What the hell was Nancy going to say? He had promised her big things for the following night. Well, one, to be precise. He stifled a smile. She was such an innocent, but even she would begin to wander if time after time he couldn't perform. It had never happened before either with Agnes or anyone else. It was bloody worrying. Surely to God he wasn't going senile, at his age. It must be the situation, the – atmosphere. It was all wrong. Shagging in the front seat of a car wasn't exactly the ideal set-up, and he had already experienced the results of trying it in the house during the day. What he needed was a better venue. Surroundings more conducive to romance. And Nancy's house was no good. Her old mother looked as if you couldn't scratch your arse without her whipping out the rosary beads for a novena. Then a glow of satisfaction lit up Dermot's face. If he couldn't go to Nancy, then Nancy could come to him, when the Winter Cook had gone home, Agnes was out at her meeting, and Patrick was fast asleep in bed.

chapter twelve

The room in Limpy McGhee's house near the Mass Rock was silent apart from the muffled snores of it's occupant, who was hidden in his bed under a swathe of blankets, from the bottom of which his cracked black boots poked. Through the newly-cleaned windows, the corners of whose panes still held the dirt of years, the sunlight fell on the empty floor and on the hindquarters of the dog. It lay at full stretch, long face resting on its paws, vapid eyes half lidded as it regarded the scene of devastation before it. There was hardly an item of interest left in the room following Limpy's great clearance in anticipation of hordes of the paying public. No more boxes, bottles and heaps of clothing among which to root, no discarded crusts to gobble or makeshift battlements behind which to dodge a missile. And the walls were the only perpendicular structures left against which the dog could relieve himself. In fact, nothing of interest at all. Even the persistent smell of dog urine had gone, replaced by the stench of Jeyes' Fluid, which Mrs Healy had instructed her husband John, on pain of death, to sprinkle liberally around Limpy's abode. This was something she had wanted to do for many a year, but in fact was only second choice after her preferred option, a hand grenade, but even she agreed, on her better days, that this solution might be a little harsh. Now the dog hardly stirred himself all day, although when the heat rose and the smell of the disinfectant got too much for him, he would slink outside and find a place out of harm's way where he could lie in the sun. The dog gave a low, sorrowful whine and Limpy moved to find a more comfortable position on his bed.

The somnolent atmosphere was suddenly shattered by the door bursting open and crashing against the wall. The dog leapt to his feet, teeth bared and hackles rising. Limpy gave a jump and uttered an oath. In the doorway the sunlight was partially blocked by the bulky figure of the Winter Cook, wrapped in an old brown overcoat and with a woollen hat of the same colour pulled down over her ears and sticking up at a peak on the top. Seeing her pass through the village, Pig Cully had said,

"What the hell does she not look like?"

John Breen had replied,

"That's the latest fashion, Cully. Designer dog turd."

As she strode across the room towards the bed, Mrs Megarrity shouted,

"McGhee, ye wee maggot! Get up out of that!"

"What the hell – ?" he groaned, surfacing from the sea of blankets.

Another stride took the Winter Cook within reach of the Miracle Man, and she grasped him by the shoulder of his grubby shirt and shook him.

"Five hundred pound, ye conniving little git! 'Ye couldn't ever lend me a couple of bob?' ye said, and 'I'm down on my luck, Lizzie. I'll pay ye back the minute I get two pounds close enough together to count.'" She reeled off a litany of his stock phrases for extracting money from her. "Tried to keep it a secret from me, didn't ye?"

Limpy kneaded the sleep from his eyes and then rubbed his hands through his tousled hair.

"Jasus Christ, Lizzie, ye near had the heart jumping out of me. Is that any way to come into a man's domicile? And me trying to get the beauty sleep to look good for the pilgrims?"

"I'll give you feckin' pilgrims! I'll take yer head off at the waist! Where's the money?" She began to look around the room. "Ye can't have drunk it all by now."

"Five hundred pound, Lizzie? Where in the hell would I get money like that, would ye tell me?"

"Don't play the innocent with me, John McGhee. From one of them reporters, that's where. And ye were going to keep the whole damned lot for yerself. Ye must've cadged five times that amount out of me over the years. By God!" She raised her hand as if to strike him and he cowered back in the bed.

"It was only a promise, Lizzie. He'll hardly hand it over. Ye know what them boys is like."

"Under the mattress," she said, grabbing the striped ticking and yanking it upwards. Limpy gave a cry and tumbled off the other side of the bed and onto the floor. With a wary eye on the Winter Cook, the dog came over and sniffed his master. Holding up the mattress with one hand, the Winter Cook poked around the underside of it with the other before dropping it again.

"Where's the money, McGhee? What've ye done with it?"

"I swear, Lizzie, I've never seen five hundred pound in my life."

Sweeping up the pillow from the bed, Mrs Megarrity whacked Limpy round the side of the head with it.

"Ye lying little toad! Ye've already been given it – by a fella called Fergus Keane. I want my share of it now! Half!"

Limpy struggled to his feet and then began to back away as his sister came round the bed towards him.

"Now Lizzie, ye know I would give ye the shirt off my back if you needed it, but – "

"The shirt off yer back, is it? And what would I be wanting

that for, only dusters? Never mind the feckin' shirt, give's the money!"

She swung at him again with the pillow but missed as he stepped back smartly. The dog had moved off to a safe distance. Although he had rarely seen the Winter Cook, he knew her sort and that definitely wasn't his sort.

"Ah, Lizzie, I wish I could. God knows, I do. But ye see – I gave it to somebody that needed it more nor me. A worthy cause, Lizzie. As God is my witness."

Rushing forward, she grasped Limpy's shirt front and rammed him against the wall. Her big meaty fist was raised level with Limpy's nose and pulled back ready to deliver the conclusive point in the argument. The top of her woollen hat wobbled like a jelly.

"I'm the best worthy cause there is around here. Hand over the money, ye little twister, or I'll give ye a bad leg even a miracle won't fix."

"You're choking me, for Jasus' sake. Lizzie I swear, I gave the money away. All of it."

For a few seconds the Winter Cook stared at him, her look alternating between bafflement and ferocity.

"Ye – gave it away? The whole five hundred pound?"

"I swear to God, Lizzie, on our mother's grave."

"Ye – are ye feckin' mad or what? Who d'ye give it to? Come on, cough up!" She shook him like a terrier shaking a rat and his dentures clattered together.

"I can't tell ye that, Lizzie. Now let go of me, will ye?"

A fistful of fat fingers brushed the tip of Limpy's nose.

"John McGhee, you tell me where that money went or I'll knock ye good-looking. As God is my witness."

"Don't be hitting me now, Lizzie," he whined, "I'm an old man."

The Winter Cook's fist pressed against his nose and moved it sideways.

"I'm going to count up to five, John, and then it's Goodnight Irene!"

"All right, all right, I'll tell ye, just don't hit me."

The Winter Cook eased the pressure on his chest and he wriggled free from her, massaging his neck where his collar had tightened round it like a noose.

"Come on then, give."

Her brother composed himself for a moment and then gave a smile which was almost beatific.

"I gave it all to the Church," he said. "To Father Burke. Lovely man."

"You – what?" Mrs Megarrity bellowed.

"I thought that was only fair, seeing as how the miracle got me the money in the first place. Ye know, 'What does it profit a man if he gains the whole world and loses his own soul'." He lowered his head and looked up past his eyebrows at her, a contrite expression on his face. "Was that the wrong thing to do, Lizzie?"

"Good God Almighty, you've hardly been inside a chapel in yer whole life."

"It's never too late, darlin'."

"Don't you darlin' me."

"Well, I can tell ye one thing, this miracle has made me realise there's people a lot worse off nor me."

"Ye're damned right there is. Me!" But then she regarded him for a moment and her fierce look faded a little. She said in a softer tone, "I wouldn't have thought ye had it in ye, John McGhee. I have to admit that was a fine thing to do." Her features momentarily clouded. "Ye wouldn't be lying to me, would you? If I thought for a minute you were lyin' – "

"Lizzie, would I lie about a thing like that? I'm just glad it's going to do some good for somebody."

The Winter Cook put her head to one side and looked at her brother, long the black sheep of the family.

"Ye know, despite your rough ways, I always thought there was a good streak in ye." She rummaged in her handbag and brought out a five pound note. "Here," she said and ruffled his hair, "get yerself a wee drink. You're a man any sister would be proud of."

Young Patrick McAllister sat up in bed with a smile on his face and his arms around two packets of crisps, a bar of chocolate, a bag of wine gums, a packet of peanuts and a large bottle of lemonade. He looked down at the collection again and gave it a squeeze just to reassure himself that it was real. Parents were difficult to work out sometimes. Mum was always telling him not to eat sweets and things. They were bad for him. They would ruin his teeth and make him fat and he wouldn't be able to eat his dinner – which was good for him and his teeth and wouldn't make him fat. And sometimes Dad would tell him that too, though not as often as Mum. Now, when Mum had gone out somewhere, Dad had said he should go to bed early as he had to get up for school in the morning and had given him all this stuff although he didn't go to bed early any other nights. Maybe all this was for keeping the secret about Dad and Miss Quinn from Mum – the time they were doing something with the furniture and Miss Quinn had got hot and had to take some clothes off. Dad had asked Patrick if he had kept the special secret because it was going to be a surprise for Mum and he had told Dad he had kept it a secret except for Mrs Megarrity and Dad had said that didn't matter because she knew about it already and she could keep a secret too.

He looked down at the riches before him and wondered which one he should start on first and should he eat everything before he went to sleep or keep some for the morning. But if he took anything to school they would all want a share and he would get hardly any and he didn't feel like sharing because they didn't share and they tried to eat things secretly by sneaking them out of their pockets and up to their mouths and chewing quietly. He lifted the chocolate bar and tore away the wrapper, revealing the thick chocolate beneath, then slowly bit into it. Next he took the cap from the lemonade bottle and had a drink of that before deciding that crisps and chocolate would make a nice mixture.

When he had eaten some of the crisps he took another swig of lemonade, looked at the packet of peanuts, made a hole in the paper and poured some into his mouth. This was better than doing homework. He had tried to tell Dad he had homework to do, but when he had been ignored he hadn't said it again. Dad had just told him to hurry up and get to bed and make sure he went to the toilet first so he wouldn't have to get up again. He said that it didn't matter about Patrick brushing his teeth after he had eaten the sweets and before he went to sleep because it wouldn't do any harm for one night, and for a few seconds Patrick worried about the army of little bugs with drills and picks that would be banging away at his teeth all night. But only for a few seconds. The chocolate bar and the crisps and the peanuts and the wine gums were rapidly being washed down by the lemonade. He burped twice and then tried a third one at a higher pitch.

He was quite important now, and that was probably why he'd got the new bike and these sweets from Dad. And another time, Mrs Megarrity had said not to tell when he saw her drinking from the little bottle that smelt like the bar and was good for her health. But she hadn't given him any sweets, only a fierce look. Somebody at school told him that Mrs Megarrity had about a hundred kids and they would come and take you away if they didn't like something you did. That's why there were so many of them.

Patrick finished off one packet of crisps, had another drink of lemonade and opened the second packet. He was beginning to feel a bit full up and he pulled up his pyjama jacket and looked at his stomach, wondering where everything was going. He put the lemonade bottle to the side of his mouth and squinted down at his stomach to see if it got bigger as he drank but it didn't and then the drink went down the wrong way and he coughed and spluttered. He finished the crisps and peanuts, although he didn't feel like eating much more. The chocolate bar seemed more difficult to chew now, and there was no lemonade left to wash it down so he swallowed the last of it in two big lumps that he thought were going to stick in his throat and when they came to waken him in the morning he would be dead because the chocolate had blocked his tubes and then his Dad would be sorry he had given him so much to eat and his Mother would wish she hadn't gone out without tucking him in and kissing him goodnight. Unknown to Patrick, there was a chance that his wish would be fulfilled. At the meeting in the chapel house to discuss the Mass Rock site, Agnes had just said that the best way to get Dermot to change his mind was for them to put their proposals to him as a committee, and that they should go and see him right away, as she knew he would be at home and at a loose end.

Dermot slowly and quietly opened the door to Patrick's room and by the light from the hallway saw his son fast asleep in the bed. Beside it on the floor lay the empty lemonade bottle and the sweet wrappers. Smiling, Dermot gathered the debris then shut the door quietly before walking back down the hall to the sitting-room, where Nancy Quinn was stretched on the couch with her skirt rucked up round her hips.

"Dead to the world," Dermot told her. "He won't bother us this time."

She held her arms out for him to come to her and after they had kissed long and passionately she rubbed her nose against his and said,

"Well, what d'you think of the idea? I read it in a magazine.

'How to spice up your love life.' I'm sure it'll work. And it'll make it more – " she craned forward again and gave a little bite at his chin, " – exciting."

"I don't know, Nancy. Sounds bloody daft to me. Maybe I've just developed some kind of – physical problem I can do nothing about."

"Don't be silly, Dermot. It's all in your mind. Trying to do it in a car. That's enough to put anybody off. I've been thinking about it."

"So have I," he said, slipping his hand up her leg. "All the time."

"No, not that. The answer. Look, what we'll do is this. You leave the room and I'll take my clothes off and hide somewhere. Then you come in pretending to be some kind of wild animal – that's what it said – a lion or something – and then you find me and – take me all of a sudden. Oh, Dermot, it'll be fantastic!"

Dermot's eyes widened a little as he imagined it. Maybe she had something and anyway, it couldn't hurt.

Nancy said,

"Have you got a shaggy rug or something like that – to put over you? Make it more realistic. A big hairy animal coming to get me. Oh God, I can't wait!"

The more he thought about it, the more Dermot warmed to the idea. That had obviously been part of the problem between him and Agnes, no excitement in it. Just the same dreary old routine every time. If Nancy wanted a big hairy animal, by God that's what she would get.

"Right!" he said, and jumped up. "Let's do it!"

"We'll both be on our hands and knees, all right? And you've got to come in and get me."

Dermot made a growling sound, said,

"You just be ready, that's all," and went out of the room to find a suitable disguise and prepare himself. Nancy went behind the couch – she did not want to be too hard to find – took her clothes off and got down on all fours to await the call of the wild.

In the hallway, Agnes held open the door to allow the four people who accompanied her to enter – Father Burke, Maggie Nolan who joined all parish committees as a matter of course, Master Boylan, the retired headmaster of the local school, and wee Mrs Laverty with the funny eye and six children.

"If you would like to go through to the sitting-room," Agnes was saying, " – the door at the end there – I'll make some coffee. I'll find out where Dermot is and then we can all hear what he has to say."

Led by the priest, the group went down the hallway and into the sitting-room, where everyone except Father Burke took a seat on the couch. He placed himself apart, on an armchair by the fire, in order the better to emphasise his position as chairman of the committee. As a trickle of polite conversation began between the priest and Master Boylan – the two women were evaluating the style and quality of the furnishings and fitments whilst examining them for dust – behind the couch Nancy was going rigid with shock. She had rolled up her clothes and stuffed them under a cabinet at the other end of the couch, and now she could not reach them without moving and risking detection.

In the bedroom Dermot put the finishing touches to his animal costume, a large goatskin rug held on by a belt round his chest, and over his head a shaggy cushion cover. It had been a bit of luck finding that. Apart from a chink of light from the aperture at his neck, he could see nothing, but that would only add to the excitement, which had already produced the desired effect on him. He would need to be careful he didn't catch it on the furniture. Nancy had been right after all. This gave a whole new perspective to things. On his hands and knees he tried a few thrusting movements and, feeling pleased with these, he crawled out of the bedroom and down the hallway towards the sitting-room. Reaching up to the handle, he quietly opened the door and paced forward into the room with all the vigour and bearing of a male African lion.

"Ahrgh!" he called as he moved towards the middle of the room, feeling before him as he went. Master Boylan looked round slowly. There was nothing he hadn't encountered in a lifetime of teaching. The eyes of the two women widened as they turned in their seats to find the cause of the noise – a moving goatskin rug with a bare backside sticking out of the after end. By the fireplace, and unable to see Dermot, Father Burke drew a faint smile across his lips. One would have expected a child to have been in bed at that time of night. At the end of the couch nearest Dermot, wee Mrs Laverty drew in a sharp breath as she saw the naked haunches fringed by the rough hair of goatskin.

"Jasus!" she whispered and crossed herself. At her side, Maggie Nolan bit her lip in excitement and pressed her spectacles tight against her face to ensure optimum vision. Although she had kept up hope all these years, Nirvana had been no more than a dream. How often was such an opportunity afforded a spinster woman.

"Ahrgh!" Dermot voiced again, and added a growl calculated to raise the hackles on any female of the species within hearing distance. Father Burke, seeing the bare backside coming into view and guessing at the appendages that swung beneath, thrust himself back into his armchair to whisper,

"Good God Almighty!"

By this time Nancy was almost prostrate behind the couch, her limbs trembling and her breath coming in gasps. But with slow deliberation and infinite caution she began to move towards her clothes beneath the cabinet. Halfway across the room

Dermot paused to sniff an unfamiliar odour before loping forward, his ears pricked for sound and his body tensed in anticipation. He could stop and take the cushion cover off his head, but that would spoil the fun. And besides, it would be all the better when his searching hand unexpectedly came across the cool smooth flesh. He gave a little shudder and put one probing hand in front of him. The audience watched with the paralysis of fascination as Dermot's fingers closed around Maggie Nolan's ankle and with a grunt of satisfaction his hand rapidly slipped up her leg while at the same time he let out the triumphal mating cry of his species. Maggie Nolan's eyelids fluttered and her eyes rolled heavenwards. Master Boylan, who had only ever understood such matters in terms of animal and insect behaviour, watched this with a detachment that suggested he might later write a treatise on it. And then a number of things happened almost at once.

Father Burke jumped up and shouted,

"Enough!"

Dermot leapt to his feet in front of Maggie Nolan who saw what she had never seen before and fainted at the sheer physical impossibility of it. More coolly circumspect, wee Mrs Laverty made a judgement that favoured Dermot. From the hallway Agnes came sweeping in with a trayful of drinks and an apology on her lips. She took in the scene, screamed and threw the tray in the air, a cup of hot coffee splashing over Nancy's buttocks just as her hand at last closed round her bundle of clothes. She sprung up from behind the couch, startling everyone, especially Father Burke and Master Boylan who had thrust upon them a new and enlightening experience. Agnes screamed again at the sight of the naked Nancy and the realisation of what it all meant. As Maggie Nolan struggled to consciousness, aware that her last chance was fading fast, Dermot whipped the cushion cover from his head, blanched at the sight that met his eyes and clamped the cover over his groin.

"You – !" Agnes flung at him, but could find no more words and gave another scream in their stead. Behind her the door opened to admit Patrick who, blinking against the light said,

"Mum – I feel – sick," and immediately threw up over the cups and saucers and slices of cake that lay scattered on the floor.

chapter thirteen

In the morning of the last Saturday in May, the narrow road to the chapel and the Mass Rock beyond had vehicles nose to tail for a hundred yards or more on either side of the gate into the Mass Rock field. Just inside the gate and behind an old kitchen table that had paint splashes and a four-inch saw-cut in it, John Healy sat collecting entrance money. For want of anything more formal, he wore an old cap with the skip pulled down and the crown up, at the front of which a rubber band held a piece of paper bearing the word "OFFICIAL" in John's tortured handwriting. Slung across his chest was his money pouch, a handbag of his wife's in black and red shiny plastic. On the side of the table was pinned a notice which said, "MIRACLE SITE. ENTRANCE £2. MIRACLE MAN VISIT £1. BOTTLE OF WATER 50p." As the field was on a slope, the table, the chair and its occupant all inclined steeply towards the road, although now and then John Healy would lean the other way to compensate, giving the impression that he was a victim in the last stages of some grave paralysis. Despite his discomfiture, he smiled gently to himself as he gathered the coins and notes across the table and dropped them into his official receptacle, trying as he did so to calculate the percentage of the take he would get from Dermot McAllister and how long it would have taken him to make the same amount of money from raising sheep. His wife had already been out twice that morning to conduct a financial audit, including the takings for visits to the Miracle Man, which John Healy kept separately in his pocket. After all, it was only fair that Limpy got something out of all this, seeing as how the old bugger had started the whole thing off. And the old bugger himself was very much in evidence, wearing a double-breasted suit that was very well tailored, although unfortunately not for Limpy, a suit that could have graced an Edwardian drawing room and, by the appearance of the frayed cuffs and mildewed seams, had probably done so. His hair was plastered down on either side of a middle parting, his lurid tie sported a huge knot and his chin and jowls shone from the unaccustomed attention of a razor blade. He was just now showing a group of visitors around his house and environs, as he put it.

"Here we are, ladies and gentlemen, this is my humble abode." A few of them looked at the small, dilapidated building and nodded in agreement. "It was on this very spot I discovered that the Virgin Mary had done a miracle on me. So, follow me and I'll tell yez the whole story."

Limpy's big black dog, which had long craved a bit of excitement in its dull life by way of having new people to bite, now found itself overwhelmed by an embarrassment of riches, as a consequence of which it appeared that the beast did not know where to begin and had in fact bitten no-one in the last two weeks. Limpy, though, had put this down to the visit by the Virgin Mary and claimed it a greater miracle than the curing of his leg.

People were spread in a semi-circle around the Mass Rock, some praying on their knees, while others stood and looked around them aimlessly, the dark rock with its small and indecipherable carving having failed to hold their attention for more than a few minutes. Children ran here and there between the adults and a pair of them had to be pulled away from the dam of stones they had started to build across the stream, beside which a piece of cardboard stuck on a twig proclaimed, "NO DRINKING THE WATER". A few of the pilgrims filled bottles with the holy water, one woman glancing round in John Healy's direction before stuffing a full bottle at the bottom of her bag and arranging a scarf over it.

At the table two well-dressed men stood, one holding a camera and with a bag slung over his shoulder.

"This is where it happened then, is it? The miracle," the one without the camera said in an English accent. As he spoke he drew a pen and a notebook from his pocket. "We're from the Press."

John Healy sat as straight up as he could in the circumstances and smiled broadly.

"Right there, gentlemen," he said and pointed towards the Rock, "and there's the holy stream. And over there," he nodded towards Limpy's house, "is the very man it happened to. Good value, at two pound each, gentlemen. Three pound if you want to meet the Miracle Man himself." He held out his hand. The man with the notebook gave a little snickering laugh then nodded to his companion who put the camera to his eye and pointed it at John Healy.

"The Press don't pay," the reporter said. "And we don't charge for putting your picture on the front page of a national newspaper either."

"The – front page," John Healy said. "Well." He straightened his cap, stuck out his chest and gave a big smile.

"Oh, very likely," the reporter said. "Unless of course a world war or something happens between now and Monday morning."

The cameraman pressed the button, apparently unaware that the lens cap was still on the camera, and said, "That should come out nice."

"And your name is?" the reporter asked, pen poised above his pad.

"John Healy, farmer – " he indicated the field with his hand, "and agent for the site owner. It was me that told the parish priest about it in the first place, and – " But the two men were already moving off and walking up the hill towards the Mass Rock.

Outside his house Limpy was giving a demonstration of his walking abilities both before and after the miraculous event. His progress across the yard in the pre-miraculous state was so slow and tortured that some of the onlookers wondered why he had not formerly been at least confined to a wheelchair, if not a stretcher and counted that too as a minor miracle. Out of the crowd that was gathered around the foot of the Mass Rock a fat woman pulled two crying children and, followed at a distance by her husband, she went towards the table where John Healy was lost in thoughts of national acclaim. On the way, she shouted at the children to stop their bloody crying and cuffed their ears, this having the opposite effect to that which she had intended, so that when she addressed John Healy, he could hardly hear what she said for their bawling.

"Hey Mister!" she shouted in a strong Belfast accent. "See this here? This is rubbish, so it is! Miracle site my arse! It's just an oul' bit of a rock. An' there's nothin' for kids to do!"

Behind her, the man said,

"C'mon Chantelle, let's go now," in a voice so quiet that it was barely audible above the noise from the two boys. John Healy stared at the woman, quite speechless in the face of such an onslaught.

"Where's yer toilets?" she demanded.

"I – we haven't – got any – yet." And then he added, "They're under construction."

"Ha!" the woman said, "I didn't think yez had any. There's a law against that, ye know. There's a wee lad up there pissin' in that stream and them ones goin' to drink that water hopin' for a miracle. Bloody disgrace! Would ye shut yer bake! You've got my head turned, so yez have," she bawled at the boy who was making the loudest noise. "We've come miles and miles to see this," she told John Healy who, having regained a little composure made so bold as to reply,

"Well, I didn't ask ye to come, Missus."

"It was in the paper!" She bawled. "`Miracle Site' it said. The only bloody miracle is you haven't been lynched yet." She stabbed an index finger on the table. "I want my money back!"

John Healy tried to stare the woman out and think fast. This was serious. McAllister hadn't mentioned anything about people wanting their money back.

"Well, this here's a religious site," he ventured. "We're not allowed to give refunds."

The Belfast woman advanced a large fist across the table and shoved her face closer to his.

"Well, ye'd better start right now, Mister, otherwise you'll be in need of a feckin' miracle. Twelve pound."

She opened her hand to receive the money.

"Twelve? You mean six." He began to rummage in his bag.

"Twelve! Four threes is twelve! Me an' m'man and the two wee lads."

"But – the kids got in for free."

The woman said in a quiet yet menacing tone,

"Twelve pound, Mister – or I'll wrap that feckin' table round your neck!"

The glance from the husband that met John Healy's eyes assured him that the woman was quite capable of adapting furniture in this manner. With bad grace, he dug the money out of his bag and slapped it into the hand of the woman who turned abruptly, dragging her children after her and saying to her husband as they headed for the gate,

"Didn't I tell ye we should've gone to the Giant's Causeway

– but, oh no, you had to go and see a feckin' miracle site."

John Healy leant back in his chair and gave a sigh. This miracle business wasn't quite as easy as it had first appeared. Then after a moment's thought he took five pounds out of his official collecting bag and put it into his unofficial pocket. It was a well-known commercial principle that the owner had to stand the cost of dissatisfied customers.

At the Glens Hotel, things were going no better. Following Dermot's public display of a chimera at rut, Agnes had swiftly departed with Patrick and without a further word to Dermot, who was now sulking in his tiny office, only to be disturbed at frequent intervals by telephone callers enquiring about accommodation, the arrival of new guests and the complaints of those already in residence. Mrs Megarrity had just left him, having announced the arrival of three more guests – one from the Irish Press, one from the Cork Examiner and a small man from London who, she said, "looks like a bookie's runner – a weasly-faced little bugger, and a crook to the back bone, if I've ever seen one. Not that I'm prejudiced against any man." Now she was fending off two English newspapermen who had stayed overnight and were complaining about the state of the bedrooms, the lack of service and the poor meals.

"I wouldn't even have the nerve to throw food like that in the bin," the smaller of the two men said, "except after dark when the neighbours couldn't see it." The other one sniggered. Mrs Megarrity's eyes narrowed and her face took on the snarling features that had turned the legs of braver men to jelly.

"That's bloody typical, that is. Yous English coming over here to Ireland to bite the hand that feeds yez. I cook good, plain food here, and it would suit yez better to be eating grub like that than pollutin' yourselves with that novel cuisine that wouldn't feed a sparra." On seeing her antagonists raised eyebrows she tossed her head and said, "Ah yes, that surprised ye, didn't it? I know a thing or two about hot cuisine, so I do, so ye needn't try and put one over on me. My grandmother, I'll have yez know, cooked for some of the crowned heads of Europe – and recipes were handed down. I'll say no more."

"Perhaps," the small one ventured to his friend, barely able to keep his face straight, "that's why royalty's a bit thin on the ground on the Continent."

As she turned away, the Winter Cook said,

"We're not here, mister, to cater for people with weird tastes in food."

"No," one of them said whilst she was still within earshot, "I think the best you could manage here would be cooking for people with no taste at all."

Margaret Garrison, now financially secure for the foreseeable future due to the sale by Cissy of some of the shares through a reputable broker, was eager to make the acquaintance of these two English sophisticates, whose views and tastes would undoubtedly be so very much in keeping with her own. In the sitting room she tried telling them about her year in London with the Hennessys, describing it in terms more suitable to a grand tour of Europe and talking as if she would even now be welcome at all the great houses and was intimate with every doorman and head waiter in the best clubs and restaurants of London. But the two young men were not at all interested in the ramblings of this old woman, the highlight of whose life seemed to have been a few months spent in London many years before either of them had been born. Nevertheless, Margaret was glad of the diversion from the terrible business of Mr Rowan who, she had reluctantly had to admit to Cissy, must have been cheating them during all those years. For her part, Cissy was growing into her self-appointed role as financial manager and had taken to reading the Financial Times, for which she had placed a daily order in the Inisbreen Stores. A world of which she had previously not had the slightest inkling was slowly opening up to her, and she read with increasing interest, if yet little understanding, of profits and losses, rights issues, yields and earnings per share. She had also spoken to a notable lawyer in Belfast, with a view to taking legal action against Mr Rowan.

"Ah, Mr Rowan," the lawyer had said. "His name is known to me," but did not elaborate. A meeting with the lawyer had been arranged to take place in two weeks, but when Cissy had asked Margaret if she wanted to accompany her, Margaret had said,

"I'm sure you'll be perfectly capable, Cissy."

Her confidence growing by the day, Cissy had replied,

"Oh I didn't expect you to take part, Margaret. I just thought you might have liked to do some shopping in town while I was at the lawyer's office."

The hotel's other permanent resident, Mr Pointerly, who was usually in a torpor of half-remembered incidents of long ago, set in a landscape peopled with characters whose features and qualities were as much a product of his imagination as they were of his memory, was yet again engrossed in thoughts of what had happened at McPhee's house that fateful night. Of course, there would always be setbacks in any venture and finding that young reporter there had been quite a shock, but at least it did prove the point. He gave a shiver of anticipation and allowed himself to slip into his little daydream in which, instead of a gilded youth, McPhee would be waiting for him in some sun-dappled bower by the river bank, or as he walked on the strand he would hear a call from the pine trees. Like Jack Armitage at boarding-school. He had been a true friend, and there had never since been anyone quite the same. Those winter days when they had sat naked before the fire, toasting their muffins, heads together and dreaming aloud of their golden futures. And now, when he thought he had the McPhee chap all to himself, he found this young man intruding on the relationship. Well, he wasn't just going to give up. "Faint heart never won . . . whatever." Anything worth having was worth fighting for, so the first thing he had to do was get rid of this interloper so that he himself could command McPhee's full attention.

For a long time Mr Pointerly sat in his armchair by the window, his chin cradled in one hand, his long fingers playing a little tattoo on his cheek. Every now and then he would pull a face and then shake his head. At times he looked as if he were dropping off to sleep and a long sigh would escape his lips. Then at last he got up from the armchair, stretched himself and was about to walk out of the lounge when he saw a copy of the Northern Reporter lying on a coffee table in the middle of the room. He stopped and looked at it and then after a moment returned with it to his chair. Twice he read the article on the Miracle Man by Fergus Keane, a smile slowly forming on his lips, so that by the time he had finished the piece for the second time, he had a wide grin on his face. Then taking the loose change from his pocket, he counted it, put it back into his pocket and left the room, still holding the Northern Reporter.

At the telephone box outside the Inisbreen Stores, Mr Pointerly paused and looked around him, as though someone might be watching his every movement, but the village street was empty. He had some difficulty opening the door with its heavy return spring, but once inside he quickly turned to the bottom of the newspaper's back page, where the address and telephone number were given. Slowly and with deliberation he pressed the numbers given in the newspaper and then waited with fingers tapping until the telephone was answered by a woman's sing-song voice saying,

"Northern Reporter, can I help you?"

"Eh, yes," Mr Pointerly said, in a tone of voice that was not his normal one. "I'd like to speak to your editor on a matter of some importance."

"What is it in connection with, Sir?"

"It's in connection with these so-called miracles at Inisbreen."

"Well, if you have an opinion on that, Sir, and you care to put it in a letter, Mr Martyn would be happy to consider it for publication."

"My dear young lady, I may well put my opinions in a letter in due course, but at this moment in time I wish to speak to Mr Martyn on the subject as a matter of urgency. This is the Bishop of Down and Connor."

At that moment, as he sat in O'Neill's snug sipping a pint of stout and a glass of Bushmills whiskey, the Miracle Man's attention was otherwise engaged in matters of a most pleasurable kind. In his inside jacket pocket, nestling happily over his heart, he had noted, was the letter he had received that morning. It was an unusual event for him to receive anything in the mail except buff-coloured envelopes whose contents almost certainly demanded urgent payment, envelopes which he promptly stuffed unopened beneath the pile on the mantelpiece. But this morning he had sat staring at the light-blue envelope with its neat writing and Inisbreen postmark, as if by doing so he might discover who had sent it to him. Now, with a smile of deep satisfaction, he took the single-page letter from his pocket, unfolded it carefully, almost reverently, and held it at arms length to read it yet again. "My Dearest John," it said, "I was surprised and overwhelmed by your letter and your generosity. Over all these years we have had to remain apart. Feelings which I thought might have gone long ago began to return the day we talked on the strand. When I read your letter and saw what you had done, those feelings came back to me even more strongly. We should never have bothered about my parents disapproval, and anyway it doesn't matter now. There's only Margaret and I think maybe I can handle her. If you are interested in meeting again, nothing would make me happier. Although we did have some bad luck financially, things are all right now and I need to return your money. Please contact me as soon as possible. Yours ever, C."

With a jaunty step Limpy walked across the bridge at Inisbreen, looking around him at the green and brown hills, the various shades of colour on the trees and the brown river that rushed to the sea, sights that had passed unremarked a thousand times, and yet today he was looking at them afresh. It was a wonderful feeling. He smiled and nodded at a stranger who stood in a doorway and then held the smile for three or four white gulls that came squawking and swooping low over the bridge. Since the miracle, everything had just got better and better. First the curing of the leg itself, then the money, and now this. After forty years. Who would've believed it? It was nearly a miracle in itself. Turning left from the bridge, he went down the road that ran alongside the river and led to the Glens Hotel and the salmon fishing net that ran out from the rocks beyond. For the third time since leaving O'Neill's pub and the sixth since leaving home, he slipped his hand into his inside pocket and felt the other letter he carried, his reply to Cissy. This time he had gone to the trouble of getting a new envelope, although Frank Kilbride at the Inisbreen Stores had taken some persuading to sell him one from a packet of twenty-five, and had charged him extra for what he had called "a handling charge and the commercial inconvenience". No doubt the store owner would sell the packet of envelopes at the normal price and hope that the buyer didn't notice that one was missing. Limpy paused at the entrance to the Glens Hotel and looked up and down the road. Neither on the road nor on the bridge was there anyone else in sight. Quickly he went inside, his hand in his jacket clutching the letter. He glanced sideways towards the residents' sitting room and saw that the door was closed. The letter rack was at one side of the stairs and as he went towards it, he took the letter from his pocket. At the bottom of the stairs he stopped and looked up and then along the corridor that ran towards the kitchen at the back of the building. There was no point in letting everybody know your business, and especially not Lizzie. But he had no sooner slipped the envelope between the trellis of straps and the faded green baize of the board than a hand clumped down on his shoulder and he gave a little jump of fright before turning round.

"Mr McPhee, very nice to see you. I really must apologise about that little – intrusion the other night. No harm done, I hope?"

"Ah, Mr Pointerly, it's yerself. No, no harm done." Limpy began moving towards the front door. "I'm sorry, now, I can't be staying to talk, but I've got one or two urgent bits of business that need attending to."

"Oh, that's a pity, that really is a pity. I was thinking that we might have a drink and, you know," he winked at Limpy, "a little chat."

"Oh we will, Mr Pointerly, we will certainly. Never let it be said I turned down a drink with any man," he winked, "or a little chat. I'll see you soon, Mr Pointerly. God bless ye." Limpy had recently taken to bestowing blessings on all and sundry as he took leave of them, considering it an appropriate action for a man of his spiritual significance. No-one had objected and Mr Pointerly certainly gave a broad smile.

"Yes indeed, Mr McPhee."

As the door closed in front of a happy Mr Pointerly, a voice from behind said in a sharp tone,

"Good-day to you, Mr Pointerly. And how are we today?"

"Ah – Mrs Megarrity. Yes, fine, very well indeed. I was just this minute talking to your brother." He pointed at the door.

"Oh, I saw him," the Winter Cook said and glanced at the letter rack, "but I don't think he saw me."

"Fine man, fine man. He and I have got quite – friendly recently. Really quite – close."

"Close, Mr Pointerly?"

"Yes, Mrs Megarrity, close. We share the same interests, if you know what I mean." He gave her a knowing look. "Neither of us married, you know? Tell me, was he always – that way?"

"What way would that be, Mr Pointerly?"

"You know." Mr Pointerly inclined himself to the left.

"Ah, we always put that down to the bad leg. He's never been any different since ever I remember him." Mr Pointerly smiled broadly. "You know, that's very good to hear. Very good indeed." Turning away from the Winter Cook he went towards the sitting-room, nodding and saying to himself, "Yes. We're obviously two of a kind, he and I. Two of a kind."

Mrs Megarrity looked after him for a moment, shook her head and said,

"Silly old fool."

Then with a quick look around her she plucked the envelope from the letter rack and shoved it into the pocket of her black dress before hurrying away towards the kitchen.

It took over a minute for the steam from the kettle spout to loosen the adhesive on the envelope flap, during most of which time Mrs Megarrity stared in disbelief at the name on the front of the envelope and kept repeating it.

"Cissy Garrison? Cissy – Garrison? Jasus tonight, why would he be writing to her?" She half closed one eye, stared with the other and drew in air through her pouted lips. "By God, I knew he was up to something, the little git."

The flap was at last open. With eager fingers she drew out the letter – written on coarse, lined paper torn from an exercise book – unfolded it and began to read it in a low voice.

"'My Most Dearest Cissy – ' My Most Dearest – ? Jasus

Christ of Almighty, what's this? 'Thank you for your beautiful and esteemed letter. I'd like you to keep the five hunnerd pounds – ' Oh – my – God! Oh – my – good – God Almighty! That lowdown connivin' lyin' feckin' little rat! Five hundred pound to that wee hallion!" The Winter Cook put a hand out to steady herself against the wall. "God save us entirely!" She drew a deep breath, braced herself and read on, "' – an if I had ten times that amount of money an ye needed it an even if you didnt sure Id give it you.' Ten times – Is he mad or what? 'We shountve split up all them years ago but thats water under the bridge now.' Split up? What the hell does he mean, 'split up'? Oh, by the Lord Jasus, when I get my hands on him I'll feckin' split him up, so I will, from head to toe." The Winter Cook gave such snort of indignation that the letter flapped in her hand. She set her jaw, clenched her fists then tackled the final sentence. "'Maybe theres still time for us, Cissy, and if your still intrested we could meet tonight at seven beside the old house on the strand of fond memories. Your ever loving Johnny."

With glaring eyes the Winter Cook stood with the letter held before her, flapping in her shaking hand.

"Johnny, is it? I'll give him ever-bloody-loving. That wee trollop. The man's got a bit of money for the first time in his life and she's lifting her skirt trying to chisel it out of him. Well, not while I'm around, Miss Cissy feckin' Garrison." Mrs Megarrity tore the letter and envelope into small pieces, lifted the lid of the stove and threw them inside. She had just taken her little bottle of whiskey from her apron pocket and removed the cap when she stopped and stared into space.

"Jasus tonight! 'Neither of us married', he said. And 'Two of a kind', he said. Two of a bloody kind! Mother of God, he's not content with having a wee gold-digger round his neck, he has to have a homersexual as well!" Slowly her eyes narrowed and her face took on a pugnacious look. "Well, they might be able to put one over on my John, but now they're dealing with

Lizzie Megarrity and that's a whole different matter." And to celebrate her new-found status as defender of the family honour, not to mention the family assets, Mrs Megarrity took two large slugs of the liquid which young Daniel McAllister knew smelt like the bar and was good for her health.

Father Burke's housekeeper, Mrs McKay walked along the shore road towards the village, her big shopping basket bumping at her side, her woollen hat pulled down over her ears and her overcoat buttoned to the throat even although the weather was warm and there was no sign of rain. "Ne'er cast a clout till May is out," she had always believed, and she wasn't going to be lulled into a false sense of security just because of the fine weather. It was a blessing to be able to get out of the chapel house for a little while, perhaps to meet a friend or two along the road or drop in on someone for a cup of tea and a chat, but above all to get away from Father Burke. The man was driving her mad, God forgive her. What with his talk of selling the car and taking to a bicycle, his insistence on plain food for both of them, and above all his obsession with this miracle business at the Mass Rock, she wondered how much longer she could take it.

Hour after hour he would sit in his study, calling for tea and yet more tea while he pored over the various plans he had sketched for the Mass Rock site and tried to engage her in discussion on methods of raising finance for the project.

In almost any other situation she would have been able to handle it. She hadn't been a housekeeper to priests for nearly thirty years without being adaptable. But, God knows, her stamina had almost gone, sapped by his constant harping on the same things, and above all by a steady diet of the likes of boiled fish, turnips, and porridge, without so much as a sniff of a coq au vin or a cream bun to break the monotony. If only she could have the Canon back. He'd had his faults, of course, but he'd also known how to enjoy himself. In such a situation, she would normally have resorted to prayer. In this case, she was in something of a dilemma, as she felt that Father Burke, by the nature of his profession, would be given preference by The Almighty in any dispute. This whole miracle thing was getting out of hand entirely. It had been a bit of a novelty at first and good for a laugh when that old eejit McGhee had said he'd seen the Virgin Mary. No doubt there had been many a thing he'd seen on the way home from O'Neill's pub after dark, but they were never there in the morning. One thing was for sure, whoever the Good Lord chose to do a miracle on, it wouldn't be a flea-ridden old reprobate like him. And that Mary McCartney, she was no more than a simpleton. You may as well say Peggy May had seen a vision. So Father Burke, the man from Dublin who looked down on the locals as a bunch of witless peasants, swallows the whole thing hook, line and sinker and no doubt was already considered a laughing stock by every priest in the country. Each and every day there were people knocking on the chapel house door and calling on the 'phone – which of course she had to answer, as he was engaged in matters of much greater importance – asking how to get to the Mass Rock and had the Virgin been seen again and had there been any more miracles, and then hordes of sensation-seekers descending like flies on the Mass Rock site itself. God save us, the next thing, there'd be bus-loads of disabled people flying round the roads and piles of crutches left outside the chapel gates. One reporter had actually tried to push his way in at the front door of the chapel house when she'd told him that Father Burke wasn't in, and that even if he had been in he wouldn't in a month of Sundays talk to anyone from the scurrilous rag that he worked for, with naked women draped across the pages. And now to add insult to injury she had to walk to the village for all her shopping from the Inisbreen Stores where everything was two prices from that robber

Kilbride – no more rides to Ballymane in the Canon's big car and afternoon tea at Adare's Hotel – and her with the housekeeping money cut to a pittance because of the Father's crazy economies. Where was going to be the end of it all, that's what she wanted to know.

In this mood of righteous indignation, Mrs McKay approached the front door of the Inisbreen Stores, only to stop abruptly and stare first at one window and then at the other. Gone were the buckets and spades, the dying plastic swan and the fishing lines. The pyramid of cans and the pile of custard packets had also been cleared away, along with the notices of dances and auctions. In their stead, both windows were filled with small plaster statues of the Blessed Virgin, Saint Patrick and the Sacred Heart, as well as crucifixes, holy water fonts, great bunches of rosary beads, little Celtic crosses with each having stuck on its pedestal an oblong of paper on which was typed "INISBREEN" in uneven lettering, a sheaf of stickers for car rear windows saying, "Catholics Do It For The Love Of God" and various other religious artefacts. A poster on each window proclaimed, "INISBREEN MIRACLE. GENUINE SOUVENIRS HERE. BARGAIN PRICES", and underneath was a crude drawing of what Mrs McKay took to be a gorilla in a dress and with a tea-towel on its head, above which a dinner plate seemed to be floating, and from the gorilla's mouth a balloon of speech extended, saying, "Peace be with you."

Mrs McKay gave a snort of rage and, clutching her shopping basket tight to her chest, she marched into the general store. There was no other customer inside except a boy of about twelve who was being served at the hardware counter by Frank Kilbride.

"Mr Kilbride!" Mrs McKay said when she was only halfway across the floor. "What is – that?" She flung an arm out in the direction of the shop windows.

In his usual laconic fashion, Frank Kilbride glanced up and said,

"I'll be with you in just one minute, Mrs McKay, after I see to this young man here."

Mrs McKay pulled herself to a halt at the counter and shoved aside the boy, who hastily retreated to a neutral corner.

"Never mind that. I want to know what those – things, those objects – in the window are. What're they supposed to be, Mr Kilbride?"

"Well now, Mrs McKay, they're supposed to be souvenirs. That's what they're supposed to be. Didn't you see the notice in the window? 'Souvenirs', it says."

"Souvenirs? I've never heard the like in all my born days. Those are religious objects, Mr Kilbride. You can't sell them in a – a – store, for God's sake! It's a sacrilege!"

Peggy May had come out from the back shop at the sound of the commotion and stood scratching one of her breasts. The eyes of the boy in the corner grew wide.

"D'you not like them, Mrs McKay?" she said. "I think that Jesus one's got a lovely wee face. Did you see my drawing of the Virgin Mary with the halo? I did that all myself, so I did."

"Mr Kilbride," the housekeeper said, in as official a tone as she could manage, "as a member of the parish household – and as Father Burke's representative – I demand that you remove that effrontery from your windows immediately."

"What's an effrontery?" Peggy May asked. "Have we got an effrontery in the window, Mr Kilbride?"

"Mrs McKay you're a decent woman and I don't want an argument with you, but you must understand. This is a business and there's people out there that want a souvenir of the place where the miracle happened, and it's my job to provide it for them."

"Provide yourself with a nice thick lining to your pocket,

you mean. My God," Mrs McKay said, "selling religious articles like that – and you not even a Catholic!"

Frank Kilbride gave her a long, steady look and said slowly,

"Well now, Mrs McKay, I'm not a woman either – but I still sell knickers and brassieres."

The boy sniggered into his hand and Peggy May grinned vacantly.

"Oh!" was all Mrs McKay could utter for a moment. And then, "Oh! I've never heard such talk in all my life!" She blessed herself. "You should be ashamed of yourself, Frank Kilbride. And especially in front of these children. Ashamed!" She gathered her basket to her bosom. "Well, you haven't heard the last of this, I can assure you." She turned abruptly and stalked towards the door, raising her head so that her eyes might be averted from the effrontery in the windows.

"Oh, I'm sure I haven't," the storekeeper said, half to himself. And then as Mrs McKay slammed the front door behind her he added in a sing-song parody of his own voice, "Good afternoon to you, Mrs McKay. Thank you for your custom, Mrs McKay. Call again soon, won't you?"

chapter fourteen

Young Dippy Burns rode his old bicycle with unusual vigour as he went through the village and over the bridge at the far side, head low and thrust forward, his legs like two great piston rods driving up his knees almost to touch his chin. He was on his way to see Father Burke at the chapel house on a matter of great importance. About two weeks before, while examining his genitals, Dippy had noticed a distinct redness in the folds of skin. With some difficulty, he held back from seeking guidance on the matter from his favourite book, the medical encyclopaedia, which he had been in the habit of reading at frequent intervals. After all, he reasoned, everything that was a little out of the ordinary wasn't necessarily an illness. Determined to give time to the self-healing process he had read about, he had ignored it for three days, even deliberately looking away when passing water. On one occasion this had caused him to wet the trousers of the man standing next to him in a pub toilet, and Dippy had narrowly missed having another subject for the healing process, a broken nose. When at last he had brought himself to look at the affected organ, he saw that not only were the symptoms still there but that they had actually become worse. A long study of the medical book confirmed his worst fears. He had tertiary syphilis. There was no doubt about it. The symptoms were unmistakeable. How he had contracted it was a mystery to him as the book didn't list any activities in which he normally indulged.

One day, when the itching had got just about more than he could bear, and while aware that nothing could stop the progress of this dread disease, he decided that a disinfectant might take some of the discomfort away. From the bathroom cabinet he took out his sister's bottle of mouthwash and, holding the affected part over the wash basin, doused it liberally with the contents, his face screwed up against the expected stinging sensation. There being no reaction from his tortured flesh, he examined the bottle. On the other side a piece of paper stuck to it said, "Inisbreen Holy Water". While it did not result in the instant disappearance of his symptoms, the water did seem to have a particularly cooling effect on the inflammation and so Dippy took himself off to bed, content with the thought that, if these were to be his last hours on earth, at least he would be free of pain. On waking the next morning he found to his amazement that the itch and every other sign of the ailment had gone completely. He had heard about Limpy McGhee's leg, of course, but tertiary syphilis? That was something else entirely. It had to be – he hesitated over such an awesome word – it really had to be another miracle. Nothing else it could be. And the person to contact was Father Burke. He'd know what to do.

On offering to show the parish priest the subject of the miracle, Dippy was quickly assured that that would not be necessary. In any event, Father Burke said, any claims of miracles had to be medically examined before they could even begin to be considered. He himself would be more than happy if it were shown to be a miracle cure, as he was convinced of the power of the Mass Rock and the water that had sprung from its base. So, he would 'phone the doctor immediately, he said, to arrange a time for an examination to be carried out. As he crossed the hall to the telephone, Father Burke was accosted by Mrs McKay, who had been listening outside the study door whilst dusting the picture frames.

"And what does that one want, Father, if you don't mind me asking? I wouldn't believe a word he swore to."

"Mrs McKay, this is a private matter! I would be grateful if you would attend to your duties in the kitchen – and shut the door behind you."

When the housekeeper had stumped off to the kitchen and banged the door shut, Father Burke dialled Doctor Walsh's number and after a few moments delay, the telephone was answered and he was put through.

"Good morning to you, Doctor Walsh, this is Father Burke here. I believe we may possibly have another miracle cure on our hands and I would be very grateful if you could find time to examine the person in question."

From Doctor Walsh there was a long, weary sigh that ended in a kind of croaking groan.

"Listen, Father, despite the rubbish printed in that Northern Reporter rag the other day – with whom, incidentally I have already lodged a complaint – I do not believe that that McGhee person underwent a miracle cure."

"Ah now, I wouldn't be expecting you to make that kind of judgement, Doctor. That's for the Church to decide. No, no. I would simply want you to assess the person's current state of health."

Doctor Walsh gave another sigh and said in a monotone,

"Indeed. And who is it this time?"

"A young man who claims to have had a complete and virtually instantaneous cure by the application of the holy water from the spring at the Mass Rock."

"I see. And from what ailment does he claim to have been cured, might I ask?"

Father Burke cleared his throat. It was a delicate subject whatever way you approached it.

"He had, eh – tertiary syphilis, apparently."

There was a little choking cough from the doctor.

"Tertiary – syphilis? Is that right? And who, might I ask, is the unfortunate victim of this extremely rare disease?"

"Young man by the name of Cornelius Burns, Doctor. In his twenties, I should think. D'you know him?"

"Cornelius Burns, eh? Not the fellow they call Dippy, by any chance?"

"I do believe he did refer to himself in that way. You're obviously familiar with the case. That's good."

"It is, is it? I don't suppose you know why they call him Dippy, do you?"

"I'm afraid not, Doctor. I've only just made his acquaintance."

"Well I'll tell you why," Doctor Walsh said, as his voice grew louder. "Because he's not half wise. Dippy Burns could no more get tertiary syphilis than I could get pregnant. Apart from passing water, I doubt if he even knows what functions his genitals are capable of performing. He's in my surgery at least once a week, and if you can name an illness, he's had it. One day it's an ingrown toe-nail, the next it's terminal cancer. He's had diseases of the spleen, the liver, the bladder and the brain, and only the last one comes within a mile of being probable. And sometimes – just to make it more interesting – he has two illnesses at once. He's a walking medical textbook!" Now Doctor Walsh was shouting down the telephone. "Good God Almighty, he's even had beri-beri and denghi fever – and he's never been out of the county! In short, Father, the man is a raving hypochondriac, and he's driving me round the bend with him! Would you please – please – refrain from doing the same! Goodbye!"

Father Burke was left staring at the telephone receiver after the line had gone dead. Exactly fifteen seconds later, Dippy Burns shot out of the chapel house front door as if a pack of devils were after him and he had to support himself on a gatepost to regain his breath, proof, if proof were needed, that the emphysema he had long suspected of clogging his lungs, at last had a fatal grip on him.

Pig Cully was leaning halfway across the hardware counter in the Inisbreen Stores, admiring the contours of Peggy May's buttocks under the tightness of her short skirt as she bent low to sort the packages and small boxes that filled the lower shelves. Further along, Frank Kilbride stood near the top of a ladder, emptying the remains of one box of screws into another, re-wrapping metal items in greaseproof paper and tidying the stock that crammed the shelves.

"And what did ye say to her then, Frank? By Jasus I would've given her a piece of my mind if it was me, the old bitch."

"I told her I was only supplying what people wanted. This is a business, not a charity, I said. I don't go round her house telling her what she should have in her cupboards."

"Damned right, Frank. That's what comes of working with them priests. They think they own ye. Ye wouldn't be wanting a wee hand there, Peggy May?" He gave his little chirruping laugh. "You can decide the spot."

"Oh, ye'd only have to wash yer hands afterwards, Mr Cully. This is dirty work, so it is."

Pig Cully squeaked.

"That's just what I want, Peggy May, a bit of dirty work."

"Give over, Cully," Frank Kilbride told him good-humouredly.

The bell tinkled, the door opened and closed and there stood Limpy in what passed for his Sunday best – an old, pin-striped brown suit, a white shirt gone grey around the neck and a silver and maroon brocade tie stiff with age. His damp hair was slapped flat to his head. On his feet he wore a pair of heavy black shoes that in harder times he had soled with the tread from a car tyre. The slabs of rubber having regained their curvatures, when Limpy walked he seemed to rock forwards with a nodding motion. In the damp weather he left tyre tracks on the pavement.

"God bless all here," he said, determined to consolidate his role as a symbol of living Christianity. Frank Kilbride looked round, swayed and almost fell from the ladder.

"Jasus!" Pig Cully said when he glanced from beneath his cap, and Peggy May popped her head above the counter and stared.

"Is that you, Mister McGhee?" she said.

"None other, Peggy May," he said. "None other." He rocked towards the counter, looking from one side to the other as though acknowledging a cheering crowd. "Mister Kilbride," he said grandly, "give me a bottle of yer best whiskey, if ye would. Black Bush would fit the bill, I daresay."

Pig Cully adjusted his cap upwards, the better to see the phenomenon that stood before him. "Black Bush, is it? Ye given up drinking the parafeen, McGhee?"

"Not at all, Mister Cully, not at all. I'm celebrating a windfall, as ye might say. And any of them that counts themselves friends of mine would be more than welcome to participate in the said bottle, so they would. In other words, the drinks is on me."

Pig Cully snapped his cap peak down over his eyes again and said,

"The drink's is on you? Ye must be wanting the bugger on tick."

"No credit here, McGhee. You know the rules," Frank Kilbride announced, still up the ladder, but poised to descend.

"And who asked for credit?" Limpy said and drew a huge

roll of notes from his pocket, pulled off a twenty and slapped it on the counter. "Take it out of that!"

Frank Kilbride came down the ladder at speed.

"Jee-sus, McGhee." Pig Cully squeaked. "Ye've never robbed a bank, have ye? Where in the hell did ye get all that? There must be – "

"Never you mind, Cully, never you mind," Limpy said and then with a broad grin, "If yez must know, I sold my life story to a magazine. `Exclusive' the man said. Wanted to give me a cheque, but I says no bloody fear. It's cash or nothin'."

Frank Kilbride was examining the note against the light. Peggy May said,

"Is it all right, Mr McBride?" and he nodded in surprise and went off to fetch the whiskey.

"He just came up and offered ye a bunch of money, just like that?" asked Pig Cully.

"Oh, he wanted to offer me less, but says I, `Listen here, boy, this isn't just any old story. This here's of – national importance.'" He nodded, pleased with the phrase. "'You don't get a miraculous cure every day of the week.' So he had to up the ante."

"Bloody hell," was all Pig Cully could reply.

"Ye got that whole bunch of money for tellin' your life story, Mister McGhee?" Peggy May asked.

"Indeed I did, Peggy May. That and a lot more besides."

"Jeez-o! I wonder how much I would get for telling my life story."

"A lot more," Pig Cully quickly volunteered, "if ye'd some juicy bits in it. That's where I'd come in."

Frank Kilbride put the bottle of whiskey on the counter. He was grasping the twenty-pound note like the hand of an old friend.

"Was there anything else while you were here, Mr McGhee?"

"Oh, Mister McGhee now, is it?" Pig Cully said.

"Well, let's see, you could throw in a handful of them cigars and I suppose I'd better take a half dozen of stout as well."

"Shouldn't ye be setting a more sober example to the citizenry," Pig Cully enquired, "you being a friend of the Virgin Mary and all?"

The storekeeper said sharply,

"The man's entitled to a drink now and again. What else can I do for you, Mr McGhee? How about a few of these cream cakes here – lovely with a cup of tea – and that would just about round off the twenty nicely."

"You'll get rid of them buns yet, Kilbride" Pig Cully told him. "They must've been there this week or more. Sure the flies has half of them ate. You get the flies for free, McGhee."

"I'll have you know this is a hygienic establishment," Frank Kilbride was saying as Peggy May swiped at a gorging bluebottle and sank the back of her hand into the yellow cream.

"Ah, to hell with poverty," Limpy said, giving a magnanimous wave of his hand. "Throw in the buns as well."

From round the corner of the shore road a small procession appeared, Father Burke striding out at its head and all of those behind him carrying hastily-made placards proclaiming, "Stop the sacrilege", "No Profit From God", and "God – Yes, Mammon – No!" Mrs McKay and her sister that was married to the water bailiff followed directly behind the priest, then two nuns on holiday from Belfast, three old men who had been press-ganged on the road, two women from the Legion of Mary and six or seven children who were not paying attention and kept bumping into the people in front of them. By way of conducting those behind him, Father Burke began waving his arms and then in a wavering voice he launched into "Faith of Our Fathers" about an octave below the range of those who followed him. They joined in as best they could. In this manner they marched towards the Inisbreen Stores, in front of which they made a ragged halt and turned to face it, still singing. With an increasingly grave look on his face, Father Burke examined the contents of both windows and then as he walked to the door he thrust his hand into the air, fingers extended upwards, in order to encourage the choir to greater efforts. Without his lead their voices subsided and they finished at the end of the next verse. This revealed the lone voice of a small boy singing a different tune which was quickly silenced by a cuff on the ear from a nun who felt that, in the absence of Father Burke, she had to exert some authority, as she was for the moment Christ's senior representative on this particular patch of earth.

Peggy May, Pig Cully, Limpy and Frank Kilbride behind the counter had been staring through the front window at the gathering outside. When Father Burke entered, his black soutane swirling round his ankles, Pig Cully sat on the bench and seemed to retreat under his cap, Limpy smiled and edged in front of the whiskey and stout bottles, while Peggy May scuttled behind the counter again. Frank Kilbride stood with his arms folded and waited.

"Mister Kilbride." The priest had stopped in the middle of the store.

"Father Burke."

"Mister Kilbride, I wish to protest in the strongest possible terms about that – sacrilege – in your windows. I demand that you get rid of them forthwith."

"I'd be more than happy if I could, Father. If you're offering to buy them all, I could do you a good price."

"Of course I'm not offering to buy them! I want them removed from your window immediately! They're an affront to the Catholics of this parish."

Peggy May was confused.

"I think the Jesus one's got a lovely wee face. I'm buying one for our Jennifer."

Kilbride said,

"Father, people are coming from miles around to see the miracle site at Inisbreen – instigated by Mister McGhee here and your goodself – and some of them want souvenirs to take home with them. Where's the harm in that? They tell me that Lourdes is heaving with souvenirs."

Father Burke was a little taken aback at a Protestant quoting Lourdes as a precedent.

"Lourdes? What's Lourdes got to do with anything? This is Ireland, and the Church has to sanction the sale of any religious objects."

"Are you saying you're going to tell me what I can sell in my own shop? I think not, Father."

The subject of the miracle kept smiling but shifted uneasily, due to the proximity of the whiskey and stout. Under his cap, Pig Cully appeared to be asleep.

Outside, the band of protesters had given up any pretence of singing and were moving around restlessly, the supervising nun scanning the group of children for signs of the bad behaviour that she knew must be there somewhere, the public display of which would bring instant opprobrium and eventual ruination on the whole Catholic Church.

"Mister Kilbride, you can't just go putting religious articles in a shop window. It's not something I'd normally mention, of course, but after all – you're not even of our religious persuasion."

The storekeeper gave a tight little smile.

"Ah, you have a monopoly on God then, do you, Father?"

The priest looked a little flustered. Trust a Protestant to use a devious and specious argument like that. In other circumstances, he might well have made a good Jesuit.

"Of course not. But you Presbyterians don't believe in miracles – or worship the Virgin Mary. She's – ours."

In an attempt at mediation, Limpy McGhee said,

"Well now, Father, maybe the Virgin Mary's not that bothered. I mean, I'm not even sure if I'm a Catholic, and she still did a miracle on me, so she did."

The priest's face suddenly went pale and his cheeks sagged against the bones beneath. For a few moments he stared at Limpy.

"You're not – what?"

"Not a Catholic, Father. Well, not that I know of for sure."

Frank Kilbride smiled and Pig Cully squinted out from beneath his cap.

"But – how can you not know if you're a Catholic or not? Were you baptised?" the priest asked, trying to keep an even tenor in his voice.

"I couldn't rightly say, Father. My mother died when I was a nipper and when I was ten my father ran off with a gypo woman that sold pegs round the doors. I'll need to ask Lizzie. She knows all them things."

"But – I mean, how can you not be a Catholic? You're supposed to have had a miracle happen to you, for goodness sake."

"Well, all I can say is, she never asked me what I was. It was just bang! and she'd done the job. Anyway, Father, I believe in miracles now. I'd say that probably makes it all right, wouldn't you?"

Father Burke looked a little dazed. Good God! Why had nobody told him the man might not be a Catholic? And what was the Bishop going to say when he found out about this? He would be the laughing-stock of the diocese, he would be drummed out of the priesthood. The young priest drew himself up, turned to Frank Kilbride and with as much composure as he could muster said,

"Mr Kilbride, I can assure you that I am going to take this matter further. Good day to you." Then he turned and went quickly out of the store.

From underneath his cap came Pig Cully's squeaking laugh.

"Hey, McGhee! Does that mean you'll get your limp back?"

Limpy's hand closed round the neck of the whiskey bottle.

"Devil the bit, Cully. When the Virgin Mary does a miracle, it stays done," he said, but just to be on the safe side he made the sign of the cross, albeit backwards and with his left hand.

When Limpy left the Inisbreen Stores, the bottle of Black Bush sticking out of his jacket pocket and carrying the stout and the cream buns in a white paper bag, he headed down the street for the bridge and beyond it the Glens Hotel. Unfortunately he would have to tell Lizzie about the five thousand from the newspaper – "Five – thousand – pound", he said very slowly, while shaking his head in disbelief – because she was bound to find out sooner or later. Still, it was only fair, after all she'd done for him over the years. For sure, she'd be looking for her cut, but he'd try and beat her right down, tell her he had a lot of bills to pay, was as near as dammit getting thrown in jail over the head of it, all the usual old stuff that worked a treat every time. And they'd have a good drink of Black Bush to celebrate. Things were looking just champion now – except for Cissy. One day she was all on for a meeting and when he says yes please, she doesn't show. It wasn't even as if the letter got lost in the post. He paused on the bridge and looked down at the few sailing boats that bobbed at anchor near the banks of the river. Still, maybe it wasn't surprising, having second thoughts after forty years. A big step for any woman to take. He'd maybe leave it a few days and then send her another letter. See if she'd come round to his way of thinking. She always had been a shy wee thing.

Limpy went up the path at the side of the hotel and along the lane to the back door leading directly into the kitchen. Without knocking, he opened the door and went in. Mrs

Megarrity, who had been sitting by the stove having a nap, jumped to her feet and was about to make some pretence at working until she saw who it was.

"Jasus tonight! It's you! Would ye knock that friggin' door before ye come in. I thought it was McAllister, an him an me at daggers dawn."

"Ah, I'm sorry about that, Lizzie, but I was rushing in with some good news." Limpy placed the bag of stout and buns on the table and then slowly withdrew the bottle of whiskey and held it up for his sister's approval before setting it too on the table. Mrs Megaritty almost purred at him,

"Good news, is it? Well, never mind yer good news. I've got some for you. D'you remember that five hunnerd pound you so charitably gave to the Church?"

"Oh – yes – that five hunnerd. Now Lizzie, I don't like to be talking about that. It's not right for a man to blow his own trumpet."

"Well, allow me, boy, because there's going to be dynamite up yours in a minute, you lowdown, connivin', lyin' little get! Church my arse! Ye gave that money – five hunnerd pound, for the love of Jasus! – to that wee runt Garrison! An' me giving ye a fiver to treat yerself to a drink on the strength of it. Do ye deny it? Do ye?"

Limpy, who had been making a slow retreat towards the door under this heavy fire, adopted the submissive posture and wheedling tone that had been his salvation so many times before.

"Well – ye see – Lizzie, I didn't want to embarrass the woman by letting everybody know her business. She didn't ask me for the money. I heard she was in a bad way financially and I sent it to her – because she was – an old friend."

"She was in a bad way financially?" His sister bellowed. "An' what the hell way d'ye think I've been in for this last twenty years, running around here with the backside out my knickers? God knows, I never asked for much, but to have to come down that road every morning looking like I've been robbing scarecrows – "

But Limpy was not listening to his sister's sartorial history. A few facts had at last come together and from these he had made a deduction. "Ye nosey old bitch! Ye opened my letter, didn't ye? Is there nothing sacred around here?" He flung an arm up in a dramatic gesture. "Has a man not got the right to privacy, prosperity, to the pursuit of happiness and – "

The Winter Cook fairly flew at the diminutive orator and caught him firmly by one ear which she yanked upwards.

"The pursuit of five hundred pound is all you're going to be doing, John McGhee. C'm'ere!" She led him by the ear to a chair at the table, then shoved him into it. "You," she said, giving his ear one last tug before releasing it, "are going to write a letter."

"Ah!" The Miracle Man held a cupped hand over his throbbing ear. "Ye're a hard and vicious woman, Lizzie Megarrity, so y'are."

"Not half enough for your kind," she said from the far side of the room where she was taking paper and a pen from a drawer. "Now, ye're going to write a little note to Cissy Garrison – the one that's got our money, remember? – and tell her to meet you in one of the rooms at – " she glanced at the clock, " – four this afternoon, and to bring the five hunnerd with her. Number twenty-six is empty. That'll do just fine. C'mon, get writing. And ye'd better lay it on thick, about how desperate ye are for the cash and if she doesn't hand it over, ye'll end up in the jail. I'm sure ye know the kind of thing."

"But Lizzie, I don't need to get the money back because I've – "

"Ye'll just do as ye're told, or ye'll have two legs needing miracles doing on them! Here." She shoved the pen into his hand then tapped the top of the notepaper. "'My Most Dearest Cissy'. Jasus save us."

Oh well, if she was too busy chasing five hundred pounds to be interested in five thousand, that was her look-out. When she eventually did find out about it and wanted a share, she could whistle for it.

When Limpy had written the letter and gone – without his bottle of Black Bush – because "ye need to keep a clear head for this work, John McGhee" – the Winter Cook sat down at the table, poured another whiskey and set about writing one more letter. This one said, "Dear Mr Pointerly, Now's the time. I've waited for you long enough. Meet me in Room 26 at a quarter to four. There's a big bed and plenty of space. Get yourself ready. When I walk in that room, I want to see you as nature intended. Yours for ever, John McGhee. PS. No holds bard."

"Well now," she said with a smile, "we'll see who gets five hunnerd pound and what the wee gold-digger thinks of her true love after this." She poured herself a generous measure of whiskey and raised the glass. "Ye crossed the wrong woman this time, Cissy Garrison," she said aloud, then sat back contentedly in her chair and savoured the free whiskey.

chapter fifteen

In Room 26 of the Glens Hotel, Mr Pointerly could not get his clothes off fast enough. His hands were trembling so much from excitement that his fingers found difficulty in undoing his belt buckle and for some time the buttons on his shirt defied his most determined efforts. He kept starting on one garment and then abandoning that to walk up and down the room, stare at the bed with a shiver of anticipation before commencing to attack another article of clothing.

"Oh, my Lord," he said breathlessly. "My Lord! I knew it would happen eventually. But so suddenly."

Near the dressing-table, he stood in a kind of daze, with one shoe off and the corresponding sock rolled down, his belt dangling loose and one arm in his jacket. He was smiling and frowning alternately. As if at a signal, he suddenly began tearing at his shirt front to open the buttons, at the same time kicking out one foot in an attempt to remove the shoe which he had loosened. He proceeded round the room in this manner until, tiring in one leg, he began to kick out with the other, before realising that he had already removed the shoe from that foot. With a few more contortions, all his clothes had been removed, revealing his long, skinny body. He shivered, gathered up his clothes and went quickly towards the door that led directly to the bathroom.

As Limpy entered the back door of the hotel and went towards the service stairway at the rear of the building, his sister the Winter Cook lingered in the upstairs corridor near to Cissy Garrison's room. Twice she had tiptoed to the door and bent forward to listen at it. She looked at her watch, a cheap digital one which gave the appearance of having been run over by a steam roller, and for which her son had swapped a catapult at school. Only the hour digits could be seen with clarity, as the minute figures had a habit of degenerating into hieroglyphics. This resulted in frequent banging of the watch on the kitchen table, following which it might momentarily show any time in twenty-four hours or none at all. The Winter Cook screwed up her eyes. It looked like 3.58. And then the door opened and Cissy Garrison came out. She was wearing a checked skirt and a pink tulle blouse made for someone of more ample proportions than herself and whose ruffed collar was so high that it obscured the lower part of her face. A pair of goggles might have completed the outfit and led the casual observer to think that the visored Garrison sister was about to embark on major welding operations.

"Well, hello there Miss Garrison and how are ye this evening?"

The Winter Cook blocked the way for Miss Cissy to proceed to Room 26.

"Very well thank you, Mrs Megarrity."

"I was wondering, Miss Garrison, if I could have yer opinion on something. Ye see, I'm planning to cook a special farewell meal for me leaving for the summer break, and with you and yer sister – and Mr Pointerly, of course – being such long-time residents, I thought I would ask yez what ye'd prefer. Now, I've got a list here somewhere – "

"Well, that's very kind of you, Mrs Megarrity, but I do have to meet someone and – I think I may already be a little late."

She tried to move to one side and past the Winter Cook who deftly side-stepped into the space.

"Oh, it'll hardly take a minute, Miss Garrison. If I could just find this list."

The door from the corridor into Room 26 opened slowly and quietly as Limpy looked around it to find that Cissy had not yet arrived. He came in, closed the door behind him and gave a smile, before going over to the bed and testing it with his hand for softness. The bed got a nod of approval. Then Limpy broadened his shoulders, thrust his arms in an embrace around an imaginary Cissy and threw her sideways, so that she lay back in his arms looking up at him.

"I have always wanted ye," he said in a whispered but dramatic tone. "Ye should've been mine years ago. And yet – " the back of one hand was pressed against his brow, "the fates would not allow it." He turned away, eyes downcast, a tragic prince deep in his winter of discontent. "Kinset – Kisnit," and then in a sub-whisper, "Whatever the feck they call it."

He flung out one arm and in doing so appeared to be supporting his paramour with the lightest of touches from the other. "But – it is never too late." Getting into the swing of things, he flung her upright again. "Come away with me now! Be mine for ever! No longer will I have to say – " he flung out both arms, abandoning his imaginary partner to the laws of gravity and at last giving full voice to his emotions, "Where are you, my love, where are you?"

"I'm here! I'm here!" Mr Pointerly shouted as he burst through the doorway of the bathroom and went prancing across to the bed.

"Jasus Christ of Almighty!"

Limpy staggered back, bumped against the bed and sat down heavily upon it. As he looked at the gangling septuagenarian bearing down on him, arms outstretched and appendages bouncing as he ran, Limpy's face was rigid with astonishment. Mr Pointerly stopped, looked at Limpy on the bed and said,

"So keen, McPhee, so keen!" and flung himself on top of the Miracle Man who had barely the time to utter a shout of protest.

And then, having been suitably delayed by the Winter Cook, Cissy walked into the room. With the door half open behind her, she stared and stared at the naked back of Mr Pointerly as he grappled with the figure beneath him.

"Oh my goodness!" Her little hands fluttered nervously and she almost dropped the envelope that she carried. She gave a long, shuddering, "Oh!" and then said, "Mr Pointerly! What on earth are you doing?"

The old man gave a jump and rolled sideways, revealing a red-faced Limpy beneath.

"John! What – is this? Mr Pointerly, please!" Miss Cissy said and turned her head away as Mr Pointerly revealed a full-frontal view of himself.

"Cissy!" Limpy tried to struggle to a sitting position, but was defeated by Mr Pointerly's legs. "He's gone crazy! What the hell are ye doing, ye old fool?"

"Aha!" the voice boomed from the doorway behind Cissy. "Who would've believed it? A senior citizens' vice ring in Inisbreen. I suppose it was going to be three in a bed."

"Mrs Megarrity! I'll have you know that I am no part of this – charade! I simply came here to talk to this – " she waved a dismissive hand at Limpy, " – person, on a private matter."

The trembling Mr Pointerly, in pulling his legs up in an attempt to lend himself a degree of modesty, merely succeeded in exposing even more of his anatomy.

"It's all a – terrible mistake," he said weakly.

"However," Cissy continued, as if Mr Pointerly had not spoken, "I was obviously wasting my time. I'm hardly surprised at this one," she jerked her head at the naked contortionist, "but you, John. I can see now why you never married." She took a step towards the bed. "This is obviously what you wanted – as well as to humiliate me. Well, have it. God alone knows how you got it in the first place."

She flung the envelope and it landed on the floor near the bed.

"Cissy, no! Listen to me!" Limpy managed to break free and sit upright. "It's not like ye think!"

"Don't ever speak to me again, John McGhee," Cissy said, and taking up a regal pose reminiscent of that of her elder sister, she pushed her way past the Winter Cook and hurried off down the corridor.

In three strides Mrs Megarrity crossed the floor and scooped up the envelope.

"I'll take care of this, I think."

"Lizzie! This is all your doing!"

"You," she said, poking the envelope at him, "had better get your backside out of here before McAllister shows up. And could I remind ye," she said to Mister Pointerly, who lay huddled on the bed with a dazed look on his face, "that ye'll be expected to dress for dinner tonight."

Fergus Keane knocked on Limpy McGhee's door and waited. In his hand he clenched a rolled-up copy of the Daily Times which he was slowly beating against the side of his leg. After a few moments, the door scraped open and Limpy said in a doleful voice,

"I'm sorry, I'm not open for visitors until – ah! it's yerself, young Fergus. I thought it was one of them nosey gits of visitors. Come on in."

Fergus stepped gingerly into the room and was surprised to find that it had been changed into a place which was at least reasonably suitable for human habitation if not quite a desirable residence.

"What is this, Mr McGhee?" Fergus unrolled the Daily Times and held up the front page, on which there was a photograph of Limpy below a headline proclaiming, "'VIRGIN MARY WINKED AT ME,' SAYS MIRACLE MAN."

"Ah yes," Limpy said and gave a half-hearted laugh. "I told the man that was my best side."

"But Mr McGhee, you've given your story to another paper! I gave you five hundred pounds for an exclusive in the Northern Reporter."

Despite the melancholy look on his face, Limpy managed a little smile. He nodded slowly to the young journalist.

"Well, that's right, Fergus, my deal with ye was exclusive. Exclusive of sufficient cash. The agreement I have with the Daily Times is – well – inclusive of more cash."

Fergus threw the newspaper to the ground.

"So, for the sake of a few extra pounds, you break our agreement? That's great. Thank you."

Limpy bent and picked up the newspaper.

"Did they never teach you tidiness at home? Listen, the reason I went back on our agreement wasn't for a few extra pounds."

"It wasn't?"

"No, it was for five thousand pounds." He fixed the young reporter with a steady gaze. "I had to take it, Fergus son."

"Five – thousand pounds?" Fergus gasped. It was doubtful if the whole Northern Reporter company was worth that much money. "But, what am I supposed to do? I told my editor I had an exclusive, and he's expecting a series of articles." Fergus looked crestfallen. "And that five hundred pounds – it was my own money."

"Ah, ye never went and spent yer own money, did ye? If I'd've knowed that, young Fergus, I'd've never taken it off ye. What the hell sort of paper's that ye work for, ye have to use your own money?"

"My editor – Harry Martyn – he wouldn't give me the money. He – didn't believe your story."

To the young reporter's surprise, the old man simply shrugged and said,

"Well, he's not the only one."

Limpy went over to a chest of drawers which was of Victorian vintage and yet appeared to have the lacerations of a millennia upon it.

"I was going to get in touch with ye anyway. I've got something for ye."

Grasping a drawer handle he pulled. The drawer did not move, so putting his foot on the front of the chest of drawers he applied both hands and tried again. For a few seconds he heaved, before the drawer suddenly yielded and he went staggering back across the room and almost collided with Fergus.

"God damned dog. Would you believe he's pissed on that chest of drawers too?" Limpy rummaged in the drawer he had liberated. "Made all the food damp." He plucked out a buff envelope. "I was bloody glad when them biscuits was done, I can tell ye. Here." He thrust the envelope at Fergus.

"What's this?"

"It's yer money back, plus a wee bonus."

Fergus, who had intended to demand the return of his five hundred though with little hope of obtaining the full amount, looked suitably taken aback.

"A – bonus? For what, Mr McGhee?"

Limpy, having put the end of the drawer in its place, rammed it home with a kick of surprising agility for one of his age.

"Well now, Fergus, you set me on the road to fame and fortune, as ye might say, so there's an extra hundred in there, just as a wee token of my appreciation for what ye've done."

"Oh but Mr McGhee, I couldn't possibly take a hundred

pounds from you. I mean, you must need it yourself and I would – "

"Ah, it's of no account to me," Limpy said gruffly. "Not now, not now. Not – " he gave a little sigh, " – not when the one object of my heart's desire won't even listen to my heart-rendering pleas." Slowly he shook his head. "What's the point, eh? It's hardly worth going on, so it isn't."

"I don't understand, Mr McGhee."

This time, Limpy gave a great sigh, this and his depressed state serving to wring the maximum sympathy from Fergus Keane.

"Miss Cissy Garrison, resident of the Glens Hotel – and one of the finest creatures ever to set foot on this earth. That's why I took the five thousand. I never had enough money before to – ask her to marry me." A forlorn look came upon his face and his shoulders drooped. He could have been eliciting money from his sister, the Winter Cook. "Her and me – we go back over forty years, so we do. And now – " he grimaced, but managed to hold back a flood of emotion, " – just when I thought her and me was getting together at last, she thinks I'm – one of them queers. It was all the fault of that old eejit Pointerly. Didn't you see him in here the other night at his carry on." He bowed his head and slowly drew it from side to side. "Now Cissy never wants to clap eyes on me again – living nor dead."

Fergus swallowed to dispel the lump that had come to his throat.

"But, that's so unfair. That stupid old bugger Pointerly, he wants to be – "

"Ah now, the man means no harm, Fergus. He's lonely, just."

Fergus took a step nearer to the old man.

"Is there – anything at all I can do to help, Mr McGhee?" Limpy gave a brave laugh.

"Don't be concerning yourself with an old man's troubles,

son. Away you go and write your stories." He winked. "I'll make sure you get enough information to keep you going – five thousand or no five thousand."

Fergus stood outside Limpy's closed door and gazed across the field, the damp skin around his eyes cold where the wind blew over it. Poor Mr McGhee. Probably his last chance at happiness, pulled away from him like – a rug from under the feet of a drowning man. Fergus's fists clenched by his sides. There must be something he could do. Here he was with the great power of the press coursing through his right arm, his hand wielding the pen that was mightier than the sword. What was its purpose, if not truth and justice, the righting of wrongs, the championing of the afflicted? Oh, there was something to be done all right, and he was the man to do it. Because if that bastard Harry Martyn had coughed up in the first place, Mr McGhee wouldn't have these coals of – well, these burning coals heaped on him. Turning quickly away, he almost tripped over Limpy's dog, which was about to cock his leg at him. The animal looked up at him with its sleepy eyes and as Fergus aimed a kick at it, the dog neatly side-stepped and narrowly missed ripping a large piece from Fergus's trousers with its long yellow teeth. It had been too long at the game with Limpy McGhee to be caught out by an amateur.

Fergus lingered for some time in the telephone box, kneading his hands together as he tried out various approaches to Harry Martyn. He, Fergus Keane, had been on the verge of success. A scoop, no less. A great story with all the right ingredients – religion, medicine, a lonely old man restored to full health, a stream of holy water, crowds flocking to the miracle site and the prospect of more miracles to come. Despite what Harry Martyn had said, Fergus knew it was a story that could run for months. He had discovered it and brought it to the world, and all Harry Martyn could say was that it was boring and couldn't he get a sex angle on it. The man couldn't lift his mind out of the gutter. And if he had paid up in the beginning, they'd still have an exclusive, and pieces with Fergus's name above them would be getting syndicated in newspapers the length and breadth of the country, if not the globe. It was all Harry Martyn's fault and, God damn it, he was going to tell him so in no uncertain terms.

When the telephonist answered, Fergus said,

"Get me Harry Martyn, right away!" but on hearing the gruff tones of his editor on the line, some of the young reporter's courage ebbed away.

"Mr Martyn – eh – this is Fergus Keane. And I must say, Mr Martyn – I'm not very happy." Firmness, that's what was needed. He wasn't going to be brow-beaten by a man that didn't know when to sign a cheque for one of the best stories that had ever appeared in a newspaper.

"Keane?" The voice fairly boomed down the line, not at all the sound of a man who was about to be put in his place. "Fergus Keane? You're not very happy? You're not very happy? Listen, you jumped-up ink squirter, I'm not very bloody happy! In fact I'm not happy at all. I've had a doctor on from this Inis-whatever-the-hell-it's-called, who says he's going to sue the Reporter! Sue, for Christ's sake! Do you realise what that could do to us? Close us down, that's what!"

Suddenly Fergus began to tremble and he had to support the telephone receiver with his other hand.

"But – Mr Martyn – I don't understand. Sue for what?"

"What the hell d'you think? For what you wrote about him."

"But, I didn't give the doctor's name in the piece."

"He said he's the only doctor in the area and it would be obvious to anyone with half a brain that he was the man referred to. What you wrote was, quote, 'Garbage from beginning to end,' unbloodyquote. I have also, Keane, had the

Bishop of Down and Connor himself on the 'phone, demanding your immediate resignation, due to the – I've written it down here – the 'totally unwarranted imputation that the Church has accepted the happenings at Inisbreen as the workings of divine intervention, and the clear implication that the Church authorities, including myself, are a gathering of gullible dockheads'. I think he meant dickheads. What've you got to say about that, Mr Keane who's not very happy?"

A red flush of anger swept over Fergus's face and neck, and he found it difficult to speak.

"I – don't understand, Mr Martyn. It's true! Mr McGhee's leg was cured and other people have seen the vision and – I might've exaggerated a little about the doctor, but – "

"Keane, this story's been nothing but trouble from the beginning. I told you it would be. So, you're off it! D'you understand? Off! I want you back here, like, yesterday!"

"But, Mr Martyn, I can't just – "

"Back here, Keane. I've got at least a month's worth of filing for you to do."

"Mr Martyn, I – " Fergus gulped and took a deep breath as the brainwave hit him. "If I was to come back now, I couldn't follow up the sex angle on this story."

The line from Ballymane fell silent. Then at last,

"What sex angle, Keane?"

"Oh, Mr Martyn, you wouldn't believe some of the things this Miracle Man's been up to." Fergus smiled. Now he was on a roll. "In fact, I'm beginning to think this is the real reason they call him the Miracle Man."

"Really?" There was the sound of a mouthful of tea being slurped and Harry Martyn enquired in a purring monotone, "What sort of things exactly was he doing, Keane?" Then he added urgently, "If you haven't got enough change for that telephone box, give me your number and I'll ring you back."

"Well, at one time he used to – oh, look, I've got to go, Mr

Martyn. My contact has arrived. She's – wow! can't imagine those two together. Be in touch soon, Mr Martyn. Bye!"

"But Keane – !"

"Call you tomorrow," Fergus shouted as the telephone was halfway to the cradle. And then he leant back against the side of the box, looked up at the cobwebbed light bulb and trembled at the sheer brilliance of what he had just done.

Nancy Quinn was a devout Catholic, at least when she was in the chapel, at school or in proximity to any person or thing that she felt had even a vague religious connection. Amongst her possessions was a bottle of holy water from the miracle site at the Mass Rock. She had brought the water away with her after a visit to the site, where she had knelt and prayed fervently for her current desires, namely a greater understanding by her ageing mother of the dress and mores of females in their mid twenties, the demise of a teenage pupil – she left the precise method to the wisdom of the Lord – who had groped her from behind in the crush for the exit at school lunch break, and a red Porsche, most especially a red Porsche. With this last item she was prepared to offer some help, as she now felt in a good position to put pressure on Dermot to part with some of the cash that he undoubtedly had piled up in his bank account. She would not even press him for a new car. A nice second-hand one would do just as well. And as she had been called into the headmaster's office the morning after the unfortunate incident with Father Burke and the church committee and been given her walking ticket because she was "not a fit and proper person to teach young Catholic children", she felt that guilt should play a significant part in persuading Dermot that she was deserving of such a present.

At the time, Nancy had taken the water to put into the water-font in the hallway of her mother's house, but the bottle had lain forgotten on her dressing-table. Now, with the various reports from locals of its efficacy in treating everything from lumbago in humans to mange in cats, her mind turned to Dermot's "problem", which had certainly been temporarily solved by his wild animal act. She had at least noticed that much as she had leapt to her feet with the hot coffee scalding her buttocks. But at their first attempt since then – in the fateful living-room they had flung their clothes off in joyous celebration of their new-found freedom – expectation had followed excitement in starting high and quickly flagging. The question she asked herself was, would the water work for Dermot and therefore by extension, so to speak, for her also? Going with a rich man was all very well – except for that nosey old bitch who called herself a cook – but if this was going to happen every time they tried to make love, then it was just not worth it. There were only two consolations. One, she fancied, was her increasing proximity to Dermot's money. The other was that, with the influx of reporters into the hotel, there was one very nice-looking young man who had arrived the day before and who had wasted no time in chatting her up. Not that she would allow such a thing to affect her relationship with Dermot, of course, because that was founded on mutual love and respect.

As they lay together on the couch in Dermot's living-room, Nancy broached the subject of the holy water as a cure for his problem and he at once grew red in the face.

"Don't be so bloody stupid," he said and then mumbled something about superstition and sacrilege. Nancy snuggled closer to him.

"Darling," she said, and whispered in his ear her vision of what it would be like when his problem had been overcome. At this, Dermot began to get a little flustered.

"For God's sake, Nancy, have a bit of sense. A thing like that would never work. Holy water would have the exact opposite effect to an aphrodisiac. I mean, I don't ever remember fancying being groped by a nun."

But being a teacher, and therefore used to explaining things simply and persuasively to those who were reluctant to open their minds, she said,

"Dermot, darling, in a situation like this, the wish is father to the action. If you really want it to succeed, it will. All you need is a little faith – and holy water."

And so, before he went down to the bar to serve for the evening, she had him undress and lie on the couch. While he lay there with his eyes closed and his hands clenched by his side, as though about to undergo a painful experience, she began to work on him, teasing flesh here and arranging there, like an undertaker preparing a corpse. She had even thought to warm the bottle of water by the fire before applying some of the contents, and this in such an expert manner that one might have thought it was not the first time she had done something of the kind. A few pleasurable groans escaped Dermot's lips before Nancy, having applied the liquid to every part of his anatomy that might have even the slightest bearing on the problem, straightened up, swept back a fallen wisp of red hair and said with some satisfaction,

"There." The task had been accomplished. Now all that could be done was to await results.

About an hour after Dermot had gone down to serve in the hotel lounge bar, Nancy rang down to him.

"Well," she said, "have there been any results yet?"

"For God's sake, Nancy," he hissed into the telephone, "I can't speak now!"

"Well there's no need to bite my head off! You could just say 'yes' or 'no', couldn't you?"

"No. I told you it wouldn't bloody work!"

"Don't you feel – anything? I would've expected something to happen by now. It is holy water, after all."

"Well it hasn't. Goodbye."

It was just after ten o'clock. Nancy was sitting watching

television and wondering if she should just give up and go home, when she heard the outside door of the flat closing. She glanced at the clock and frowned. There was the sound of footsteps in the hallway before the door was opened and Dermot came in.

"Dermot! You haven't – finished for the night, have you?"

"No, Nancy, I haven't finished for the night. I asked somebody to take over for a few minutes."

"Why did you ask – Oh, Dermot! Something's happened, hasn't it? I knew it! I knew it would work! If you've got faith, anything can happen." Nancy jumped to her feet. "Oh my God! How long've you got?" She began to pull open the buttons on the front of her dress. "We'll need to hurry!" She gave a shiver of excitement. "Well, come on then," she said, kicking her shoes off, "don't waste time. Thanks for not waiting until you'd finished in the bar, Dermot. I would probably have been gone."

Without taking his eyes from Nancy, Dermot had hooked both thumbs inside his trousers and underpants and pulled them both down around his knees. Nancy glanced down with a smile which quickly turned into a grimace. Her hand went to her mouth.

"Oh – my – God! Dermot!" She leant forward and peered at Dermot's groin. "You'd need a magnifying glass to – "

"Exactly!" Dermot almost shouted. "You and your stupid bloody idea! What the hell am I going to do? If it keeps going like this I'll be reclassified as a castrato. Look at me." Nancy put her hand to her mouth in order to stifle a smile.

"There's – not that much to look at, actually." She emitted a little whining sound that should have been the beginning of a laugh but she pressed her fist hard against her teeth.

"Oh, very funny. Very bloody funny. Have a laugh about it, why don't you." He yanked his underpants and trousers up to his waist again and started for the door. "I've got to get down there again, before they rob me blind." He turned and shook a finger at Nancy, who was only controlling her laughter by not looking at him. "If this is permanent – if I've got to go round like this for the rest of my life . . . You'd better think of something, Nancy – and pretty damn quick!"

Dermot left the room, slamming both the living-room and outside doors behind him, while Nancy appeared to have been suddenly overtaken by the gravity of the situation. And shortly afterwards she did indeed think of something. She thought of the good-looking young reporter with the dark hair who was in Room 27 on the floor below. Nancy wondered if she should go along that corridor on her way out and perhaps stop to make a neighbourly enquiry as to his health and general well-being.

chapter sixteen

They knew that there must be something wrong with Limpy McGhee when he didn't turn up at O'Neill's bar for his nightly drinking session. Although he had lately taken to drinking of an evening in the bar of the Glens Hotel, he invariably finished off with a visit to O'Neill's. They said he couldn't rest easy in his bed until he had had an argument with somebody – anybody would do – then insulted them and stamped out in a temper. And so everyone who came into O'Neill's that night was asked if he had seen Limpy in the Glens Hotel bar or on the road from his little house near the chapel, but nobody had done so. When it drew near to closing time and he had still not been seen nor any sightings of him reported, it was decided that he had either passed away from a surfeit of drink or had taken off for England with his new-found wealth. It was just the sort of damn fool thing he would do, they thought.

Had they seen what Limpy was doing at that time, they would scarcely have believed the evidence of their own eyes, for not only was he sitting at home during pub opening hours but he was cold sober, a combination which the man himself would have sworn was beyond his powers of endurance. He had been sitting this way for a good part of the evening, the dog rising from his resting place now and then to mooch around the bare floor, sniffing for the ghosts of the bones and other titbits that were once strewn among the rubbish. Even when he cocked his leg and left his calling-card on the corner of the far wall, Limpy took no notice. His mind was on other things.

After all these years – over forty, it was – he had almost got Cissy back again. Almost. All of a sudden his life had been changed at the thought of it. And he'd got a bit of money, too. Maybe even enough to put a deposit on a wee house. After all, he couldn't bring a decent woman back to a place like this. But then Lizzie had to put her oar in and bugger up the whole thing. There was no harm in that old fool Pointerly, it was Lizzie's doing entirely. So now Cissy thought he was as queer as a nine-bob note and wouldn't even look the road he was on. And just when she was ready, willing and able to take up with him again. Now he would have to find some way of enticing her back, of convincing her that he wasn't a horse's hoof after all.

It was almost midnight before the idea came to him. As the immensity of it became apparent, he wondered how he could have sat racking his brains for so long and not seriously considered it before. It combined diversion and practicality, it would give him a status worthy of his role as a miraculous symbol and a commercial asset, and if he played his cards right it would certainly bring Cissy running back to his side. With a broad smile, Limpy jumped to his feet and rubbed his hands together. There was a lot to be said for thinking and no denying the power of the brain when it was let go at full tilt. Weren't the McGhees famous for it, sitting around considering weighty matters, "cogertating", as his old uncle used to say, whilst those that were weaker in the head did the labouring work? He reached to pat the dog's head. The animal, which had been lying half asleep near the bed, was so surprised at this unaccustomed show of affection that it immediately got up and went to a corner of the room, from where it sat and watched its master with eyes full of suspicion. The last pat on the head it had received – after it had relieved itself against the leg of the bed – had been swiftly followed by a boot up the backside.

Limpy had never owned a car or had a driving lesson in his life, having obtained his driving licence in the days before the advent of the driving test. His only means of automotive transport had been an ancient tractor which had long ago expired and been abandoned at the back of his house. For a time he had tried an old bicycle, but due to his bad leg he had had to swivel across the saddle at every pedal stroke, and ended up throwing the bicycle in a ditch along the road, saying that it was "for nothing but sawing the arse off me". Whenever he wanted to go anywhere more than two or three miles away he either took the bus or cadged a lift, and on those rare occasions when he had bought a few sheep or a pig, he reluctantly paid someone to transport them home. Now he was behind the wheel of his first car, a huge old Ford, propped up on the seat by two cushions which the garage man in Castleglen had kindly given him when it had become obvious that otherwise Limpy would have been unable to see out of the windscreen.

Behind the showroom, in the yard where they kept the vehicles that were waiting to be scrapped – or sold to customers like Limpy McGhee – the salesman had held out his arm and said,

"There she is, sir! The very limousine for a gentleman such as yourself. And only just come on the market, since his Lordship took delivery of his new one." He had lovingly patted one wing of the old car, but carefully, as a shower of rust falling from the wheel-arch might have deterred even the most ardent of buyers. "She's a beauty right enough, sir, and solid as a rock."

"His Lordship? What lordship?"

"Ah, please sir, if you would, forget I said that. Erase it entirely from your memory. Slip of the tongue, sir, a fox's pass, as you might say. I couldn't possibly reveal the name. And if I could," he had winked at Limpy, "I would have to charge you twice the price for her."

Limpy had cast his eye along the once-graceful lines of the old car, from the black paint slapped over the rusting sills to the wheels without hub caps.

"Undersealed, sir," the salesman had nodded at the black paint. "Essential in this climate. Salt air, you know."

"Oh, I'm well aware of the depredations of rust on metal, so I am," Limpy said. He shifted his gaze to the wheels. "What about them things that should be on the wheels there? Hub caps, is it?"

The salesman had smiled and given Limpy's elbow a squeeze of sheer admiration.

"Ah, you've been holding out on me, sir, haven't you? I'd venture you know more than a thing or two about motor vehicles. So you'll recognise a car that's been used for what we in the trade call 'off-road work'."

Limpy smiled and nodded. Of course he did.

"His Lordship there, he's very big on off-road work, I can tell you. Shooting parties, point-to-point meetings and the like. Only the very best vehicles are up to it, as I'm sure you know. And if I was able to tell you the names of some of the gentry that've sat in this conveyance – well." He gave a toss of his head, still in awe at the import of the information he held in confidence. "Now, you're obviously a man with an eye for a bargain, so there's no point in me coming in at a big price. Rock bottom, sir, best offer, and only because you're a gentleman that appreciates a quality vehicle." And then a lowering of the voice and a confidential tone. "I'd hate to have to let it go to some of the shit-kickers we get in here." He had paused for a moment, clearly considering if it was worth laying his job on the line to give such a good deal to this fine gentleman. "Listen," he said, "forget seven fifty, disregard six hundred. And you might say I'm robbing myself, but – " his palms came together in a loud clap – "five hundred!"

"I'll take it," Limpy had said, already imagining himself driving through Inisbreen in the car, like a nabob on an elephant. And then he had slapped the car dealer's upturned palm in the time-honoured manner of those striking a bargain and paid his five hundred pounds.

Later, he had roared out of the yard, clutch slipping and black smoke belching from the exhaust – "his Lordship's a terrible man for oil, sir," – just managing to navigate through the streets of Castleglen without mounting the pavement or running down any pedestrians. Now he was driving the twelve miles on the mountain road between the town and Inisbreen, where the only things he could kill would be himself or a few sheep, the big engine roaring through a hole in the exhaust and the thud of the worn shock absorbers loud at every bump in the road. What would their faces not be like in Inisbreen when he rode in on this yoke? And how long would it be before he could get Cissy Garrison to talk to him again and have the pair of them riding around in luxury, a second lordship now at the wheel and his ladyship by his side.

"Jasus McGonagle!" Dan Ahearn said when Limpy brought him and Pig Cully out the side door of O'Neill's pub, "that's one helluva vehicle, McGhee. You could get half a dozen of sheep in the back of that bus." He clapped his hands together and shook his head in amazement. "Tell me this, now. Would she be hard on the fuel?"

"Oh, easy enough, Dan, easy enough," Limpy told him, as

if from a lifetime of automotive experience. "She'll do me rightly for a runabout, so she will."

"Damn me, a runabout! It's yerself has the style, McGhee."

With cap down over his eyes and hands thrust deep into his trousers pockets, Pig Cully was inspecting the old Ford. He gave one of the wings a kick and a shower of rust fell to the ground.

"How much did ye pay for her, McGhee?" he demanded.

"Five hunnerd," Limpy told him, with a shrug of indifference.

"Ye were robbed, McGhee. It's got terminal tinworm. A feckin' pile of rust on wheels."

"Ah now, I wouldn't say that, Cully," Dan Ahearn said. "I wouldn't say that at all."

"She's damn all of the sort, Cully. I know a class vehicle when I see one," Limpy said, and patted the fading paintwork. "And once I get this thirst off me I'll take the two of yez for a run in her. Then yez'll know what a motor vehicle should be like."

In O'Neill's snug, Limpy ordered pints of stout and whiskies for the three of them and insisted on paying, an action which met with no resistance from either Cully or Ahearn. When young O'Neill brought the drinks in, a rare honour in the pub, Limpy asked him,

"Are there any of them newspapermen in the bar, son?"

"A whole rake of them, Mr McGhee. Been there since opening time. Drinking like there was no tomorrow, so they are."

"Good business for ye, son, good business. That's because I'm what's known as a commercial asset." Limpy did not quite know what a commercial asset should feel like, but he knew that it felt a lot better than his previous status had done. He stuck out his chest beneath the old suit he had taken to wearing and assumed an air of importance. "Don't ye be letting on to them I'm in here, son. Even a public figure has to have a bit of privacy now and again."

Pig Cully grunted and said "Jasus," under his breath.

"Is that your vehicle out there, Mr McGhee?"

"It certainly is, son. Just purchased today. D'you like her?"

"Oh, she's some machine, Mr McGhee. That's the kind of thing I'll be getting one of these days. By Christ it is," he added, showing that, out of earshot of the Mother, he could be just as much a man as any of them.

"Ach, yer mother wouldn't even let ye buy a kiddie car, O'Neill," Pig Cully told him. "She has ye under the thumb good and proper."

The young man's face went red and he banged the glasses down in front of Pig Cully.

"We'll see about that, Mr Cully, so we will. We'll bloody well see about that," he said and stalked out of the room.

When Limpy had downed his stout and whiskey in double-quick time and ordered the same again all round, he leant on the table, eyed his two companions and said,

"Boys – I've got an announcement." He cleared his throat. "I'm planning on throwing a party." He looked from one to the other to see their reaction. Dan Ahearn seemed a little confused by this and turned for guidance to Pig Cully, who slowly lowered his front chair legs to the floor and pushed back his cap to reveal his little piggy eyes.

"A party, McGhee? What for?"

Limpy leant back in his chair and took on what he supposed was a regal air.

"To celebrate my good fortune, of course – and to have a bloody good time. A good-going party, boys, with plenty of music and drink and grub. I'll be paying. What d'yez think?"

At the sound of the magic phrase "I'll be paying", Pig Cully's interest noticeably quickened and there was a slap as Dan Ahearn's hands came together in confirmation.

"I think ye might just have something there, McGhee. A party, eh? When were ye thinking of having it?"

"Saturday night, Cully. At your house," Limpy said.

"At – what?"

"At your house. There's not enough room in mine to swing a cat."

Dan Ahearn said,

"Now there's a thing I never rightly understood. What for would anybody be wanting to swing a cat?"

The other two men ignored him.

"Well, maybe ye've got a point, McGhee." Cully's face took on a lascivious look. "Some of us might be wanting a bit of privacy before the night's out, ye know what I mean? So, who were ye thinking of inviting to this party, then?"

Limpy glanced at the other two men and suppressed a smile.

"Oh – anybody that's seriously interested in having a good time. I've been going over her in my mind, so I have." He leant forward and jabbed a finger on the table-top. "And I tell yez, I'm going to have the best damned party ever seen this side of Ballymane."

"And I can invite anybody I want?" Pig Cully inquired, his interest now thoroughly aroused.

"Ye certainly can – as long as it's female."

"Well then," came the reply, "I'll be inviting – Peggy May."

"That, my friend," Limpy said, "is your purgative. And what about you, Ahearn? Ye want to come to the party of a lifetime – food, drink, women, dancing? Could ye stick the pace?"

Despite being in his early fifties, Dan Ahearn's experience with women was largely confined to his sister and his late mother. The thought of being in close and lengthy proximity to eligible females appeared to be more than he could take in at one sitting. He grimaced and his big bony hands kneaded each other.

"Jesus McGonagle," he said softly. "A party – with women?" He shook his head at the enormity of the thought. "By jeez, that's a big one, boys. I'll need to do a bit of thinking on that, so I will."

"Well don't be thinking too long on it," Pig Cully told him, "otherwise Saturday will've come and gone." He gave one of his squeaking laughs. "D'you think he'll need a few tips, McGhee? ye can bet he still thinks it's for stirring his tea with."

"Not after Saturday night, he won't. I tell ye, boys," the little man slapped his hand on the table, "she's going to be one hoor of a party!"

The following morning, Father Ignatius Loyola Burke knelt in the front pew of the otherwise empty church of Saint Patrick and Saint Brigid in Inisbreen, his breviary held open before him, head inclined upwards towards the large cross that hung over the altar and his lips moving in silent prayer. Outside, a stiff breeze that had blown up the glen from the sea swayed the trees back and forth, throwing moving shadows on the stained-glass windows. The silent prayer on the priest's lips rose to a murmur then fell again, while at the back of the church the door-latch rattled as a gust of wind blew over and around the tall gravestones that crowded near the entrance like eager catechumens. The priest's lips stopped moving and slowly his head was lowered until he sat staring at the blurred pages before him. He gave a long sigh, and the shoulders that were normally held well back sagged beneath his black soutane. The words of the breviary, prayer of any kind, had suddenly fled his mind and his face contorted into a mask of anxiety.

It had all seemed so straightforward when he had first learned that he was to be a parish priest, albeit in a place called Inisbreen that he had never heard of and that did not even appear on some maps. Here was the opportunity to make his mark, and before he had even got to Inisbreen he had begun drawing up plans as to how he was going to organise everything from the Legion of Mary to the bingo sessions. He had seen enough in his previous two parishes, witnessed the poor management of affairs by lackadaisical parish priests, to have learned how it should be done properly. All he needed was a parish of his own. And now he had one. Yet somehow things didn't seem to be working out quite the way he had imagined. Matters were arising of a type that he had never encountered. He could always call on advice from the bishop, but he was reluctant to do that, and in any event he was dubious about the quality of such advice. He must show that he had the skill and resolve to succeed on his own, but that was proving to be more difficult than he had anticipated.

The major problem, of course, was these people. They were a different breed from those he had been used to in the South. Up here they didn't take too well to being told what to do and they had more of a tendency to talk back, to question every aspect of his parish management, but not so far – thank God – the teachings of the Church itself. It must be the Scots blood in them, that rebellious – almost Presbyterian streak, he shuddered – that characterised the type the world over. That business about the graveyard was a typical example. It was a disgrace, and he had told them so from the pulpit in unequivocal terms the second Sunday he had been there. The place was overgrown like a jungle, so that a man would nearly need a guide to lead him to a grave. Oh, they had told him that every now and again they "had a go" at it. And the very next week – quite coincidentally, of course – they had done just that, a horde of them descending on the place one Saturday morning, men, women and children with scythes and sickles and rusty shears, hooking and hacking indiscriminately until he feared that he would have to go out with a sack to gather up severed hands and feet. When they had finished, it had looked worse than before they had started, with bare patches in some places and chopped-off clumps of grass and weeds in others. The answer, he had told them, was to have professionals come in and do it properly, but all they could say was what was that going to cost and who was going to pay for it.

And that was only half the problem with the graveyard, for it was almost full, and with the river on two sides, the road on another and the adjacent farmer unwilling to part with any land, he was at a loss to know what to do. Of course, suggestions were not in short supply. These had ranged from a ban on burials and a switch to cremation – this from a farmer who offered to sell him what he called "a beautiful wee incinerator at a giveaway price" – vertical burial, which would have the added advantage of requiring only very small and therefore cheaper gravestones, and from one old woman, who no doubt had a vested interest, the idea that a series of novenas should be said, asking the Lord to suspend all deaths in the parish until a solution could be found to the problem. So, how had the Canon handled problems like these, which must have been around for years? Was it possible that the wily old man had after all known just a little about running this parish?

Now, to add to his burdens, there was this so-called miracle, and it looked as if that was going to turn out the worst of all. When he had met McGhee that first night, seen how he walked naturally and heard about his life-long affliction, it was obvious that something remarkable had happened. The lady in white and the subsequent appearance of the stream seemed to confirm it. And there had been other signs. People who had apparently been cured of minor ailments. No woman with an issue of blood, it was true, but one who had claimed the overnight cure of boils on her buttocks. Everything pointed to a miracle. But how had he been supposed to know that McGhee might not be a Catholic? The man couldn't possibly be the subject of a miracle on a Catholic site if he didn't believe in the basic tenets of the Faith. Father Burke thought that perhaps he should've smelt a rat – or rather a cat – when the old woman had claimed a miraculous cure for the mange in her ginger tom. As much as he hated to admit it to himself, it was becoming increasingly plain to him that the whole thing was a fake, either at the hands of McGhee or someone else.

He had invested a lot of time and effort in it, had drawn up plans, and had even managed to persuade the Bishop that it was genuine. If it ever got out that it was a hoax, his career in the Church would be ruined and he would be a laughing-stock in chapel houses the length and breadth of Ireland. In a few short weeks he had gone from a state of mild depression at the thought of coming to Inisbreen, to euphoria at the opportunity afforded him by the miracle, and now he was back to depression again. He stood up abruptly and shrugged as if to throw off his unwelcome thoughts. He had planned to go directly from the chapel to Ballymane, where he could perhaps cadge a lunch at the chapel house before conducting his afternoon's business in the town. Now a kind of depressive torpor had overtaken him and he did not feel up to it at all. What he needed was to go home, lie down in his room and have Mrs McKay bring him up some tea and biscuits. That had always made him feel better, even as a child, when his mother would come up with cake and a glass of milk and stay a while to stroke his forehead and tell him how proud she was of him and what an illustrious future he had in prospect, in contrast to that waster of a father of his.

During his drive to the chapel house, Father Burke was engrossed in further thoughts of failure that only served to deepen his gloom. By the time he had put the car in the garage, let himself in the front door and hung up his coat, he had more or less decided that his only way out was to give up the priesthood entirely. It wasn't so difficult when he thought about it straight out like that. He would simply leave Ireland quickly and for good and go to some remote South American country, where he could live the life of a peasant and where his mother would never find him.

"Mrs McKay, whenever you've got a minute, would you get . . . " The young priest stopped and stared. Then he looked away, blinked and slowly returned his gaze to what had brought him to a dead halt in the doorway of the kitchen. On the table, which had been set for one, were the remains of what must certainly have been a sumptuous meal. In one corner was an empty soup bowl flanked by three vegetable dishes containing what remained of sweetcorn, broccoli and asparagus tips. The skins of two baked potatoes propped each other up on an adjacent plate. In a casserole dish the chicken bones and ruby-coloured sauce suggested a coq au vin, while the plate behind it showed the last vestiges of a mammoth slice of Black Forest Gateau. Worse was to come. In the middle of the table was a wine bottle – Chateauneuf du Pape, he could read it from where he stood – and it was completely empty. In the ashtray there was further cause for horror where two cigarette butts had been extinguished. And finally, beside the pepper and salt cellars – the best silver-plated ones from the china cabinet – was an empty brandy glass, held in the hand of the sleeping Mrs McKay whose mouth and legs were both wide open.

Father Burke put his hand out to support himself on the door jamb. The whole world seemed to be falling about his ears. And could he believe what his eyes were telling him?

"Mrs McKay!" he said, and his words came out in a high-pitched tone. He tried again in a deeper voice. "Mrs McKay!"

This time she stirred, blinked her eyes open and sat looking at him with a glazed expression for a few moments. Then she gave him a lopsided smile.

"Ah it's yourself, Father. I didn't expect you back until this evening."

In the circumstances, thought Father Burke, her speech was surprisingly clear. Perhaps she was used to heavy drinking.

"That, Mrs McKay, is patently obvious. This is absolutely disgraceful behaviour, not to mention an abuse of parish funds."

The eyes of the housekeeper narrowed and she seemed to gather a cloak of sobriety around her. "Parish funds, is it?" Her lancing tone reminded the priest uncomfortably of his own mother's combative style. "Parish funds, indeed. I'll have you know that all of this – " she swept her hand above the table, " – all of this was bought by yours truly out of the reduced wages that I've had to endure since the Canon, God bless him, left this house." Her look defied him to answer, but he made bold.

"Perhaps so, Mrs McKay, perhaps so," Father Burke said quickly, "but there can be no excuse for such a show of drunken excess in a Catholic – indeed a Church – household. It's a disgrace." He felt he no longer needed the support of the door and clasped his hands gravely before him. "Mrs McKay, I'm sorry, but I'm going to have to consider your future here very seriously indeed." The housekeeper leant on the edge of the table and rose a little unsteadily to her feet. "Future, Father? What future?" she said. "Underpaid, overworked, running in and out day and night like a scalded cat to answer the 'phone to people wanting to know about miracles. Walking to the Inisbreen Stores to get robbed by that Frank Kilbride now that the car – " she drew a sneer onto her face, " – is for restricted use only." The young priest fidgeted with a button of his soutane. This was a point of some sensitivity. "And another thing while I'm at it," Mrs McKay continued, warming to her task, "the food I've had to eat since you came here isn't fit for a donkey. Porridge and turnips and carrots! I don't know what kind of food they serve in the chapel houses of the South, but it's not what I'm used to and it's not what I'll be having from now on." She lined him up and fixed him in her sights. "If this is some idea of making sacrifices, then perhaps you should go and live in a monastery." There was a short silence, during which time the young priest stood looking at the older woman as though he was about to burst into tears.

"And now," she said, taking a deep breath and smoothing down the front of her dress, "if you will excuse me, I've got work to do."

She turned away from him and began to gather up the plates. For a little time Father Burke hovered in the doorway as if he had something to say but could not quite find the words. At last he said in a subdued voice,

"Mrs McKay, I may as well tell you that, due to recent events in this parish, I don't feel that I can continue my work here. In fact," he cleared his throat, " I have come to the conclusion that this is not my true vocation and that I should leave the priesthood entirely."

Mrs McKay stopped gathering the plates. For a moment she stood with her head slightly lowered before slowly turning to face Father Burke. She regarded him with soft, motherly eyes and said,

"Well now, Father, that's a very big decision. A very big decision indeed, and not one that should be taken in the heat of the moment." He made as if to speak, although in truth he had little to say, having got no further than the blind resolve to rid himself somehow of his intolerable burden. Then the housekeeper said quietly to him,

"Father, maybe if you would care to go up to your bedroom and have a wee lie down, I'm sure you must be exhausted, I could bring you up a cup of tea and a nice piece of cake. How would that do?"

As Father Burke gave a silent nod and turned towards the stairs, he felt the first glimmer of hope that things might just work out after all. They always had done when Mother had taken charge.

Because of the influx of reporters to the Glens Hotel, for the first time ever during the off-season, Mr Pointerly and the Misses Garrison had been placed at the same table, and they showed even less signs of pleasure than normal at the forthcoming meal. Cissy sat with her eyes screwed up in concentration, as though she were making detailed calculations, while her sister and Mr Pointerly made minute rearrangements to the cutlery and studied the pattern of blotches on the table cloth to see what breed of creature would slowly emerge from the soup and gravy stains. Only one of the other tables was occupied, although a number were reserved for reporters, some of whom were still queuing outside the toilets on each of the two floors. One squat, grey-haired reporter from the Galway Telegraph, who looked like nothing so much as a granite chip, had simply come out of a toilet on the first floor and immediately joined the end of the queue again, having shrewdly calculated that the waiting time for the toilet almost exactly coincided with that between his attacks of what he called "the Kerry two-step". In front of him a tall man with a grave face held his legs tightly together and breathed carefully while frequently consulting his watch.

"Did you guys ever stay in a place like this in your entire life?" the American reporter at one table asked his two companions, one of whom was a Londoner of Asian extraction who was determined to find a sex angle in the miracle story. The other was Mr Patel, who had come to England from India with his BA Eng. Lit.(failed) and to his surprise had quickly landed a job as a reporter on a daily tabloid. The Londoner said,

"Not me. There's a chippy on the Commercial Road that runs it a close second, though."

Mr Patel was more positive.

"They say that there are eating-houses in Calcutta where the holy man blesses you before you go in, and if you manage to walk out, he demands a fee." He gave a smile which was not returned by his companions. "I think perhaps we will see a holy man with a begging bowl when we leave here."

After a few moments consideration the American said,

"God dammit, you know what? I think I'll forget this miracle story and write a piece about this place. Except they'd never believe it back home."

The Londoner looked at a notepad he had been scribbling in and said,

"How about this? 'No Sex For Miracle Man Who Loses Stiffness After 68 Years.' What d'you think?"

"Jee-sus," the man from the Boston Globe-Tribune breathed and shook his head. "Listen, you guys, what d'you say we get the hell outa here and find somewhere that serves food fit for human consumption?"

"But I have not seen any other place near here," said the man who was almost a graduate in English literature.

"Look, I don't care if I've gotta drive from one end of the country to the other. I just want something decent to eat. What d'you say, Lou?"

"Lee," the Londoner said, without looking up from his notepad. Then he tapped his pencil against his teeth and asked, "What about – 'The Night The Senior Citizen Fell For The Virgin'? I'm with you, Don. Lead on."

The American pulled a face and said, "Dan. And how about you, Shrivna – eh – Mr Patel? You wanna join us?"

"Ah, this is the famous American pioneering spirit, no? Even if there is nothing there, you will find it." His eyes grew wide. "Yes. Perhaps even in this wilderness, there might be a curry house somewhere."

Rising from the table the American said,

"A curry house? Hell, no. I'm looking for an improvement on lunch, not a repeat performance."

As the three men walked through the foyer they met Dermot who glanced at his watch and said,

"Good evening, gentlemen. Are we not dining in tonight?"

Dan Kowalski, the American, shook his head and said,

"No sir, we're not dining in tonight. We haven't recovered from lunch yet. Tell me, where d'you get your cook? Dyno-Rod?"

"Ah – yes – very good." Dermot gave a little laugh then leant forward to say in a low voice, "She's not the best, I know, although she has her moments." Mr Patel rolled his eyes. "But she's only here in the off season."

Mr Patel said to Lee,

"I think this means that everything is off, yes?"

"Look," Dan Kowalski said, "is there anywhere else around here we could get a meal?"

"Well, you could try the Strand Hotel about five miles away, on the road to Castleglen. But it's their off-season too."

"Their cook isn't a sister of this one, by any chance?" Kowalski said.

"Well, if she is, she doesn't admit it. Ha ha."

The American started for the door, saying to Lee and Mr Patel,

"Okay, guys, let's go."

"Oh, by the way – guys," Dermot said. The three reporters stopped. "There isn't that much to do around here in the

evenings."

"You've noticed," Kowalski said.

"But tomorrow night, there's something that might be of interest to you. The Miracle Man, John McGhee? He's holding a big party. I won't be able to make it myself, but I'm sure you'd be very welcome. Apparently it's open to all comers. You could do worse than go along? Meet the man himself, have a few drinks, enjoy yourselves, and you never know," Dermot forced a laugh, "you might even pick up a good story for your newspapers."

The three journalists glanced at each other and variously

recalled venues from Tierra del Fuego to a Finnish forest in midwinter that had been more full of promise. Dan Kowalski said,

"If we're not whacked after playing dominoes, we'll maybe give it a try. It'll be the first time we've been able to clap eyes on this guy since we arrived here."

"Well, you can't miss it. It's in the house about quarter of a mile past the bridge. Big place, red roof, front gates rusted away. I'd say it should be at full steam about eleven o'clock or so."

When the three journalists had gone out of the front door, Dermot smiled and said,

"And then about twelve o'clock maybe you'll get a story that'll keep you writing all night." And he laughed and rubbed his hands together.

Ten minutes later, when the Winter Cook came banging through the door into the dining-room with fourteen plates of soup on her trolley, she stopped and surveyed a room that was empty save for her three regular diners. Slowly she shook her head and said,

"Jasus tonight, they've all gone. I told McAllister we were feeding the buggers too well!"

chapter seventeen

Limpy McGhee's big old Ford squeaked to a halt in the car park at the side of the Glens Hotel and gave a muffled bang before the engine shuddered two or three times and stopped. A few curses were laid on the head of a certain car salesman in Castleglen as Limpy fought to open the car door which, suddenly yielding, almost threw him face first out of the car.

"By Jasus!" he said, shaking his fist at the car, before slamming the door shut. A shower of rust flakes fell from the underside of it to the ground. Nevertheless, he stood for a moment, looking back and admiring the sweeping curves of the bonnet, the rake of the windscreen, the places where the hub caps should be. He was sure Cissy would be impressed.

Going through the little gate at the side of the hotel back yard, Limpy quickly took himself to the door leading to the back stairs, all the while keeping his eyes on the kitchen door further along the building, from which his sister Lizzie might well emerge at any moment. Safely inside, he was about to take the stairs to the first floor, when he stopped and rubbed his chin, scraped clean of stubble with a cut-throat razor he had sharpened on the back step of his house. Then opening the door to the hallway which led to the foyer, he looked out before walking quickly and quietly to the foot of the stairs, all the while listening intently and glancing around him. Leaning to one side, he looked through the open doorway into the empty sitting-room. He gave a little smile.

On the foyer table beside him, there was a brass bell, a newspaper waiting to be collected and a vase of dried flowers which had shed most of their petals and now looked more like a corn stook. Limpy pulled a face and tiptoed back down the hallway to the dining-room, where he poked his head round the door. And when he looked at the nearest table, he gave a big grin and crept into the room.

Standing outside Cissy's bedroom door, Limpy slapped his hair flat and straightened the mauve and puce tie which, not possessing an iron, he had laid under his mattress the night before in a vain attempt to flatten the kinks in it. He held up the bunch of dried flowers which he had taken from the dining-room table and gave a smile of satisfaction at the neatness of the fresh newspaper wrapping. Then he knocked lightly on the door. At first there was no reply, but after he knocked again, a little louder this time, a sleepy voice from within said,

"Yes, who is it?"

Limpy's reply was a further knock. After a few seconds the door was slowly opened and Cissy peered out.

"Oh, it's you. Well, I'm sorry, John, but I've got nothing to say to you. Please leave."

The door began to close but Limpy stuck his foot in the gap.

"Cissy, wait a minute now. I just want a word. I brought ye these." He thrust the bunch of flowers through the gap and into her hand. "Look, can I come in for a minute? I don't want the whole world knowing my business. Only for a minute, please."

"No, John, I don't – "

"For old times' sake, Cissy. For what we once meant to each other? I've got something important to tell ye."

Cissy looked at the old, lined face under the slapped-down hair. Then she slowly opened the door.

"Only for a minute, mind. And you'll stay by the door. I remember old times too, John McGhee."

Limpy gave a low chuckle.

"Ah, we had some good times, Cissy, eh? D'you remember when . . . "

"Just say your piece, John."

"Cissy, look. What happened in that bedroom with old Pointerly, that was none of my doing. That was a set-up job by Lizzie – Mrs Megarrity. You of all people should know I'm not like that."

Cissy looked away from him and her hand tightening on the bunch of flowers made the newspaper crackle.

"People can change. It's the best part of forty-five years."

"Ah Cissy, that's near a whole lifetime. Why didn't we do something, you and me?"

"You know the answer to that as well as I do. My family would never have allowed it."

"Well then we should've said to hell with them. And it's not too late now, Cissy. Look – " He took a step towards her and she moved backwards. "I've arranged a party on Saturday night – specially for you. It'll be a great night, darlin'. Music and dancing and a wee drink or two. Ye used to love parties, didn't ye? Tell me ye'll come to it."

"A party? For me?" She looked down at the flowers and began to pick at one with a tiny fingernail. "I – don't know. I mean, I haven't been to a party for – " Cissy slowly shook her head. "For half a lifetime."

"Then ye're long overdue for one." He stepped forward quickly and caught her by the arm. She did not resist. "Say ye'll come, Cissy."

"I – I really don't know, John. You know what Margaret's like and – "

"To hell with Margaret! Cissy Garrison, it's about time ye were yer own woman." He looked earnestly into her face. "C'mon, what d'ye say? For the first time in yer life, break free!"

Into Cissy's eyes crept a little twinkle of excitement which had not been there for a very long time.

"Well – I don't know. It would be nice, I suppose. And it has been such a long time."

Limpy clapped his hands together.

"That's my girl! Now ye're talking." He gave a little skip. "Boy, this is going to be one helluva night, I can tell ye!"

"Where's it going to be, this party? Oh, I hope Margaret doesn't throw one of her tantrums. You've no idea, when she gets started."

"Never you mind about Margaret." He gave a knowing smile. "And I'll provide the transport there and back for you. Chauffeur driven." He rubbed his hands together. "Ah, it'll be just like old times, Cissy, so it will. Just like old times. Leave everything to me."

"And – I'll need to think of something to wear. I'm sure I haven't got a single decent thing and – with us never going to social events, or anything . . . "

"Never worry about that. If ye put one of them bin bags on ye'd still look beautiful. Ye'll be the belle of the ball, Cissy."

Cissy lowered her eyes and gave a little smile.

"Oh, get away with you, John McGhee. You're as full of blarney as ever you were. Now, off you go and let me have a look through this bunch of old things I've got in the wardrobe." She gave a little sigh and said half to herself, "I just know I'll have to go to Castleglen to buy something new."

"I'm going, I'm going," Limpy said, hardly able to contain his excitement. Cissy looked at him for a moment.

"And for goodness sake, John McGhee, you haven't changed one bit." She turned and, lifting a brush from her dressing-table, she came over to him and began brushing his hair, saying, "Look at you. You're like something the cat dragged in." While he stood beaming, she put a parting in his grey hair and swept back the sides to give it a semblance of neatness. "There. That's a bit better. Now, off you go. But before you do – " She took the flowers from the paper and with a smile and a shake of her head she handed them to him. "It was a nice thought, but you can take these back down to the dining-room where they belong." She opened out the newspaper and began to smooth it. "And I'm sure Mr McAllister would like to read today's newspaper on – " Cissy stared at the front page of the Northern Reporter. "Oh – my God!"

"What? What is it?" Limpy came round beside her and looked down at the newspaper. Across two columns at the top of the page it said, "Amazing Sex Life of Miracle Man," and underneath in smaller type, "by Fergus Keane".

"Ah – Jasus," he said softly.

Cissy was rapidly scanning the article beneath, with phrases such as "many lovers" and "love nest on the hill" leaping out at her.

"Oh," she said and threw the newspaper from her to land on the floor. "How could you – embarrass me with this?"

"Ah now listen, Cissy, listen. Don't believe a word of that. He made it all up. Ye see, I told him ye thought I'd gone queer, and how bad I felt when ye wouldn't see me again. So the boy's only trying to do me a favour – get me back in your good books, like."

"Good books? Good books? John McGhee, you get out of this room at once! I never want to speak to you again! Ever!"

"Ah Cissy, don't be like that. Ye know there was never nobody but you."

Cissy marched to the door and flung it open.

"Out – you – you – gigolo! I wouldn't go to a party with you if you were the last man on earth!"

With fingers from both hands squeezed into the one small

handle, Limpy hauled at the door of the telephone box, using all of his strength and more than a little of his weight against the strong spring. No sooner had he got the door open far enough to dart inside than it came slamming back and threw him against the far side of the box. Angrily he kicked the bottom of the door.

"Bugger!" he said and then he began rummaging through his pockets, bringing out one coin from this pocket, two or three from that one, until he had a small pile on the shelf before him. He lifted the receiver, screwed up his eyes as he concentrated on remembering the number, before slowly and deliberately pressing the required buttons.

"Hello? Georgina, is that you?" he shouted into the receiver. As he recognised the voice, he smiled. "This is Johnny McGhee from Inisbreen here. Listen, Georgina, I'm having a party on Saturday night, and everybody and his brother's going to be there. It'll be the best bloody party this side of Ballymane, so it will, and I want ye to come – and bring yer girls with ye."

In the kitchen of the Glens Hotel the pots fairly rattled together as Mrs Megaritty nested them before putting them away in the cupboard under the sink. Wee Henry, who had brought the fish order and was now sitting at the table drinking tea and eating a sandwich that looked as if it had been cut with a hatchet, knew the signs well. Mrs Megarrity was on the warpath.

"What a set-up," she was saying. "What a bloody set-up. It's Soddomin Begorra all over again. I tell ye, that McAllister wants doctoring. Throwing out a decent wife like that so's he can put one up that little tart."

Wee Henry appeared to choke on a piece of bread but he made no comment.

"And now her at it behind his back with one of them bloody Englishmen. I knew all along she was nothing but a hot-arsed little scut. And her a convent girl too."

"Aye, them sort's often the worst," Wee Henry agreed absent-mindedly, and then, after proper consideration, "or the best, depending on your point of view."

Mrs Megarrity turned and gave him a look that had the little man's heart shrivelling inside of him. He gave a series of rapid blinks.

"For some people. I'm not – "

"Drunkards and fornicators every one of them! My mother, God rest her, would turn in her grave if she knew I was threw in with a crew like this – and me always wanting to be a nun when I was a child."

Wee Henry stared over his huge sandwich, his eyes widening as his brain struggled to imagine Mrs Megarrity in a nun's habit.

The Winter Cook pointed to the door into the hallway, which was slightly open.

"But I've got the wee bitch taped, so I have. There's something going on up there while he's down in the bar, and I'm just watching and waiting." She wagged an admonitory finger. "Watching and waiting, Wee Henry."

The Winter Cook continued with her work, attacking the dirty dishes with unaccustomed vigour while glancing frequently at the open door. Having fought his way through the outsized sandwich, Wee Henry proceeded to roll himself a cigarette so thin that it appeared to have scarcely any tobacco in it at all and when he lit it, the end flared momentarily like a Roman Candle. Now and then the Winter Cook would mutter something to herself and jab with the dish-mop at a particularly offensive plate. Then suddenly she stiffened and craned forward, watching something through the gap in the doorway.

"I knew it!" she said at last in a loud whisper. "There she goes now, and him up two minutes ahead of her." She quickly untied the strings of her apron, sweeping it from her waist and onto the table. "I'm going to put a knot in her knickers once and for all," the Winter Cook asserted. "You just see if I don't." She began to tiptoe towards the door.

No more than five minutes later, Mrs Megarrity came rushing back into the room and closed the door behind her, leaning against it and breathing heavily. There was a look of triumph on her face as she said,

"They're at it in number twenty-seven, hammer and tongs. The very same room they had to send for Doctor Walsh for them honeymooners last year. I told him a bucket of cold water round them would've done the job just as well, but no, it had to be injections. Now, Wee Henry," she said, grasping his arm and hauling him to his feet, "you're going to make a 'phone call."

"Me, Mrs Megarrity? Why me?" In his sudden ejection from his chair he had bent his roll-up, which now hung dejectedly from his mouth.

"Because McAllister would recognise my voice. Ye're going to be the man next door to them, wanting something done about the din they're making. Come over here."

By the shoulder she dragged him trotting behind her as she stalked across the room to where the old telephone was mounted on the wall. "Now, when McAllister answers in the bar, you tell him ye're in room twenty-five and there's a racket next door in twenty-seven and he'd better come up right now and do something about it. Have ye got that?"

"Yes but, Mrs Megarrity, he'll recognise my voice."

"Not if ye put on an English accent, he won't."

"I – don't think I want to do this, Mrs Megarrity. I mean, I've never – "

"Look," she said, catching the little man by the collar and propelling him towards the telephone, "either you 'phone McAllister right now or ye've slapped yer last haddock on my slab!"

For a man who had never been further than Dublin, Wee

Henry's imitation of an English accent was surprisingly good. Dermot tried to explain that he could not leave the bar unattended, but Wee Henry was very insistent, saying that his headache was being made ten times worse by "the devil of a noise coming from next door", and he demanded that Dermot do something about it "forthwith". Wearily, Dermot said that he would come up immediately and put a stop to it, and yes, he agreed that a decent hotel wouldn't tolerate such behaviour for a single moment.

When the shouting began, Mrs Megarrity was listening at the kitchen door, with Wee Henry half crouched behind her, as if suddenly overcome by the immensity of what he had done. As it was a warm day and some of the bedroom windows were open, three people strolling past the hotel at that moment also heard the commotion, and much to the entertainment of its occupants, the noise also came echoing down the back stairs to the bar below.

"You little bitch!" they heard Dermot shout. "I turn my back for five minutes and you're jumping into bed with somebody!"

"No, Dermot, listen, it's not like that."

"It's not like what? You're standing here in your underwear and he's just legged it down the corridor!"

"He never laid a finger on me!"

"It wasn't his finger I was on about."

There was a pause before Nancy was heard to retort,

"Well, we know why you could mistake it for a finger, don't we?"

There was a chorus of "Ooohs" from the crowd in the bar and gestures of knives being stuck between ribs.

"Is it any wonder, looking at you. You're like a beached whale!"

"Oh, you pig! You told me you adored puppy fat!"

"Puppy fat, darlin', not a sack of mongrels!"

The people in the street and in the bar below and even the Winter Cook and her vassal at the kitchen door, heard the sound of the ensuing slap. "Bitch!" "Bastard!" "Randy little whore!"

"Oh!"

In total silence the listeners waited for the rejoinder. "Bloody – impotent old lecher!"

Breath was drawn in sharply. Someone remarked that the teacher was now ahead by a good length, and in view of the previous remarks, the metaphor was generally taken to be a horse-racing one.

"Right, get your fat arse the hell out of here. I don't ever want to see you in this hotel again."

"Listen, I wouldn't come anywhere near you again even if your arse was studded with diamonds – which would be it's only attraction!"

Then came the sound of protest from Nancy and two sets of feet walking quickly. Everyone in the bar glanced up at the ceiling as they followed the progress of the pair. Along the corridor, down the flight of stairs to the half-landing, back through the short passageway, shouting at each other as they went. They were heading for the front door of the hotel. Without a word of co-ordination, the occupants of the bar rose as one and moved swiftly and silently towards the two windows of the lounge, those behind standing on chairs or kneeling on tables in order to see over the heads of those in front. Some went to the doorway and lounged against it, trying to look as if they had been there all day. In the kitchen, the Winter Cook and Wee Henry drew back a little from their observation point as the shouting and the thundering of feet on the stairs grew closer.

Nancy came out of the front door of the hotel and bent over to adjust one of her red high-heeled shoes, which John Breen said later should have told Dermot that she was up to no good.

The men in the doorway and at the window of the lounge bar craned forward the better to see this rear elevation, and it might have been thought by some that she lingered just a little longer than was strictly necessary over this adjustment. Then, having taken her keys from her handbag, she turned and walked slowly past the glens Hotel lounge towards her car, exaggerating her hip movements and tossing her long red hair. On reaching the car, the ex-teacher at the Catholic primary school who as a pupil herself had once been one of Sister Monica's Little Saint Brenda's in the Legion of Mary, half turned and gave a v-sign to the men inside, who smiled and gave a rousing cheer.

In the kitchen, Mrs Megarrity gently closed the door and said,

"There's a good job well done. That little trollop. Isn't it well seen what they say? 'Them that live by the sordid, die by the sordid.' I think this calls for a wee celebration, eh?" From beneath her apron she drew out a quarter bottle of whiskey, removed the cap and held up the bottle.

"Yer good health, Wee Henry. And ye can be sure of one thing." She gave a wicked smile. "Yer secret's safe with me."

Father Burke stared out of the window as he contemplated his future, not only as newly-appointed parish priest at Inisbreen, but as any kind of priest anywhere. The thought of his mother's reaction to his inevitable disgrace he thrust firmly into the deepest recess of his mind. It was too awful to contemplate. It was now all too clear that this man McGhee was a fraud who had tricked everyone into believing that he had been the subject of a miracle, and this for the worst possible motives – money and self-aggrandisement. That a bunch of gullible natives had fallen for it, he could understand, but that he himself with his trained, analytical mind should have succumbed to this fakery was beyond comprehension. When

McGhee admitted that the miracle was a fake, as he surely would, the disaster would be complete. Mrs McKay had managed to persuade him to delay his decision to leave the priesthood, but it was only a matter of time before Bishop Tooley would be on the telephone asking for his resignation. Then his only honourable course of action would be to seek refuge with a silent order of monks, where even the most inquisitive of men would not be able to ask him any awkward questions. Father Burke had a momentary picture of himself with a suitcase, trudging along the road out of Inisbreen in the rain and vainly trying to thumb a lift, with cars swishing past, people laughing behind fogged-up windows. Such a promising future, and now all turned to ashes in his mouth. He moaned and held his head between his hands.

Mrs McKay startled him by coming into the room without knocking.

"More prayers, Father?" she said briskly. "You might leave a little of the Lord's attention for the rest of us who'd maybe need it a bit more than yourself." She set a tray down on his desk. "I've brought you a nice wee cup of tea – and a piece of your favourite cake."

"Oh – yes, thank you, Mrs McKay."

For a few moments the housekeeper looked at the young parish priest.

"Father Burke, you can't keep anything from me. I've been in this trade too long. You're still worrying yourself sick over this miracle business, aren't you?"

He glanced quickly up at her and then away. It was almost like being in the presence of Mother, and at some of those times he had felt that his mind was an open book to her. Father Burke's shoulders sagged and he lifted both hands in an attitude of despair.

"Mrs McKay – there's no getting away from it, I've been a fool. Now there's nothing else for it. I'll just have to pack my bags and go – after I confess to the Bishop that the man's a fake." He looked up at his housekeeper and smiled ruefully. "I do believe you might just have suggested that possibility to me at the outset."

Mrs McKay placed the tea and cake before the priest and then sat down on the chair at the side of his desk.

"Well, you might be right, Father, you might be right. Who knows. But, did you ever think – maybe it doesn't matter all that much whether it was a miracle or not?"

The young priest turned and spoke round a mouthful of cake.

"What d'you mean, it doesn't matter? Of course it matters."

"Begging your pardon, Father, but the Canon used to say 'The Good Lord works in mysterious ways'. And if this has strengthened some people in their religion and brought others back to it – not to mention putting a bit of extra money in the plate – well, maybe that's not such a bad thing – whatever it was."

"But – Mrs McKay, you were dead against the whole thing from the beginning."

"Oh, I know I was, Father, I know. But I've been giving it some thought. And anyway, that was then. This is now. The Canon would say you've got to go from where you're at."

"The Canon was obviously full of handy little sayings. Mrs McKay, what are you suggesting? That we turn a blind eye to fraud?"

"Not exactly, Father. Not exactly. And of course, we don't know that for sure. I mean, you could go ahead and denounce the whole thing as a fake and that you'd made a terrible mistake, been taken in by an old eejit like Limpy McGhee. You could do that, Father. Tell the parishioners – tell the Bishop – let all the newspapers and television know. But, whatever you or anybody else says, at the end of the day the people'll make up their own minds, and there's nothing any of us can do about that. Because there's people out there, Father, who are getting some kind of – well – comfort out of this. They maybe need to believe in it, you know?"

Mrs McKay shrugged and looked into the soft brown eyes that were now regarding her with rapt attention. Father Burke sighed and said,

"There is a certain logic in what you say, Mrs McKay. I can't deny that. If people want to believe in it – if it strengthens their faith – then no doubt they will, regardless of what the Church says."

"And then, Father – wouldn't that be a kind of miracle itself?"

Father Burke slowly nodded.

"I daresay anything that gave the people of Inisbreen a greater faith in God and made them attend Mass more regularly could be described as verging on the miraculous, yes."

"And you wouldn't want to be the one standing up and saying they were all wrong, Father, now would you? Especially if there was no evidence to the contrary." Mrs McKay shifted her gaze to the window and through it to the sunlit field where some cattle clustered around a drinking trough. "And the Bishop had given it his approval."

"The Bishop, given his approval? I hardly think in the circumstances – "

"If he did, Father. I mean, if he – visited the Mass Rock site, for instance. That sort of thing."

"Mrs McKay," the priest said with a smug little smile, "I do believe I have some powers of persuasion – otherwise I would hardly have followed this vocation – but at this juncture, given what has unfolded, I don't think that even I could persuade the Bishop of Down and Connor to come and visit the Mass Rock, far less give it his official approval as a possible miracle site."

Again the housekeeper looked away from Father Burke and

out through the window her eyes following the road between the hills that led to Ballymane and eventually to Belfast.

"Maybe not, Father," she said slowly. "Maybe not. But there might be somebody else that could."

chapter eighteen

Mr Pointerly had been walking up the village street early on Friday afternoon when, much to his surprise, the little fat fellow with the cap pulled down over his eyes swaggered – or perhaps it was staggered – over to him and said that there was going to be a party at his house on Saturday night "with a few of the boys", and he was welcome to come along. Of course, he had accepted with alacrity, imagining all sorts of delights awaiting him when he got there, and for the rest of that day and most of the Saturday, he could think of little else. When had he last been to a party with "a few of the boys"? Probably not since that time in London, years ago, when someone had recommended that he go to a bar near Covent Garden – the "Gay Hussar" was it? – and he had met a nice young man who had invited him to a party in a house nearby. But it had been a dreadful affair, all dim pink lights, cheap wine and people dressed in the most outlandish clothes imaginable. What with the lipstick, the rouge and the coloured hair, the whole thing had reminded him of nothing so much as a circus. One of them, who must have been all of sixty and was wearing a sequinned dress and a pearl choker, had said, "Irish, darling? I didn't know there were any of us left over there. I thought Saint

Patrick had banished all of us with the snakes." Now Mr Pointerly was striding out along the road to Pig Cully's house, in the expectation that this party would be a more gentlemanly affair than the last one and conducted with suitable decorum.

If Limpy was feeling any sadness at the absence of Cissy Garrison, then he was certainly keeping it well hidden. In Pig Cully's house, hastily cleaned for the occasion, Limpy and his two joint hosts had worked their way through a crate of stout and the best part of a bottle of Bushmills by the time the first guests arrived. In the large living-room where the event was being held, the sideboard was covered with bottles containing alcohol of every imaginable type, whilst the table beside it attested to the fact that the Inisbreen Stores had been cleaned out of cakes, buns and pastries. Frank Kilbride had seldom had such an opportunity to get rid of old stock. In the corner, Cully had set himself up to play a selection of records, ranging from old seventy-eights of Dame Nelly Melba and Count John McCormack to a whining Country and Western singer who sounded, Limpy declared, "as if he had his bollicks caught in a gin-trap".

After an elderly couple, whose idea of a good night was mugs of cocoa and a few hands of gin rummy at home, there arrived the two saturnine Burns brothers with their tanned leather faces and white bald heads. They merely nodded in reply to Limpy's greeting, took a whiskey each and found places near the corner, where they sat in silence, staring and sipping. Pig Cully looked around the room, shook his head and said,

"A real humdinger of a party."

Suddenly the record on the radiogram struck up with "After The Ball Was Over". Ignoring the irony in this, Limpy marched over to Dan Ahearn, bowed deeply and said in a tone of exaggerated politeness,

"Would you care for to dance, Mr Ahearn. I kept this one specially for you."

"Well jeez-o, Mr McGhee, very nice of you to ask, I'm sure," Dan Ahearn replied in kind. "I don't mind if I do."

And so the two men, grasping each other like wrestlers, stumbled off around the floor, more or less in time to the music. Pig Cully poured himself another drink, shook his head and pulled his cap further down over his eyes.

"D'ye come here often?" Dan Ahearn asked.

"Naw, only in the mating season."

"And what d'you think of the band?"

"Oh, they're awfully good. Yer man there playing the scratches is marvellous."

"Excuse me."

"Why, what've ye done?"

"No, excuse me," the voice said, and a hand tapped Dan Ahearn's shoulder. It was Mr Pointerly, who had just arrived. "This is an excuse me, isn't it?" He beamed at Limpy. "I thought you and I might have a little – " He made a walking movement with his fingers.

"Ah – Mr Pointerly. How did ye – know about the party?"

"Oh, your friend over there – Mr – Tully, is it? He told me I'd be very welcome. 'A few of the boys', he said." Mr Pointerly gave a smile and a little wave to Pig Cully across the room, while behind Mr Pointerly's back, Limpy shook a fist at Pig Cully.

"My dear Mr McPhee," Mr Pointerly said in a confidential whisper, "I really must apologise for what happened the other evening – in the hotel. I believe I interpreted your note a little too literally."

"My – note? Oh – yes. Well, don't you worry about it, Mr Pointerly. At least now ye know I'm not a horse's hoof, like yerself."

"Oh. I – well, I thought when I saw you dancing with – " He

indicated Dan Ahearn, who stood looking at them vacantly.

"Ah no," Limpy chuckled, "that was only a wee joke to make Mr Cully there jealous. I'm straight as a die myself." Limpy leant close to Mr Pointerly and was subjected to the full force of his after-shave lotion, which Dermot said retailed in the Inisbreen Stores at a quid a gallon, ten percent discount if you brought your own bucket. Limpy appeared to gasp with excitement. "Mr Cully over there, he's yer man, Mr Pointerly. Keen as mustard, he is. But shy, Mr Pointerly, shy. Needs the experienced touch, if you get my meaning."

"Really?" Mr Pointerly's face lit up.

"But, don't go whipping nothing out, Mr Pointerly. Some of these older ladies haven't seen fresh meat in a long time."

"Thank you very much indeed, Mr McPhee," the old man said, giving Limpy's arm a squeeze and then moving directly towards Pig Cully in the corner.

"No bother, Mr Pointerly. If I can do a friend a favour – "

On the turntable, the needle ran through the last few bars of the tune.

"Yer next dance please!" Dan Ahearn bellowed, entering into the spirit of things.

In the corner, Pig Cully had at last escaped the attentions of Mr Pointerly by telling him that it must have been his cousin that McGhee meant. He himself was as straight as a brush shaft. At this, Mr Pointerly had fluttered his eyelids and gone to get a drink and look for Cully's non-existent cousin.

In the next fifteen minutes the number of people at the party doubled. One of the first to come in was Peggy May, resplendent in a cerise taffeta dress. It had come from a jumble sale, the original owner having been a good six inches taller, and Peggy May's needlework in shortening the dress had left the hem looking as if it were held up with baler twine. Her make-up clearly owed a debt to the local method of whitewashing a cow byre, applied as it was without thought of expense or expanse. Her lipstick was dayglo bright, her orange eyeshadow gave the impression of twin suns setting each time she blinked and two green disc earrings stuck out from the sides of her head. The ensemble was designed to impress, and it certainly had this effect on Pig Cully, who pushed his cap back, took a long look at Peggy May and exclaimed,

"Holy heavens!" then quickly glanced round to make sure that Mr Pointerly was out of earshot. "Hollywood comes to Inisbreen, eh?"

Dan Ahearn cocked his head to one side, looked Peggy May up and down, then drawled,

"What're ye talking about, Man? She looks like a set of feckin' traffic lights."

"Ye're right," Pig Cully said, rubbing his hands together, "and they all say 'Go'!"

From O'Neill's pub which they had left in good time to return before closing if the party was no good, came five or six men including Johnny Spade with his rolling walk and "Hiya McGhee", followed by young Moore who, as a matter of course, made a playful snatch at Limpy's crotch. The men got themselves a drink and something to eat from the table then ranged themselves on the seats around the walls. Pig Cully had cornered Peggy May by the sideboard and was attempting to persuade her that neat whiskey was the best thing to ensure that she kept a clear head the next morning. Beside the window, Limpy put another record on the radiogram and started it playing with a thump of his hand. As a fiddle struck up with "She'll Be Coming Round The Mountain", he let out a whoop and set off round the floor, hopping stiff-legged on one foot while the other pawed the air in front of him. One by one the others began to clap in time to the music, and the more they clapped and whooped, the greater the energy and antics he employed. And when the noise from the partygoers was almost drowning out the music and Limpy was whirling and whooping like a thing possessed, the four prostitutes from Ballymane walked into the room.

The one at the front, who was the eldest and was obviously the leader, was wearing a skirt so short that in other circumstances it might have qualified as a broad belt. Her bleached hair was done in an extravagant bouffant style above a fat face heavy with powder, fly-swat eyelashes and cherry-red lips in a perfect Cupid's bow. Beneath an apparently see-through crocheted jumper her huge breasts strained and shook as she teetered across the floor in shoes with vertiginous heels. She was followed by the three others, two of whom were plain in looks if no less garish in appearance than the first. The last woman was the youngest, no more than twenty-two or -three, and despite the heavy make-up was by far the prettiest of the four. As the ladies of pleasure lined up as if for inspection, the men did not know where to look first, whether at the lacy jumper of the big woman or at the pretty face and long slim legs of the youngest of them. Pig Cully had abruptly left Peggy May and was staring in open admiration at the four women. Young Moore's mouth gaped open before he managed to whisper,

"God Almighty! D'y'ever see anythin' like that in yer life?"

"Johnny McGhee," the big woman said through a huge smile. She extended a fat hand festooned with jewellery. "Delighted to see you again, lover. Thank you so much for inviting us." She shook his hand and then held it. "And aren't you the big celebrity now? My girls and I have been following every word in the papers, so we have. Isn't that right, girls? And what's this we've been reading about you in the Northern Reporter?" Her smile grew even wider and her eyes narrowed to emulate it. "I think you've been holding out on us, Johnny."

"Ah now," Limpy said, "ye don't want to believe all ye read

in the papers," he said with a smile of delight. "They were exaggerating as usual. It was only two women a night – not three like they said."

"Oh, you are a one, Johnny. I can see I'll need to keep a tight grip on you," Georgina said. "It's not every day I get my hands on a man that's both good-looking and rich!" She threw back her head and gave a deep, husky laugh, Dan Ahearn's staring eyes moving in unison with the shaking of her great bosom.

"Jay-sus McGonagle!" he breathed and one of his legs began to tremble.

"Ye're very welcome, girls!" Limpy cried, flourishing his free hand. "Just what we need to get these boys into the swing of things. Boys! These are friends of mine from Ballymane. Georgina," he indicated the fat woman, "Dolores and Pamela," he nodded towards the plain ones, "and Lucille." Lucille gave a sly smile and cocked a leg which made more violent the shaking in Dan Ahearn's corresponding limb. In the corner, Peggy May feigned disinterest in the brazen show by the four women.

"Cully! Throw on a record there and let her go, boy!" Limpy shouted, and wheeling the big woman round he backed her onto the space on the floor that had been cleared for dancing. With half an eye on the three spare women, Pig Cully hastily set a record in motion. As the first notes of the accordion band blared out, Limpy shouted,

"Take your pick, boys," and was almost whirled off his feet in the arms of Georgina. Young Moore and Spade leapt forward like greyhounds out of traps, Moore to face Lucille and Kiernan in front of Pamela. Pig Cully and Dan Ahearn collided in their rush to Dolores and there was pushing and tugging of jackets before Dan Ahearn broke free and grabbed her hand to pull her onto the dancing area. The old couple had observed all of this with equanimity, while Mr Pointerly sat with his long nose in the air and wondered which one was Mr Tully's cousin.

Consoling himself with another drink, Pig Cully trudged back to the sideboard to stand near Peggy May, who pointedly ignored him.

As the evening progressed, the living-room – large as it was – gradually filled with people, so that the area left for dancing became smaller and the dancers were more tightly packed. Any communication had to be shouted above the noise of laughter and whooping and the music from the radiogram which someone had turned up to full volume. Beside it, an old man sat swaying at the window, his elbow on the sill and his chin supported by his hand. Blearily he opened his eyes. Not six inches from him, on the other side of the window, he saw a sallow face with slant eyes looking back at him. He sprang back.

"God Almighty!"

His elbow slipped off the sill, which his chin hit with a thump and he fell to the floor.

"Ye're drunk, ye old eejit," the man next to him said, helping him to his feet. "It's time ye were away home to yer bed."

"Tommy, listen to me! There's – a Chinaman out there. I swear to God. Yella face and slanty eyes."

Tommy shook his head and said to his wife,

"I think he's gone completely, Maggie. Ten minutes ago it was a ghost. Now it's a bloody Chinaman."

Two minutes later, at the door of the living-room appeared the three newspapermen, Dan the American, Lee from London and Mr Patel, whom the other two sometimes called Shriv.

"My God," Dan Kowalksi said, as he stared at the mass of swaying and writhing bodies and the wall of heat hit them, "this looks like one helluva shindig! Let's hope there's some booze left."

Led by the American, the three pushed their way round the

edge of the room, Mr Patel nodding an apology to everyone he pushed past and Lee writing in his notebook as he went. Having helped themselves to drinks at the table, they squeezed themselves into a space at the corner of the room and began to take stock of the female guests. Immediately, Lee's interest was aroused by Lucille, his eyes following her every move until she had come off the dance floor, when he stepped quickly forward and asked her to dance with him. When he had surveyed the field and made a choice, Mr Patel decided to have another drink before asking her to dance. It was pretty obvious what she was from her appearance – cerise taffeta dress, dayglo lipstick and orange eyeshadow – but he could put it on expenses, and at least he would be sure of a good time with a professional. However, his intentions were temporarily frustrated when Johnny Spade went over to Peggy May who was standing forlornly in the corner. With a great tug which almost lifted his feet from the floor, he hitched up his trousers, narrowed his eyes to a killer gaze and said to her,

"C'mon Babe, wind up yer dancing gear and let's cruise."

"Oh, I'm not very good at dancing, Mr Kiernan. Mammy says I've got two left feet and a backside like the hind end of a horse."

"Ah there's nothing to it," he said and executed a series of drunken hops. "That there's the foxtrot and the waltz is the same thing but a bit slower. Ye'll pick her up as ye go along." He grabbed her hand and began pushing his way towards the dancing area. Pig Cully, who had been fetching a drink for Peggy May, was just in time to see her go off with Johnny Spade. Pig Cully shoved the drink onto the sideboard, intent on saving Peggy May's honour at all costs, but as he turned to follow them he found Pamela standing before him, her low-cut dress revealing her full and heaving chest. Her hand ran up his arm and squeezed it.

"I don't believe I've had the pleasure," she purred. Her

other hand slipped to his waist and began to massage it. Pig Cully gave a little whine. Taking this as assent, Pamela pulled him towards the middle of the floor, where Johnny Spade was dancing with Peggy May, his elbows flapping like he was trying to take flight. Mr Patel shook his head, threw back his drink and said something to himself in Gujurati.

Dan Ahearn stood grasping the edge of the table as he swayed back and forth, a whirlygig of bottle shapes racing before his eyes. Beside him was Limpy, bathed in sweat and with his shirt open to the waist.

"By God," he took a great draught of stout from his glass and some of it ran down his chin, "this is one hoor of a party, Ahearn – and the pubs is not out yet. They'll be dancing on the roof before the night's out!"

"Did ye see that – " Dan Ahearn started, then ground to a halt. He took a deep breath and tried again. "Have ye seen that woman, that – ye know, the one with the dress." He took his hands off the table long enough to describe a vee at his chest but replaced them quickly to avoid falling on his face. "Jeez-o. Y'ever see anythin' like that, McGhee?" One hand was raised to slap the other, which couldn't be raised to meet it. "Where'n hell did ye get her from? She's some woman. D'you think – would she take a walk out wi' me?"

"I'm sure she would, Dan – if ye've got the money."

"Money for what? We'd only be going for a walk." He shook his head gravely, still barely able to believe that this goddess of love was so amply proportioned and generously displayed. "She's one helluva woman."

Blear-eyed he scanned the floor for Lucille who had just picked up Dippy Burns from where he had been wedged in a corner, observing the proceedings and wondering about the dangers of contagious diseases in such a hot and crowded environment. Lucille had had no success with any of her dance partners, who at the mention of money had decided that they were urgently required elsewhere. This time it was Lucille's turn to dump her partner when he gave her a gawky smile as they took to the floor and without benefit of introduction said straight off,

"I don't suppose ye'd know anything about tertiary syphilis, but ye'd never believe what happened to me."

In the corner near the radiogram, Limpy was sitting on the vast lap of Georgina, whose face was red from the exertions of dancing. In between sips from a concoction of various liquors, she nibbled at the ear of the Miracle Man and kept his ardour warm by gently massaging his inner thigh. Later she might work up to his wallet.

"Mr McGhee," the voice shouted above the din. Someone in the middle of the room was doing a Highland Fling, urged on by a circle of clapping and whooping spectators.

"Well, damn me, if it isn't young Fergus Keane." Limpy grabbed the young reporter's hand and pumped it. "How're ye, boy? Have ye had a drink? There's enough here to float a friggin' battleship. Georgina, this here's the reporter that made me famous," he said. "He got the scoop."

Fergus Keane was having a little difficulty staying upright and he put an arm on Limpy's shoulder.

"Mr McGhee." Fergus crooked a finger. "C'mere. Did I do it for you – or what? Eh? A friend in need is – indeed – a friend in – need, eh?" Fergus gave a drunken laugh. "No half measures, Mr McGhee. Three a night. No more talk now about you being a horse's hoof, eh?"

"Well, there's been no more talk from my woman, full stop. I'm thinking maybe ye overdid it a bit there, young Fergus. But yer heart was in the right place. I daresay she'll come round soon enough." He laughed. "All the rest of the women have."

Fergus grabbed Limpy's wrist and held his arm aloft in a victory salute.

"Three-times-a-night McGhee!" he shouted. "The Miracle Man!" And then his eyelids flickered and closed, his legs gently buckled and with one graceful if involuntary movement he flopped into the armchair beside Limpy, who looked down at him for a moment and said,

"By Jeez, it's hard work writing lies, eh?" Then he and Georgina laughed and the big woman reached over to pat the unconscious Fergus gently on the cheek.

"Lovely young man."

"Mr McGhee." A big hand shot out, grasped one of Limpy's and shook it vigorously. "Dan Kowalski. Boston Globe-Tribune. Very pleased to make your acquaintance at last, sir. You're a hard man to track down. Now, Mr McGhee, I'd very much like to do a personal and exclusive story on you and your miraculous experience. There's a helluva lot of interest in this back home, especially in Boston. Big Irish population, you know? A story like this from the old country? Goldust, Mr McGhee, goldust."

"Well, very pleased to make your acquaintance, Mr Gomulski, but I'm afraid I can't do any interviews." Limpy pulled himself up to his full height and adjusted the lapels of his suit, which was now giving off a strong odour similar to that of a very old and incontinent dog. "I've already sold the exclusive rights to an English publication – for a very considerable sum. I'm sorry, Mr Gromoski."

Dan Kowalski gave a broad smile.

"I think you got the wrong end of the stick, Mr McGhee. Let me explain. What I want to do is publish your story in North America. Wouldn't affect your English deal at all."

"It – wouldn't?"

"No sir. Look, let me lay a scenario on you. This is how I see it. I carry out an in-depth interview – you know, childhood, career, religious background, neighbourhood, how the miracle happened – that sort of thing? Take two, three days, I guess. I'd write it up then we'd run it in the Globe-Tribune and syndicate it – all over the States and Canada – South America too, I guess. Maybe one day a week for a four- or five-week series. And your face, Mr McGhee, would be on the front page of every newspaper from Saskatoon to San Antonio."

Limpy McGhee looked suitably impressed.

"Well now, that would be something, wouldn't it? And – what kind of remuneration would we be talking about here, Mr Graminski, for my story, like?"

"For that kind of thing? Oh, I guess we got to be talking about – fifty. Dollars, that is. We can work out the details later. You won't find the Globe-Tribune backward when it comes to paying out for a big story, Mr McGhee."

"Fifty? Jasus, I got a lot more than that from the English fella."

"You got more than fifty thousand dollars from an English newspaper?"

Limpy staggered back two steps and sat down heavily in Georgina's lap. They said in unison,

"Fifty – thousand – dollars?"

"Well, it could be a little more. Depends how things turn out. We'll start at fifty anyway. What d'you say, Mr McGhee? Exclusive American, Canadian and South American rights. Do we have a deal?"

Limpy's body seemed to sag under his jacket, which now appeared to have the ability to stand up on its own. In a small voice he said,

"Where do I sign, Mr Kramuski?"

About three hundred yards from Pig Cully's house, halfway up a hill that was partly covered in trees and bushes, three men, late of the Glens Hotel bar, had another drink from a whiskey bottle before starting their work. The smallest of them stepped forward. He was Seumas Kernohan, whose widowed mother had lain stricken for six years with nervous debilitation and whose only relief came from the weekly laying on of hands in private by the butcher, who was reputed to be very effective at that sort of thing. At any rate, it had always left Mrs Kernohan with a smile on her face. To one of Seumas's legs a torch was tied with the lens pointing upwards. Then he was helped up into a small tree, where a rope was passed around his thighs and the tree trunk before being tied at the back. A white garment was produced from a carrier bag and placed over the young man by John Breen. With the robe in place, a hood falling forward nicely to cover much of the face and the bottom hem reaching past Seumas's feet, the other two drew back to judge the effect.

"Switch on the torch there, Seumas."

The torch was lit, sending a glow of light upwards that caught the whole garment and gave it an ethereal appearance that was most effective in the darkness.

"Jasus!" John Breen said, "That's brilliant. I can't wait to see the wee bugger's face. McAllister'll be sorry he missed this. Raise yer arms, Seumas!" The arms were duly raised. "Spot bloody on, boy. Now, let's hear the voice."

After a clearing of the throat there came on the night air a moaning, female voice.

"Limpy McGhee, you have been telling the world a pack of lies about me."

All three of them laughed.

"Marvellous! Bloody marvellous! Right, Michael, away down and get him, just like I told ye."

When Michael Maguire rushed into Pig Cully's living-room, eyes wide with fright and hair nicely standing on end, he shouldered his way through the crowd to where Limpy was gulping down a large glass of whiskey held in his two shaking hands. The prospect of a cheque with his name and "Fifty Thousand Dollars" written on it was more than his fuddled brain could encompass without a huge leap of the imagination, assisted by a large measure of alcohol.

"McGhee! Come quick! There's a – woman in white out there – all glowing and floating in the air! And she's asking for you!" Michael Maguire grabbed the little man's arm and pulled at him. "Come on for God's sake, McGhee, and make it go away. It's frightening the bejasus outa me!" Limpy blinked a few times and then fixed the messenger with an imperious gaze. "A woman in white, did ye say? Floating in the air?" "And asking for you, McGhee. Asking for you."

"And where is she?"

"Up at the Mass Rock. Come on for feck sake!" The old man's eyes drifted heavenward and he said with reverence in his voice,

"It's her. I knew she'd come back." He rose swaying to his feet and said to Georgina, whose look of wide-eyed innocence and amazement was a stranger to her face, "Excuse me, Georgina, but the Virgin Mary's asking for me."

Then with regal if unsteady gait he walked slowly behind Michael Maguire who bulldozed a way for him through the throng of people, a Saint John the Baptist preparing the way for the Messiah. Within a few seconds, the record that had been playing was abruptly stopped and from one group of people to another the message crackled around the room like an electric current. Then as one man, the occupants of the room surged towards the door, all except Mr Patel who, in the sudden silence could explain better to a bewildered Peggy May the necessity of her providing him with a receipt for the services which he hoped she was about to supply.

Outside, the night was clear and a bright moon sailed in a cloudless sky, throwing a wan light over the crowd that moved in silence out of the house and through what Pig Cully referred to as "the back garden", a plain grassy patch formerly littered with abandoned domestic appliances and farming implements.

Ahead of them, dragged at a half run by the pointing Michael Maguire, went Limpy, his jacket flapping out behind him like dark angel wings in the cool breeze.

"Where did ye say she was, son? I can't see nothing." His breath wheezed in his chest from the exertion.

"Up there it was, Mr McGhee. On the hill."

He pointed to an area halfway up the hill and behind the Mass Rock, in front of which was an extensive thicket of whin bushes, into which even the most wayward of sheep would not have ventured. In like manner, the reporters too held back and simply watched alongside the other partygoers as Limpy ducked under the thorny branches and disappeared.

At that moment, the white-clad figure suddenly glowed against the blackness of the hill high above, appearing to float amongst the branches of a tree. The crowd gasped in unison and some raised their arms to point. Limpy popped up between the whin bushes. His arms rose up before him as though he was about to fly up and join the apparition. Michael Maguire had now melted into the darkness.

"Limpy McGhee!" The voice floated down on the breeze. From the people below there was a buzz of chatter that quickly died to silence. Limpy bowed his head.

"Yes, your holiness. It is me, Limpy McGhee. Recipier of the celestial transplant, for which I thank you most sincerely."

"Limpy McGhee, I would like you to do something for me."

The Virgin Mary seemed to be having difficulty keeping her voice at an even tenor.

"Whatever ye say, yer holiness. Just you name it."

The crowd strained forward as the breeze snatched away some of the words of this historic conversation. There was an awkward moment as the apparition suppressed the urge to laugh and then regained control of itself to say, in a slightly deeper tone of voice and now tinged with the local accent,

"I want ye to tell all of the people about yer miracle. Spread the word far and wide. I want ye to . . . "

The remainder of the words were made indistinct by a sudden gust of wind. The little old man leant forward and put a hand to his ear.

"What – did ye say? Give's that again – yer holiness." He tried to move towards the apparition but was held back by the thickets of jagged whin.

"I want ye, Limpy McGhee," the Virgin and the tree behind her were now shaking, "to convince – aah! Bastard!" With a cracking of twigs and branches the holy apparition did a half somersault and came to rest with a pair of boots pointing skywards, head and arms hanging down and trousers exposed to the crotch by the leg-mounted spotlight. The cowl of the garment had fallen away to reveal the contorted features of Seumas Kernohan who was shouting,

"Breen, get me down! The rope's cutting the feckin' knackers off me! Ah, Breen!"

From the spectators below, a great gale of laughter suddenly swept up the hill on the breeze, followed by shouts of, "Heaven's up that way, your holiness!" and "She's carrying a torch for ye, McGhee!"

But Limpy McGhee was oblivious to all of them as he threw himself forwards, oblivious to branches, thorns and rabbit holes, his two small fists clenched before him, his face drawn in anger at the insult to his patron and himself. For a few moments he disappeared beneath the bushes and then suddenly was free of them, clawing his way up the hill. Upside down, Seumas Kernohan saw him coming, and the ever-tightening constriction of the rope and the speed with which Limpy approached made the fallen idol all the more anxious to be set free.

"Breen, you hoor! Where the hell are ye?"

The faint sound of laughter drifted up from a clump of bushes at the bottom of the hill.

"When I get my hands on ye," Limpy shouted, "I'll kill ye, Kernohan! I'll rip yer innards out, so I will!"

But in the darkness, and with another tangle of bushes before him, the old man could not get near to where Seumas Kernohan was trapped.

"McGhee! Have ye a knife on ye? Get me down, for feck's sake, before I'm ruined!"

Limpy stood in front of the whin bushes, chest heaving as he gasped for breath.

"To hell with you, Kernohan. Ye can get your bloody self down. Or maybe if ye pray hard enough a miracle'll happen and ye can fly down."

And with that Limpy turned and, skirting wide around the bushes, trudged back down the hill, ignoring the alternate pleading and insults from the Virgin Mary up the tree.

From their grandstand view of the whole proceedings, the crowd was moving back to Pig Cully's house, talking and laughing, some shaking their heads in disbelief while others wiped away their remaining tears of mirth. Here and there individuals replayed the scene, taking on the roles of the Virgin Mary and then Limpy with upstretched arms and finally the upside-down Kernohan. At the back of the retreating crowd, Dan Kowalski and Lee walked along in silence, by the light of the moon Lee scribbling his emerging story beneath the headline, "TRANSVESTITE VIRGIN FALLS FOR SEXYGENARIAN".

The American slowly shook his head and said,

"God damn, the whole thing was a fake! Would you believe how crude that was, Louis?"

"Lee," the other man said, without looking up.

Dan Kowalski suddenly stopped and grasped Lee's arm. Some people bumped into them as they walked past.

"Why'n the hell didn't I – ? You know what? Us reporters, we're supposed to be smart, aren't we? Sophisticated, worldly-wise, all that crap. But I reckon we're no different from these people. We needed this story as much as they did, only for a different reason."

Lee stopped beside him but continued looking at his pad.

"Same shit, same reason," he said. "Doesn't work if you think you're better than your audience, Don."

"Jee-sus! I've just signed up that old guy for fifty grand." He spun round to look back up the hill. "Where'n hell is he? I gotta get that paper back."

But in the wan light of the moon Limpy McGhee was nowhere to be seen. In the copse near the top of the hill, Seumas Kernohan was being helped to the ground by his fellow conspirators, their humour long since vanished at the thought of Dermot McAllister's reaction when he heard about the mess they had made of the job they had been well paid to do.

As the crowd approached the house, Fergus Keane, tousled-haired and still tipsy, came pushing his way against it, plucking at people's sleeves and asking,

"What's happened? Eh? Can somebody tell me? What the hell's happened?"

Too busy laughing and talking, they ignored him. So, as the crowd drew away from him, the young reporter was left standing on his own, with only Kowalski and Lee between him and the dark horizon. As they approached, Fergus half ran to meet them.

"What happened here?" he shouted. "I'm from the Northern Reporter."

"Dan Kowalski, Boston Globe-Tribune."

Fergus Keane's eyes widened and he stared at the big American. God Almighty, the Boston Globe-Tribune? Did this man know that he, Fergus Keane, had broken the story? You could bet that American newspapers were always ready to give a chance to a bright young journalist. How many times had he seen that in the movies. But the American said,

"Some newspaperman you are. You missed the main event, kid."

"Look," Fergus said, "I was the one that broke this story in the first place."

"Well, Mr Newspaperman, I reckon you were taken for a ride, and then some. Turns out our miracle man's a big fat fake. There was a guy up in those trees there, pretending to be an apparition of the Virgin Mary, until he fell on his ass and gave the game away. Damndest thing I ever saw. I wouldn't be surprised if that old guy doesn't get lynched."

chapter nineteen

"Mrs McKay?" Father Burke came rushing into the chapel house kitchen, his black soutane swishing around his ankles. His eyes were bright, there was the hint of a smile on his face and his drooping shoulders of recent days had given way to an upright posture that recaptured his old enthusiasm and determination. Mrs McKay looked up from stirring a pot whose contents gave off an aromatic smell that had the young priest's nose twitching.

"Minestrone soup, Father," she said. "And then we're having beef olives with asparagus and broccoli for the main course – if that's all right."

"Fine, Mrs McKay, fine. Have you seen my plans for the Mass Rock site? There were six big sheets, rolled up together with an elastic band around them. Can't find them anywhere and I've got work to do on them. I'm going to put them on display when the Bishop makes his visit, to demonstrate how much effort we've put into this."

Mrs McKay noted the "we" but refrained from smiling.

"Big white sheets, were they? Done in black felt tip pen?"

"Yes, yes, that's the ones. Have you seen them?"

Mrs McKay suppressed a smile and slowly began to stir the pot again.

"Was that the same ones you told me to throw them in the bin, Father."

"In the – bin? Ah, Mrs McKay, you never did."

"'If I never see them again it would be too soon' you said. 'Put the lot of them in the bin.'"

"But, Mrs McKay, I wasn't myself. Surely you realised that." He lifted his hands and then dropped them in despair. "I'm never going to get them done again on time."

Mrs McKay gave him a mischievous look and then said,

"Just as well I didn't throw them out, then, isn't it? They're in the cupboard under the stairs."

"Oh, thank you, Mrs McKay. You're a gem." For a moment it looked as if he was about to grasp her by the shoulders and kiss her, but then he cleared his throat to remonstrate with himself. Smiling in anticipation, he bounded through the doorway like a little boy, the housekeeper saying after him,

"And Father, I don't want to see you up half the night at those things like you were before. If you get sick, it's me has to look after you."

She heard his laugh echoing from the cupboard under the stairs before he shouted,

"All right, Mrs McKay, I'll bear that in mind."

It was only half-an-hour later that Father Burke's re-awakened interest in the Mass Rock miracle was dealt a blow that left him white faced and a little unsteady on his feet. Slowly he walked across the hall to the kitchen, shaking his head in disbelief.

"Mrs McKay. I've just had a 'phone call from Mrs Dargan."

"That's nice for you, Father," the housekeeper said without looking round from the sink.

"No, no. She told me that – last night – outside the house where John McGhee was having a party – there was supposed to be an apparition of a woman in white up on the hill, asking for McGhee – and it turned out to be one of the locals dressed up." The young priest looked at his housekeeper, his face contorted with puzzlement, anxious that his housekeeper, his new mother substitute, would explain all of this to him, tell him that everything would be fine and she would make the hurt go away. His drooping shoulders, so recently thrust back in renewed enthusiasm, were once more in evidence.

"I knew it," he said forlornly, "I knew it was a hoax all along. And what's the Bishop going to say now – after the Canon persuading him to visit the Mass Rock?" Then his eyes narrowed and he looked intently at her. "Mrs McKay – Mrs Dargan seemed surprised that I didn't know about it already."

Mrs McKay pulled open a drawer and began to rummage among the cutlery.

"I do believe the milkman said something of the sort this morning, but sure you couldn't believe the half of what they'd swear to in this parish."

"And you didn't think you should tell me? I mean, you let me carry on under the delusion that everything was fine and that – "

"Now I wouldn't go reading too much into that, Father. You know what the boys around here are like. It was probably only a bit of fun."

"Oh no, this was no bit of fun, Mrs McKay. It was him all along, this Seamus Kernohan. But I'll bet someone put him up to it." He punched one hand into the palm of the other. "I should've stuck with my intuition. I just knew it was a fraud. I just knew it." He turned away. His shoulders seemed to have sagged even more, his hands kneading each other in front of him. "Thank you for trying to spare me, Mrs McKay, but it's no use." He paused in the doorway but did not look back. "I'm going to pray now, and then I'll have to think how I'm going to tell the bishop that his visit will have to be cancelled – and that he'll need to find a new parish priest for Inisbreen." As he went disconsolately across the hall to his study, he said to himself, "I wonder if they serve tea and cake in the monastery."

Father Burke was not the only one who sensed impending disaster following the discovery of the fake Virgin Mary at Limpy McGhee's party. Dermot had hastily arranged a meeting with Frank Kilbride and now as the evening sun threw long shadows across the valley they sat in Dermot's car on the road to Castleglen and looked down to where Inisbreen sat astride the river at the end of the sandy bay.

"That bunch of feckin' eejits," Dermot said again. "Why the hell did they have to cock it up on this of all times? And just when things are building up nicely. God, they're fighting to get into the miracle site, the hotel's booked solid for weeks and you must be making a fortune from those bloody awful souvenirs you're selling."

"Just supplying a need, Dermot. Just supplying a need. But how long is that going to last now? Inisbreen'll be a joke from one end of the county to the other and before we know it business'll be back to where it was before you thought this up."

"Oh you needn't tell me. I know, I know. I've thought of nothing else since I heard about it." He thumped his fist off the steering wheel. "And that was to be it. Just one last time, in front of all those witnesses and with the newspapers there and all." He gave a sigh and looked down to where the tree-covered slope gave way to the ground containing the Mass Rock, the field which had first given him the idea. "Frank – we've got to do something to save this."

"Well, the first thing you'll have to do is tell Kernohan and the other two to keep their mouths shut."

"D'you think I'm stupid? I've already done it."

"Well, we better hurry up and decide what we're going to do next. And there's no way we can keep this quiet. The story's all round the place already." He shook his head. "I even had

Peggy May going on about it this morning, giving me her version – which amounted to, 'That wasn't very nice of them boys to play that trick on Mr McGhee.' Dermot, we'll never get another chance like – "

But Dermot's thoughts were racing in another direction.

"What? She said what?"

Dermot had turned and was leaning towards Frank Kilbride, staring into his face.

"Who?"

"Peggy May. Tell me again what she said."

"'It wasn't very nice of them to play a trick on Mr McGhee.'"

Dermot relaxed back into his seat, a smile slowly came to his lips and he slapped a big hand onto one knee. "That's it, Frank. That's the get-out, d'you see? The boys were simply playing a trick on McGhee. Nothing to do with the other – real – appearances. They didn't do it before, weren't there, knew nothing about it. Simple."

"But there weren't any real appearances."

Dermot sighed.

"We know that, Frank, but we've got to make sure nobody else does, mh? It's perfect. Just a bunch of the local lads getting pissed and having a bit of fun at Limpy's expense. Well done Peggy May!"

Frank Kilbride considered this for a few moments.

"Well, I suppose it could sound plausible."

"Plausible? Frank, it couldn't be better. Especially if we get – " Dermot paused for dramatic effect, " – the boys to admit it themselves."

"Admit it? Who to?"

"To the press, of course," Dermot said, and then almost shouted, "God damn it, why didn't I think of that before? What we need, Mr Kilbride, sir, what we need is – a press conference. A bloody press conference! Let's use them for a change. I'll call a press conference – and we'll have Limpy McGhee there and John Breen and company." There was a pause and then Dermot added, "And – one Father Ignatius Loyola Burke."

"Burke? After what happened between you and the piano teacher? He wouldn't come within a mile of it."

"Oh, I think Saint Patrick'll be there all right – if it's put to him in the right way. He's got as much invested in this as anybody, perhaps more. Number one, he's been backing it right from the start. I know for a fact he's been to see the Bishop at least twice trying to persuade him it's genuine. Now if it appears it's been a fake all along – and I happen to know he's worried as hell about that – he's going to look a complete eejit. And priests aren't supposed to be that gullible – only their parishioners. That's number one. Number two. I don't think he could resist the opportunity to blow his own trumpet."

"Well, maybe. How come you know so much about him?"

Dermot gave a little chuckle and started up the car.

"I think you're forgetting, Frank. His housekeeper – Nora McKay? – she's a cousin of mine."

"Ah, Christ, you haven't told her, have you? We agreed that we'd – "

"Of course I haven't bloody told her! But she's told me plenty about our venerable parish priest, and I reckon we've got him by the short and curlies. Besides, I think he's earned a little time in the limelight. We probably couldn't have got this far without him. This thing's got a momentum of it's own, now. You wait and see, he'll jump at it."

Limpy blinked in the unaccustomed light of early morning and set off down the path that led from his house to the road. Beside him the big black dog walked obediently enough, led as he was by the long piece of string his master had looped through his collar, although the dog too was used to lying late and might well have been wondering upon what new adventure they were now embarked, especially since Limpy carried in his other hand a battered suitcase. One clasp was broken and a piece of rope was tied around the middle of the case, which bumped against Limpy's leg. When he had first thought of quitting Inisbreen, he had wondered how many suitcases he would need to carry all his worldly goods but had quickly if reluctantly concluded that most of what was left after the big clear-out at the river was distinctly unworldly and should have followed his kitchen table and its contents down to the sea. And he knew that if he were to throw this suitcase into the ditch now it would not make one whit of difference to the rest of his life. Not much to show for over sixty years of living.

He did not look round at the Mass Rock site as he passed. Despite the fact that his leg had been sorted by the so-called miracle, it would have been better if it had never happened. He'd been happy before, or at least not too unhappy most of the time. Now everything had changed, now he was the butt of jokes the length and breadth of the county and probably beyond. Even the dog had lately taken to pissing exclusively outside, which was welcome but disconcerting. Clearly he wasn't happy either. Now they were off to find a new billet some place where he would be unknown and he didn't much care where it was or perhaps even if he ever found somewhere. And even if he was discovered dead in a ditch, that might be a fitting end, as he wouldn't be surprised if he'd been born in one in the first place.

The car was past him by a few yards before it suddenly stopped and reversed to draw level with him.

"Hey, Mister McGhee!"

Limpy looked over at the car. It was Fergus Keane.

"Where's your car?"

"Ah, don't talk to me about cars. Bloody thing's knackered. Engine blew. And can I get a hold of that bastard in Castleglen that sold it to me? Can I buggery! They're quick enough about taking yer money."

"I'm sorry to hear that. Are you going off on a trip?"

"Aye," Limpy said without enthusiasm, "off on a trip. And what brings ye out this early?"

"I was coming up to your place. See if I could do another piece on you. Or d'you still have the exclusive with that other paper? The one that was able to bribe you away with big money?"

"Well, I've still got the money and if they want it back they'll have to find me first. But why the hell would ye want to do an article on me now?"

With surprise the young reporter looked at the old man.

"About the miracle, of course. What else?"

Limpy started walking again, so that Fergus had to let out the clutch and creep alongside him.

"What miracle? It was them boys all along. It was – a fluke – a freak – a – I don't know what the hell it was, but it was no damned miracle. There's nothing to tell any more. So away ye go home and write about things people want to read, hurling matches and – council meetings and stuff."

Limpy had not stopped walking.

"But it was a miracle!" Fergus shouted. "I believed that and so did you – and you still do!"

"Aye, well, nobody else does, so there's an end of it."

Fergus continued to reverse the car as Limpy plodded along with the dog on one side and the case on the other. Then Fergus said all at once,

"You're not just going on a trip, are you? You're leaving! For good!"

"So what of it? I'm a free agent."

Immediately Fergus slammed the gears from reverse into first, sank his foot on the accelerator and roared off down the road, spraying gravel on the dog which bore it with a fortitude that would have astounded Limpy had he not been sunk in the gloom of his thoughts. Fifty yards away the car slithered to a halt, nose into a gateway, reversed and came flying back up the road to stop beside Limpy. The passenger door flew open.

"Get in!" Fergus commanded. Limpy stopped and looked at him. "Get in." And when the dog made to jump up on the seat, the young reporter said, "Oh no, not in here. In the back for you – and no pissing on the seats."

"I'm going to the bus stop," Limpy said. "Just drop me anywhere near there."

Fergus stopped the car by the side of the road and began to reverse into a gateway.

"It's the other way," Limpy said. "Into the village."

Fergus's words were almost lost as the car roared off in the direction from which they had just come.

"You're not going to the bus-stop. You're going home."

"What? By Jasus – You listen to me, Fergus Keane. I'm catching the bus to Ballymane, an' neither you nor – nor – the Virgin Mary herself is going to stop me."

Fergus Keane laughed.

"Mr McGhee, you're almost as pig-headed as me. So, where're you going?"

"I'm going to Ballymane and then – we'll see. What is it to you anyway, where I go?"

They had reached the path which led to Limpy's house and Fergus pulled the car in and switched off the engine.

"Because you should be here, where you belong. Whatever anybody else says, a miracle did happen up there. Your leg was cured, wasn't it? And there are crowds of people coming to see the miracle site, aren't there?"

"That's as good a reason for leaving as any," Limpy mumbled.

"The point is, they've decided that a miracle has happened. This isn't just about you any more, Mr McGhee. It's much bigger than that now. I was the one that brought the story to the world. But you're the man that started it all off. The Miracle

Man." Fergus put out his hand and gripped Limpy's arm. "This is where you should be. This is where you belong."

Limpy looked out of the window and gave a shrug.

"I don't know nothin' any more. For a while there I thought I was landed. Leg fixed, bit of money, getting back with Cissy. Now everybody thinks I'm a fake – and she thinks I'm a sex maniac, thanks to you and your bloody front page headline."

"Yes, I know, I'm sorry about that, but I was only trying to help." Fergus turned and looked earnestly at Limpy. "I don't think you're a fake, Mr McGhee. I believe you. Stay here and make the rest of them believe you."

Such an intensity of feeling shone out from the young man's eyes that Limpy smiled in embarrassment.

"Ye're a good lad, Fergus. Ye've been with me since the beginning and ye've held yer ground. Which is more than I can say for most." He sat for a few moments looking out at the wooded hillsides and the green fields on either side of the river. Then he clapped a hand on his knee and declared, "Okay, I'll give her another go, young Fergus, on your say-so." He snorted. "Stay and do my Miracle Man act for the natives, although I'll take no pleasure in it now. Still, I suppose it's a small enough price to pay for the celestial transplant."

Fergus gave a secret little smile. Sometimes the thought of how persuasive the Press could be was almost overwhelming.

Dermot sat in his little office under the stairs and hoped that Father Burke wasn't going to bring up the subject of Nancy Quinn. As it was he felt bad enough about it, wished he'd never got involved with her – never even met the damned woman – except to buy the Mass Rock field from her, of course. Agnes and Patrick had not returned and there was little immediate prospect of their doing so, although he did have the beginnings of a plan formulating in his mind. And it was nobody's fault but his own. He might have known better than to trust a woman who at all times carried a spare pair of knickers in her handbag. Dermot picked up the telephone and dialled the local number. At the other end, the telephone rang and rang. He was about to give up when it was answered by Father Burke saying abruptly,

"Chapel house. Yes?"

Dermot drew a deep breath and then said in his brightest hotelier voice,

"Good morning! Is that Father Burke?"

"Yes," the priest replied.

"Father, this is – Dermot McAllister. I know you're a busy man, Father, but if you could give me just two minutes – "

"I don't have anything to say to you, Mr McAllister – except goodbye."

"The Virgin Mary, Father," Dermot said quickly, before Father Burke could put down the telephone. For a few seconds there was silence on the line and then the priest said,

"What?"

"The Virgin Mary, Father. The one that appeared to Limpy McGhee last night? I'm afraid the newspapers'll be plastering that across their front pages tomorrow, not to mention the television. You can just imagine it, can't you? 'Ex parish priest hoaxed by spoof virgin,' and 'Bishop sees cardinal in virgin crisis.' You have my sympathies, Father, because I know how much you've supported the miracle theory from the beginning. Through thick and thin, in fact."

There was a little choking cough from the parish priest before he said,

"Thank you very much for your concern, Mr McAllister, but I have no wish to discuss the subject with you."

"Well, if you say so, Father. But it was only because I have a genuinely high regard for your integrity that I thought you deserved to know about the press conference. Get a chance to redress the balance, sort of thing. Give your side of the story, you know? Still, in the circumstances, I can understand why – "

"Just a minute. What press conference?"

"The one that's being held in the hotel this afternoon at four o'clock." Dermot had a sudden flash of inspiration. "In time to catch the evening television news and tomorrow's first editions. We're going to have John McGhee there and those fellas that played that horrible trick on him last night. Something has to be done, Father. I mean, if stories like that get around, it could undermine the credibility of this whole miracle thing – and make us the laughing-stock of the country. So the boys are going to say how sorry they are, that they didn't mean any harm, and Limpy McGhee'll forgive them and tell everybody that his vision and the miracle were absolutely genuine."

"You're saying – that was only a practical joke last night?"

"Well of course it was, Father. And I said to those fellas, 'Look, boys, I like a joke as well as the next man, but you've gone too far this time.' I just knew I'd have to do something about it. Somehow I felt a sense of responsibility. I don't know why."

"Mr McAllister, I must say, that's a bit rich coming from a man who charges the faithful to get into the Mass Rock site to worship – not to mention some other aspects of your personal behaviour."

Dermot gave a heavy sigh.

"Charging to get into the Mass Rock site – perhaps that was a mistake. But I'd just paid out for that field and I had to try and recoup some money from it somehow. I couldn't put sheep back in there with people crawling all over it. I've been giving it some thought and I've been considering donating the site to the Church. In fact, it might be a good time for you to tell the Bishop, when he makes his visit. And then maybe by that time I'll be in a position to make an announcement about Burke Hall, too."

With a broad smile, Dermot waited in the ensuing short silence.

"Burke – Hall? What d'you mean, Mr McAllister? What is that?"

"Well, we really need a proper chapel hall, Father, especially with all these people visiting Inisbreen. So, I was considering giving a bit of land and a cash donation to start off the fund-raising, so that a new hall can be built, and who better to name it after than the man who first recognised John McGhee's experience as a miracle."

"Burke – Hall," the young priest replied. "I – I don't know what to say. It's a very nice thought, Mr McAllister. Very nice indeed."

"A lot of people I've talked to say it's no more than you deserve, Father. Anyway, we can discuss all that later. The main thing is to have a successful press conference this afternoon. But we don't have the experience to put the religious argument, your kind of ability to get into the cut and thrust of debate with that journalist rabble. We're only amateurs. They'd wipe the floor with us." Dermot paused for a moment and then said,

"Inisbreen needs you, Father."

At the other end of the line Father Burke cleared his throat and when he spoke, his voice had a determined edge to it.

"Four o'clock, did you say? That doesn't give me much time to prepare, but if I was to get onto it right away – I think I should be able to put something together. After all, the Bishop would never forgive me if I failed in my duty to put a good case for the Church and against that grubby materialism of the press."

A little later in the morning Dermot sat leafing through the bundle of cheques from banks in London, Dublin, Belfast, Cork and Limerick and he had every reason to smile. In two weeks he had taken more money than he would in six in his busiest period at the height of the summer. He put the cheques aside and started on the substantial pile of notes, sorting them into fifties, twenties, tens and fives before beginning to count them. You couldn't beat cash. Most of the newspapermen had been surprised and annoyed when he told them that he didn't accept credit cards. They seemed to think that he was under a legal obligation to do so and probably believed that if they were to wave an American Express or visa card at an Amazonian Indian in return for his services as a guide, the native would produce a sales voucher and an endorsing machine from his loincloth. The Miracle Man's leg had certainly brought a small economic miracle to the Glens Hotel and there was every prospect of more if the crowds kept coming. The bandwagon was rolling now and there would always be enough eejits claiming they had been the subject of miracle cures to keep it on the move. Dermot squeezed the thick wad of bank notes. If the press conference went well – and Father Burke's presence would make all the difference – if they could pass last night's incident off as a joke, they would be in with a good chance. He smiled. If that was the case, it couldn't have turned out better if he'd planned it himself. What was needed now, though, was some proper organisation. If entrepreneurs like himself and Frank Kilbride were to have a chance of bringing some economic prosperity to Inisbreen – and to themselves, of course – there would need to be some changes. A decent road, for a start, and a car park at the miracle site. The commercial possibilities were endless. Already he had spoken to Mrs Standish, the Summer Cook, about an idea he had had for a new dish at the hotel – Lamb McGhee – which would be a leg of lamb marinated in Bushmills whiskey, Limpy's favourite drink. She had said that she thought it might not be in the best of taste, so to speak, but she would give it a try if that's what he wanted. And he had thought up a dozen other ideas in the last week, all of them potential moneyspinners. Dermot leant back in his chair and imagined a steadily growing pile of cash in his bank account.

He was in the middle of adding up a column of figures when the telephone rang. He glanced at it but kept adding. If one more guest rang up to complain about the hardness of the bed or the poor television reception, he would tell him to pack up and get the hell out of it. Who needed them? There were plenty more. He stopped counting and looked at the ringing telephone. No, that wasn't the way to maintain a steady flow of customers, keep them happy – and relieve them of the maximum amount of cash. Lifting the receiver he said smoothly,

"Good afternoon, the Glens Hotel, how can I help you?"

"Dermot?"

He felt a little shiver of recognition tinged with excitement run down his spine.

"Agnes? Is that you, Agnes?" He found himself smiling. "God, there's a coincidence. Would you believe it? I was just thinking of 'phoning you. How's Patrick and that lovely mother of yours?"

"My mother's just fine. Look, Dermot, after what you did to me, I shouldn't ever speak to you again. But – it's Patrick."

"What about Patrick? What's happened to him?"

"Nothing's happened to him. He's perfectly all right, except that – well – he's missing you – although God knows why."

Dermot settled a little more into his chair and smiled broadly.

"Well, I could come down and see him, I suppose, but I'm run off my feet with the amount of business this miracle thing has generated. I suppose you've heard about it?"

"Of course I've heard about it. It's been in all the papers and on tv."

"You wouldn't believe it. I've taken more money in a week

than I would in six during the summer." He gave a little laugh. "I'm up to my knees in cheques and banknotes here. Help!"

Agnes was silent for a few moments, possibly calculating the implications of six week's takings coming in every week.

"Indeed. And what's this I hear about the bishop coming to the Mass Rock?"

Dermot looked surprised.

"How did you hear about that?"

"Dermot, you're not the only person I know in Inisbreen. Is it true?"

"So I'm told. And the sooner the better as far as I'm concerned."

"Since when did you take such an interest in Church affairs?"

Dermot laughed.

"Let's just say that I'm tackling business with a religious fervour."

"Oh, I might've known you'd have some smart answer."

"And we're holding a press conference at the hotel this afternoon."

"A press conference? Why?"

"Oh, some of these reporters are starting to put the story about that the miracle wasn't genuine. And you can imagine what that would do for business."

"Oh, I thought you'd be too busy with that little tramp Quinn to be worrying about business."

Dermot drew a deep breath. It was just as well he had anticipated a phone call like this. "Agnes, listen, what can I tell you about that? I realise how much it must've hurt you and – "

"Have you any idea of the embarrassment I felt? The disgrace of it – and Father Burke and the others there to see the whole thing! I'll never be able to show my face up there again."

"Ah God no, Agnes, no. Sure, weren't you the injured party? It's me they're down on. And I deserve it, God knows I do – for being naive, if nothing else. Listen, can you imagine the turmoil I've been through since? I swear to God, if I hadn't had those few drinks – well, more than a few, I suppose – nothing would've happened. Not that anything did happen, mind you, but I tell you what, Agnes, it's the last time I offer to help anybody with their personal problems. The little bitch. And you know what, at the heels of the hunt, it was money she was after! Wanted me to buy her a car, for God's sake! A Porsche! Could you believe that? Jasus, the woman's got a slate loose. And the best of it is, Agnes, it turns out – she's as bent as a wooden half-crown! A lesbian! Mrs Megarrity found her in one of the rooms here – in bed with a female reporter! Absolutely abloodymazing. It shook me, I can tell you. So, Miss Quinn got fired out the door sharpish." He gave a little pause, both to catch his breath and to give Agnes time to digest the facts. And then in a plaintive tone he added, "Agnes, why didn't you ever tell me I could be such an eejit?" There was no answer from Wexford. "Look, to hell with my pride, I've got to say it. I need you and Patrick here to look after me, stop me making a damned fool of myself."

"Hmph, those are probably the truest words you've ever spoken in your life. But you never listened to me before. Why should you start now?"

"Oh I did, Agnes. God, I did, believe me. Many's the time I said to myself 'Dermot, that woman's got the wisdom of two, so she has.' But I just didn't let on I was listening to you. Around here a man's got to have at least the illusion of independence. No, I need you here, Agnes, I need you here to keep me on the straight and narrow, I need you to work here beside me, I need you to – well, count the money. If business carries on like this, I won't be able to handle it on my own. And once the extension is built, well – "

"What extension?"

Dermot smiled to himself.

"Oh, didn't I mention it? I'm planning on having an extension built to handle the extra business. I'm beginning to think we're sitting on a goldmine here." Dermot paused and then said in his huskiest voice, "I'll make it all up to you, Agnes, if you'll just tell me you'll come back home."

The line fell silent. Dermot thought he caught the sound of a sigh from the Wexford end, but he couldn't be sure.

"I – don't know. I'll have to consider it. If you think I'm just walking back in there to start up where I left off – "

"Anything you want, Agnes. Just you name it. It's no more than you deserve. Can't you just picture it, though? You and me in business together. Boy, would we make some team."

"Well – just supposing I was to come back and help with the hotel – no bar work, mind you, I wouldn't lower myself to do that – I would need to be a partner. A full partner, Dermot, with an equal say in the running of the business – and that means the whole business."

"Agreed, Agnes. Fifty-fifty, right down the line."

"And the place would need to be redecorated to my specification."

There was a slight pause from Dermot.

"Done, Agnes, done. I always said you had better taste than me."

"And that Mrs Megarrity. I want her out."

"Well, we could certainly discuss that." Dermot was getting the distinct feeling that he was no longer in the driving seat, or at the very least he had acquired a co-driver. Yet in some curious way he rather liked this unusual sensation.

"Not discuss it, Dermot, do it. I don't want her on the premises."

"Okay, it's done, Agnes. She's as good as gone."

"Well, I'll consider it."

"Good. That's good. So, when will you call me?"

"When I've considered it."

"Fair enough. Well then, I suppose I'd better start preparing for this press conference this afternoon. Because I'll tell you what, unless these reporters go away convinced that the miracle was genuine, you needn't bother coming back here, because I won't be here myself."

chapter twenty

The two small boys stopped at the telephone box outside the Inisbreen Stores and pressed their noses against the glass to look at the funny man inside who was waving his hands and talking to himself. Seeing them stare at him, Fergus Keane stopped in mid oration, pulled a face and shouted,

"Clear off, you little buggers!" and although they could not hear what he said, they got the message and ran off down the street waving their arms and silently acting out Fergus's conversation with himself. In the telephone box, the ace reporter sighed and tried again.

"Look, Mr Martyn, I'm sorry. That story about the Miracle Man and all those women, I – well – I made it up. But you did say you wanted a sex angle on it. I mean, I was under a lot of pressure." And then in an aside to himself, "Yes, that's it. Under pressure." That sounded good. Journalist on the front line, barely able to keep pace with the fast-moving story. Fergus shrugged. "You know what it's like in this game, Mr Martyn."

But Harry Martyn was not the editor of the Northern Reporter for nothing, and after a few moments Fergus found himself replying,

"Very well, Mr Martyn, if that's what you want. I won't

even wait till the press conference this afternoon. I'll come back to Ballymane right away and you'll have my resignation on your desk this evening."

It would be a tragic end to a promising journalistic career. The door of the telephone box was suddenly pulled open by a woman wearing carpet slippers and with a purse in her hand, who said,

"Excuse me, but if you're able to talk to somebody without using the 'phone, you could just as easy do it out here and let me in there."

Fergus gave an embarrassed grin.

"I'm – going to use it now. I was just – practising."

"Well then maybe you should get a grown-up to do it for you, son," the woman said and banged the door shut.

Fergus drummed his fingers on the glass of the telephone box as he waited for the Northern Reporter's telephone to be answered in Ballymane. Firmness, that's what was needed. And he had it – until the telephonist's perky voice said,

"Good morning, Northern Reporter, how can I help you?"

Fergus replied and then before he had time to draw breath, Harry Martyn was on the line.

"Good morning, Mr Martyn. Fergus Keane here. I was – "

"Keane! Where the hell are you? What've you been doing? Why haven't you 'phoned? If you're going to tell me you've been on this miracle story, you'd better have some damn good stuff! Do you realise how long it's been since I've heard from you? And no contact number! Unforgivable, Keane. Un-forgivable!"

"I – eh – I was going to – "

"What the hell's wrong with you, man? Have you been drinking or what?"

"Well – the last time we talked you – you didn't seem too happy with what I'd been doing. I know you published my last piece but – I thought that I was maybe – " why did he have to say it, why did he have to give voice to something that he had kept suppressed in his sub-consciousness, and to Harry Martyn of all people? "I thought I was going to – get the sack." There, he'd said it now and that almost guaranteed that it would happen.

"The sack?" Harry Martyn chuckled. "Me sack you? Keane, Keane, please, do I look like a man that would sack anybody? Do I? Listen, I've never sacked anybody in my life. Well, perhaps one or two left in debatable circumstances. Some resigned, others left without a word of explanation, one or two departed under what I suppose you could call a cloud and there was one fetched away by the police, but sacked? Never. I believe in developing my people, Keane, and if they fail to make the grade, I blame myself. Oh yes I do. Y'see underneath this bluff exterior, this carapace that one develops in the inksquirter's trade, I'm really just a pussycat, a soft touch for every sob story in the book." He gave a little snorting giggle. "Besides, your uncle owns too many shares in the Northern Reporter. Ha ha. Not that you don't deserve sacking, Keane, being incommunicado like that. Oh, you've got a lot to learn, boy, but I'm the man to teach you. Now, this miracle story. The last piece you sent in – the sex angle bit – that was good, but I think you've just about wrung it dry. Time we pulled the plug on it, before we get into the realms of fantasy, eh?" The editor of the Northern Reporter slurpped at a large mug of tea. "Not unless you know for a fact that this guy's having a gay relationship with the priest, or the Virgin Mary's landed on a Martian spaceship in his back garden."

The ace reporter gave a silent sigh. What ever happened to truth and objectivity in journalism?

"Oh but Mr Martyn, I'm sure there must be other angles we can find. They're having a press conference this afternoon. Something's bound to come out of that."

"No, Keane. Take it from me, that's a sure sign the story's

running out of steam and somebody's trying to breath new life into it. Now, if there were to be one or more spectacular cures, for instance, that would give it some extra mileage. But unless anything big happens, in a few days time it'll be forgotten. A dead duck. One more miracle story that bit the dust, along with weeping Madonna statues, Christ's face in the middle of a turnip or the piece of driftwood that looked the dead spit of Saint Patrick."

"But, Mr Martyn, there must be some substance to it, otherwise the Bishop of Down and Connor wouldn't be paying an official visit to the site."

Harry Martyn's slurp of tea ended more abruptly than usual.

"Are you absolutely sure about that, Keane?"

"Oh yes, an official visit, in two weeks. I 'phoned his office this morning to confirm it." Like he would've said something like that without checking his facts first. How much did Harry Martyn really have to teach him? When he spoke after a few seconds, there was an edge to the editor's voice that had the young reporter standing a little more erect in the telephone box.

"Keane, listen to me. This is what I want. Number one – a piece on this miracle from the point of view of the people who believe in it. Number two – why they believe it – anybody that's been affected by it – strengthened their faith – cured of something – changed their lives – whatever. Get out there and dig up some human interest stories, all right? I want stories about – "

"But Mr Martyn – I thought you just said it was a dead duck?"

"Keane! For God's sake, man, use your loaf! We've got a religious controversy here, right? Dynamite! There's a bishop saying one thing – the miracle's kosher, mh? – and on the other hand we'll have those cynical Fleet Street hacks saying its only the wild imagination of a bunch of Irish peasants. Now, who the hell buys our newspaper, eh? Who d'you think my money should be on? Look, if the Church is involved at bishop level, this is big, Keane, big, big, big – and I want you to go out there and get me a big story. I want the human angle, I want real-life drama, I want facts. But more than facts, Keane, I want a story for the front page. The lead story."

"The – lead story? Yes sir, Mr Martyn."

"And, Keane?"

"Mr Martyn?"

"Easy on the expenses, son. This isn't the Daily Express, you know."

"Easy on – ? No, Mr Martyn. I mean, yes Mr Martyn. I'm on my way."

"And what's them things supposed to be?" the Winter Cook said in the kitchen of the Glens Hotel, poking a grubby finger at the plates that were lined up on the table below the window.

"Vol-au-vents," said Mrs Standish, the Summer Cook. She carried on cutting ham sandwiches which she placed on doily-covered plates. The Winter Cook turned and fired a snarling look at the back of the woman who had been brought in over her head, as if she, who had cooked for hundred-strong gangs of navvies, couldn't even throw a few bits of sandwiches together for a bunch of reporters. That was bad enough. What was worse was that the woman was English, married to a retired businessman with more money than you could shake a stick at and her only doing it for "a little diversion", while there were others, who would remain nameless for the sake of decorum, who needed the money to keep body and soul together not to mention put a bite of grub into the mouths of five ravenous kids.

"Volley whats?"

"Vol-au-vents, Mrs Megarrity. Vol-au-vents. If you call

yourself a cook, I'm surprised that you have to ask what they are."

At the open window above the table a dirty face appeared, and then another, before Mrs Megarrity noticed and angrily waved the boys away.

"And what d'you mean by them remarks? I'll have ye know that I was a cook here for many a long year before you came and put your neb in. And I didn't need any of this fancy English grub to do it, neither."

"French, actually," the Summer Cook said, bringing the knife-blade down onto the cutting-board with a snap. The Winter Cook swung her head from side to side and mouthed at Mrs Standish's back, "French, actually."

An arm snaked in the window and a dirty hand swiftly removed a plate of the contentious snack. Mrs Megarrity was engaged in more weighty matters.

"I don't give a tinker's fart if they're from the Vatican. People round here like good plain grub, not these pansy bits of pastry and wee things on sticks. Those fellas'll have them swallied up in ten seconds flat and then be looking for a proper bite of grub. Jasus tonight, if this is what yous live on in England, no wonder yous're not fit to dig yer own roads."

A large knife in her hand, Mrs Standish turned to face the Winter Cook a second after another plate of vol-au-vents disappeared out of the window.

"Mrs Megarrity, I do not have time to bandy words with you. If you have a problem, go and see Mr McAllister. Otherwise I'd be grateful if you would start putting those plates of sandwiches onto trays. The press conference is due to start in half-an-hour." There was the sound of crockery clinking and both women turned towards the window. "What was that?"

"Ah – it's that bloody cat again. If I get my hands on it I'll wring its neck for it. Mangy skitter of a thing." The Winter

Cook waddled over to the table and with bad grace began to lift the plates. "Maybe it took a fancy to your volley-vongs." From outside the window there was the sound of retching, followed by a spitting noise. "It'll be about the only one around here that will."

Fifteen minutes later, the big room in the Glens Hotel was rapidly filling with journalists from newspapers, two from radio stations and a BBC television crew who were busy setting up their camera and sound equipment at the back of the room so that they could shoot over the heads of the attendees. The room had a small stage at one end and in the middle of the ceiling was suspended a large mirror ball which would spin and throw little spots of light on the heads of the dancers below, "like bloody electric measles," Pig Cully had said. One night, when the bulb in the spotlight had blown just before a dance, Dermot McAllister had paid Dippy Burns three pounds to stand at the back of the stage throughout the evening and shine a torch onto the mirror ball. It was, Dippy Burns maintained, from this feat of human strength and endurance that he had first contracted osteo-arthritis, which had left him permanently weak in one arm. Fortunately, it had never spread to other parts of his body, although when he advanced his theory to Doctor Walsh, Dippy was informed that in certain circumstances the disease had been known to affect the cranium and he had rushed home to look that up in his book too.

At most functions, the tiny stage usually held the three musicians who called themselves the Hot Shots – although they were universally known as the Toss Pots – with their cracked-voice singer who also twanged a guitar, a drummer thrashing the life out of his skins, and a burly farmer who wrenched tortured notes from a cheap accordion and smiled while doing so. Now it had on it five chairs behind a small table. In front of the stage had been arranged four rows of seats that were now occupied by the representatives of the press and radio, among them Fergus Keane. Much to the surprise and delight of the journalists, two of the hotel girls were busy taking orders for drinks, "Courtesy of Mr McAllister". The air was filled with a hubbub of talk and laughter, chair legs scraping as journalists turned to fire well-honed pleasantries at their colleagues on rival newspapers. Another two waitresses appeared bearing large trays crammed with sandwiches, sausage rolls, pork pies and what was left of the vol-au-vents. A number of locals had also come in to stand at the back of the room, and within a few minutes they too were munching sandwiches and quaffing Dermot's free drinks. What with the food and drink, the chatter and the general air of expectancy, the atmosphere was more like that of a party. When Dermot stepped onto the stage and looked around the room, he smiled and gave a series of little nods of satisfaction. So far so good. In order to get their attention, he banged a glass on the table and little by little the talk and laughter subsided.

"Ladies and gentlemen," he said, although there were no females amongst the journalists, "I would like to welcome you all here this afternoon. Please feel free to eat and drink your fill." He smiled as he slowly surveyed the room. "Now, following recent events, but most particularly the events of Saturday evening last, a local man, Mr John McGhee – popularly known as the Miracle Man, of course – our parish priest Father Ignatius Loyola Burke and one or two other people, wanted the opportunity to meet the Press and give their views and other information that would maybe help you to write accurate accounts of the miracle and the events surrounding it. The various people involved will make statements and then there'll be an opportunity for questions. So first of all, let me introduce – " Like a showman, Dermot turned to hold out an arm towards the door beside the stage, " – Father Ignatius Loyola Burke!"

Journalists exchanged glances, smiled and shook their

heads. The door opened and the parish priest walked in smiling, glancing from side to side as he went, as though expecting a round of applause. He carried a fat folder under his arm. His hair had been combed to perfection, his face was ruddy from washing, and the new soutane that he wore had a fresh, satiny sheen and fold-marks from having been in a box. Father Burke took a seat at the table and from inside his folder drew out a sheaf of papers.

"Thank you, Father," Dermot said. "Next we have Mr John Breen, Mr Seumas Kernohan and Mr Michael Maguire."

Again the door opened and the three men came out sheepishly, firstly John Breen, followed by Kernohan and then Maguire, all three of whom were wearing their best suits and with their hair plastered down, as if they were appearing in court, which each of them had done on various occasions. On mounting the low stage, Maguire tripped and fell against Kernohan, almost bringing him down too. As he passed, Dermot smiled and patted Maguire on the shoulder, perhaps a little harder than was necessary.

"And finally the man who started it all – the Miracle Man himself – the pride of Inisbreen – Mr John McGhee!"

There were a few ragged cheers from the back of the room, then the door opened and the Miracle Man walked into the room.

Limpy had taken great pains to prepare himself for his first appearance before the television cameras. He was wearing a brown pin-stripe suit and a mangled yellow-and-red tie that made it look as if he had been sick down the front of his moss-green shirt. Stuck in his breast pocket was a handkerchief which looked as if it had last been used to give the semblance of a polish to his black boots. Glistening like a set of fairy lights, globules of water clung to the fringes of his hair, which, normally bushy from lack of combing and having only a nodding acquaintance with shampoo, was slapped down tight against his head, a crooked middle parting giving him the look of one who had just surfaced from a deep-sea dive. His eyebrows were suspiciously black and there was an unaccustomed ruddiness to his cheeks. Reporters and locals alike stared at Limpy, done up, as Lee whispered to Mr Patel, "like a pox doctor's clerk". Even Dermot stared, before rolling his eyes and giving an almost imperceptible shake of his head.

"Good-day to yous," Limpy said with a beneficent wave of his hand as he took his seat. "Yous can start shooting any time you're ready." He stretched his neck and posed for the television camera at the back of the room, where a few more of the locals had crowded in and were now standing on tiptoe to see what was going on at the front. Then at a nod from Dermot and clutching a piece of paper, John Breen slowly got to his feet, glanced nervously around the room, cleared his throat and began reading in his drawling voice.

"This here's a statement by me, John Breen, about what happened last night outside the house of Francis Cully about eleven o'clock p.m. Me and Mr Kernohan here and Mr Maguire – having considerable quantities of drink taken – decided to play a wee trick on our old friend – " he turned and nodded gravely at Limpy, who obligingly smiled for the assembled multitudes, "Mr John McGhee. We therefore proceeded to get a sheet, a length of rope and a torch to do the job, and went to the hill near Francis Cully's house. Mr Kernohan here – " Seamus kept his head lowered, " – was dressed up in the sheet and then he was tied to the tree, with the torch up his leg. Mr Maguire was then sent to the house to tell Mr McGhee that a woman in white was floating in the trees and asking for him. Mr McGhee came out, because he thought it was genuinely the Virgin Mary." In confusion as to whether he should bow his head or bless himself, John Breen tried to do both simultaneously and merely succeeded in poking a finger in his eye. "The crowd followed Mr McGhee out, and then due to bad workmanship, Mr Kernohan here fell off his perch and ended upside down, which gave the game away."

There was a ripple of laughter around the room, and John Breen smiled nervously, as though reluctantly accepting congratulations.

"The whole thing was just a joke, so it was, and we didn't mean no harm to our friend Mr McGhee." Kernohan and Maguire nodded gravely. Limpy smiled and waved a dismissive hand. "And of course," John Breen added quickly, "we didn't mean no disrespect to the Virgin Mary herself neither. We've known her all our life." He looked at his piece of paper, said, "That's it," and sat down quickly.

From the front row, a journalist wearing a suit in which it appeared that both he and a companion had slept the night before, stood up and said,

"Mr Breen, you said that you and your friends – "

"Questions at the end, please," Dermot announced briskly. "Next, Mr John McGhee will make his statement."

Now in the crowd at the back of the room stood Pig Cully, Dan Ahearn and Frank Kilbride, who had taken the unprecedented step – at Peggy May's insistence – of closing the Inisbreen Stores and taking her to the press conference. Beside them, and entirely hidden by those around her, Cissy stood on tiptoe as she vainly tried to see the stage. Then, as Limpy got up to speak, she said something to Frank Kilbride, who helped her climb onto a chair, from which position she could see everything at the front of the room. Behind her, with Mr Pointerly in attendance, her sister Margaret tugged at the hem of Cissy's skirt and hissed,

"Cissy! Get down at once! You're making a complete fool of yourself!"

With one hand grasping the collar of his jacket, Limpy began,

"Good afternoon, ladies and gentlemen. Very decent of yous to come along today."

The Press, their attention once more directed at Limpy, once again began to chuckle and nudge each other. Cissy stood on her chair, her eyes wide and shining as she looked at her former lover. Unaware of the object of her sister's affection, Margaret merely looked up at her in puzzlement. Mr Pointerly's attention was given over to glimpses of Limpy between the heads of other people.

"Yous've heard," Limpy said, "what my esteemed friend here, John Breen, told about the incident that took place the other night, regarding a practical joke the Virgin Mary took part in – or ratherly a version of. I accept his apology forthwith, and I'd like to state categorally that no way does it affect my leg's standing – " Limpy gave the limb a resounding slap, " – as a miracle subject. It was cured by the Virgin Mary herself when she personally appeared to me at the Mass Rock. I remember the whole thing as clear as day, and she didn't look nothing like Seumas Kernohan with a sheet on and a torch up his leg. No sir. And anybody that says it was, well, it's a pack of damned lies."

Father Burke nodded and said,

"Exactly so."

Before Limpy could continue with his speech, a tall man with red hair who had pushed his way towards the front, said,

"Mr McGhee. John Thompson, the Daily Times."

"Hiya, Johnny boy," Limpy said, sticking up a thumb. "How's it going?"

"Mr McGhee. Not only because you've broken our agreement by holding this press conference, but also because I now regard you as a faker and a fraud – despite what we've already heard here – I have to inform you that our agreement is at an end and that I'll be demanding the immediate return of the money already paid to you."

At once a hubbub started amongst the crowd in the room, with people leaning this way and that or standing on tiptoe to see who had spoken. One journalist shouted, "Piss off, Thompson!" and another chipped in, "Yeah, let the old fella keep your fiver."

At the back, the Winter Cook snatched off her waitress's cap and ground it in the palm of her hand.

"Did yous hear that? 'A faker and a fraud' he says. Jasus tonight, he's insulting John McGhee and every man and woman in Inisbreen!" To enable her to look over the heads of the crowd, she grasped the shoulders of the man in front of her and hoisted herself, almost pulling him backwards to the ground in the process. At the table, Father Burke shot a worried glance at Dermot, who gave him a reassuring glance and began to walk along in front of the stage, towards where John Thompson stood.

"A faker and a fraud?" Limpy shouted. "I'm no bloody fraud! An', boy, ye want to watch yer step! Ye're as good as calling the Virgin Mary herself a liar, so ye are!" Limpy looked upwards, as if attempting to intercede with the Mother of God to stay her wrath from the head of this blasphemous Englishman. Then Fergus Keane stood up.

"I'd like to say something," he said.

"Young Fergus Keane! Ye're very welcome! Now here's the boy that'll tell the truth of it! The first man on the job. Tell away, Fergus!"

The young reporter stood for a moment, nervously fingering the notebook that he held before him. In front of all these journalists from the length and breadth of Ireland and beyond, here was his chance to make his mark. He took a deep breath and began.

"Fergus Keane, the Northern Reporter. I was the first journalist to break this story, as Mr McGhee said. I was with him when he first discovered the stream coming from the bottom of the Mass Rock. And having talked to Mr McGhee, I decided that, in my experience – " he paused in order that his journalistic colleagues might have a chance to marvel at the knowledge and wisdom of one so young, " – he was genuine, that a miracle really had happened to him."

Limpy was nodding vigorously and holding up a thumb to the young reporter.

"You could say that Mr McGhee is a somewhat sad, even pathetic figure of a man. He certainly drinks too much and his house is – well, let's say it could do with some improvement. Like, knocking down. And some people have even said that the Virgin Mary would never choose a person like that to be the subject of a miracle."

The room was now in complete silence. Limpy leant across the table, the wide eyes in his grave face staring directly at the young reporter.

"Well, I know from personal experience that Mr McGhee is as honest as the day's long and I would suggest to some of you doubting Thomases that the Virgin Mary knows a lot more of what she's about than the rest of us put together."

"I don't buy that for one goddamed minute," the American voice said from the middle of the room. "After last night, I'm beginning to wonder if this isn't just a scam to get money out of the newspapers and pull the tourists in." Dan Kowalski jabbed a finger at his chest. "Well, you can count the Boston Globe-Tribune out, my friend." He turned to Mr Patel and said, "And to think I almost believed this bunch of crap."

Within a few seconds the room was in uproar as journalists shouted questions at the stage, talked and argued amongst themselves, while locals threw catcalls at them from the back. Here and there scuffles began to break out as men exchanged harsh words, and to one side of the room the Winter Cook was shouldering her way between people, shouting,

"Where's the man that insulted John McGhee?"

Father Burke got to his feet and held out both arms, waving his hands for silence and calm.

"Gentlemen, gentlemen, please!" he shouted but could hardly be heard above the rising din. "Gentlemen! I have a statement to make!"

He began to read from his notes, although nobody took the slightest notice of him. Still standing on her chair, Cissy was leaning forwards on the shoulders of the man in front of her. With a look of concern, she was watching Limpy, who sat at the table, his chin sunk to his chest, his narrow shoulders sagging. He should have followed his instincts and left Inisbreen when he had intended to, then he couldn't have been persuaded by Dermot McAllister to take part in this stupid bloody press conference.

"John!" Cissy shouted, her voice so thin and reedy that even Margaret standing behind her could barely hear it. Near the stage, Dermot had reached John Thompson, had him gripped by the elbow and was talking close into the man's ear when Mrs Megarrity at last burst out of the crowd and reached the two men. It was a straightforward punch to the journalist's jaw that she delivered, the swing starting somewhere about the Winter Cook's waist and arcing to come in at an angle, the force of the blow propelling John Thompson into the BBC camera which crashed to the floor. Pieces broke off and scattered amongst the feet of the crowd.

"Ye'll not call my brother a fake and a fraud!" the Winter Cook shouted as Thompson lay on the floor clutching his jaw. With an anguished look on his face the cameraman got to his feet, went rigid for a few moments then turned and kicked the wall. Now he was shaking with anger.

"Do you – do you know – how much that cost?" he said. "Have you any idea what you've just done, you stupid, stupid bitch?"

As the Winter Cook glowered at the cameraman and pulled

back her arm ready to deliver another haymaker, Dermot yanked her away. The man from the BBC, who either did not know the price of the camera or felt that it was too horrific for words, contented himself with an anguished wail and a rhythmic punching of his fist against his leg.

Looking round the room, Dermot could see the anger and tension on the faces of the locals, some of whom would just be spoiling for a fight with these reporters who had been throwing their money around and treating the villagers like they had straw sticking out of their ears. He started pushing his way towards the stage. He would have to calm everyone down before there was a riot. And it was obvious by the way that he stood transfixed on the stage that the great orator himself Father Ignatius Loyola Burke was going to be of no help whatsoever. From her perch at the back, Cissy was now frantically calling out,

"John! John!" in a high-pitched wail whose constant repetition threatened to exhaust her meagre physical resources. Margaret looked on, totally bewildered at the outlandish behaviour of her sister, who at last began to clamber down from her chair. In a second, Cissy had disappeared into the milling crowd. Being small, she was able to slip along the wall and arrive at the stage. The three men from the Virgin Mary Repertory Company had quit the stage, ready to join any fray that might break out below. Limpy sat with bowed head, seemingly oblivious to all that was happening before him. He only looked up – and then with surprise – when the younger Miss Garrison poured onto the floor the water from a heavy carafe and then with it began a slow and steady banging on the table. At first it was not heard above the general din in the room. She thumped the table even harder. One by one people stopped talking and then turned towards the source of the noise. She kept up the banging until she had the full attention of everyone in the room and there was silence.

"Dis-graceful!" she said, her weak voice clearly heard in every part of the room. "Dis-graceful! You should all be ashamed of yourselves!" She was shaking with emotion, yet in her small, gentle face her eyes were pinpoints of determination. "How dare anyone say that John McGhee is a fraud! He is not a fraud! He's as honest a man as you'll find in Ireland! Honest and kind and trustworthy. A gentleman!" she said. "And I know!" Her voice moderated a little, and suddenly she seemed near to tears. "I – know."

Margaret Garrison listened to this in amazement, to the extent that she entirely forgot herself and clambered onto a chair, using the broken television camera as a step. The man from the BBC sat in the corner, his face in his hands, wondering how he was going to explain to his boss how his camera had sustained more damage at a minor press conference than it had during three months in Beirut. On the stage Limpy sat looking at Cissy with open admiration, the black dye on his eyebrows and the pink on his cheeks beginning to trickle down with the beads of sweat caused by the stifling heat of the room.

"For over – forty years," Cissy continued, "I've known – and admired – John McGhee." Now she was looking directly at him, as he was at her, and their looks seemed to form a channel of mutual affection. She appeared to be speaking only to him. "And all those years ago – " her little chest heaved, " – I made the biggest mistake of my life. I let him go – even although I loved him dearly."

As if from one body, there was a little sigh from the crowd and a smattering of conversation that quickly died into silence.

"Twice recently I almost did it again," Cissy was saying, "but I'm not going to make the mistake the third time." She leant forward, staring at Limpy who sat with his mouth open, his face a perfect picture of delight. "John McGhee," she said, holding his eyes with hers in a steady gaze while each person in the room waited expectantly. "John McGhee – " her little hand stretched out towards him, as though searching for something in the dark, " – will you marry me?" Deathly silence. Around the room eyes widened and breaths were held. From Mr Pointerly there was a forlorn look as he had his worst suspicions confirmed and then Margaret Garrison's eyes fluttered and she toppled like a felled oak onto the BBC cameraman who had been contemplating the remainder of his career as a toilet attendant at Broadcasting House. On the stage Limpy looked at Cissy blankly for a moment, unable to comprehend the enormity of what she had just said. Then slowly his head began nodding, until he finally managed to get out,

"Ah – Cissy – yes ma'm! Yes indeed, I certainly will marry you! Oh yes!"

At the back of the room Dan Ahearn clapped his hands together and said, "Jasus, if that doesn't beat all!", Mrs Megarrity let out a long wail and slumped against the wall and then a great cheer went up from the crowd, journalists and locals alike, and then another, followed by clapping and shouts of "Good man!" and "Well done McGhee." A journalist in the middle of the room started pushing his way towards the stage, waving and shouting, "Mr McGhee, Mr McGhee – an exclusive! You and your bride-to-be! Your life stories. All right?" Oblivious to all of this, and with his eyes fixed firmly on Cissy, Limpy stood up, went to her and gently put an arm around her shoulders.

With heads bowed a little or tilted to one side, the crowds watched this, smiling somewhat embarrassedly at the show of affection by the elderly couple. At the back of the room, Dermot beamed and inclined his head towards Frank Kilbride, saying out the side of his mouth,

"You'd better get back up to your shop, Frank, and take on two new assistants. I think you're going to be needing them."

In a corner, Mr Pointerly was using a newspaper to fan the

face of Margaret, who lay on the floor, pretending to be still unconscious as a result of the sudden revelation of Cissy's romance and impending marriage. Someone tried to push past Mr Pointerly and he turned and looked up. It was the young reporter, the one he had surprised in McPhee's house that night. He obviously hadn't got the sack after all and anyway surely he too must have suffered a similar disappointment over this McPhee business with Cissy Garrison.

"Hello there," Mr Pointerly said to Fergus, dropping the newspaper, which fell onto the chest of the recumbent Margaret. She opened one eye, saw the departing Mr Pointerly and then closed her eye again in the hope of attracting some other male to administer first-aid. As they reached the door, Mr Pointerly said to Fergus,

"Well, this is a turn-up for the books, eh? Makes one wonder who's who and what's what."

Already Fergus's brain was racing, a story forming, dramatic headlines flashing before him.

"Eh, yes, I suppose you might be right."

"Listen," Pointerly said, gently taking hold of Fergus's elbow, "I was just thinking of slipping off for a quick one, you know?" He made a show of surprise at Fergus's supposed reply, and said with mock innocence, "A drink, of course. Care to join me?"

"Well you know, I didn't drink hardly at all before I came here," Fergus said, "but – there's something about this place drives you to it. Certainly, Mr Pointerly, I think I could just do with a stiff one."

"Oh – jolly good!" Mr Pointerly said delightedly. As they made their way through the doorway towards the foyer, Fergus gave a little smile to himself and said,

"You know, I was thinking the other day of doing an article on the sex life of the older gay man in Ireland. You might be just the very one to talk to on that, Mr Pointerly."

Outside the Glens Hotel the brown river flowed placidly under the bridge, past where the boats swung lazily at anchor on one side and the hotel on the other, out beyond the sandy point and into the calm green waters of the bay. Along the river and by the shore, seagulls swooped and cried, while wagtails strutted and ran and speared for food in the sand. Above the bay and the green hills and the low meadows where the sheep lay at their ease and the cattle waded to their bellies in the water, puffy little white clouds hung motionless in the blue sky. Near the river a glistening chestnut horse ran in a field to come suddenly to a halt and stand stock-still looking at nothing. And at the front door of the Glens Hotel, the fat black cat ambled out to sit in the sun, which shone without distinction on the saints and sinners of Inisbreen.